Praise for Minerva…
THE ACAD…

"[A] pitch perfect Regency …. Readers will be hooked." (THE MUSIC OF LOVE)
★Publishers Weekly STARRED REVIEW

"An offbeat story that offers unexpected twists on a familiar setup."
(A FIGURE OF LOVE)
Kirkus

"[A] consistently entertaining read."
(A FIGURE OF LOVE)
Kirkus

Praise for THE MASQUERADERS series:
"Lovers of historical romance will be hooked on this twisty story of revenge, redemption, and reversal of fortunes."
Publishers Weekly, STARRED review of THE FOOTMAN.

"Fans will be delighted."
Publishers Weekly on THE POSTILION

Praise for Minerva Spencer's *REBELS OF THE TON* series:
NOTORIOUS

★A *PopSugar* Best New Romance of November
★A *She Reads* Fall Historical Romance Pick
★A *Bookclubz* Recommended Read

"Brilliantly crafted…an irresistible cocktail of smart characterization, sophisticated sensuality, and sharp wit."
★Booklist STARRED REVIEW

"Sparkling...impossible not to love."—Popsugar

"Both characters are strong, complex, and believable, and the cliffhanger offers a nice setup for the sequel. Readers who like thrills mixed in with their romance should check this out."
—Publishers Weekly

"Packed full of fiery exchanges and passionate embraces, this is for those who prefer their Regencies on the scandalous side."***—Library Journal***

INFAMOUS

"Realistically transforming the Regency equivalent of a mean girl into a relatable, all-too-human heroine is no easy feat, but Spencer (Outrageous, 2021) succeeds on every level. Lightly dusted with wintery holiday charm, graced with an absolutely endearing, beetle-obsessed hero and a fully rendered cast of supporting characters and spiked with smoldering sensuality and wry wit, the latest in Spencer's Rebels of the Ton series is sublimely satisfying."
—Booklist STARRED review

"Perfect for fans of Bridgerton, Infamous is also a charming story for Christmas. In fact, I enjoyed Infamous so much that when I was halfway through it, I ordered the author's first novel, Dangerous. I look forward to reading much more of Minerva Spencer's work."
—THE HISTORICAL NOVEL SOCIETY

Praise for Minerva Spencer's *Outcasts* series:

"Minerva Spencer's writing is sophisticated and wickedly witty. Dangerous is a delight from start to finish with swashbuckling action, scorching love scenes, and a coolly arrogant hero to die for. Spencer is my new auto-buy!"
-**NYT Bestselling Author Elizabeth Hoyt**

"[**SCANDALOUS** is] A standout...Spencer's brilliant and original tale of the high seas bursts with wonderfully real protagonists, plenty of action, and passionate romance."
★Publishers Weekly STARRED REVIEW

"Fans of Amanda Quick's early historicals will find much to savor."
Booklist STARRED REVIEW

"Sexy, witty, and fiercely entertaining." *★Kirkus STARRED REVIEW*

Praise for S.M. LaViolette's Books:

"Lovers of historical romance will be hooked on this twisty story of revenge, redemption, and reversal of fortunes."
★Publishers Weekly STARRED REVIEW

"A remarkably resourceful heroine who can more than hold her own against any character invented by best-selling Bertrice Small, a suavely sophisticated hero with sex appeal to spare, and a cascade of lushly detailed love scenes give Spencer's dazzling debut its deliciously fun retro flavor."
★Booklist STARRED REVIEW

"Readers will love this lusty and unusual marriage of convenience story."
NYT Bestselling Author **MADELINE HUNTER**

"Smart, witty, graceful, sensual, elegant and gritty all at once. It has all of the meticulous attention to detail I love in Georgette Heyer, BUT WITH SEX!"
RITA-Award Winning Author JEFFE KENNEDY

More books by S.M. LaViolette & Minerva Spencer

THE ACADEMY OF LOVE SERIES

The Music of Love
A Figure of Love
A Portrait of Love
The Language of Love
Dancing with Love*
The Story of Love*

THE OUTCASTS SERIES

Dangerous
Barbarous
Scandalous

THE REBELS OF THE *TON*

Notorious
Outrageous
Infamous

THE MASQUERADERS

The Footman
The Postilion
The Bastard

THE SEDUCERS

Melissa and The Vicar
Joss and The Countess
Hugo and The Maiden

VICTORIAN DECADENCE

His Harlot
His Valet
His Countess
Her Master*
Her Beast*

THE BELLAMY SISTERS

PHOEBE*
HYACINTH*

THE WILD WOMEN OF WHITECHAPEL

THE BOXING BARONESS*
THE DUELING DUCHESS*

Novellas:

THE ARRANGEMENT: The Duke's Treasure
THE BACHELORS OF BOND STREET: A Second Chance for Love

*upcoming books

S.M. LAVIOLETTE

CROOKED SIXPENCE BOOKS are published by
CROOKED SIXPENCE PRESS

2 State Road 230
El Prado, NM 87529

First printing March 2022

10 9 8 7 6 5 4 3 2 1

Photo stock by Period Images
Printed in the United States of America

Prologue

St. Giles, London
1794

The most important person in John's world was dying right in front of him, and he couldn't do anything to help her.

"Gran?" he whispered, his hand shaking as he wiped the greasy, unhealthy-looking sweat from her brow.

Her eyes flickered open. They were sunken and red-rimmed, the whites a sickly yellow. "Sorry, John… so… sorry."

"Sorry 'bout what, Gran?"

"For—" She coughed, an awful hacking sound that made his own chest hurt just listening to it.

John kept a hand on her shoulder, needing to touch her. It had been hours since she'd last been awake; he'd felt so *alone.*

"I want to tell you, but"—*cough, cough, cough*—"dangerous." She sucked in a noisy breath.

"It's awright, Gran, you don't need—"

"Ask Kennedy."

"Kennedy?" John hadn't heard the name before.

"He's not as bad as—" She doubled over in a fit of coughing, blood spraying from her mouth.

"Gran!" John shrieked, and then froze, like a mouse in front of an alley cat. What should he do? What did she—

"I'm so sorry," she mumbled again and then slumped back onto the cot, her breathing even more ragged than before.

"It's awright, Gran," John whispered. "Please… just sleep so you can get better."

She'd been apologizing anytime she opened her eyes—for what, he didn't know—and he just wanted her to *stop.*

Like a serpent, her hand shot out and closed around his arm, surprising a yelp out of him. "Take the gown and go to him, John. He'll know—" Her body convulsed with the violence of her coughing.

"Gown?" John repeated.

But her eyes rolled back in her head, and she became still.

"Gran?" He shook her. "*Gran!*"

John whimpered with relief when she groaned and moved restlessly beneath the thin, sweat-soaked sheet. He scrubbed a tear off his cheek and sagged back in his rickety chair.

It was July and the weather in the tiny garret was so hot that John's eyeballs were sweating. There was no window in their section of the attic, so the only breeze came from the room next to theirs, which had only one tenant, a disagreeable man named Dolan.

Dolan scared him, even though he was small and wiry and not much bigger than John—who at five feet was exceptionally tall for his age. Not that he was sure exactly what his age was since Gran got confused about things like years and dates.

"How is she, boy?"

John's head whipped around at the sound of Dolan's voice, as if thinking about him had summoned him.

That's what his Gran said about the Devil: *don't think about him, John, or he'd come calling.*

Dolan might not be the Devil, but he was unwanted, all the same.

"I asked you a question, boy," Dolan snapped.

Looking into Dolan's eyes made his stomach curdle like he'd swallowed sour milk. "Sleepin'," he said, proud that he sounded defiant rather than scared.

Dolan gave a sharp bark of laughter and approached the bed. "That ain't sleep, boy—she's unconscious. You need a doctor."

That's what John thought, too. But he didn't have the money to pay one—even if he could convince one to come to Pigeon Alley, one of the most unsavory parts of St Giles.

"But I reckon that would be throwin' away money," Dolan said. "A quack would just tell you to take your leave of 'er." He tried to pat John on the shoulder, but John flinched away before the man could touch him.

"Why so skittish, young lad?" Dolan asked in a voice he probably meant to be friendly, but John saw the greedy, nasty glint in his eyes.

John couldn't think of anything to say, so he just shook his head.

Dolan glanced around their small, gloomy lodgings, his gaze settling on Gran's sewing bag—the only item of value in the room. The scissors in the bag, which John wasn't allowed to touch, were Gran's prized possession. Without them, she'd not be able to do her work.

There was also a thimble, some sharp needles in a little tin box, and a leather pouch that contained something John had never seen because his Gran had stitched it shut.

"This is yours," she'd said when he'd asked what was inside.

"Why can't I open it?" he'd asked, more than once.

"Someday you will."

"When?"

"Someday."

That was all he could ever get out of her.

Even though he'd been curious for years, now he couldn't bring himself to care about whatever was in the pouch. His eyes slid back to Gran. And he knew, with sick certainty, that she'd die if he couldn't get a doctor.

John wished he could ask his Gran what to do, but it was down to him—he was the man of the family.

"I have something—maybe enough to pay a doctor," John blurted before he lost his nerve.

Dolan's eyes glittered with interest. "Oh?"

"Gran's scissors." He half expected her to leap from the bed at his suggestion, but she didn't even twitch.

"Let me see them," Dolan said, no longer smirking. Maybe he wanted to help? John needed *somebody* to help.

He dug around in the bag, pushing aside some bits of cloth, a small notebook that Gran had kept, even though she couldn't read, her needle tin, the leather pouch—and at the bottom of the bag was the thick felt case with the scissors. John glanced at his Gran as he took them from the bag. Normally he'd never be so bold, but she didn't even shift on her cot when he handed the valuable item over to Dolan.

Dolan unwrapped the felt and held the fancy-handled scissors closer to the smoky tallow candle. "These're fancy—she must 'ave pinched 'em."

"Gran don't steal!" John shouted, even though he'd wondered how she'd afforded such a nice pair.

Dolan chuckled. "Calm down, lad, I was just teasin'. These'll be enough to get Feehan over 'ere to take a look."

Feehan was a butcher who lived several streets away and had once lanced a boil on John's knee. He was a filthy, frightening mountain of a man, but Gran had summoned him for that, so she obviously trusted him.

John held out his hand for the scissors.

"Nah, you don't want to go out on the street wiv somefink, so rum, do ye?"

That was true, but John also didn't want to leave anything valuable—or rum, to use Dolan's street cant—with the unpleasant little man, either.

"Just tell the butcher that Jake Dolan says you can pay."

John hesitated, not liking the thought of leaving the scissors or his Gran, but what choice did he have?

"You want me to sit here while you go—keep 'er company?"

Dolan's kind offer made John feel bad that he didn't like or trust the man.

He nodded again and then forced himself to speak up like a big lad, like Gran always said, "Thank you."

Dolan took the chair where John had been sitting. "Go on, now. I'll watch 'er. You best be runnin'."

John turned and ran.

***

It took John almost three hours to track down Feehan, who wasn't at his shop, but at a rat pit on the far edge of St. Giles.

The huge butcher wouldn't leave with John until the terrier he'd put money on took a nasty bite from a rat and was out of the running.

Because of his loss, Feehan was in a foul mood and grumbled as he shuffled after John, moving so slowly that John had to chew his tongue to keep from shouting at him to hurry. Something told him that the nasty butcher would only go slower, or worse, not come at all.

"You'd better have the balsam to pay me, boy," Feehan threatened in between wheezes.

"I can pay." John didn't tell Feehan he didn't have money, but barter was just as good. At least he hoped it was.

When they got to John's building Feehan stared up at it and swore. "Bloody hell! You're on the top floor. I remember this place. Old lady Fielding—you're her brat, ain'tcha?" He scowled and sighed when John nodded. "Well, get on with ye."

John bolted up the steps, suddenly terrified that Dolan might have taken the scissors and left his grandmother alone. After all, he didn't know the man. What if—

But when he reached the top floor, breathless and sweaty, he found Dolan standing on the landing, almost as if he'd been waiting for him, his rat-like features pulled into a sad expression, but his eyes as sharp as ever.

"She died, boy—not long after you left."

John pushed past him, and Dolan grabbed his arm. "You don't want to go in there, lad."

"Lemme go!" John shouted, squirming.

"You don't need to see her. It ain't pretty, boy."

Dolan's sleeve rode up, exposing his wrist, which John couldn't help noticing was already bleeding from what looked to be scratches. John opened his mouth wide and bit him as hard as he could.

Dolan gave a bloodcurdling scream and released his grip; John sped through the darkened room and came to a stumbling stop in front of Gran's cot.

Her eyes were wide open as they'd not been in days, her expression one of terror. On the floor was the dingy, flattened cushion that had been beneath her head when John left. It was damp with blood and something that looked like vomit.

A huge hand clamped on his shoulder. Unlike Dolan's grip, Feehan's was unbreakable. "You owe me—I don't care if she's dead. I made the trip."

John couldn't seem to find any words.

"The boy lied if he told you 'ee 'ad money, Feehan," Dolan said, coming up to stand beside the butcher, cradling his bloody wrist.

"I did not!" John looked for Gran's sewing bag, but it was gone. He whirled on Dolan. "Where is it?"

Dolan sneered. "What the hell are you talking about?"

"Gran's scissors and her bag! You took it!" John launched himself at the loathsome, grinning man, surprising Dolan enough to knock him to the attic floor.

He was pummeling the small man when something hard struck him on the back of the skull and his head exploded with pain and white sparks.

John lost track of time, only coming back to himself when Feehan shook him so violently it felt like his head would snap off.

"Why, you little bastard! You lied to me." The butcher slapped him hard. "Nobody lies to me and gets away without payin'!" Feehan hit again, this time with his fist and not his palm, and everything went black.

The next time John came to, he was tied to the chair with torn up strips of sheet and the cot was empty.

"Where's me Gran?" he demanded of Dolan, who was digging through the old crate where Gran had kept a few bits of food when they'd had any.

"Gone. It's too bleedin' 'ot to leave 'er lyin' out."

"That ain't what I asked! Where is she?"

Dolan ignored him.

"Where's me Gran?" John hollered, struggling against his bonds when the man wouldn't answer. But the old sheets, when twisted and used like ropes, were tougher than he'd expected.

"Where's the scissors?" he yelled, his vision red and his body trembling with rage.

Dolan finally turned around and came closer; his eyes so cold that John recoiled. "Feehan wouldn't take the scissors so I paid 'im outta me own pocket." His already slitted eyes narrowed even more. "That means you owe me."

"You're lying!"

Dolan slapped him hard and then raised his fist when John opened his mouth to yell again. "You'd best shut up if you don't want another."

John blinked away the pain, furious when he felt tears on his cheeks.

"What do ye got to repay me, boy?"

"I can w-work," he stammered. "I'll run messages and clean out stalls and—"

"I run me own messages and I ain't got no stalls."

"I'm big—I can work. I can—" He flinched as Dolan ran a finger down John's jaw, his eyes glittering in a way that made him feel like puking.

"Yes, what a big boy you are. Why, I remember the first time I saw you, not long after yer ma died. You was just a babe and dressed as fine as a fivepence." He gave an ugly laugh as he tugged at the filthy collar of John's shirt. "Not so fine now, eh?"

John tried to concentrate on what Dolan was saying, but his body was shaking with fear.

"I recall yer ma, she was a right flash piece." He licked his lips in a way that made John sick. "I reckon anyone could be yer da—"

"Gran said me da was called Joe—"

"Joe and Mary?" Dolan hooted. "Ride up on a donkey, did they? Was you born in a manger?"

John glared up at him, too angry to even speak.

Dolan scratched his ear. "Mary was swellin' wiv somebody's brat before she died. I reckon yer da is either Kennedy or Bower. They used to 'ang about with Mary back then, but I don't recall no *Joe.*"

"You're a liar!"

He leered down at John. "Yer ma had lots o' men, but none that wanted to marry such a worn out jade."

"They were married! You're a liar!" John couldn't stop screaming over and over and over, until even he couldn't understand the garbled words. He just knew that he needed to stop Dolan from talking. He needed to keep him from wrecking John's memories—which were all he had left—with his vicious lies.

Dolan slapped him. "Shut up, you little bastard before I—"

"What's goin' on 'ere, Dolly?" somebody demanded.

Dolan yelped and spun around.

The voice belonged to an immense man dressed in fine, bright-colored clothing that was blinding in the dingy room. "Can't keep a wean under control wi'out tyin' 'im to a chair?"

"You go ahead and laugh, Alfie. You won't fink it's so funny when 'ee bites *your* 'and."

Alfie turned to John. "You bite *my* hand and I'll break your 'ead, boy."

John quit squirming as Alfie towered over him, his gaze speculative and his green eyes as hard as the stained glass in the church where Gran forced John to go some Sundays when she was well enough.

"So, you're young John Fielding, eh?" Alfie's eyes flickering over John in a way that made him feel like an animal up for auction. "Don't look much like yer ma."

"You knew me Mam?" John blurted.

Alfie leered. "Aye, I knew 'er." He made a thrusting gesture with his hips and laughed; Dolan joined in with him, the sound as ugly as they were.

"That's a lie! She never—"

Alfie backhanded him, his arm a blur.

John flinched back before the blow made contact, so Alfie's enormous paw only clipped his ear. But it still hurt badly enough to make his eyes water.

"You shut yer gob, boy. I 'spect you've a lot to learn," Alfie muttered, scowling down at him briefly before turning to Dolan, "So, 'ow much you want for 'im?" Alfie asked. "'Ee's too big to be a lily white."

John gawped up at Alfie. Lily white? Surely, they weren't talking about selling *him* as a chimney sweep? "You can't sell me! I'm not—"

Alfie lifted his fist, and John shut his mouth.

The giant turned to Dolan. "I'll give you a couple'a twelvers for 'im."

"Two shillings?" Dolan squawked. "That won't be enough to—"

Alfie's hand shot out.

Unlike John, Dolan wasn't fast enough, and the blow caught him full in the head, knocking him to the floor. "You shut yer gob, too. Or did you forget 'ow much you owe Fast Eddie? By rights I oughta just *take* this boy."

Dolan cowered in a way that John would've enjoyed if he weren't so terrified of the giant himself.

"Yeah, yeah, sorry 'bout that, Alfie. Er, I'll take the money. Fanks, Alfie."

Alfie grunted and then pulled a knife from a sheath on his belt.

John yelped and cringed when Alfie leaned toward him.

Rather than hit him again, Alfie just chuckled. "Calm yersel, little man. I din't pay for ye just to snuff ye." He cut John's hands and legs free. "Do I need to tie ye? You gonna run, or you gonna come nice-like?"

John opened his mouth to ask where they were going, but one look in Alfie's hard eyes told him that would only earn him another cuffing.

"I won't cause no problems."

Alfie winked. "There's a smart lad."

"Where's me Gran?" John risked asking.

Alfie frowned at him but turned to Dolan. "Where'd you send 'er?"

"A gent from St. Bart's came for 'er."

Alfie's hand shot out and his huge paw wrapped around Dolan's throat. "Where's the balsam?"

Dolan's mouth moved, but only gasps came out.

"What?" Alfie asked, leaning closer.

Dolan must have said something because Alfie tossed him on the floor like a rag doll and then bent to yank off his shoe. Coins rolled onto the floor, and Alfie scooped them up and dropped them into his coat pocket.

Alfie turned to John. "Yer Gran's gone—already buried." He grabbed John's shoulder and shoved him out the door. "You keep your mouth shut and don't ask no questions. You only need to remember one fing from now on: you belong to Fast Eddie. "

John didn't know it then, but in the years to come he'd discover that Alfie hadn't exaggerated—he belonged to Fast Eddie: body, mind, and soul.

Chapter 1

Twenty-Four Years Later
London
1818

John leaned against the lamppost and watched the three women alight from the carriage. He'd left his horse in an alley a few streets over and walked the short distance to avoid the chaotic congestion that always marked Bond Street, the *ton's* favorite fashion haunt.

He'd been watching the three women for weeks; watching *her*, really. At first, he'd had a reason to spy on them—an unpleasant, criminal reason, but a reason, all the same. But now…

Well, somehow watching her had become a habit. John told himself that was because he had nothing pressing to do. For the first time in years—hell, for the first time in his life—he was his own man and could do whatever he damn well pleased.

Apparently, what he pleased was stalking a spinster and her two youthful charges.

John barely noticed the younger women—Ladies Melissa and Jane—even though both were, objectively, more attractive than their aunt, Miss Cordelia Page.

But it hadn't been Miss Page's face or body that had first drawn John's interest. To be honest, he'd barely noticed her when he'd started watching the three women. He never would have bothered spying on them again after the first time if Miss Page had not done something to intrigue him.

It had been the type of scene that had played out all over London all day, every day, for centuries: a group of boys tormenting a street cur; poor boys picking on something weaker than themselves and being cruel for reasons of their own—or no reason at all.

Miss Page had been the only one in her party who'd noticed the yelping dog and the boys pelting it with stones, their voices loud and raucous. She had stopped in the center of the walkway while her companions walked on, unaware that they'd lost her.

By the time the two girls and their footman had noticed she was gone, Miss Page was confronting the five jeering boys in the alley, her hands on her hips, her body between them and the cowering dog

She'd had no clue about the danger she was facing.

John had run toward her when he'd guessed what she was doing, but he'd been too far away and would never have made it in time.

Fortunately, the footman was closer, and he reached the fray in time to launch himself between Miss Page and a sizeable rock. The servant took the projectile in the chest and the young ruffians ran when they saw what they'd done.

The footman would have a bruise but was not otherwise the worse for wear.

Meanwhile, the woman—oblivious to the danger she'd just faced—picked up the cringing animal and cradled it in her arms, regardless of dirt and disease, holding it as if it were the most precious thing on earth.

John had stood frozen at the opening of the alley and gawked, as though *he'd* been the one hit with a rock. A dog. She had risked herself for a filthy old dog that would probably die, anyhow.

Women of her class didn't do such things.

Except now John knew they did. Or at least *one* of them did.

After that, he'd found himself following the trio again the following week. And the week after that.

John didn't follow her *every* day. He wasn't that bad.

Yet.

It wasn't as if they went anywhere interesting or exciting. Today they were going into a modiste's shop. The last time it had been a bookseller. The time before a modiste *and* a bookseller. Upper-class women appeared to do little other than shop. Even ones like Miss Page who were unmarried, impoverished gentlewomen dependent on their wealthy relatives' whims and kindness.

To be frank, John was bloody fed up with his irrational obsession with the woman. He had never been fixated on a woman in his life. He'd learned early in life that wanting things was the fastest road to disappointment. The more you wanted something, the more disappointed you'd be when you couldn't have it. Or when it was taken away.

All he'd ever allowed himself to want was revenge: revenge against the man who'd abandoned John and his Mam, leaving them to die in the gutter.

Revenge was cold and consuming and implacable; it was an emotion he could understand.

What he was experiencing right then—a gut-clawing yearning—was unlike anything he'd ever felt before.

He'd tried arguing himself out of his obsession, but his brain refused to listen. He wanted Miss Cordelia Page more than ever with each day that passed.

John had no earthly idea why he was so transfixed by the woman. He didn't want to just bed her, although that idea had certainly taken root the more he'd watched her; he also felt a compulsion to—God help him—*know* her.

What the hell did that even mean?

Everyone John had allowed himself to get close to was dead and that had taught him a valuable lesson: keep people at a distance.

John hadn't invited Miss Page into his head—he didn't want her there—and yet she'd inveigled her way in. It was bloody annoying.

He'd allowed one person into his life in the past two decades, his ex-employer, Stephen Worth. The only reason he'd allowed Worth in was because the man had rescued John from Hell and then given him a job.

He'd also given John a reason to live: revenge.

Revenge had been enough for years.

Until now.

Miss Page had not rescued any other dogs, but he'd seen other acts of kindness. She always had a penny for a street sweeper, a kind word for the servants who fetched and carried, and she was patient with her spoiled nieces even when they were petulant or rude to her.

She was a poor relation—a woman who was tolerated only so long as she was useful—and yet she faced her servitude with humor and good-natured acceptance.

If there was one thing in life that John knew plenty about, it was servitude—and he'd never faced it with good humor or acceptance.

Just what made this woman so bloody cheerful all the time? And why did she intrigue him so much, like a shiny object that he could see, but never quite well enough to make out the details? John *needed* to get closer.

He paused beside a lamppost to watch her from beneath the brim of his hat.

As far as John could tell, she possessed only a handful of dresses while the two girls—his stepsisters, not that anyone would ever believe such a relationship existed—never wore the same garment twice.

It wasn't surprising that the girls did not resemble him. Not only did they have a different mother, but—as the legitimate daughters of a duke—they had also enjoyed an entirely different life—one of ease and plenty.

John could just imagine the dainty girls' reactions if they ever learned that he was their bastard half-brother.

The thought made him grin, a gruesome sight that caused an approaching pedestrian to stumble and careen into a pair of young bucks.

"On the tipple this early?" one dandy jeered after the older man.

Then the fop spotted John and his taunting smile slid from his face faster than a whore dropped her knickers. "Oh, beg your pardon," he murmured, scuttling out of John's way.

John ignored both his horrified stare and his apology and kept his eyes on the three women, who were disappearing into the modiste's shop, where they would most likely be for hours. And when they came out? They would climb into their carriage and go to some other shop.

Was he really going to wait around for hours just for a glimpse that lasted no longer than a few seconds?

John sighed. Yes, he was.

He pushed himself off the lamppost and crossed the street to one of tea shops that catered to the throngs of Bond Street loungers.

The hum of conversation inside the crowded shop leaked from the room like water from a cracked mug when he entered. John paid no attention to either the sudden silence or the staring eyes and lowered his big frame into a spindly chair near the bow window.

He ordered a pot of tea that he had no intention of drinking and commenced to wait.

***

Cordelia was careful to mask her true thoughts on the hat that her niece, Melissa, was currently modeling. Hiding her feelings was something Cordelia did well. She had learned it was wiser to ignore Melissa's whims rather than confront them head on.

"It *is* a fetching bonnet, my dear." *For a lady of the night.* "However, that shade of red will not flatter the apricot muslin you are planning to wear to Lady Northumberland's *fête champêtre.*"

Melissa scowled at her reflection and plucked off the dreadful hat, handing it back to the hovering shop clerk. "I suppose you are correct. What about that one?" She pointed to a far more appropriate straw and pale green voile concoction and the clerk went to fetch it.

Satisfied that she'd steered Melissa into a more suitable direction, Cordelia turned to her younger niece, Jane, who sat slouched on a settee, her nose in a book. Her pelisse, bonnet, gloves, and reticule lay scattered about her on the plush divan, as though she were a volcano that had erupted, spewing women's garments far and wide.

"Jane, darling, won't you please choose a hat?"

Jane glanced up, her blue eyes unfocused behind thick, smudged spectacles. "I beg your pardon, Aunt Cordy?"

"A hat, my dear. That is why we are in a millinery shop, among all these hats. You must select one."

Her smooth brow wrinkled. "Must I?"

"If you care to attend Lady Northumberland's party tomorrow."

Jane appeared to be giving her words serious consideration.

"You have already accepted the invitation, Jane. It would be unkind to change your mind at this late date. Besides, you wanted to see her conservatory for yourself."

"That's true." Jane pursed her lips and grudgingly closed her book. "Can you not choose something for me?"

The shop bell jingled and Cordelia turned to find Eldon Simpson, the Earl of Madeley, looking very much like a fox surveying a henhouse.

Well, drat.

"I thought I recognized His Grace's carriage in that dreadful snarl outside." The earl spoke to Melissa, although his eyes flickered to Cordelia, to whom he gave the slightest of nods.

Melissa flushed in a way that made Cordelia's heart sink. How could her niece not recognize a cold-blooded fortune hunter when she saw one? That was a foolish question and Cordelia knew it. Her sister's children had been sheltered and cosseted from the moment they'd been born. They had no clue what dangers the world held for pretty—seemingly wealthy—girls.

Cordelia approached the handsome earl, whom she knew to be one step away from being chased by shopkeepers bearing pitchforks, torches, and unpaid bills.

"Good afternoon, my lord." She masked the chill in her voice with a pleasant smile.

"Good afternoon, Miss Page." He glanced at Melissa and then Jane. "Will you ladies be gracing Lady Northumberland's party tomorrow?"

"That is why we are here, to select new hats," Melissa said.

Jane had already inserted her nose back in her book and appeared unaware of the handsome lord's existence.

The earl's eyes widened; all the better to show off their sky-blue color. "Hat shopping? I adore it above all things."

Melissa laughed. "Will you be going to the party, my lord?"

"Why, I wouldn't miss it for the world, Lady Melissa."

Cordelia suspected the earl would rather be boiled in oil than attend such an insipid affair, but he was so strapped as to make finding a wealthy bride—immediately—a necessity.

"Oh, dear," Cordelia said in the diffident tone that she knew people expected of spinster aunts. "I'm afraid we are running terribly late."

Melissa cut her a narrow-eyed look. "Surely we needn't leave just yet, Aunt."

Cordelia gave her niece a vague smile. As a poor relation, she was adept at appearing impervious to slights, irritated sighs, or withering looks. "I recall seeing something the exact shade of your gown at Madame Lisette's. We must make haste and see if the hat is still available." She didn't wait for Melissa's answer and turned to Jane, helping her younger niece collect her scattered possessions before ushering her toward the door. "It was a pleasure seeing you again, my lord." She nodded at the hardened rake and gave her seething niece an encouraging smile. "Shall we go, Melissa?"

Lord Madeley bowed over Melissa's hand. "I shall see you again soon, Lady Melissa."

Melissa waited until they were out on the street again before hissing, "That was very rude, Aunt Cordy!" She sounded remarkably like her mother—Cordelia's elder sister—the Duchess of Falkirk.

Jane pushed her smudged spectacles further up her rather beaky nose—she bore more of a resemblance to her regal father than her beautiful mother—and scowled at her sister. "Oh, don't be such a cat, Mel. Anyone can see Lord Madeley is nothing but a hedge bird."

Cordelia had to bite her lip to keep from laughing. "Jane, that is hardly a polite thing for a lady to say."

"I'm sure she learned it from Charles," Melissa said.

Cordelia suspected Melissa was right. Unlike most young men his age, Charles Merrick—the duke's son and heir—did not find it unmanning to socialize with a female.

Cordelia was waiting for the two girls to climb into the barouche when a vast expanse of great coat-covered chest appeared in front of her. Cordelia looked up and up and up to a man so big that his towering form blocked the sun and left his face in shadow.

"I believe you dropped this." The deep voice did not sound entirely English.

The footman, Marcus, who'd been helping Jane settle into the carriage, turned, saw the stranger, and puffed up like a belligerent rooster. "Here then; what do you want?" He attempted to thrust himself between Cordelia and the interloper but failed when the huge stranger did not budge.

Marcus was a big man, but he looked like a boy next to the giant.

The stranger turned in profile to cut a dismissive glance at the footman, and Cordelia gasped as sunshine illuminated his face.

Heat surged up Cordelia's neck at her ill-bred response.

Rather than be insulted by her reaction, the man appeared to be amused, his lips twisting into something that might have been a smile, although it was difficult to say given the way his scarred cheeks pulled in such unnatural directions.

His coal-black eyes burned into her. "Is this yours?" he repeated.

Cordelia knew she should at least glance at whatever he was attempting to return, but she couldn't look away from his gaze. Aside from the savage scars radiating out from both corners of his mouth, he was handsome in a stern, unsmiling way. His nose was the high-bridged regal beak that was so prevalent in England's oldest families—or at least it had been regal before it had been broken and poorly set.

His most unusual characteristic after his scarred visage was his hair, which was a glossy black and long enough to be worn in a queue. Outside of a few military units that still adhered to the custom, it was unusual to see long hair on a man.

"Ma'am?" He raised a jet-black eyebrow at her and she wrenched her gaze from his face and looked down to see a rose-pink glove in his huge hand.

Cordelia blinked; his *six-fingered* hand.

"Aunt Cordy?" Jane poked her head outside the carriage. She looked from the giant to his hand. "Oh, that is my glove." Her open smile made Cordelia even more aware of her own rude, open-mouthed gawking.

The stranger cut Jane a dismissive look as he handed her the glove.

"Thank you, sir," Jane said.

But his eyes were already back on Cordelia.

She exhaled the breath she'd been holding and fixed a gracious smile on her mouth. "Yes, thank you, sir." She was pleased that her voice sounded so much calmer than her flustered brain.

His nostrils flared slightly, and he gave an abrupt nod and turned, his graceful movements a surprise for such a massive body.

Cordelia couldn't help watching as he cleaved oncoming pedestrian traffic like a human axe, the people he passed cutting him furtive, anxious glances.

And then he turned down an alley and disappeared.

"Goodness," Cordelia murmured, her legs strangely weak, her mind a whirl.

"Did you see that, Aunt Cordy?" Jane leaned toward Cordelia, her blue eyes wide.

She was formulating a gentle chastisement about ladies not commenting on the disfigurements of others when her niece continued. "I have never met anyone other than me, Charles, and Papa like this, have you?" She held up her right hand.

Cordelia looked at Jane's six-fingered hand, grateful she had misjudged Jane's interest in the stranger.

It just so happened that Cordelia *had* met two others with the distinctive extra digit on their right hand and both were the duke's natural offspring. Could that mountain of a man possibly be related to the Duke of Falkirk? Her sister's husband was notorious for sowing his seed far and wide, perhaps—

"Have you seen anyone else with six fingers?" Jane asked again.

Cordelia could hardly mention her father's infidelities, so, instead, she sat back against the plush velvet squabs, oddly exhausted by the brief encounter, and said, "No, Jane, I haven't."

***

John waited until he'd turned into the alley to look at the small square of embroidered linen in his hand, *C. F. P.*

Thanks to his investigation of the duke's family, he knew the initials stood for Cordelia Frances Page. He also knew she was the Duchess of Falkirk's much younger sibling and had come to live with her sister several years before. Miss Page had grown up in a modest country squire's house, close to the Duke of Falkirk's family seat, and was in her early thirties. She had no beau in London or in the area around the duke's house, which was where she spent most of her time when she wasn't launching a niece into society.

John ran his thumb over the raised needlework. It had been easy to pluck the handkerchief from where she kept it tucked in the wrist of her left glove. While John was not a skilled pickpocket—or cly faker as it was called in street cant—he'd done his share of it when he'd been a lad, until he'd grown too large to blend in.

Tiny violets and even smaller green leaves encircled the initials. The workmanship was exquisite. John raised the handkerchief to his nose and inhaled. The small cloth had a scent, although not of violets. Whatever the fragrance was, it was sharply aromatic, and John could not identify it. He inhaled deeply and held the breath in his lungs, savoring it like he would a fine brandy.

John knew that women of Miss Page's class—when they were not shopping or attending balls or parties—spent their time employed in activities like needlework.

But not the type of needlework his Gran had done—stitching garments for a tailor by the dim light of a tallow candle until her eyes were too weak to see, her fingers too bent and stiff to ply a needle.

John shoved aside the broken shard of memory and pictured instead the woman who must have labored on this tiny square of fabric.

The sun had been at his back and had thrown her face into relief. Her eyes were a kaleidoscope of greens and browns with a hint of gold. But it wasn't the color that made him take notice so much as the expression in them. Large and slightly up-tilted at the outer edges, they seemed to be smiling, even when they had looked up at him.

And people never smiled when they looked at John.

Her lips were not bow-shaped like those so admired by poets, but full and mobile. They'd stood so close that he'd seen small brackets around her lips—lines made by smiling and laughing. Although she probably didn't know it, hers was a mouth made for sensual pleasures.

Her figure was not the slim, fragile type so admired by the *ton*, but then John was not a member of that august assemblage. She was voluptuous—his preferred type of female body—and he could imagine how well she'd fit in his arms and had done so far more often that he'd liked.

Her wide hazel eyes had taken in his scars with a thoughtful expression that had startled him. It wasn't the look he normally saw on women's faces. No, the usual reactions were either fear or a combination of morbid attraction and sexual curiosity.

John had long ago become accustomed to people gawking at his face, and it didn't bother him. And why wouldn't people stare at him? He was hideously scarred.

But Miss Page had looked beyond his scars—or at least it had felt that way—making him feel like a book she'd opened and begun leafing through. Could she see the things he'd done? The things he was still doing. The things he had planned for her family.

The whimsical notion was utterly unlike him. It was far more likely that Miss Page was merely more self-possessed than most people. What had looked like thoughtfulness had probably been a polite mask of shock and revulsion. He knew women of her class were taught to conceal their feelings.

John gave vent to an exasperated groan when he realized he was standing in an alley, like an infatuated dunce, thinking about the blasted woman. Again.

It didn't matter how often he told himself that she was just another impoverished spinster, a woman of average beauty well past her prime who was nothing special.

No, that argument was as toothless as an old crone.

He wanted her. Badly.

John scowled and shoved away thoughts of the woman, carefully tucking away the handkerchief he'd stolen as he approached the lad holding his horse.

He took the reins and tossed the boy a coin.

The lad, no older than ten or twelve, tilted his head back and stared up a good two feet at John. "'E bit me, sir." He held out a scrawny limb as proof. His arm was stick-thin with pasty skin stretched over bone, the half-starved body of a street urchin. There was an undeniable U-shaped imprint of equine teeth on his small forearm.

John wasn't surprised; the big dun colored stallion was an ugly, irascible beast. Much like John, himself.

He swung himself into the saddle and looked down at the lad's upturned face. "He bit you, but you did not let him go?"

"No, guv." The boy's pinched face was serious and his gaze was steady, even though most grown men quailed beneath John's stare.

John tossed him another coin. "If you want to get bitten again, come to Berkeley Square; I have need of a stout stable lad."

The boy grinned, and the expression exposed a set of teeth that were two shy of the normal complement. "Aye, guv."

John snorted at the boy's enthusiasm and wheeled his mount.

"You didn't say which 'ouse, guv. I know all the swell's 'ouses—I used to be a lily white," he said, trotting alongside him.

John had pegged the lad for a chimney sweep, thanks to his soot-stained face. "It's the biggest house on the square."

"But ain't that the Duke of Falkirk's house?"

John smiled grimly and kneed his horse into a canter. "Not anymore."

Chapter 2

St. Giles
1798

John was chewing on a stale currant bun, watching the smaller children scramble for their share of food, when Des Houlihan grabbed a boy named Ben Watkins by the shoulder.

"Food ain't for the likes of you, Watkins!" Des barked, flinging Ben's body across the room.

Everyone but John laughed when Ben fell into a tangle of legs and arms.

Des towered over the cringing boy. "You'll get food when you earn it." He spun on his heel and headed for the door, stopping when he spied John staring at him.

"What're you lookin' at, Fielding?" Des stalked toward him, clearly expecting him to cringe, too.

"I ain't lookin' at nothin'." John glared at the hateful man, refusing to look away. He'd shot up over the last two years and could look Des right in his piggy eyes.

Fast Eddie had noted John's unusual size and had put him to fight against other boys twice, and once against a dog. It had pleased Eddie when John had won all three times and he'd given John a twelver and promised him more fights.

But John knew Eddie wouldn't be happy if he attacked Des Houlihan, because Des was Eddie's brother.

And so he backed down.

"You keep them Hell-black eyes offa me before I knock 'em right outta yer head." Des raised his fist to cuff him and John prudently dropped his gaze to the filthy floor. "Know yer place, Fielding."

John's body didn't unclench until Des left the dirty, cramped room that the youngest of Fast Eddie's employees—the kiddies, as child thieves were called—called home.

Des had disliked John since his first week, either because John was so big and Des so stunted, or because John had had the brass—not to mention stupidity—to ask if Des knew a man named Dolan.

Des had knocked him across the room. "Dolan works for Eddie and that makes him none of yer business. It ain't for the likes of *you* to be pryin' in Fast Eddie's affairs."

Des hadn't realized it, but he'd given away a piece of Eddie's *business* by telling John that Dolan worked for him—something he hadn't known before.

But the hateful man was right about one thing; it was dangerous to pry so openly.

That was the last time John had brought up Dolan directly, but that didn't mean he'd stopped looking for the man who'd likely murdered his Gran and nicked her bag.

John would *never* stop looking for Dolan.

The sound of whimpering pulled him from his dark thoughts. Ben was cowering in a corner, cradling his arm like it was an infant.

John sighed and strode over to the younger boy, dropping to his haunches to examine the scrapes and bruises on his arm and face. "Did that bastard bust yer arm?"

Ben shook his head and then winced at the pain it caused.

The other boy was lucky it wasn't broken. Just last week, Des had smashed the ankle of a kiddie named Tommy after discovering that Tommy had held back a few pennies from his daily take. Tommy had laid around after Des broke his leg, moaning and begging for food for three days before he'd disappeared. Two days after that, Tommy's body had washed up on the muddy banks of the Thames at low tide.

There had been two lessons to take away from that episode.

One, never steal from Fast Eddie.

Two, if you can't work, you weren't worth keeping around.

John had felt sorry for Tommy, but he'd hadn't shared his food or helped the other boy because Tommy had been a nasty little toad who'd bullied the younger children.

Ben, on the other hand, was gentle, timid, and not too smart. But he was kind, and John had seen him share his food with the smaller kiddies more than once.

John handed the boy a bun. "Here."

"But Des said—"

"I don't care a damn what that cunt says," John snarled.

Ben recoiled but clutched the bun and vigorously nodded his thanks.

Mismatched boots and a filthy green skirt appeared next to John, and Lily slid down beside him. "What's this, then? Got a new pet, John?"

John scowled at her, and she laughed. Lily laughed a lot, although, as far as John was concerned, there wasn't much to laugh *about.*

Lily was too old to be living with the rest of them, but, for some reason, she was still in with the kiddies instead of working in one of Fast Eddie's brothels, where girls usually went after they'd reached a certain age.

It had been Lily who'd first approached John when he'd first come to live with the kiddies. At first, he'd worked alone picking pockets—and not successfully, either. Lily had convinced him to join her sham after the boy she'd worked with had been moved on to another job.

Without her help, John would probably have ended up like Tommy—dead in the river.

"Ben's comin' with us tomorrow," John said to Lily, speaking even though his mouth was full, something his Gran would have slapped him for. But everyone here chewed with their mouths full and nobody cared. They cared more that there was something they *could* chew.

"Oh! You're the boss now, eh?" she teased, her voice full of good humor.

John didn't answer, so Lily turned to Ben. "You can come with me an' John, we've got a good wheedle goin'."

That was an understatement; John and Lily both brought in more money than any of the others, even the older ones who lived on the floor above them. John didn't fool himself that it was thanks to him. No, it was all thanks to Lily.

When she'd first approached him, John had been ashamed at the thought of being rescued by a mere girl. But he'd quickly swallowed his pride and done what she'd told him to do. Lily was the reason he'd eaten so well every day and grown so big and strong.

Even though Des hated him, he wouldn't act on that hate because John was a good earner, and in Fast Eddie's organization, only two things mattered: doing what you were told and bringing in money.

John ate the rest of his bun while Lily explained to Ben that tomorrow he'd be throwing his body beneath a carriage driven by a toff.

"What?" Ben demanded, eyes bulging.

Lily laughed and nudged John in the ribs. "Remember what you called me when I told yer that, John?"

John smiled faintly. "I said you were as mad as a mudlark." He still thought so, even though he'd flung himself beneath carriages more than a few times, although that wasn't what he was best at.

"Mad as a mudlark is right." Lily laughed, and even Ben, usually too scared to find much humor in anything, laughed with her.

Lily nudged John again and handed him a bun. Her gray eyes, her best feature by far, were uncharacteristically serious. "You shouldn't a given yours away—you're too bleedin' big to go without. Take it. You need it more'n I do." There were dark smudges beneath her eyes and she looked tired; yet she was trying to give him food that she needed. Why Lily was so good to him had always been a mystery.

"I'm not hungry."

"Liar." But she laughed and took the bun back.

She ate in silence for a moment before she leaned close and said, "Des said I'm goin' to Jenny Holloway's."

John's jaw dropped, and he turned to stare at her. Jenny Holloway's was one of Fast Eddie's whorehouses—the meanest, dirtiest, roughest one.

"When?"

"Friday."

"That's only two days away!"

Lily nodded.

John scrambled for something to say, but there was nothing. To refuse to go was… well, unthinkable. Even if Des just tossed her onto the street—instead of into the river—there was nowhere else to go and Lily would end up whoring or starving.

"I—I never thought they'd make you go," he said lamely.

"I didn't either—not with Des always tellin' me I'm so ugly and lame, to boot." She laughed, but there was no humor in it this time. "Well, I guess I ain't ugly and lame enough."

"You're not ugly," John retorted, his face heating with shame because he'd once thought exactly that. It was strange, but after working alongside her, hearing her laugh, and seeing how kind she was, John couldn't remember why he'd ever thought she was ugly.

Lily patted his knee, as if *he* was the one who needed comforting. "My knight protector."

John scowled and blushed. "I don't understand, Lil. Why would they send you away? Don't all the money you bring in matter?"

"Des said run goods—even like me—is worth a packet."

John knew that was true enough. Rich men were mad for run goods—street cant for virgins—and paid ridiculous sums.

"Des said the punter won't care 'ow ugly I am if it's dark enough."

"He's a rotting whore's son!" John spat, anger burning like acid in his gut. "I'm going to kill 'im one day, Lil—I swear it."

"Hush, you! What would 'appen if somebody 'eard?"

John was so bloody tired of living in fear, of taking the cuffs and kicks that Des constantly inflicted on those who were weaker. And he was sick of watching the few people he liked—like Lily or Ben—being treated like rubbish.

Sending Lily to Bella's—the nicest of Eddie's brothels—would have been bad enough. But sending her to Jenny Holloway's was beyond cruel. The girls who worked at Holloway's looked worn and ill and dead inside. Lily had so much life in her; how long would that be true?

"I'll be fine, John, don'tcher worry." Lily leaned over and gave him a peck on the cheek, the action making his face hot and causing all the other kiddies to snigger.

John didn't think Lily would be *fine* at all. None of them would—not unless they could get away from Fast Eddie before he used them up like bum fodder and then threw them away.

John felt like his head would explode the more he thought about Lily's grim future.

And there wasn't a damned thing he could do to stop it.

Chapter 3

London
1818

The footman who opened the door to John's house on Berkeley Square was the only man he'd met in England who was bigger than him.

The younger man gave John a grin of pure joy. "Good afternoon, Mr. Fielding."

John grunted and handed over his hat and gloves.

The footman, Fredrick, or Daft Freddie, as John had heard one of his other footmen call the giant—right before John had sacked the man—talked slowly and moved with the careful deliberation of a child.

Frederick had shown up for a footman position, even though John hadn't advertised for one. Indeed, he'd not advertised for any servants and yet their number seemed to be increasing weekly, mainly because John appeared to have difficulty saying no. Especially to somebody like Frederick.

When John's aged butler, Sims, had brought Frederick to his library, it had put John in mind of a cow being led to slaughter. Frederick's big hand had trembled when he gave John his letter of reference, a brief missive on expensive paper that was written in the spidery hand of somebody ancient and signed by a Lady Mildred Leslie.

John had looked from the letter—which attested to Frederick's eleven years of excellent service from boot black to footman—and back at the behemoth, who was clutching his battered hat in a death grip.

He'd opened his mouth to tell Frederick Brown that he didn't need a footman but found himself telling the man he could start work immediately.

Frederick had bobbed up and down like an amorous pigeon. "Thank you, my lord. Oh, thank you."

John had scowled, uncomfortable with so much gratitude. "Fielding is my name, there is no *my lord*." He'd been desperate to get the man out of his library before Frederick had tried to kiss his hand.

Now, as John strode across the calacatta marble and headed up the massive semi-circular stairs, he had to admit that it wasn't only Frederick's gratitude and adoration that made John uneasy; it was his fragility.

Although Fredrick, who was as big as an ox, looked nothing like Ben Watkins—who'd been skinny to the point of emaciation and barely five feet tall—the big footman was as gentle, harmless, and ultimately defenseless as Ben had been.

Trying to protect the vulnerable and wounded was nothing but a recipe for pain, and John dearly wished he could scour the impulse from his mind—tear it out completely, right down to the roots. After all, look what John's worrying had done for poor Ben: nothing.

He realized his hands were clenched into fists and he loosened them as he reached the second-floor landing, where yet another footman loitered. Although loiter was an unfair word as the man was struggling to move a heavy marble pedestal for a broom-wielding maid.

When they saw John, the footman bowed awkwardly around the heavy object and the maid dropped a jerky curtsey.

John ignored the pair and entered the library, which was the only room he liked.

The unadorned pedestal outside the library wasn't the only bare thing in the massive house. There were blank walls and bare floors in all the rooms in the giant mansion, thanks to the prior owners, who had stripped it bare.

But if his house was empty of possessions, it was full-to-the-brim with servants. It had not been John's intention to hire *any* servants, but it seemed his intentions were beside the point.

He'd arrived at Falkirk House carrying only his valise and looking forward to some solitude. He hadn't even reached the top step before the front door had opened.

"Who are you?" John had growled at the ancient man gaping up at him.

"Sims, butler to His Grace of Falkirk for fifty-two years, er, sir." He'd clutched the oversized door handle as if it were a lifeline, his slight, bent figure swaying from side to side.

John had been gob smacked. Just what the devil was he supposed to do with such a fossil? Why the bloody hell hadn't the acquisitive Duchess of Falkirk—who'd supervised the stripping of the house—taken the ancient codger with her?

John's uncharacteristic moment of indecision had stretched into several. All the while the butler had submitted to his glare, blinking owlishly up at him.

"You *are* Mr. Fielding, sir?" The old man had asked when it seemed the two might stand frozen on the front stoop until pigeons roosted on them.

"Aye, I'm Fielding." John had stepped foot, for the first time, into his new home, which he'd not even looked at before buying it. He'd not purchased the house because he liked it and wouldn't have cared if it was falling to pieces. He'd purchased it to humiliate his father, the Duke of Falkirk, whose money trouble had forced him to sell the London mansion which had been in the family for generations.

John knew all about his father's *money trouble* because he was the one who'd created it.

"Are you the only servant here?" John had asked.

The butler's white bushy eyebrows had hovered over his old eyes like low-lying clouds."There are seven of us, sir. There is—"

John held up a hand, and the man had stopped speaking, his rheumy eyes riveted on John's six-fingered hand. "You may provide me with a list of names and positions tomorrow. Right now, I hope a cook is among that number because I am hungry."

That had been three months ago. And twenty-three more servants ago, for a total of thirty.

The house was now dust-free and John enjoyed splendid meals served by at least five servants. Yes, his employees took prodigious care of their sole resident, even when he ordered them not to.

At least three nights a week—sometimes more—John combed the city's underworld, carrying on his search for Dolan, which he'd been able to begin in earnest after he'd stopped working for the banker, Stephen Worth, last fall.

When John returned home after venturing into the stews—usually in the wee hours of the morning—he always found a footman waiting up for him, a fire crackling in his chambers, and, most interestingly, a small pot of hot chocolate on his nightstand.

Chocolate.

John snorted as he threw himself into his leather armchair—the only chair sturdy enough for his enormous frame—recalling the first morning he'd seen the mysterious, steaming pot.

Of course, he'd not touched the blasted chocolate.

At first.

Then one morning, after a particularly rough night, he'd taken a sip—but only to settle a tickle in his throat, mind. It had been the equivalent of drinking something unspeakably beautiful—like a spectacular sunset. Who would have guessed that such a substance existed?

He had since concluded that chocolate was better than brandy, not that he would admit his preference to anyone.

John stared into the leaping flames in the massive library hearth and contemplated ordering a pot.

Although it was March in London, it felt like December. The recent cold snap matched John's mood, which was bleaker than usual now that he'd forced himself to stop following—well, *stalking*—Miss Page.

The weather was reminiscent of Boston, Massachusetts, where he'd spent five years working for the disgustingly wealthy banker, Stephen Worth, before coming to Britain a little over a year ago.

For most of last year John had striven to bring about Worth's clever plan—a plan that had worked brilliantly and earned revenge not just for Worth, but also for John, not to mention yielding an obscene amount of money for both, in the process.

He'd spent some of his newfound wealth to acquire this splendid house, which should have gone to John's half-brother, the Marquess of Gaulton and future Duke of Falkirk.

His mouth twisted into what passed for a smile and he stretched out his legs and tugged off his cravat. Why not be comfortable? He had nowhere to go today. Indeed, his days had been uncomfortably empty since he'd stopped following Miss Page.

John sighed and felt a twinge in his right ribs, reminding him of last night, when a so-called promising lead on Dolan had led him to an unsavory gin house on the waterfront.

Not only had the promising lead not materialized, but John had—mortifyingly—fallen prey to a trio of cudgel-wielding lads who'd been waiting for him when he'd left the pub.

He'd gathered his wits quickly enough, fortunate to escape with nothing worse than some bruised pride, torn clothing, and the loss of his wallet. To be honest, the worst part of the whole affair had been the destruction of his favorite pair of boots, which had been ruined when he'd stumbled into a ditch overflowing with the contents of an untold number of chamber pots.

Without money to hire a hackney, he'd needed to walk all the way home in his shitty footwear and tattered clothing. John deserved every bit of misery he'd received. Looking for a murderous scoundrel in the stews of London two decades after the murder was beyond foolish; it was madness. But then, how else should he spend his time? Join a gentleman's club? Practice his sparring and swordplay?

No, he wasn't some toff who needed a club. He already had a hobby—two, actually: finding bloody Dolan and stripping the Duke of Falkirk of his last, finest, possession: his famed family seat, Chelmsford Park.

John couldn't *buy* the estate—it was entailed. But he could make matters so dire for the duke that he and his son would be forced to engage in the legal fiction known as Common Recovery to break the entail.

And *then* John could get his hands on Chelmsford, and he would have everything. Surely taking away the duke's prized possession would sate his hunger for revenge?

At first, he'd believed that forcing his father to sell Falkirk House would be enough. But he felt nothing as he glanced around the magnificent, if a bit worn, library that surrounded him.

Shouldn't he *feel* something, even if only pride of possession? After all, he'd grown up in the stews and yet all this was now his.

John's gaze flickered over the intricately carved floor-to-ceiling bookcases, most of which were only sparsely populated with volumes.

He'd purchased both the property *and* its contents, but that had not stopped the Duchess of Falkirk from stripping the house of anything of value.

John could have taken the matter before a court—and he'd have won, too—but he didn't care. In fact, it amused him to discover what a grasping, greedy bitch the duchess was beneath her proper, cool veneer.

Instead of ordering chocolate, John poured himself a whiskey and then paused in front of a portrait, one of the few the duchess hadn't stolen. It was some long-dead ancestor, as was evidenced by the six-fingered hand that was peculiar to the Merrick bloodline. Judging by the man's dress, he'd lived early in the last century.

The painting had suffered extensive water damage, no doubt the reason the prior owners had left it behind. The brilliant scarlet and silver of the man's buckled pumps and skirted coat were disfigured by warped, blackened lumps of mold or mildew. His pale blue eyes had somehow escaped the assault and looked out on John with an expression of weary disappointment, as if finding himself in the company of a baseborn criminal was merely another insult in a long line of many.

John tossed back his drink and smirked at the haughty face. "Don't worry, *Your Grace,* after I take Chelmsford, you'll have plenty of family for company." He set down the empty crystal glass with a thump, revived by the sudden blast of hatred that coursed through his veins.

He'd spent too much time mooning over Miss Page and not enough getting things done. But he was done making an idiot of himself; tomorrow he would get back to the business that had brought him to Britain.

Destroying his father.

And the best way to get to the Duke of Falkirk—who'd fallen ill and been bedridden since the financial losses John had inflicted on him the year before—was through his father's precious son and heir: Charles Merrick, the Marquess of Gaulton.

Tomorrow, John would set about bringing down his half-brother, the man who'd received all their father's love and led such a pampered, luxurious life.

Chapter 4

St. Giles
1802

John wiped the blood and sweat from his face the moment the official called the fight and dropped his hand. He ignored the screaming and jeering of the punters as his trainer, Marvin, clapped him on his shoulder.

"Good fight, John. Fast Eddie wants a word."

"Now?" John glanced around but didn't see the crime lord.

"Not 'ere and now," Marvin said, jerking his thumb up to where an enormous wicker basket was suspended above the sawdust covered floor where John's opponent was still weakly writhing. "After this next bout."

By *bout* Marvin meant the cockfight that would take place once they removed the boards that covered the pit. The basket above them—which was so loosely woven that the human occupant's hands, elbows, and legs poked through the gaps—held some poor bugger who'd not been able to pay his gambling debts.

Eddie liked to lower the basket close to the fighting cocks, whose metal rippon spurs would often slash both basket and occupant, to the great amusement of the men who came to watch.

John had to shove through the blood-thirsty crowd—earning a few more blows in the process—to get to the small, grimy room where Marvin could stitch up any bad wounds and John could clean up.

He sat on a keg while Marvin yammered about the fight and smeared some foul-smelling salve on the worst of his injuries. John blocked out the man's droning, instead wondering about what Eddie wanted to see him about. Although the boss never missed one of John's fights, he rarely spoke to him afterward. The last time he'd done so, he'd made a point of reminding John that he could fuck for free at any of Fast Eddie's brothels.

His suggestion had been more than that; it had been an order.

Eddie didn't care that John didn't like brothels or that plenty of women wanted him; women who had a say in their bed partners. All he wanted was for John to do as he was told.

John had known that Eddie wasn't offering free whores out of the goodness of his heart; he did it to bind John closer to him, to force him to become like the men who'd given up on having a life other than the one Eddie let them have.

John would have thought that having to move into Eddie's own house; working for Eddie's top two lieutenants; and eating at Eddie's dinner table every night would be enough for the man.

But no, he wanted to own John's cock as well.

Is that what this little talk would be about? That John had rejected Eddie's offer the last time. If that was the case, then John would do what the man wanted and go to one of his whores.

It had been a small, worthless form of resistance, in any case. Especially when John did so many other, far viler things for Eddie without batting an eyelid.

The door opened and the very man he'd been thinking about interrupted his thoughts.

"Here's my lad!" Eddie flashed him a tight, vicious grin that sent chills down his spine. It didn't matter that John towered over Eddie or that his employer had the slender build of a dandy; the man's eyes were pits of Hell for all that they looked as blue as a summer day.

John bowed his head. "Eddie," he murmured.

Eddie slapped him on the shoulder, his grin only growing as he wrapped his hands around John's biceps and failed to span them. "Christ, but you're a bloody ox!" He laughed and shook his head in amazement. "Are you sure you're not a few years older than you claim to be?" The way he smirked at John made him feel like the other man was enjoying some private joke at his expense.

Eddie barked a laugh when John merely stared. "Never mind. Here, this is a bit extra—to show you what happens when you make me happy." He slid a fat purse into John's hand. "And when you make me *money*."

John glanced down at the money in surprise. He usually received his pay with all the others, and he'd rarely received additional money for a fight.

When he saw Eddie was frowning at him, he hastened to say, "Thanks, Eddie."

Eddie smiled again. "Good lad. And good work on Charlie Pinker, too. You helped remind him where he hid my money."

Pinker was a man who John had beaten so badly he'd probably never eat, walk, or talk normally again. John knew he should feel something at what he'd done—shame, horror, or even amusement, which is what Eddie's men Jessup and Brown had obviously felt since they'd laughed and joked while they'd watched John thrash the petty crook.

He felt nothing. And he felt nothing when Eddie said, "I'm going to need you to go over to the Crown and Ferret tonight. They're holding a man in the cellar who owes me fifty quid. I want you to get it out of him."

John knew what that meant: he was to beat the man. Not because he could pay—they never could—but to demonstrate that nobody stole from Fast Eddie without retribution.

"After you've taken my money from his hide, I want you to finish him."

John blinked, raising his eyes from the pouch of money in his hand to meet Eddie's icy blue gaze.

"You understand me, lad?"

"You want me to kill him." It wasn't a question.

Eddie studied John's face as if he were looking for something—probably signs of fear or rebellion. He nodded at whatever he saw, apparently satisfied. "You want Jessup or Brown to go along? Or can you handle this?"

John knew what that meant, too. When Eddie gave a man a job to do, he was putting his trust in him. Asking for help was not a good idea if you wanted to rise through the ranks.

"I can do it, Eddie."

Eddie patted his shoulder and smiled again, the expression never coming close to his eyes. "After yer done, you go to Bella. I told her to expect you and give you somethin' special."

John had to force himself to say, "Thanks, Eddie."

Eddie's eyes narrowed. "She said you didn't come around the last time. You ain't turnin' up your nose at a gift from me, are ye?" His blue eyes glittered like frosted glass.

"No, Eddie."

"Good, good." He squeezed John's arm hard enough to leave marks. And then he asked, "How's Lily doin'?"

John wasn't stupid; he knew that Eddie's question was a not-so-subtle reminder that Lily could either flourish or suffer, depending on John's behavior.

"She's good with the kiddies, Eddie—she teaches 'em lots."

"She likes it back there, eh?"

John swallowed. "Yeah, she's real grateful to you for movin' 'er out of Holloway's and back with the kiddies."

Eddie's gaze was knowing, and he smirked in a way that made John want to smash his face. They both knew that Eddie had only taken Lily out of the whorehouse because John had begged him to. Now Eddie would have Lily's happiness to hold over John's head and make him obey orders without question.

"That's good—I'm sure she'll do me proud," Eddie said. "I'm sure you both will. You go on, now. Get the job done and then enjoy yourself tonight."

***

Ma Brannen—who ran the Crown and Ferret for Eddie—looked about a hundred years old and was as vicious as a viper.

She grinned at John when she saw him, exposing only four teeth. "I made a packet offa you tonight, lad!"

No wonder she was smiling.

"Eddie sent me," he said, even though she had to know that.

She scowled when she realized he didn't want to celebrate the money she'd won on his labor. "Follow me," she snapped, leading John through the back of the bar and into a kitchen so filthy it made his hair stand on end. At the back of the room was the sort of heavy door that concealed a keg room.

Ma unlocked the door and then hesitated. "I've got full kegs in there—don't be breaking anything."

John ignored her, took the candlestick, and pushed open the door. There was a man—a big one—huddling in the corner, shivering in the cool room. Piles of shit and vomit told John the man had the shakes from blue ruin.

He turned to Ma. "Close this door and wait outside until I call for you."

Her eyes narrowed; she didn't like being told what to do—not by a sprout, but she was smart enough to know Eddie wouldn't be amused if she disobeyed.

"Aye."

She slammed the door, and John turned, setting down the candlestick before approaching the cowering figure.

"Oi!" He kicked the man's shoe when he didn't look up.

The face that turned toward him was covered in a beard so full it was hard to see any skin.

"Eddie wants 'is money," John said, already taking off his coat because he knew the man wouldn't just hand it over—not that he probably had any.

The bundle of rags shifted until the man faced him, his feverish gaze telling John that he was hurting for more gin. "I ain't got it."

John began rolling up his sleeves.

The man squinted up at him. "You're John Fielding, ain'tcha?"

"Who wants to know?"

"I seen you fight. I used to be a fighter, too."

John snorted in disbelief.

"Aye, you can laugh, but I was somefink in my day. You don't remember me, do ye?"

"No."

He gave a bitter laugh. "Small surprise in that, I reckon. It's me—Alfie. I'm the one who brought you to Fast Eddie and saved you." The man sat up and threw his chest out, or at least he tried to, but collapsed in a bout of coughing.

It took John a moment to find the resemblance; it was there, but it was faint.

"Remember?" Alfie asked anxiously.

"I remember you hit me, threatened me, and bought me for two shillings."

Alfie quailed at the derision in John's voice and cringed back as John bent down and grabbed him by the coat, dragging him to his feet.

"But, I saved ye! Dolan wanted to sell ye to flesh-brokers—like 'ee did 'is own niece."

At the sound of Dolan's name, John paused, reeling back from the foul stench that came out of Alfie's mouth.

"Have you seen Dolan lately?"

Alfie blinked, clearly surprised at the direction the conversation had taken. "Er, Dolan?"

John shook him until his remaining teeth rattled. "Yeah, Dolan."

"No, I ain't—"

John punched him in the stomach. "Don't lie."

Alfie tried to bend over and protect his gut, but John held him upright, pinned against the wall.

He sobbed and squirmed. "I'm not lyin'."

Memories of that long-ago day flooded him and John hit the other man again, and again, until bile and vomit dribbled from Alfie's mouth.

"That fucker killed me gran—and then stole from us. Tell me when where 'ee is."

"It's been years." Alfie wept piteously, snot and tears glistening in his ragged beard. "I saw 'im for the last time a week after I got you."

"Where?"

"I don't remem—"

John hit him again, this time over the heart, even though it hurt his already sore hand.

Alfie screamed and John let him slide down to the floor and put his boot on his chest, holding him pinned. "Where?"

"'Ee wanted to sell somefink to Eddie."

"What?"

"I don't—"

John lifted his foot to kick him in the side.

"It was somefink 'ee prigged!" Alfie yelped.

"Somefink 'ee stole from my gran?" John asked, menace dripping from his quiet words.

"It might 'a been—I tell you I don't *know*. All I know is that 'ee went into Eddie's 'ouse and never came out—that's the last time I ever saw 'im. Please," he wept. "Please don't 'urt me anymore."

John glared down at the former bully in disgust. "Does Dolan 'ave any family?"

"Nah, 'ee 'ad a sister and a niece—I tole you, 'ee sold her."

He'd beaten enough men to know when they were telling the truth; Alfie knew nothing about Dolan.

Furious at finding yet another dead end where Dolan was concerned, John glared down at Alfie. "You owe Eddie a lot of money—it's time to pay up."

Alfie wept openly. "I ain't got it—you know I don't. I'd be drinkin' if I did."

That was true enough.

"You used to work for Eddie—doin' my job, right?" John asked, huffing as he grabbed Alfie and hoisted him to his feet again.

"Yeah, yeah, I know what you 'ave to do."

John punched him with his other hand this time, but even that hurt, and he cursed Eddie for sending him out to do this on a fight night.

He caught his breath and stared at the pathetic excuse for a man. What was the point of this? Why break his hands when he was just going to kill him, anyhow?

John let Alfie slide to the floor while he unrolled his sleeves and put on his coat.

"What now?" Alfie asked.

John ignored him and pounded on the door.

It opened, but instead of Ma, it was one of the bar wenches who waited.

"Hi John!" She grinned up at him, thrusting her bosom at him. "Remember me?" She slid a hand up his chest. "I'll be off in less than an hour."

John remembered her. He'd had too many gins one night and had given in to her pestering and fucked her in the alley behind the Crown and Ferret. She'd smelled unwashed and had squealed so loudly when she came that his head had rung for an hour afterward.

"Go open the back door," John said, ignoring her question, offer, and the affronted squawk sound she made when she realized he wasn't interested.

He turned back to Alfie, who was trying to make himself as small as possible, but looked like an oversized grasshopper with his lanky body and long knobby legs pulled up in front of him.

"Get up," he barked.

He was pleasantly surprised when the man got to his feet; he'd been sure that he'd need to carry him.

John dragged him out of the keg room, past the fuming serving wench, and out into the alley.

"You're takin' me to the river, ain'tcha?"

John didn't bother to answer.

When Alfie struggled, John delivered a few well-aimed punches and then heaved the man over his shoulder.

Christ! He looked skinny, but his bones were made of iron.

It was lucky the docks weren't far off, but even so, it was a miserable journey.

"Please, lad," Alfie moaned. "Please let me go."

John had to laugh. "Go where?"

"You could give me to one of the king's men—you know they'll take anyone."

That was true, His Majesty's navy was so desperate for sailors they'd probably take a corpse.

"You worked for Eddie—you know what he'd do to me if he learned I didn't obey," John said.

"He'd never know! I'd be gone."

"Why should I risk my neck for you?" he asked, not that he had any intention of doing so.

"I could tell you where to find yer da."

John stumbled and then stopped. "What did you say?"

"Yer da."

John snorted. "I remember you and Dolan enjoying a laugh about me Mam—about how she was a flash piece and either of *you* could be me da." John now knew that was true—that his mother had once been a whore for Eddie and that she'd started off at Bella's but ended up at Holloway's before she'd died.

"I lied! She belonged to Lem—'ee was right possessive of 'er."

"Lem who?"

"I'll tell ye if you let me go."

"You'll tell me or I'll beat it out of you."

Alfie shook his head. "I'll take it to my grave."

John shrugged Alfie off his shoulder and the other man dropped to his knees.

He whimpered and gazed up at John. "Please."

"Who are you talking about?"

"It was Lem Kennedy—him and Gerry Bower were always 'angin' about yer ma."

"Where are they?"

"Bower's dead—died years ago—but Kennedy was alive last I 'eard. 'Ee went back to Dublin after 'ee ran afoul of Eddie."

"Me da worked for Eddie?"

Alfie nodded. "All of 'em did—yer ma, Bower, and Lem."

"What happened?"

"'Ee stole somefink from 'im"—Alfie raised his hands—"I swear I don't know what. You know 'ow Eddie is—'ee don't tell anyone anyfink, 'Ee likes to keep everyone 'oo works for 'im ignorant. I *swear* I ain't lyin'."

John believed him; Eddie's secretive ways were legendary. He didn't trust *anyone*. And Alfie—once a favored minion of Eddie's—was a good reason why he didn't trust.

John kicked him; not hard, but hard enough to get him upright.

"You promised!" Alfie whined when John shoved him toward the docks.

John actually hadn't promised, but the knowledge that Eddie had known his parents—had used them just like he was now using John—burned in his belly. "Keep walkin'," he growled.

Alfie dragged his heels and carried on so loudly that he didn't even notice when John stepped up behind him and cracked him on the base of the skull.

The big man dropped like a felled tree, and John worked quickly, wrapping him in burlap sacks he found near an oyster boat.

Once Alfie was trussed up good and tight, John quickly found one of the men who lurked around the docks looking for drunks to overwhelm and sell to the press gangs.

Ten minutes later, and with a quid in his pocket, John made his way toward Bella's, where he would take the whore that Eddie was forcing on him. After all, it was no hardship, and letting Alfie go was already enough rebellion for one night.

John was no fool. He'd taken an irrevocable, dangerous step tonight when he'd disobeyed Eddie's order, and there was no turning back.

He would keep working for Eddie, but only until he found Dolan and made him pay for murdering his Gran. After that, he'd take Lily with him and they'd run away. Maybe they'd go as far as Dublin to look for the man who might be his father.

Or maybe they'd run even farther. John would go as far as he needed to run to get beyond Eddie's reach.

Chapter 5

London
1818

Should I m-move the philosophical meeting or re-schedule it for another n-night?" Cordelia's nephew, Charles, the Marquess of Gaulton, asked when Cordelia told him about Jane's indisposition.

"No, you needn't move your meeting," she assured him.

"Perhaps I should ch-change the night—so that I might help you k-keep Jane occupied." He pulled a face at the thought. "Or do you need me to escort M-Melissa somewhere? I'll do it."

Cordelia chuckled at his martyrish look. "Not at all, Charles. I shall stay home with Jane and I've sent word to Lady Tewkes, who will chaperone Melissa to the rout along with her two girls. We won't even notice a dozen scholars bickering in your library." She smiled across the breakfast table at him and spread some strawberry preserves on her toast.

Only Cordelia and Charles usually shared breakfast as the girls were late sleepers. She treasured these tête-à-têtes with her nephew, especially on the mornings when they rode in the park together, which they'd done that morning.

"But why should Cordelia need her own hack in London?" her sister, the duchess, had demanded when Charles had told his mother that he was having three ladies hacks brought to London.

When Cordelia had opened her mouth to say she would be fine using one of the girls' mounts when they weren't using them, Charles had spoken first.

"B-Because she enjoys r-riding, Mama, and that is r-reason enough."

Cordelia had known by his heavy stutter how much the minor disagreement had cost her peace-loving nephew.

His mother had noticed, too, and had backed down in response to his unusual show of mettle.

As a result, Cordelia rode with Charles at least three mornings a week. Riding had always been one of the ways in which she was every bit as good as her sister. It was a small thing, but when a girl found herself constantly compared with a sibling who was beautiful, wealthy, and a duchess, she clung to whatever scraps she could find. For a few hours every week Cordelia could shed the mantle of aunt and chaperone and excel at something.

Charles's voice brought her back to the present. "We have a new m-member joining us tonight."

"Oh? Would I know him?"

"I think n-not. He is a man of b-business and has only recently c-come back to England."

"What is his name?"

"Mr. John F-Fielding." He paused, took a sip of coffee and then looked up at her. "I should t-tell you he is rather unusual l-looking."

"Unusual?"

"Well, he's quite the l-largest man I've ever seen, and he also has some rather br-brutal scarring on his face."

A face flashed into her mind's eye at her nephew's words, but Cordelia dismissed the ridiculous thought; surely that was not the same man Charles meant—that would be an astounding coincidence. Besides, thanks to the War, there were many badly scarred men. It could not be the same man she'd thought of again and again.

"Somebody you met at Brooks?" she asked.

"No, it was at the coffeehouse we f-frequent. He is quite unusual."

"Oh?"

"He is from B-Boston and I believe he is a m-merchant of some sort, although he speaks and d-dresses like a gentleman. It was quite f-fortuitous that he was sitting at the next table and was w-was lured in by the subject we were discussing. He shall come tonight, so I could introduce you and you may put him to the question, if you like."

"I'm sure Jane will keep me far too busy to socialize. In fact, I am going to the bookshop this afternoon to fetch several more volumes for her."

Charles laughed. "I pity you, Cee. It will not be a f-fun evening discussing s-soil composition and drainage. If you should b-become bored, you can always j-join us in the library."

Cordelia had to smile at the offer, not sure which conversation would be the drier one—plants or political philosophy.

***

John was reading yet another indecipherable tome on natural philosophy when he saw Miss Cordelia Page.

At first, he wondered if he'd imagined her—as he'd done often over the past weeks. But no, it really was her. She was standing near a clerk who had brought out a ladder and was scaling it to bring down a book. She took the book and thanked him with a warm smile.

It was ironic that John had run into her without having to stalk her. In a bookstore, of all places. If you'd told him ten years ago—or even five—that he would one day voluntarily enter a bookstore, he would have laughed.

He'd only learned to read five years ago—and not by choice, either.

"You work for me now, John, and I won't tolerate an ignorant employee," Worth had told him. "Besides, to do the job I hired you to do, you will need to consort with all levels of society. We already know you can mix with the lowest. It is time to expand your range."

In addition to reading, Worth had engaged tutors to teach John proper diction, politics and world affairs, which bloody fork to use at a dinner table, and *dancing*.

If their positions had been reversed and if *John* had been the wealthy banker who had rescued a savage, surly convict, John would have given himself the sack before the first week was out. But Stephen Worth was as tenacious as a bulldog on a pork chop, so John could now read and write just like any of the swells clogging up Hookham's.

Well, maybe not *just* like them; he still had to use his dictionary frequently. Even so, he loved reading. Especially novels. He had tucked three into the pile of indecipherable political philosophy books he was buying today.

He pretended to read while watching Cordelia Page from beneath lowered lashes. She was skimming the shelves, dragging one slender kid glove sheathed hand over the spines, her full lips moving as if she were repeating a name or phrase. Her search took her higher and higher until her head was bent all the way back and she stood on tiptoes. She reached above her and the action caused her gown to ride up, exposing a sliver of ankle. John stared, riveted.

She lowered her arm with a frustrated sigh and looked around for a clerk.

John shut his book with a snap, tucked the stack under one arm, and closed the distance between them in a few strides.

Her eyes widened when they landed on his face and he knew it was recognition he saw in them rather than horror.

Ah, yes; she remembered him.

That knowledge sent a warm wave of something—pride, pleasure, anticipation, or all three—surging through his body.

"Which book do you need?" he asked.

Her cheeks tinted a subtle pink and John could almost *hear* her thoughts: A gentleman would not approach a woman if they'd not been introduced.

But then, he wasn't a gentleman.

After a brief hesitation, she said, "The one about fertilizer use in Lancashire, if you please."

John blinked at the title but turned to locate the volume she wanted and plucked it from the shelf.

"Thank you." She took the book and bit her lip, the shy gesture erotic. Her gaze lowered to the books he held and she turned her head to read the spines. "Philosophy?" she asked, looking up at him.

John nodded.

Her eyes widened slightly. "I don't mean to be forward, but are you by any chance a member of my nephew's club?"

John caught himself just in time. "Who is your nephew?"

She laughed. "I suppose that would be a good thing to mention first." She extended a hand. "I am Cordelia Page, and my nephew is Lord Gaulton."

John looked down at her hand. Her glove was a pale gray that matched her coat—or whatever it was females called such over-garments—and the kid leather looked paper thin, as though she had worn it many times. Her fingers shook slightly and John realized he was staring, so he took her hand in his, amazed that his hand was easily twice as big as hers, not to mention ungloved.

"A gentleman always wears gloves." Worth had nagged more than once. "Ladies consider naked hands unseemly."

John had ignored him, like he usually did. But now, looking at his scarred, work-roughened hand, he wished he'd taken Worth's advice; his huge paw looked barbaric holding her delicate fingers.

When he looked up, he saw that she'd been looking at their joined hands as well. What was he supposed to do with it? Kiss it? Shake it, as the Americans did?

Miss Page took the decision out of his hands, both literally and figuratively, by deftly withdrawing her fingers. Her touch was so light that it was as if a butterfly had landed on his palm and then, just as quickly, taken flight.

John knew he should say something. Anything. Although he wasn't usually very talkative with women, he was never as big a dunce as this.

She gave him a look that brimmed with humor, encouragement, and… interest.

Nobody ever looked at him like that. People looked at him with fear, disgust, and some with morbid curiosity, but never as if he were more than the sum of his scars and monstrous size.

"You are Mr. John Fielding, I think?"

That's what you are supposed to say, you idiot—your name.

He frowned to hide his mortification. "Yes, I am."

Her lips quivered as if she were holding back a smile—or even laughter.

John experienced something he could not recall feeling before—a fiery face. By thunder! He was a grown man, and he was blushing. He couldn't blame her for laughing.

"If you'll excuse me," he bit out, dropping an abrupt bow before turning and striding away, his back prickling, as if he could feel the weight of her gaze.

Good God. He'd not behaved like such a bumbling oaf since—since, Lord, he couldn't recall ever acting so oafish.

***

Once again Cordelia admired the enormous man's catlike grace, unable to pull her gaze away from his immense back and shoulders as he strode away. The moment he turned the corner, she sagged against the shelf.

Never in her life had she been near a man who affected her so physically. Oh, he affected her mind, too—why else would she have blurted out such a forward question about him knowing Charles? She cringed at the memory of her gauche words. Yes, he'd breached the barriers of politeness a proper lady kept erected, but she'd behaved just as improperly.

It wasn't her behavior so much as her body's response that was the most unnerving. And fascinating. Heat, intense physical awareness, and a punishing yearning for *something* had flooded her as she'd looked up into his black, unreadable eyes.

Cordelia was no chit in her first season; she'd felt flickers of physical desire when she'd fancied herself in love with her neighbor, Peter. She could still recall the sensations she'd experienced the few times Peter had kissed her; it had been as if something inside her had unfurled—like a flower. But *that* feeling had been gentle. Not like today.

What she'd felt today—and, indeed, both times this fierce stranger had come near her—was what it must feel like to step into a lion's den.

Cordelia bit her lip. Oh, when she put the feeling into words it sounded foolish and hysterical—much like the laughter that had bubbled up inside her when he had steadfastly refused to speak, instead holding her pinned against the bookshelves with eyes that could not possibly be as black as they appeared.

He couldn't have spoken more than ten words. She had never been in the presence of such a taciturn yet utterly entrancing man.

Cordelia didn't know if he looked at everyone with such intensity or if it was something he reserved for women. Not that she had any illusions about her appeal to men—especially not to such a virile specimen as Mr. Fielding.

Virile. Now there was a word she could not recall using before, but it certainly applied to him. And it had to be *him* rather than his clothing because his garments—greatcoat, buckskin breeches, top boots of excellent quality but only adequately polished, and a simply tied cravat—were much the same as any other gentleman.

But not his hands.

Ah, yes; he'd not been wearing gloves. Cordelia had never encountered a gentleman in public who was not wearing gloves.

But bare hands alone could not account for the reaction she had to him.

Of course, there was his face…

Today, unlike the first time, when he'd been somewhat in shadow, she'd clearly seen the angry slashes that began at the corners of his mouth and radiated outward. The scars were puckered here and there, meaning that the stitching of them had been uneven.

His lips—shapely and full—had been compressed in a forbidding line that suggested they were incapable of smiling or laughing. And the deep, broken parenthesis that bracketed his mouth spoke of a grimness that went deeper than mere flesh.

He must have been very handsome before the cuts and damage to his nose. Indeed, he was still handsome, but in a way no sane woman would contemplate getting close to. He reminded her of a caged lion she'd seen at Astley's menagerie, the savagery that emanated from him bone deep and part of his very makeup.

Cordelia knew women were often attracted to men with less than sterling reputations—rakes, rogues and the like—but Mr. Fielding did not fit into those categories. He was not recklessly dangerous like Lord Madeley, a man who was quite willing to destroy a woman's reputation in pursuit of his own pleasure.

No, Mr. Fielding was just plain *dangerous.* She suspected his exceptional size in and of itself would incite other men to violence. After all, men—like animals—seemed driven to establish dominance and challenge the larger and more powerful members of the herd.

And yet, for all that his exterior was so ferocious, the way he'd touched her hand had been gentle and respectful, as if she had bestowed some great honor on him. He had the façade of a barbarian, but she sensed something almost… fragile beneath the savagery.

You have windmills in your head.

Cordelia snorted and exhaled the breath she hadn't been aware she was holding. No doubt she *was* a fool, and a deeply misguided one at that. Her forwardness had probably rendered him speechless. All he'd done was fetch a book for a short, plump, dowdy spinster and Cordelia had repaid his kindness by behaving like an entranced schoolgirl.

Suddenly, she remembered he would be under the same roof as her that very evening.

Cordelia felt both relief and anticipation at the thought; she would have a second chance with him, an opportunity to seek him out and behave more normally than she had today.

Or, far more likely, you can make an even bigger fool of yourself.

Chapter 6

St. Giles
1802

But John, you need to keep some money for yourself—you can't keep giving it all to me," Lily protested as John pressed that night's earnings into her hands.

"Take it," he said, using the deep, commanding voice that came naturally to him after a year of working as one of Fast Eddie's bullies.

Lily just laughed at him. "You think that tone o' voice works on me?" She gently cuffed his ear. "I remember when you were still in short pants."

John glanced at her stomach, which was full and rounded and looked ready to pop. "Take the money for you and Ben and the baby."

Her eyes softened, and she laid a hand on her swollen belly. "Me an' Ben do awright for ourselves."

"I know you do—but soon there will be another mouth to feed."

"You need the money for you—to get away." She spoke the last words in a whisper.

John didn't tell her he'd given up on that dream when she became pregnant. He might have scraped together enough money for two people to run, but he didn't have enough for four. Besides, Lily had made it clear that she didn't want to leave. It was the only life she'd ever known, and the thought of running away terrified her. *Better the Devil you know*, was how she'd put it.

She was right. And where the hell had John thought he could go, anyway? Escaping St. Giles had just been a child's dream. He was Eddie's man, bought and paid for.

John tossed the money onto the cluttered table. "Take the bloody money, Lil. I've not got time to argue."

"Oh, and why is that?" she teased.

"You know why," he growled, wishing he didn't feel so ashamed about how he spent many of his evenings.

Lily squeezed his arm. "I'm just 'avin' a bit of fun. I don't think worse of you for goin' to Bella's."

Although they never talked about Lily's brief time at Holloway's, John knew she'd gone through hell before he'd been able to convince Eddie to allow her to come back and live with the younger thieves.

"You don't think I'm a pig for goin' there?" he asked quietly.

Lily snorted. "I didn't say that."

"Lil!"

When she quit laughing, she said, "I'm just teasin'. Honestly, I know the girls at Bella's and trust me when I say that you could probably sell yourself over there and live like a lord on your earnings."

John had started going to Bella's months ago—the same night he'd let Alfie free—but he still felt a twinge of guilt each time he went.

Was he becoming like the others—Jessup and Brown and Des Houlihan—men who used the women who worked there as if they were nothing but convenient holes?

John feared he was.

"Hey, now," Lily said, pushing the hair off his forehead. "I didn't mean to guilt you. Becky and Nora and Della love it when you visit. You're not like the others. You're clean, you pay extra, you don't hurt 'em, and you even bring pleasure."

John knew his face was as red as a brick. "Christ, Lil—is that what women talk about?"

She grinned. "You love hearin' that we talk about you."

Well, maybe that was a little true. It made him feel better that the young women at Bella's didn't dread seeing him. He brought small gifts and always left money, even though none of Eddie's other men paid. And it was a matter of pride to ensure that the women who serviced him received pleasure in return.

He still preferred choosing his own lovers, but he went to Bella's on fight nights or when it would look odd if he didn't join Eddie's other top men in their carousing.

"I heard Eddie made a packet on you tonight," Lily said, changing the subject.

John shrugged. There was nothing new about that, and very little to take pride in, as far as he was concerned. Over the last year, John had grown several more inches and his body was slabbed with muscle—thanks to the best food and training most days with Marvin—whereas most of the men he fought were so much smaller than him that John often felt ashamed.

But the one time he'd said anything to Eddie about how uneven the fights were, his eyes had turned to ice and he'd grabbed John by the throat.

"It ain't for you to think. *Ever.* You fight who I tell you when I tell you. You're my creature and I made you what you are and I own you, just like my dogs, cocks, horses, and whores." He'd squeezed until John's eyes had watered and he'd choked.

John outweighed Eddie by several stone of pure muscle and could have easily knocked away his hand. But Jessup and Brown, who'd stood behind Eddie, armed with knives and pistols, would have brought John down the same way he'd seen them kill dogs that tried to bite their handlers.

"The next time you get to thinking, I want you to think of your girl, Lily," Eddie had snarled when John had been close to fainting from a lack of air. "Think of how bad things would go for 'er without you around to look out for 'er."

And that had been before Lily was pregnant and with Ben. Now there were three people Eddie could hurt if John displeased him.

So, he kept his mouth shut and fought whoever Eddie told him to fight.

By the time he left Lily's room it was after midnight, but Bella was still waiting for him when he entered the gaudy parlor where the girls lounged, several of them servicing men right there—those who couldn't afford a room.

"Why, if it ain't Mr. John Fielding, 'imself," Bella mocked, her eyes flickering over him in a way that always made him feel like a horse up for auction. She walked around him in a circle, clucking her tongue. "You get bigger and more handsome every time I see you."

John wasn't interested in listening to her opinion. "I want a bath first."

She laughed. "You think I don't know that by now—a proper gentleman, you are. Come with me. I have just the thing you need."

"I know where the tub is." He went to the big communal bath every time he came to the brothel.

"Not tonight, you don't. Eddie says you get somethin' special—the entire night, not just an hour—and I'm to put you in the King's Room, with your own private bath."

John frowned. "Why?"

"Lord, boy! Don't you know better than to ask Eddie somethin' like that? If he says you get the best, then you get the best," she said as they trudged toward the stairs.

He tried to feel pleased that Eddie valued him enough to pay for the best, but he couldn't help wondering *why*. Eddie never did anything for nothing.

"Here we are," Bella said, stopping in front of double doors and then flinging open the right-hand door to the nicest room he'd ever seen.

John stared, his mouth no doubt hanging open.

Bella gestured to the enormous tub steaming in front of the fire. "See," she said. "Nice and fresh."

John grunted, at a loss for words.

"Strip down and I'll take yer togs and get the kitchen lassies to clean 'em. All on the house," she added when he hesitated.

John tried to keep his clothing clean, but Lily insisted on doing his washing and wouldn't allow him to pay her, so he wore his clothes longer than he liked so as not to give her extra work.

Bella stared at him openly while he stripped. John wasn't self-conscious about his body—how could he be when he'd spent his life crammed in with both boys and girls, without a moment's privacy—but he didn't care to be scrutinized like a side of beef. Still, he could hardly ask her to turn her back.

She grinned, her small dark eyes moving over his naked body when he stood up from pushing down his breeches and drawers. Her sharp gaze lingered on his cock, which loved the attention far more than John did, and was rising to the occasion.

"Good God, that's quite a snake ye've got there! I've 'alf a mind to come out of retirement, meself to get a ride on it."

John gawped, and she laughed until her eyes teared up. "Don't look so scared, lad. I'll not touch yer bits—not unless you ask for it." Still laughing, she scooped up his clothing and—leaving him feeling like a bumpkin—waddled from the room, her large form shaking with mirth.

John got into the tub, even though the water was so hot it almost scalded him. Although he still had to bend his knees to fit, it felt like heaven, and he was pleasantly dozing when the door opened. He looked up and blinked; not one, but two women entered his room.

John squinted, wondering if his vision was blurry.

But then they laughed, and he knew there were two.

"What' goin' on?" he asked, his voice groggy.

"You get the special treatment tonight," the brunette said—he thought her name was Becky, although he'd never had her before—pulling the sash on her loose dressing gown and exposing her lush, naked body.

John pushed himself up, suddenly wide awake.

"You stay right there," the second one—Nora—said, grinning as she disrobed and sank down beside the tub. "It's nice to see you, John."

She was one of his favorites, a buxom, curvaceous blond whose blue eyes sparkled with mischief.

"We're gonna wash you first," Becky said, soaping up a cloth.

"I can wash mys—"

"Of course you can," Nora agreed, dumping a pitcher of hot water over his head and laughing while he sputtered. "But this is all part of the *royal* treatment."

A hand shoved between his thighs and stroked his already hard cock. "Coo! This feels royal enough," Becky said, laughing.

"Close your eyes and let us take care of you," Nora whispered.

Well, why not?

John closed his eyes, laid back, and let his legs fall open.

***

"It's true what they say about you," Becky said sometime later, stroking his chest with her long, silky hair.

John had been dozing, his cock pleasingly sated after spending not once, but three times between the bathtub and the bed.

He felt more relaxed than he could recall since—well, maybe ever.

He'd never slept in a bed after lying with a woman. Usually, he was up and dressed and gone within an hour. More often, he took his pleasure in alleys or abandoned buildings. The women he knew didn't exactly have houses where they could bring him and John didn't like to bring women back to his room at Fast Eddie's house, although the other men did so frequently.

John vaguely recalled Becky had said something and struggled to gather his thoughts, his mind sluggish after a day of fighting and fucking. "What do they say about me?" he finally asked.

"That you don't talk much and hold yourself aloof."

John raised an eyebrow. "A roof?"

She laughed and slapped his shoulder. "No, you nick ninny! Aloof. It means to be a deep 'un."

"Hmph." What could a man say to *that*?

Something soft moved against his leg and John jolted. Laughter came from beneath the blankets. "It's just me," Nora said, her voice muffled and her breath hot on his thigh.

John groaned as her skilled mouth closed over his speedily filling cock and she sucked him, her pace leisurely.

"Nora loves to do that," Becky said, grinning as she stroked his chest. "Jessup said you'll be famous one day."

John frowned; Nora's pleasurable sucking was not quite enough to overwhelm the annoyance he felt at having to think of Eddie's brutal henchman. "You know Jessup?"

She rolled her eyes, making him realize what a stupid question that was. Of course, Jessup would have wanted a prime goer like Becky.

The thought of the filthy, violent man—who resembled an ill-favored carp—rutting on a woman as pretty as Becky made John's stomach turn.

"How can you fuck him?" he asked, and then immediately felt like a gudgeon for asking her such a thing. "I shouldn't have asked that," he said. After all, how could *John* beat people to death for Eddie?

She shrugged. "I don't mind. Sometimes it ain't so bad." She gave him a sly look. "You're no chore."

His face burned, which only made her laugh harder.

"As for Jessup? Well, he's as ugly as a post, but he's got power and he's used it to get me a nicer room, less work." Becky shrugged again, her hand sliding down his chest to his belly, wrapping around the base of his shaft and holding him while Nora took him deep in her throat. "What else would I be doing if I wasn't here?"

"Uh—" John tried to think of something to say, but his mind was a blank.

Becky lowered her mouth and sucked on a nipple.

"Christ!" John shouted, bucking his hips hard into Nora's sweet heat, using her rougher than he should, but unable to stop.

Becky giggled against his skin, biting and sucking the tiny nub and pumping his shaft while Nora sucked, driving him out of his mind. His balls, which already ached from too many climaxes in such a short time, snugged up against his body and prepared to—

The door flew open and banged against the wall, and Becky screamed.

John had just enough sense remaining to take his root in his hand and carefully remove his shaft from Nora's mouth before trying to sit up.

It was Ben in the doorway and his eyes were as round as coins, darting from Becky's naked torso to John to Nora as she emerged from beneath the blankets, her lips red and swollen.

"What is it, Ben?" John asked.

"John, John, John, John—" Ben mumbled, staring at the naked women while his hand dropped to the front of his breeches and he rubbed himself.

Becky laughed. "Why, he's just a simpleton!" She crawled on her hands and knees down the bed toward Ben, and his eyes bulged at the sight of her large breasts. "Come into bed and Nora and I'll show you what to do with that thing."

Both women laughed as Ben stammered, his face bright red.

"Don't tease him!" John snapped.

The women turned on him, wounded and petulant. "We're just havin' a bit of a laugh."

"He's not laughing," John shot back, getting off the bed and striding over to his friend.

Ben's eyes dropped to John's rapidly deflating cock. "John."

"What's wrong, Ben? Why are you here? Is it something about Lily?"

Ben turned back to the bed and gasped. When John turned, he saw both women were making lewd gestures at Ben and touching themselves.

John snarled, "You two get out! *Now*!"

Nora bolted from the bed so fast her legs got caught in the sheets and she hit the floor.

John took Ben's chin and turned his face away from the two harlots.

"Pay attention, Ben. Did something happen to Lil?"

A spark briefly flared in Ben's dull gaze. "It's Des, he's—"

That one word, *Des,* was all he needed to hear.

John spun and looked for his clothing, momentarily panicking when he recalled the maid was going to clean them and they might still be downstairs. But no—there they were over the chair, so somebody must have brought them while he slept.

He stumbled into his breeches and yanked on his coats and boots, not bothering with his stockings or shirt. Ben was still goggling at the naked whores, who were yelling insults at John.

"Come on, Ben." John grabbed his arm and ran as fast as his legs would carry him, one thought burning a hole in his mind: Des Houlihan was doing something to Lily, and it wouldn't be anything nice. And it was probably all John's fault because he was the reason that Lily had Des's job.

John was the one who'd begged Eddie to take Lily out of Holloway's because he knew she wouldn't survive, and Eddie had given him what he'd asked for in exchange for John's total obedience.

Des had been furious when Fast Eddie had moved him to one of his pubs—mainly because he could never bully a bar full of grown men the way he'd always bullied the children—and he'd sworn to have revenge on John.

The door to the room Lily shared with Ben was already open and Lily was lying in the middle of the floor, her eyes wide and lifeless.

Jessup was standing talking to Brown, and Des was sitting at the battered table John himself had sat at only hours earlier when he'd given Lily the money.

"What did you do to her?" John roared, launching himself on the much smaller man.

By the time Jessup, Brown, and six other men who lived in the building pried John off Des, his face was unrecognizable.

Jessup clucked his tongue and smirked. "Oh, John. You're in trouble now, lad. Nobody touches Fast Eddie's family without punishment."

John didn't care. Lily had been the best thing in his life and she was gone; the worst that could happen had already happened.

At least that's what he thought.

Chapter 7

London
1818

Jane, with a head cold, was almost as much work as a nursery full of toddlers.

For a girl who was normally so pleasant and unassuming, she became a veritable monster when confined to her bed. As a result, Cordelia spent every minute after returning from the booksellers fetching, carrying, reassuring, soothing, reading, and slaving for her normally sunny niece.

In addition to all *that,* she'd needed to get Melissa ready for her evening.

"I'm afraid diamonds are not suitable, my dear," Cordelia pointed out as gently as she could as she watched Melissa model a heavy diamond and gold necklet that must have come from her mother's jewel box.

"I am an adult now, Aunt Cordy. I hardly need *you* to tell me how to go on." Her eyes, which she'd inherited from her mother—along with her temperament—had sparked.

Cordelia was too accustomed to her niece's temper to be offended. She'd smiled and laid a hand on her shoulder. "You are a beautiful young woman, Melissa, and I would never presume to tell you how to do anything. Please think of my suggestions as advice, not orders."

Melissa's jaw had tightened and for a tense moment Cordelia had worried the gentle hold she'd always exerted over her mercurial niece might have finally given way. But the wind had turned and Melissa had heaved a heavy sigh. And then she had removed the gaudy necklet.

With that crisis averted, Cordelia had devoted what remained of the evening to Jane.

When Jane had asked for a glass of warm milk and honey—after leaving the last glass untouched—Cordelia went to fetch the beverage herself, rather than ring for it. Before she went down to the kitchen, however, she would stop on the second floor.

It was a quarter past eleven and Charles had told her the meeting would be over by eleven thirty. She paused to study herself in the large oval mirror and twitched her lace cap a fraction of an inch in one direction. And then twitched it back. She frowned. She looked ten years older wearing the hideous headgear but to *not* wear it tonight would have alerted her relatives since she'd worn a cap for years.

Cordelia grimaced at her reflection, lifted her hem, and descended the stairs, pausing on the second-floor landing; the library door was closed, and the hallway was empty.

Well, what had she expected? That Mr. Fielding would lurk in the corridor just waiting for her?

A door clicked shut behind her and Cordelia whirled around.

Naturally, it was him.

***

John washed his hands in the basin of cool water and dried them on a cloth not much larger than the monogrammed handkerchief he kept hidden in the locked drawer of his desk.

He knew he could not hide in the retiring room for the rest of the evening. Even so, he gave the thought some serious consideration.

Damn and blast, but this evening had been a mistake. Oh, not his desire to get closer to his half-brother, Charles, and try to learn about him—to find a way to complete the process of destruction he'd put in motion a year ago. No, not that.

What had been a mistake was thinking that this was the way to go about it. For the past three hours, he'd been trapped in a room with seven of the dullest men he'd met in his life. Although he only understood about half of everything they said, that was more than enough. How the devil did a man become interested in such dry pursuits?

And was any amount of revenge really worth such suffering on his part?

More than once during the tedious evening, he'd contemplated sprinting from the room and disappearing. Not just from Gaulton's house, but from London itself.

John sighed, revolted by his own cowardice, and opened the door. He froze when something moved in his peripheral vision. It was Miss Page; she was wearing a dreadful-looking mobcap and hovering at the base of the stairs, her body poised as if she were preparing to flee.

He'd made a bloody fool of himself at the bookstore and had lashed himself about his tongue-tied idiocy all day long. Now was his chance to show that he wasn't the oaf she probably believed him to be.

"Miss Page," he said.

She jolted at the sound of his voice and when she reached out to clutch the newel post, he noticed her hand was shaking.

Ah, so she was not untouched by his presence. Did she feel attraction as he did? Or was it something else—disgust, or even fear? Whatever she felt, at least she didn't run away before he could get to her.

"Good evening," he said, reaching for her hand, even though she'd not yet offered it. He'd worn gloves upon leaving his house but had promptly removed them and left them crumpled in his coat pocket before getting to Gaulton's house. He hated the feeling of leather or cloth constricting his hands.

He was glad that he'd ignored the custom because her hands were as naked as his. Her touch was as light as it had been earlier today, but this time he felt human warmth rather than cool, slick leather as he lifted her hand to his mouth.

John knew he was not supposed to put his lips on her skin, but convention be damned. Her body went rigid at the touch of his mouth and he compounded his infraction by parting his lips just enough to taste her, the faint, floral scent of her sending even more blood surging toward his rampant arousal.

He reluctantly released her hand, and she brought it to her midriff and cradled it as if it needed support.

"Mr. Fielding, what a pleasure. Is the meeting over?"

"The discussion continues, although I believe it may soon draw to a close." Good God, he bloody well hoped so.

Her expressive eyes moved over his face before settling on his eyes.

The pulse at the base of her throat fluttered and John imagined how the tender skin would feel under his mouth, how her soft, rounded body would feel beneath his hands, her eyes narrowing to sensual slits when he slid into her wet heat. What would she—a well-behaved lady—

think if she could see the contents of his mind? What would she say if she could see the things her oh-so-proper person did inside his head?

She inhaled deeply, an action that did mesmerizing things to her ample bosom, which even her prudish gown couldn't quite conceal. "And have you enjoyed the evening? I recall it is your first meeting, is it not?"

"I am enjoying it quite well. Now."

Color flared on her smooth cheeks and made her look younger. He wanted to yank the dreadful mobcap off her auburn curls and throw it into a blazing fire; why would she wear such a horrid thing?

As if sensing the animus he bore her ugly headgear, she raised her hand to her hair, her eyes never leaving his face.

"My niece is ill."

John's eyebrows shot up at this non sequitur. "The younger girl or the elder?"

"The younger. Jane."

His brain flailed for a proper response, the way a drowning victim clutched at a lifeline. He was comfortable with desire but was not so at ease when it came to expressing other emotions—as his friend Worth was so fond of pointing out.

"I hope it is nothing serious," he finally managed.

She chuckled, and the soft feminine sound knocked the air from his lungs. She looked…

Damn! John didn't know the word to describe how she looked when she laughed. Something better than beautiful. He would have said *luminous* if it wouldn't have made him feel like a pretentious tosser to use such a word.

"No, nothing serious. Jane is not happy to be here. I think her current illness is a combination of a mild influenza and a rather virulent case of homesickness."

"Home?"

"Chelmsford Park."

"Ah." John searched for something else to add to the single syllable—something innocuous that would not expose his extensive knowledge of Chelmsford, the duke, and anything and everyone connected to either.

But Miss Page appeared satisfied with "Ah" as an adequate conversational contribution.

“My niece’s heart is in the country. I do hope she will warm to London once the Season begins in earnest.”

"Where is your heart, Miss Page?"

When she smiled at his question, John realized he was having an actual conversation. Some people might even say he was engaging in flirtation. True, it was probably far below the quality of witty banter he suspected Miss Page was accustomed to, but it was flirtation all the same.

"I am a country lass," she admitted. "What about you?"

Her question gave him pause. After a moment, he said, "I suppose I prefer the country."

"That surprises me."

It surprised John, too. He might be more comfortable in London, but he'd enjoyed the time he'd spent in Cornwall.

"Not that I *know* you well enough to say, of course," she added when he didn't answer. "You just seem so,"—she blushed and waved a hand toward his person—"well, sophisticated."

John laughed. "Sophisticated is something I've never been accused of before, Miss Page."

She stared up at him, her lips slightly parted.

John doubted she understood just how provocative she looked with her plump lips in such an inviting pose.

"Miss Page?" he prodded, wondering if he'd done something wrong when she continued to stare.

"I'm sorry. I was just thinking how different you look when you laugh."

John blinked at the unexpected comment, not sure how to respond.

"I'm terribly sorry, Mr. Fielding. I don't know what made me say something so inappropriate."

"Different how?" he asked, uninterested in what was or was not appropriate.

"You looked younger."

"How old do you think I am, Miss Page?"

His question surprised a nervous laugh out of her. "Well…" She bit her lip, adorably flustered.

John took a step toward her, closing the distance between them, and reached for her.

He would never know what he'd been about to do because the sound of a door opening behind him made her gaze jump to something over his shoulder.

John turned and saw that it was the library door that had opened and Gaulton was the first to exit.

He saw John and his face lit up. "Ah, Fielding, there you are. I f-f-feared you had r-run out on us."

A tall, spindly man named Lord Deckleford chortled loudly as he pulled gloves on hands as slender and soft as any woman's. "I would not have blamed him if he did, Gaulton. Tompkins was a bore tonight. We must remember to set firm time limits for the next meeting." He shot John a look of cool condescension. "Come, Fielding, tradition dictates we buy you a congratulatory pint for surviving your first session."

A rotund wag wearing a floral waistcoat that was bright enough to have been useful as a nautical beacon clapped the taller man on the shoulder. "And we'll buy Deckleford a pint, too, because shoving an ale in his mouth is the only way to shut it."

"Not the *only* way!" An unfamiliar voice shouted from inside the library.

The men laughed uproariously.

John turned to take his leave of Miss Page, only to discover that she was no longer there.

Chapter 8

St. Giles
1802

Jessup and Brown took turns hitting John while Eddie watched. And lectured.

"I know Des is an idiot, John, but it don't look too good to have one of me own men thrashin' me brother, now does it?"

John spat on the floor to show what he thought of that.

Eddie sighed and nodded at Jessup, who hit him while Eddie continued to speak. "If you beg Des for forgiveness, I can make all this pain go away, John. Just say the words."

"He killed her. He killed Lily."

"Those aren't the words, John."

Jessup hit him again, knocking his head to the side and sending the room spinning. It was a good thing they had him tied to a chair or he would have fallen on his face.

He was vaguely aware of Eddie droning on and on. "—sends a message that Eddie Houlihan can't even protect his own brother."

John ignored him.

A hand grabbed a fistful of hair and yanked his head back. "Are you listenin' John? You made me look *weak*."

There were at least three Eddies in front of him. John spoke to the one in the middle.

"Des tried to rape her and then he killed her when she fought him."

Eddie held his hair with one hand and punched him in the face and then howled in pain.

John almost laughed. That was the thing about hitting people—there was a skill to it; you had to know how to do it or you ended up hurting yourself worse than your victim.

Eddie shook out his hand and glared at him. "I'd kill you right now if I didn't have a fight set for you in a month with Donny Baxter."

John thought it was amusingly short-sighted of Eddie to beat up his own boxer before a fight.

Unless Eddie was going to bet *against* John.

As if he'd spoken out loud, Eddie leaned down and hissed in his ear. "Just remember, it can go either way—and I don't care because I *always* make money." Eddie flung John's head away and turned to Jessup. "When he's ready to apologize, you come get me."

That was the last thing John remembered hearing for a while.

Jessup and Brown took turns knocking him out, dunking his head in a bucket of icy water to wake him up, and then knocking him out again.

Their hands must have gotten sore because the next time he regained consciousness he discovered they'd tied him facing the chair back.

"Ready to apologize?" Jessup asked in a bored voice.

"Go fuck yourself."

Jessup and Brown laughed as if that was the most hilarious thing they'd ever heard.

Brown, who spoke even less than John, leaned close. "It's like Christmas morn to me, lad. I enjoy hittin' ye."

John knew that was true; he'd seen the gleeful look in the older man's eyes whenever he'd broken somebody's bones or beaten them bloody; Brown *loved* to cause pain.

"Eddie says we can use a belt on ye—so long as we don't break your skin or leave too many bruises." Jessup held a wide leather strap in front of John's face. John had seen Jessup use it before; he'd held men while Jessup whipped them.

It seemed like the chickens were coming home to roost.

There was no denying that the following days—he lost track of exactly how many—were filled with pain.

But whenever John thought of saying *yes* to the question they asked him over and over, he remembered the nasty, smug look on Des's face as he'd stared down on Lily's body that night, as if she were nothing but rubbish.

John would chew off his bloody tongue before apologizing to Des Houlihan.

Or at least that's what he believed.

But then Eddie came to see him and he wasn't alone.

Jessup threw a bucket of water on him to wake him up. John was shivering, frozen, still tied to a chair, and had bruises on every part of his body, even the soles of his feet, which Jessup had decided he loved to beat.

"John?"

His head swung up at the familiar voice.

It was Ben, and he was shaking almost as badly as John. He dropped to his knees and crawled to John's chair. His face was badly bruised, his lip split and swollen, and he had a black eye. "John, you need to say yer sorry to Des—you *need* to say it. Or—or Eddie's gonna give me to Des to do whatever he wants, John." He collapsed into a blubbering heap after that, his sobs filling the room.

John looked up at the men who'd been tormenting him for days. Jessup was smirking, Brown looked bored, and Eddie looked mocking. Or at least his lips did—his eyes glittered with suppressed fury and John knew the other man would never forgive him for resisting, no matter how much money he could make fighting.

"'You've made me look like a fool long enough, John," Eddie said.

"If I do what you want, you won't give Ben to Des?" John asked.

"If you apologize, I won't give 'im to Des."

John's gaze slid to Jessup and Brown.

Eddie knew what he was asking. "They won't touch 'im, either."

John looked at Ben, whose eyes were darting back and forth between them, wide with terror.

He sighed. "Fine. I'll do it."

Chapter 9

London
1818

John was eating breakfast several mornings later when Sims doddered into the room bearing a silver salver.

John's mouth was full of kipper, and he raised his eyebrows at the old man.

"Mr. Stephen Worth is here, sir."

John grimaced and washed down his food with a gulp of scalding coffee. What the hell was Worth doing in town? His last letter hadn't mentioned a visit.

He pushed aside the fish bones and cut into a thick gammon steak.

Well, he could only hope that whatever the nosey, bossy American had planned, John would play no part in it. He'd had to do the man's bidding for years, but he was his own man now.

John looked up to find the butler still beside the door and barked, "What?"

Sims's forehead wrinkled ever so slightly—an almost hysterical display of emotion for the normally expressionless butler. "Did you wish me to show Mr. Worth in, sir?"

John sighed, irritated with himself rather than the old man. Naturally, the servant would wait to be told what to do. It was bloody exhausting bossing around an army of employees.

"I doubt you could stop him from coming in," John said, more than a little astonished that Worth hadn't barged in already.

"Very good, sir." Sims tottered out of the room. He'd scarcely shut the door when it opened again and Stephen Worth stood in the entrance, grinning.

"Good morning, Fielding."

John put a chunk of ham in his mouth and chewed.

"No, please, don't get up on my account," Worth mocked as John made no effort to rise. The American glanced at the chafing dishes on the sideboard. "Lord, what a spread. Are you having a party?"

John didn't bother glancing at the sideboard. He knew what it held since he'd ordered it. He knew he ate a prodigious amount of food, but then he was a huge man. Besides, the servants ate everything he did not, so there was no waste. If he didn't order all this food, the poor beggars would eat porridge—or at least that's what Sims said they all ate when the duke had owned the house.

Worth took out his watch. "It's after eight o'clock. You've become a man of leisure, I see." His hard green eyes flickered around the room, his smirk growing larger. "John Fielding eating breakfast in his natural habitat; a *breakfast* room, of all places. Tsk, tsk. Are you becoming civilized?"

John ignored his comments and forked more eggs into his mouth. There was no point in engaging in witty banter with the gregarious businessman: John always lost verbal battles—especially against a man as quick-witted as Worth. Besides, he knew his taciturnity annoyed the other man.

A footman hovered in the doorway.

"Another pot of coffee," John said once he'd swallowed. He glanced at Worth and sawed off another piece of gammon. "What do you want?"

Worth's laughter filled the small, sunny room. "Oh John, how I have *missed* you! Thank you for the kind offer to break my fast with you," he said, with no irony. "But I have already indulged before leaving home. I must confess my wife attempted to dissuade me from calling so early. Apparently, calling on anyone before noon is savage behavior here in the Metropolis. Not at all like decent, hard-working, Puritan Boston. Is it any wonder the country is on its way to Hell in a handbasket, I ask?"

John cut another piece of meat.

Worth dropped into the seat across from him. "That is quite the largest footman I have ever seen in your foyer. But his size isn't nearly so surprising as his presence in a house belonging to *you*. And a butler and young lad to hold my horse's head." He chuckled. "Tell me, John, what other servants do you employ?" He ran a critical eye over John's person and frowned. "Not a valet, I see. But perhaps that will be next?"

The door opened and saved John from having to ignore Worth's obnoxious question. John gestured to the coffee, and Worth nodded. The footman brought him a cup and saucer and poured.

"Leave the pot and go," John told the man when he'd finished. He could not seem to keep this particular footman's name in mind and had taken to calling him *hackney*—but only in his own mind—because the man's ears stuck out in a way that suggested a carriage with both doors opened.

Worth propped his elbow on the table, dropped his chin into his hand, and smiled at John.

John ate. He'd be damned before he asked the insufferable busybody what the hell he wanted. Worth could sit in his house all day without John asking him that question.

"I daresay I missed your letter of congratulations on my son's birth." Worth's eyes narrowed and his smile became a bit fixed.

John picked up the boiled egg the footman had deposited in a small porcelain cup beside his plate, smacked it down on the fancy brocade tablecloth, and rolled it back and forth beneath his flat palm as he considered Worth's words. He knew Worth's wife had given birth to a son; he could hardly *not* know, since Worth had done everything short of paying a town crier to trumpet the news.

Was John supposed to have done or said or sent something?

He mentally shrugged and peeled the broken shell from the egg.

"Has nobody taught you the proper way to eat a boiled egg, Fielding?" Worth sighed and shook his head, but he didn't bother waiting for an answer he knew would not be forthcoming. "I've come to invite you to a dinner party."

John froze, the egg half-way to his mouth. He closed his mouth and returned the egg to its special holder before giving his attention to his uninvited guest.

Worth laughed. "Ha! I knew that would get your attention. Yes, you heard correctly—a dinner party. It is exactly what it sounds to be: a party at which one eats dinner." He sipped his coffee through his smirk.

John studied him for a long moment, an action which usually flustered people. But Worth was immune.

So he picked up the egg and rolled it in salt until it was coated with clear crystals and then bit it in half and chewed.

Undaunted by his lack of response, Worth continued, "It will be a smallish affair, but the first of its kind at our new house." He lowered his cup and cocked an auburn eyebrow. "You have not seen the house since it was completed. I daresay you are curious about how it looks, given that you actively took part in its construction."

John didn't care if he never saw the inside of Worth's house. He didn't bother pointing out that he had been *active* only in the sense that he had delivered messages to the recalcitrant architect and more than a few corrupt and inept tradesmen throughout the construction process. And the messages had *not* been of the paper kind.

He finished the second half of the egg and washed it down with the last of his coffee before tossing his napkin onto the table and shoving back his chair. He was half-way to the door before Worth spoke behind him.

"So, may I tell my wife to expect you for dinner?"

John opened the door. "I'm busy that night," he said over his shoulder, and then closed the door with a decisive click, his mouth twitching with a triumphant smile; that was one way to end a conversation.

He'd just lowered himself into his comfortable desk chair—one of the few in the house that could accommodate his size—when the library door opened.

"Has anyone ever told you that you are the rudest man in England? No," Worth held up a hand to stop him from speaking, not that John had planned to. "Scratch that. You are the rudest man on two, perhaps even three continents." He strode to a scruffy, brocade-covered armchair opposite the desk and threw himself into it, causing the chair to creak ominously.

Worth was the first person to sit in the chair. In fact, Worth was the first guest he'd had in his house, full stop. But was a person really a guest if they appeared at one's house uninvited? Or would they be considered an invader?

He was pondering the question when he noticed Worth was speaking. Again.

"Are you listening to me, John?"

"No."

He took the mail from the tray where Sims deposited it and sorted through it. Most of the letters were bills, except for one from the private enquiry agent he'd hired to search for Dolan. The letter was brief and to the point: the man had discovered nothing new about Dolan.

John tossed the letter aside.

Worth heaved a gusty sigh and John looked up and heaved a sigh of his own. "I don't want to go to a dinner party, *Stephen,* and, believe me, your other guests don't want me there, either."

"You came to dinner parties in Boston."

"That was different."

"Well, yeeeees. Boston is a city in America, and we are now in London."

John ignored his levity. He opened a letter from his solicitor. Actually, it was a bill. He tossed it onto the growing bill pile.

He glanced up and saw that Worth was still in the room, waiting. "I went to those dinner parties because you paid me to," he reminded him.

"Are you saying you'd come to this dinner party if I paid you?"

"You know I'm not," he snapped, irritated that he'd been lured into a discussion when he'd sworn to himself *not* to allow Worth to manipulate him. He could see from Worth's smirk that he was amused.

"The last thing I want to do is play a game of *Let's-Stare-at-the-Savage* with a bunch of aristocrats," John said.

"Most of the other guests will be men of business."

"I get enough of men of business during the day. I hardly want to spend my evenings with them." John opened a bill for candles and stared: fifteen bloody pounds? He glanced up. "How much do you spend on candles?"

"How the hell would I know? Or care, for that matter? You're a rich man, John. *Rich.* What do you care about the cost of candles? Besides, those are household matters. Matters for a *wife* to manage."

"I won't stay rich for long if I don't pay attention to such matters, and, in case you haven't noticed, I don't *have* a wife." John set the bill aside to ask Sims about later.

All Worth's yapping made his head pound. He did not like conversing this much at any time of the day, but most especially not in the morning. He needed to get Worth out of his house before he throttled him, and the only way to achieve that involved speaking.

"Please thank your wife for her kind invitation, Worth, but give her my"—he tossed up his hands, at a loss for polite words—"tell her whatever one says at such times. See?" John demanded, smacking his leather-topped desk in frustration. "I don't even know the right bloody words to refuse an invitation. What the fuck would I say at the actual dinner?"

Worth laughed. "Well, first off, you can remove "bloody" "hell" "damn" and "fuck" from your vocabulary. Ladies do not care to listen to such vulgarisms."

John could have told Worth that he was sorely mistaken about that. He'd bedded plenty of rich society *ladies* in Boston and, without fail, they'd all loved his filthy, vulgar mouth. But that was none of Worth's business and mentioning it would only prolong his visit.

"I know you are aware of what you can and cannot say in front of proper ladies, John. You did not suffer years of tutoring in the social graces for nothing. As much as you would wish me to forget it, you are an intelligent man who knows how to engage in polite discussion."

John gritted his teeth to keep from shouting. "I have no interest in small talk—polite or otherwise—or, God forbid, *proper ladies.* You, of all people, should know that."

Worth stretched out his legs and crossed his booted ankles, assuming the comfortable position of a man settling in for a protracted conversation.

John wanted to howl in frustration. Why would Worth not leave him alone?

"You need to live your life, John. It's not healthy to shut yourself up in this house. You need—"

"I went out last night," he blurted, and then wanted to bite off his tongue.

"Spending an evening hobnobbing with thieves, bawds, and criminals does not count, John. When are you going to stop roaming the worst parts of the city like a deranged vigilante?"

"My nighttime activities pleased you well enough when they served *your* purpose," John retorted.

To his surprise, the other man nodded. "I used you abominably to pursue my goals, which were less than admirable. I have apologized for involving you in my unsavory activities, activities for which I am now trying to make amends."

"Only because your wife is forcing you to make amends."

Again, Worth surprised him. "You are correct, she is the reason I've given up revenge and begun living my life. I know you don't work for me, but I spent thousands of dollars educating you, and *you* spent thousands of hours learning. Between your money and your manners—when you choose to use them—you could gain entrée almost anywhere you wished. I would like to help you—it would be a way to apologize for using you."

John didn't want apologies. He wanted to be left alone. "When are you going to stop meddling in my life, and how I choose to live it?"

Worth regarded him steadily.

The silent approach was not only unexpected, it was also almost as annoying as Worth's incessant talking.

John sighed. "As it happens, I wasn't pursuing my investigations yesterday evening."

Worth sat up. "Oh?"

"I went to a… well, just call it a casual meeting of men."

"What men?"

"It's a club."

Worth's eyes threatened to roll out of his head. "You joined a club?" He couldn't have been more dumbfounded if John had confessed to conversing with squirrels in Hyde Park. "What club? Brook's? White's? Boodle's?"

John ground his teeth. He should have kept his mouth shut.

He was scrambling for a suitable lie when the other man's short attention span saved him the bother.

"Oh, never mind. I'm just glad you'll be speaking to other law-abiding human beings." He frowned. "Unless it's some sort of criminal club?"

"No."

"Oh, good. Anyhow, the dinner invite was only part of the reason I came this morning. The other was to ask you to join me at Tat's. I'd also like to check the progress of the new town carriage I commissioned for my wife."

John's mouth opened to say *no,* but then he looked at Worth's face and realized, suddenly, that the other man probably had as few friends or acquaintances as John.

Only a year ago, all Stephen Worth had lived for was making money and plotting revenge. Now his plotting days were over, and he had more money than Croesus.

Was Worth his friend?

John couldn't even recall what friends were anymore. Not since Lily had he been close enough to somebody to call them a friend.

And look how that had ended, John?

He thrust the unpleasant thought from his mind with practiced ease. But another memory took its place, this one from only last year when he'd heard that Worth had been caught in a mine collapse.

Everyone, including John, had believed Worth dead—or at least trapped beyond anyone's help. John had suffered a type of madness when he'd heard the news. He couldn't recall his exact thoughts, nor did he wish to, but he'd dismantled that mine timber by timber with his bare hands, not stopping until he'd found Stephen Worth's unconscious body.

Did that mean they were friends?

John scowled at the unwanted thought and glared at Worth. "Fine. I'll go to Tat's, but only to stop you from making an arse of yourself and buying some spavined nag that's touched in the wind."

Worth grinned. "We shall have a ripping good time."

Really, the man was relentless.

***

Several nights later, John was staring at his reflection and wondering just what aspect of his person Stephen Worth would critique first tonight.

John's evening clothes, which had been cut for his over-sized body by the august Weston himself?

Or perhaps Worth would comment on his stylish pewter waistcoat?

Or would he mock John's new footwear—his first pair of dancing shoes, an affectation he had always sworn to avoid?

Or maybe Worth would tease John about his cravat—

"Oh, who gives a damn what he says?" John snarled at his reflection, pleased by the menacing but reassuringly familiar reflection that glared back at him. At least his face was the same.

He still couldn't believe that he'd allowed Worth to trick him into going to this blasted dinner party. He'd sprung his trap the same day they'd gone to Tattersall's.

"So, you will come to dinner." Worth had made the statement less than thirty seconds after John had just bought two carriage horses.

When John—too stunned by his purchase to think—hadn't answered, Worth had said, "Jolly good! Elinor will be so pleased."

John's brain had been too scrambled to argue. He'd just purchased two bloody carriage horses and he didn't even have a carriage!

"Are you aware that you just bought a *mis*matched pair of carriage horses, Fielding? And you don't have a carriage, either." Worth had said, echoing his thoughts. "Don't tell me you're going to buy that whorish red curricle you were eyeballing earlier?" He'd pushed back his high-crowned beaver hat, exposing flaming red hair that was *exactly* the same color as the carriage Worth had just derided.

John had enjoyed that observation in private and ignored Worth's question for two reasons: one, he knew it irritated the other man to be ignored, and two, it hadn't been the red curricle he'd been eyeballing, but the black and white one.

Unlike the sleeker models that were being produced, the carriage that had caught John's attention had a larger, heavier body that was a shiny black lacquer with a supple leather interior the color of fresh cream, which matched the spokes and felloes.

It was the most dashing curricle he'd ever seen. It was also the only vehicle John had ever wanted. In the past, he had preferred traveling by horse.

John smiled as he imagined Worth's amazement when he finally saw the carriage and pair together. His reflection smiled back at him, the sight as horrifying as ever. He sighed and turned from the mirror; he was dawdling, and it was time to go, so he snatched up a pair of gloves and his new cloak.

He had never owned such a frivolous garment in his life. It was black superfine wool lined with matching black silk. The stiff-lipped clerk had not even asked John if he wanted the damned thing—he'd *told* him he did.

When he got downstairs, it was to find Fredrick in the foyer. John wondered if the man *lived* in the space.

Fredrick grinned when he saw John, his eyes becoming as round as an owl's as he took in his evening clothes.

"You look very fine this evening, Mr. Fielding."

John grunted and quickly made for the door.

"Don't forget your hat and cane, sir."

John grimaced, turned, and snatched both items out of his hands. And then he realized he should have put on his gloves first.

"Blast," he muttered beneath his breath, thrusting the hat and cane back into Fredrick's hands while he pulled on his gloves.

Sims drifted into the foyer in the noiseless way he had. "Good evening, Mr. Fielding."

John paused the wrestling match between his six-fingered hand and glove. The old man was all but beaming at him.

John glanced nervously from the butler to the footman. Just what the hell were they so damned happy about? "What?" he demanded.

"Have you summoned a hackney for Mr. Fielding, Fredrick?"

"I don't need one," John snapped before the footman could answer, finally getting the blasted glove onto his hand.

Sim's eyebrows crept all the way up his forehead until they almost merged with his white hair.

John sighed. "What?"

"Your shoes, sir."

John looked down at his feet and then back up. Was his own servant mocking his new footwear? "What about them?" he asked, not bothering to hide the menace in his voice.

"I surmise you are going to dine with Mr. Worth and Lady Trentham?"

It was John's turn to raise his eyebrows. How the devil had Sims known where he was going? Had he been listening at keyholes?

The man was too old and frail to sack, so the most John could do was fix him with a hard stare. "What of it?"

"That is quite a distance, sir."

"Make your point, Sims."

"Your shoes, sir. They will be ruined."

He glared, but Sims refused to back down. "Fine. A hackney."

A short time later, he was trundling along toward Russell Square.

Rather than ponder the dreaded evening ahead, John turned his mind to more pleasant matters: his two encounters with Miss Page.

A thrill shot through his body, merely thinking her name and he wanted to bang his head on something. He was a man in his thirties, not a boy. Hell, he'd not even behaved so besottedly when he'd *been* a boy.

It was irksome to think about her because he could never have her. Even if he were mad enough to ask her to marry him—*marry him!*—she was a duchess's sister and would never tarnish her family name with such an association.

As for simply bedding her. Well, that was impossible, too. She was not like the inn wenches or lusty widows he was accustomed to slaking his appetites upon. No, she was a virgin, which was every bit as exotic to John as a polar bear. More so because he would know how to behave around a bear; he'd bloody well run in the opposite direction.

Probably good advice when it came to Miss Cordelia Page, as well.

He groaned and closed his eyes; he was so tired of going around and around and around on the subject. In the past, no woman had captured his interest for longer than a few weeks and usually only a few hours.

In the past, he had spent all his time plotting and planning vengeance—not scheming how to get close to a female just so he could *talk* to her.

Vengeance.

Now that is what he *should* be thinking about. But the truth was, his plans for revenge had become stuck—mired like a wagon in deep muck—and he couldn't seem to regain either the momentum or interest to push matters forward.

He'd thought spending time with Charles Merrick would give him the fuel he needed to feed his rage, but it had just left him tired—not to mention feeling more than a little like a storybook villain in a gothic romance, a caricature of a man who endlessly blustered about his evil plans and laughed maniacally.

He hated to admit it, but he was losing interest in putting his half-brother in the poorhouse. It was the duke that he'd always wanted to hurt, but now his father was beyond John's vengeance.

There was still his search for Dolan, of course—he had not given up on that—but it was becoming increasingly difficult to make a twenty-year search the focus of his life.

Maybe Worth was right, after all. Maybe John needed something else to live for.

Chapter 10

St. Giles
1802

Des Houlihan's face would frighten children for the rest of his miserable life.

John tried to make that ample consolation for his current predicament, but it was slim comfort.

"Say it again," Des snapped, his eyes sweeping up and down Eddie's big dining room table to make sure all the ruffians were paying attention.

"I humbly apologize for what I did to you," John repeated.

Des seethed, unappeased.

"Is that good?" Eddie asked him, sounding bored.

"No!" Des shrieked through a mouth that couldn't close properly.

"What else do you want?"

"I want 'im to kneel and kiss my boot."

Eddie's eyebrows arched, and he suddenly looked interested. He turned to John. "You 'eard 'im. Get on yer knees."

A ripple of amazed laughter went up and down the table.

John didn't care. He dropped to his knees—clumsily since he was still in considerable pain—leaned down, and with no fucking about, kissed Des's boot and said, "I humbly apologize for what I did to you."

When he looked up, Des had frozen. John could tell the other man thought that it simply was not enough—that it would *never* be enough.

He knew the feeling.

"Awright, that's enough," Eddie shouted, and then banged the table with his fist to be heard over the chatter and laughter of his minions. "Sit down and eat, Des. John, get up."

John stood.

"You get out," Eddie snapped.

John was happy to oblige. Eddie had kicked him out of his house—an action that was supposed to be a punishment—and was sending him back to live in the kiddie house, yet another punishment.

John was glad to be going back to the ramshackle house, regardless of how crowded and filthy and noisy it was.

Somebody new had taken Lily's place—an old thief who was nearly blind and didn't hit his charges for amusement, the way Des had.

As for Ben…

Well, Ben dropped to his knees the minute John walked into the house. "I'm sorry, John! I'm sorry! I'm so sorry! I'm—"

"Ben!" John yelled when it was clear that Ben was working himself into a frenzy.

Ben whimpered but stopped talking.

John helped him to his feet and led him into his small room and shut the door before turning to the other man. "I want you to listen, awright?"

Ben nodded vigorously. "I'm listenin', John. I'm—"

"I've got a month before my next fight. Once that's over, me an' you are leavin'."

"Leavin'?" Ben gasped.

"Yes."

"But *where*?" Ben looked so terrified you would have thought that John was threatening to feed him to lions.

"We'll go to Dublin."

Ben's jaw sagged, and rightfully so.

"Me da lives there," John said, amazed at the drivel coming out of his own mouth. But why not Dublin? He'd given plenty of thought to what Alfie had told him that night. The other man had seemed positive that Kennedy was his father. What reason would Alfie have had to lie about such a thing?

Besides, who else did John have?

"I've got money hidden," John went on. "Not much, but enough to get us there. What about the money I gave L-Lil?" God, it hurt just to say her name. "Do you know where she kept it, Ben?"

Tears rolled down Ben's pale cheeks. "Des took it all, John. 'Ee used to come and take it every time."

John blinked. "What are you sayin', Ben? You mean that wasn't the first time Des came and bothered Lily?"

"'Ee came whenever you'd been to see 'er—somebody tole 'im." Ben swallowed. "'Ee'd take the money an' then kick me out. When I came back, Lil would cry and make me promise not to tell you. But I don't need to keep the promise now, do I, John? Do I?" he asked, becoming agitated.

"No, Ben, you don't."

The sickening, crushing truth hit him: John hadn't helped Lily by getting her out of Holloway's and giving her money; he'd only made her a target for Des. He'd only made her life more hellish. Every time he visited her, he'd brought Des Houlihan in his wake, like a plague.

He stared at Ben, who'd curled in on himself and was rocking back and forth on the rickety chair and muttering under his breath.

Ben wasn't the father of Lily's child—Des was.

How had John been so blind? He'd wondered about Lily moving in with Ben and claiming to be pregnant with his baby, but he'd never wanted to pry into her private matters.

Now it was all so clear to him. Lil would have been too terrified to tell John. Not scared for herself but scared for John—because she'd known that he'd have killed Des if he'd learned the truth.

She'd been trying to protect *him.*

John squeezed his eyes shut to keep the tears from falling. Lily had always put John's welfare before her own, and it had killed her.

"John?"

He swallowed and dragged the back of his hand across his face, mortified when it came away wet. "Yeah, Ben?"

"Do we hafta go away?"

"Yeah, Ben."

"When?"

"We need more money, so we'll have to wait until after I do this fight."

John would use his money to bet on the match. What he really wanted to do was bet all his money on whatever Eddie *didn't* tell him to do. That would be a win-win: John would make money and Eddie would lose it.

But no matter how rewarding it would be to damage Eddie that way, it would be a reckless, dangerous, stupid thing to do.

Instead, John would be Eddie's obedient dog one last time and fight the way he was told to fight. Afterward, when Eddie believed him beaten into submission, he and Ben would get the hell out.

"We're goin' to Dublin, John?" Ben asked in a small voice.

John laid a hand on his narrow shoulder and squeezed gently. "Aye, maybe Dublin, maybe America, Ben—it don't matter where we go. Anywhere will be better than London."

John would remember those words later.

Chapter 11

London
1818

Charles helped Cordelia from the carriage and turned to the coachman. "Come b-back for us in three hours, P-Powell."

Cordelia gazed up at the house they were about to enter; it was as large as Falkirk House but could not have been more than a few years old.

"I never asked where you met Mr. Worth?" she asked as he led her toward the well-lighted entryway.

"His b-bank is arranging the sale of the Shropshire house." He gave a soft laugh. "He spoke to me p-p-personally on the matter."

Cordelia was sorry to have introduced a subject that must rankle. She did not know the details of the duke's business losses last year, but she understood that Charles's personal property in Shropshire had been used to fund the failed venture.

"Did you n-n-never meet Worth's wife?" Charles asked quietly. "She was married to T-Trentham and is Viscount Yarmouth's daughter. She is your age, I th-think."

"She married Trentham before she had a Season and always lived in the country until this year."

The door opened before they reached it, and their hosts stood in the entrance.

Mr. Worth was a striking ginger-haired man who towered over his much smaller wife. For some reason, the image of a peacock and peahen popped into her head.

"Good evening, Gaulton." Worth flashed a blinding smile and stepped forward; his hand extended. Charles was nonplussed for a second before he reciprocated and the men shook in the American style.

Worth's eyes were an emerald green, which was striking with his red hair. He was a very attractive man who crackled with energy, a characteristic which was even more noticeable when compared to his mild, cool spouse.

"Welcome, Miss Page," he took her hand and gave it a gentle shake. "Let me introduce my wife, Lady Trentham."

The order of Worth's introductions was unconventional, to say the least, but the countess appeared not to notice. "Welcome my lord, Miss Page. Please come inside."

Her husband gave a booming laugh and gestured them into the foyer. "By Jove, you will think it is some quaint American custom to keep one's guests jabbering out on the front stoop."

Cordelia and Charles laughed politely and handed their possessions to the liveried servants waiting in the enormous entryway.

Suspended high above them was the most enormous chandelier she'd ever seen, some of its crystals surely weighing several pounds.

Lady Trentham followed her gaze and smiled. "My husband has something of a fetish for the unusual," she said, accompanying her up the massive marble staircase.

Cordelia could not stop staring, even though she knew it was gauche. "This is the most striking marble I have ever seen."

It was black marble shot through with stark, jagged lines that looked like lightning.

"It is from Brazil," Lady Trentham said. "Mr. Worth used to travel extensively on bank business. And like a magpie, he collected anything that interested him."

It occurred to Cordelia that perhaps Lady Trentham was one of those "things."

Cordelia smiled at the smaller woman, not quite sure how to respond to the countess's information about her husband's business. In her experience, *no* lady of the *ton* admitted to knowledge of commerce.

"I daresay my husband's work and my interest in several of his projects will repel many here in town," Lady Trentham said, as if reading Cordelia's mind.

Cordelia's lips parted and the other woman laughed and patted her arm, her silvery-gray eyes dancing with amusement. "That was dreadfully ill done of me, Miss Page. How my mother would weep to hear her daughter engage in such talk. I have rather embraced my husband's more casual American manners." It was common knowledge that Worth had started out his life as a servant before going to America to earn his fortune and then returning to marry into the very family he had once served.

A footman opened the door when they approached, and Cordelia's jaw sagged yet again.

The sitting room was monstrous—bizarrely huge, in truth. But that was not what was so staggering.

Her hostess gestured to the opposite wall. "Mr. Worth commissioned this mural last year, but it was only recently completed. The artist designed it from sketches based on my husband's recollection of the Forbidden City. He is one of the few Westerners to visit that city and the mural provides a glimpse inside." She turned to the guests who were mingling off to one side of the vast room, clustered closely together as if for safety in the cavernous space. "Allow me to introduce you to Mr. James Bowles and his daughter Priscilla."

Cordelia had to wrench her eyes away from the magnificent painting, which was so lifelike she felt as if she'd been transported half a world away.

She smiled at the timid girl. "I am already acquainted with Miss Bowles; we've met even though the Season hasn't yet begun." Cordelia could thank her sister for that—the duchess was shamelessly pressuring Charles to propose to the young heiress before the Season even began. She suspected the Bowles's presence tonight was not entirely happenstance.

Miss Bowles, who was painfully shy, merely tittered.

Cordelia turned to greet the girl's father, a hefty, ruddy-faced man, whose eyes flickered over her dismissively before settling on Charles and glinting with interest.

"You must be Gaulton. It's past time we met," Mr. Bowles boomed, reaching out to grab Charles's hand while the younger man was still greeting his daughter.

Ever the gentleman, Charles gave the gauche merchant a warm smile while allowing him to mangle his hand.

"G-good evening, Mr. B-Bowles."

The change in the older man's face was almost comical. He froze, his fist still gripping Charles's. "Good god, that's quite a stammer you've got boy. Er… I mean, my lord."

"Papa!" Miss Bowles's eyes threatened to roll out of her head.

Charles, hardened by years of teasing at Eton, merely chuckled. "I'm afraid you have the r-right of it, sir. It's a d-d-dashed n-nuisance."

The room, which had become so quiet Cordelia imagined she could almost hear the crickets in the mural stridulating, filled with relieved laughter at Charles's self-deprecating words.

The door opened just then, and yet another guest entered.

"Ah!" Mr. Worth exclaimed, striding across a floor that was covered with expensive looking rugs. "Here you are, John. I was beginning to wonder if we should have to eat without you."

Cordelia gawked to see Mr. Fielding shaking Worth's hand and giving the banker an especially sardonic look as they chatted in a low voice.

He was massive and imposing in his evening blacks and took in the occupants of the room like a predator, his dark eyes flickering dismissively over the guests—including Cordelia—before snapping back to her. His lips parted in obvious surprise.

So, he hadn't known she'd be there, either.

Worth stepped in front of him, and blocked Mr. Fielding's stunned expression from Cordelia's view.

***

John thought about grabbing Worth by the neck and dragging him out of his gaudy showplace of a house. He imagined how good it would feel to pummel the smug expression off his face.

Worth, who was attuned to John's moods—unnervingly so, in fact—grinned as John shook his hand with a crushing grip.

"Behave yourself, John," he whispered from the corner of his smirking mouth, turning his back to the rest of the guests and surreptitiously flexing the hand John had just mangled. "I'm not interfering in your business. I invited the boy for Bowles, who was nagging me to death."

John blinked. *The boy*? He gaped at Worth like a slack-jawed yokel before his words sank in. *He is talking about the Marquess of Gaulton,* not *his aunt.*

Of course, Worth would think John was angry at Gaulton's presence—he would know nothing about John's interest in Miss Page. And he must *never* learn of it.

The next ten minutes were an agony. John loathed talking to new people. He actually loathed talking to *any* people, even ones he already knew. Well, except for Miss Page. And maybe Worth, occasionally, when he wasn't attempting to boss John about.

"John, would you escort Miss Page to dinner?"

He looked up to find Worth standing beside Miss Page, who had a slight flush on her cheeks.

For whatever reason, when the introductions had been made, neither of them had corrected Lady Trentham in her misapprehension that they were strangers. Not that he supposed three brief meetings and barely a hundred words would constitute much else.

As far as John could tell, Worth did not look as if he had any ulterior motive or any tricks up his sleeve. He was simply doing the duties of a host.

John offered his arm, and she put her hand so lightly on his sleeve he had to make sure it was there before leading her toward the dining room.

"How are your studies in natural philosophy progressing, Mr. Fielding?"

John glanced down at her and saw she was smiling. There was a fetching dimple just below the right corner of her mouth.

"My studies progress much as I expected, Miss Page."

"I detect a certain irony in your response, Mr. Fielding."

His lips twitched, but he suppressed the urge to smile and make a brutal mockery of his face. "Perhaps it would be more precise to say I am progressing as I *feared.*"

She laughed, a low sultry chuckle that warmed him.

John stopped near the head of the table and pulled out her chair.

Worth was on her left, and John's name was on the placard on the right. The group was quite small, just twelve. The only people he'd met before were the Worths, Gaulton, Miss Page, and Bowles.

Bowles's daughter barely looked old enough to be out of the schoolroom and had the vapid, youthful look of a person John would go miles out of his way to avoid. She was accompanied by some Friday-faced chaperone—Mrs. Keeting—a woman who sat on John's other side.

There were two other couples, one young and one in their dotage. All four had the stiff posture, shiny faces, and not-quite-right clothing of the merchant class—John's people—and looked thrilled, eager, and nervous to be at a table with aristocrats.

Mrs. Keeting turned to John and smiled, sending strong clouds of gin breath his way. "Tell me, are you looking forward to the Season, Mr. Fielding?"

John groaned inwardly. Was he really expected to make small talk for the next two hours?

**

The evening, just like Worth's house, was unlike anything Cordelia had ever experienced.

Mr. Worth was as unconventional in his table manners as he was in every other regard. He seemed to possess the hearing of a bat and interjected his opinions freely in conversations, both near and far. He was a charismatic, attractive gentleman, so his behavior came across as that of an *original*, rather than crass.

The same could not be said of Mr. Bowles, whose booming, grating voice could probably be heard down in the kitchen. Not only was he loud, but he stalked his quarry—Charles—with the doggedness and subtly of a cat crouching outside a mouse hole.

Cordelia was eyeing the merchant with some trepidation when Mr. Fielding—who had not spoken a word for the first twenty minutes of the meal—leaned toward her.

"I believe Bowles is courting your nephew." The words were a low rumble and so unexpected that she wasn't certain she'd heard him correctly.

"I beg your pardon?"

He turned back to his plate and cut another piece of fish, using his salad fork as a knife.

Cordelia waited until it was clear that he would not repeat himself, her annoyance growing by the moment. Really! Just who did he think he was that he did not owe even the barest civility to those around him? Her ire—a creature so rarely seen that most of her family doubted it existed—emerged from its cave.

"Mr. Fielding."

He turned at her sharp tone, his fork laden with fully a quarter of the fish fillet.

"Perhaps where *you* come from, it is acceptable behavior to toss out conversational—" she fluttered her hand, searching for the correct word.

"Artillery?" One of his jet eyebrows—the only elegant feature on his savagely handsome face—arched. And then he shoved the food into his mouth in one huge bite and chewed, his eyes locked with hers.

A spark of something—mischief?—glinted in his black-as-midnight eyes and his lips *almost* lifted at the corners.

The expression was so puckish and unexpected that it robbed her of words.

What was it about this man that he could be a mannerless brute one moment and a naughty little boy the next?

It frightened Cordelia just how much she wanted to know what went on in his head.

**

Why the devil would anyone need so many bloody forks?

John glanced at the woman beside him, tempted to ask.

Miss Page was regarding him with a look that was part bemused and part amused. It was not an expression he was accustomed to seeing, and he couldn't guess what it meant.

John knew women liked men who flattered them and uttered clever quips—men like Worth—but he was not such a man. Nor did he wish to remake himself in that mold, even if that were possible.

But she hadn't asked for any of that; she had only asked him to repeat what he'd said.

Surely you can do that, *you lout?*

He sighed. Yes; yes, he could.

John leaned toward her. "I said, *I think Bowles wants Lord Gaulton for a son-in-law.*"

She studied him for a moment longer, as if pondering something.

Just when he believed that she'd was going to serve him a portion of his own behavior and ignore him, she said,"Unfortunately, you perceive matters correctly, Mr. Fielding."

"You do not approve of such a match?"

She hesitated—even John knew this wasn't a suitable subject of conversation for dinner, or between strangers—but then she surprised him and said, "I believe they are not well-suited."

"Because she is a tradesman's daughter, and he is a duke's heir?"

"No. Because they do not share similar interest or sensibilities."

He smiled at her tart tone.

She appeared annoyed, rather than repelled by his expression. "You find that amusing? You do not think some degree of compatibility is necessary between husband and wife?"

"I've never given the matter any thought."

Her lips parted in shock.

When she seemed incapable of speech, he leaned closer to her and said, "Do the women of your association join their husbands at White's? At their gaming hells? At Jackson's or Tat's or Crib's Parlor?" John was tempted to add brothels to that list but restrained himself at the last moment. "Do the men you know shop for hats and embroidery silks and pay morning calls with their wives?" He stopped, startled by his own effusion. When was the last time he'd spoken so many words in a row?

He was not the only one who was surprised. Miss Page stared at him as if he were a sofa cushion that had suddenly burst into song.

"Well?" he prodded.

"There will always be separate pursuits for each gender. What I am referring to is a harmony of intellect." Her hazel eyes were no longer smiling. Rather, they were throwing sparks. John imagined her looking equally passionate, but without the vile turban on her head and wearing considerably less than her disappointingly modest dark green gown.

He would very much like to strip her, although perhaps not entirely. No, he would leave her in stockings. Would she have the fancy embroidered ones with flowers or birds or bunnies or whatever foolishness found its way onto a silk stocking? Or would they be virginally plain with nothing to distract a man's attention from the curvy limbs they sheathed—

"*Mr. Fielding.*"

John's eyes leapt from her mouth to meet her gaze. The way she'd said his name made him think it wasn't the first time.

"Hmm?"

"I asked what you thought of my answer. There is no reason to stare so ferociously at me if you do not agree."

John was sorely tempted to tell her what he'd really been thinking when Stephen Worth leaned toward her.

"You must let me know if Mr. Fielding behaves like an unsocial lump of coal, Miss Page." Worth shot John a smirk. "That is not to be confused with his usual behavior, which is merely a *lump* of coal."

The two indulged in laughter at John's expense before Miss Page turned back to the lump in question. "He is actually behaving quite unlumpishly."

John kept his expression as bland as his face could possibly look and pointedly ignored Worth's taunting.

Instead. he stared at Miss Page, who wore a faint smile and was staring rather fixedly at *him*.

He glanced down to see if he had dropped fish or spilled wine on his cravat, but his clothing appeared pristine. He then looked over his shoulder to see if the gin-soaked chaperone on his other side had passed out in the poached hake, but she had her trembling hand on her wineglass and was lifting it to her mouth.

He turned back to Miss Page. "What? Why are you looking at me like that?"

"Since we were speaking of interests and hobbies, what pursuits do *you* enjoy?" She paused for effect. "Other than engaging in lively discussions about natural philosophy, that is."

"I have no hobbies." At least none he could confess in polite society.

"You have no hobbies." She repeated the words with no intonation.

"I work for my crust, Miss Page. Men who work for a living do not have the leisure time of the aristocracy," he pointed out.

"I believe you are telling me a falsehood, Mr. Fielding."

"You mean you *don't* believe aristocratic men have more leisure time than those who labor?"

"You willfully misunderstand me. I also believe you are misstating your own situation." She paused while a footman removed her plate. "Are you trying to claim that you spend every daylight moment toiling?"

She was… persistent. John was beginning to feel like a fox with four dozen hounds on its scent. He looked into her openly amused eyes and shrugged.

"I will take that as a *no*." She didn't wait for him to confirm or deny her assumption before continuing. "Mr. Worth is your friend?"

John glanced at Worth, who was busy charming the woman on his other side. Was Worth his friend? Was it pathetic that he wasn't quite sure what constituted friendship?

She chuckled. “That was not a trick question, sir. Tell me, when was the last time you spent time with Mr. Worth?”

“Several days ago.”

“And what did you do?”

It would serve her right if he told her they’d gone to a brothel after winning a packet in a gambling hell, getting drunk, and watching a bloody prizefight.

Instead, he said, “We went to a cattle auction.”

“Ah, so you do have a hobby.”

“Hardly that. I would call it more of an occasional pastime.”

“Are you parsing words with me, Mr. Fielding?”

“I don’t even know what *parsing* means, Miss Page.” He saw that his admission of ignorance startled her. “Would you go for a drive with me tomorrow?”

She looked as shocked as John felt.

Where the devil had the question come from?

She inhaled, and John knew she was going to offer some excuse.

“Please accept, Miss Page. I am trying to develop a hobby.”

She gave a breathless sounding laugh. “So I would be doing a humanitarian service."

John smelled imminent victory, so he behaved himself and said, "You would," while privately imagining other services. Yes, he was a dog.

“Then yes, Mr. Fielding. I will go for a ride with you.”

***

Cordelia knew by the way Charles stumbled while climbing into the carriage that he was more than a little exhausted; he always became clumsier when he was tired.

The coach passed beneath a streetlamp and she saw the taut expression on his handsome face. He caught her concerned look and flashed her a reassuring smile, his relaxed, pleasant mask quickly back in place. As a boy, he had always worried excessively about the comfort and happiness of those around him—his sisters, his mother, and even his aunt.

Cordelia was heart-sore that somebody so kind and sensitive would be forced into a marriage; if not with Miss Bowles, then to somebody like her. Many young men could marry a woman lacking in wit and intellectual curiosity and continue their own pursuits uninterrupted, taking a mistress for pleasure or seeking an accomplished courtesan for conversation and passion. But Charles was the type of man who would be loyal to his wife. And a lifetime with a woman like Priscilla Bowles—shy and sweet but dull—would be hellish.

"Did you enjoy the evening, Cee?" he asked.

"Better than you, I think."

A tired chuckle floated out of the darkness. Charles had sat between Miss Bowles and Lady Trentham at dinner. Mr. Bowles had talked to him—or at him, rather—from his seat across the table.

Although Charles had maintained his polite smile, she'd seen how much Mr. Bowles had worn on him. What would it be like to have him as a father-in-law?

At one point, Mr. Bowles had been administering a loud, lengthy harangue on the shortcomings of the aristocracy, when Charles had tipped over his wineglass.

Lady Trentham, the consummate hostess, had smoothed over the incident, blaming it on the recent fashion to dine *à la Russe.*

"I find the addition of even more cutlery to an already crowded table barbaric—not to mention downright dangerous." The smile she gave Charles was both kind and reassuring. "Mr. Worth and I attended a dinner last week where Castlereagh deposited his wine goblet on Countess Lieven's service plate. Luckily Dorothy considers him one of her closest friends and forgave him the intimacy." Her casual reference to the Foreign Secretary's gaffe caused everyone to chuckle. And that she referred to one of the top-loftiest women in Britain by her given name was enough to subdue Bowles for the rest of the meal.

Cordelia had been surprised to hear about Lady Trentham's august connections. As the daughter of Yarmouth and the widow of Trentham, her lineage was above reproach, but her marriage to Stephen Worth should have placed her beyond the pale. It was a sign of the post-war world that giants of industry could now command a place at the highest tables in the land.

That realization now brought her thoughts back to Mr. John Fielding, whom she'd been trying to forget for the past hour.

They had talked very little after she accepted his invitation for a ride in the park. After dinner finished the women had removed to a far cozier sitting room and discussed books, plays, and upcoming talks.

Cordelia liked Lady Trentham for her kindness toward Charles, but she'd also liked her on her own merits. The countess was both clever and amusing and Cordelia was excited to meet a woman her own age who did not disdain conversation beyond the latest fashion in hats.

Cordelia enjoyed attending talks on a wide variety of social issues and when she was at Chelmsford, she was as active in such causes as her sister deemed proper.

While the duchess approved of a certain amount of involvement with local charities, she frowned on many of the activities Cordelia had embraced while living in her father's home.

"Recall that you are more than the daughter of a country squire while you live under His Grace's roof. Please consider your duty to the Falkirk name before doing anything unorthodox."

By unorthodox, Ophelia meant volunteering to nurse wounded soldiers and helping at the foundling school. And so, for the past eight years, Cordelia had only partaken in activities the duchess deemed unexceptionable—like decorating the church with flowers.

Spending a few hours in the company of the outspoken, clever Lady Trentham had made her realize how much she missed stimulating interaction.

"D-Did you have a ch-chance to speak with Miss B-B-Bowles, Cee?"

Her nephew's soft voice brought her back to the present.

Cordelia's hesitation was slight, but it was enough.

He snorted. "You needn't sugar coat your opinions around me."

"She is very young, Charles. And right now, she is strongly influenced by Mrs. Keeting and her father. Given time, and with proper guidance, she will be quite pleasant."

"Pleasant," he repeated with a sigh.

It was amazing how much meaning could be injected into a single word.

"I am not c-complaining, Cee," he hastened to assure her, although she'd not spoken. "I know my d-d-duty and it is not an onerous one compared to the l-lot of most p-people."

He was right. Their lives were ones of ease when compared to most English people.

But acknowledging that fact did not make it any easier to reconcile oneself to spending the rest of one's life with a mate one could not respect or love.

Cordelia desperately wished she could remove the crushing burden from Charles's shoulders, but the only way she could rescue him from a mercenary marriage would be to contract one of her own.

Unfortunately, for Charles, the number of rich men eager to marry a thirty-four-year-old spinster of limited means and even more limited beauty was non-existent.

As much as Cordelia yearned to save her family, she was utterly powerless to do so.

Chapter 12

St. Giles
1802

John was almost finished training for the day when Eddie strode into the rank, gloomy room where John had spent most of his days since apologizing to Des.

"How's my lad doin'?" Eddie boomed at Marvin, his sharp gaze on John, who was squatting low with a beam over his shoulders, two heavy bags of sand hanging from each end.

"Good, Eddie, good." Marvin smiled nervously at his employer, eager to please. "'Ee's fit and in fightin' form."

Eddie merely nodded as he stared at John, who'd not paused his exercises.

The day was unseasonably hot and muggy, and John's body was slicked with sweat. As was usual when he trained or fought, he wore only his drawers.

Although he hated doing the squatting exercise, Marvin was right that it built endurance. But it was easy to hurt oneself by lifting too much, too quickly, and the key to getting benefit, rather than injury, was going slowly.

Eddie circled him as he worked. "'Ow much is in them bags?"

"Twenty stone, thereabouts."

Eddie whistled and paused behind John as he lowered into his last squat. "I'll bet 'ee can lift more."

When John tried to stand, he felt Eddie's weight bearing down on him. Fear fluttered in his belly as the smaller man exerted a shocking amount of pressure.

John grunted, every muscle in his body shaking as he struggled to stand upright.

"Tomorrow night you make sure Donny goes down," Eddie growled, his breath hot against the back of John's neck.

Eddie didn't let up on the pressure, but at least his words were a relief. John hadn't lost before and the thought of throwing a fight made him sick to his stomach. But the thought of what would happen to poor Ben if John didn't obey made him sicker, so he would have done whatever Eddie wanted.

"Make sure you give the punters their money's worth, which means I want at least ten rounds from you," Eddie went on. "But you put 'im down when Jessup gives you the signal. You understand me?"

"I understand," he said through clenched teeth.

"You'll stay at the house tonight because you need lots of rest before tomorrow's fight. I'll make sure you get it." John was grateful that he was facing away when he heard that unhappy piece of news.

"Understand?" Eddie asked.

"I understand."

Eddie released him and then smacked him hard on the back of the head. "Good dog."

John rose to his full height, his eyes burning into Eddie's back as the other man left the room.

***

"Tell me again what you're to do, Ben," John said, struggling to mask his impatience.

"I'm to wait 'til everyone 'as gone off to the fight. I'm to go down to Shay's dock and—"

"No," he said through clenched teeth. "Everything has changed now that I need to be at Eddie's place tonight. So you need to leave tonight—not tomorrow."

"Tonight, not tomorrow," Ben parroted.

"What are you going to do after I leave?"

Ben chewed his lip, his forehead furrowed. "I'm to go—no—first I wait until the 'ouse is quiet and go down to Shay's dock and 'ide in the oyster shed until you come."

John gave him a weary smile and patted him on the shoulder. "Good, that's perfect. Remember, don't carry a bag—nothin' to raise eyebrows if anyone were to see you."

Ben nodded but cut a mournful look at the one item in the room that he cherished above all else: Lily's music box. John had bought it for her several years ago. Ben had broken it after winding it too tightly, but he still liked to hold it, as if it brought him closer to Lily.

John sighed. "Tuck it in your coat."

"Thanks, John!" Ben's grin illuminated the grimy room.

John made him repeat the plan once more and then stopped briefly in his own room and pried up the floorboard where he kept his money.

It was fortunate that the man who would put John's money on the fight for him was on the way to Eddie's house, so he was only a little late in getting back.

Jessup and Brown were waiting for him and lounging in the big open room that John had to pass through to get to the tiny cupboard where he stayed.

The whore, Nora—whom he'd once liked before she'd taunted Ben—was straddling Jessup's lap and writhing; Jessup had his hand up her skirt, leaving no doubt what he was doing. It surprised John that Jessup would bother to pleasure his lover.

Brown had his arm around a young, doe-eyed whore John had never seen before. The girl looked terrified, her skinny body as stiff as a board in the ruffian's embrace. John pitied her. He'd seen what Brown did to women.

Jessup smirked at him. "Go to your room and stay put—someone'll bring you your food. You ain't goin' nowhere until the fight."

John scowled at the two men and headed toward his room. It was a good thing he'd already talked to Ben and placed his wager on the fight—something that had been tricky since he'd needed to go to somebody other than Eddie's men.

When John reached his room, he collapsed on his narrow cot and stretched out with a groan, his body sore, but no longer bruised and battered. Sleep would be hard tonight. So much might go wrong between now and tomorrow evening. His mind raced with all the potential disasters waiting to happen, and yet somehow, despite his worries, John fell asleep.

And while he slept, he dreamed of freedom.

Chapter 13

London
1818

John glared at the boy who was holding his horses' heads. "What the devil are you wearing, Barker?"

The stable lad's grin wavered, and he looked down at the baggy gold and crimson livery, which was easily three sizes too large for his scrawny body.

"Mr. Sims gived it to me, guv. It's the ole duke's livelry."

The outfit was not only ill-fitting; it was also gaudy, the burgundy and black reminding him of a brothel bedchamber.

John sighed, stepped up into the curricle, and took the reins.

Barker ran to the back of the vehicle and John turned in his seat to watch as he grabbed the curved handrail beside the rear step and scrambled aboard—or at least he tried to, but his baggy clothing and short stature rendered his efforts impossible.

"What are you doing?"

Barker's thin cheeks were red, and his breathing labored. "I'm your tiger, guv."

"You're my *what*?"

"Tiger. You know, guv, the—"

John gave an exasperated hiss. "Yes, I know what a tiger is." Bloody hell. He didn't know whether to laugh or cry. He could only imagine Worth's face if he were to tool around London with a tiger behind him.

He realized Barker was still looking up at him hopefully.

"You will break your neck in those clothes."

The boy seemed to shrink, his huge brown eyes growing dangerously glassy.

John rubbed his brow and had a sudden urge to go back to bed. What was he doing? Taking a female on a carriage ride? Playing house with upward of three dozen servants? Contemplating using a damned tiger?

Barker's spindly shoulders sagged and he trudged back toward the mews.

Bloody hell.

"Boy."

The narrow red velvet-clad shoulders froze. When he turned, John saw there were tears on his cheeks.

"Tell Sims I said to take you to a tailor and fit you properly. Order two suits, but not that godawful shade of red. Black and,"—John pointed to the plush leather seat—"whatever this color is called."

Baker's grin threatened to consume his entire head. "Ivory, guv."

John couldn't help laughing; the little imp knew more about decorative matters than he did. "Whatever," he said.

"Can I 'ave some gold lacing, sir?"

"No bloody gold," John retorted, only realizing the lad was twitting him when he saw Barker was grinning. Cheeky little bastard.

"Be off with you," John said gruffly, and then sprang the horses.

The gelding on the right was the same color as the curricle's upholstery and the one on the left was glossy black, like the carriage's lacquered body.

The animals were mismatched in color only; in all the details that mattered: size, spirit, power, gait, and disposition, they were identical. They pulled the curricle—including John's not insubstantial weight—as if it weighed nothing.

"You'll be the laughingstock of all London," Worth had warned him.

As if John cared.

He felt eyes watching, but, for once, people were looking at his equipage rather than his scarred face. John didn't give a damn what any of them thought—he liked the way the horses looked with the carriage, and that was all that mattered.

When he pulled up outside the Marquess of Gaulton's house, the groom who took the reins gawked with an open mouth.

The door opened when John reached the top step.

"Miss Page will be down directly, sir," the butler said. "Would you care to wait in the sitting room?"

"I'll wait here," John said, glancing around the foyer, which was a fraction the size of the one at Falkirk House and far more modern.

Personally, John liked the genteel shabbiness of the duke's old house far more than this newer one with its beige marble floor, cream silk hangings, and mahogany wainscoting, which felt lacking in personality.

He paused at the whimsical thought, but realized it was true; buildings *did* have personalities. Falkirk House reminded John of an ancient dandy who proudly sported unfashionable skirted coats, powdered wigs, and bejeweled, red-heeled pumps—fashion bedamned!

A light footstep pulled him from his musing.

"Hello, Mr. Fielding. I trust I have not kept you waiting?"

She was wearing a dark blue carriage gown with a closely fitted coat—he could never recall the names for such things—in a darker shade of blue velvet buttoned snugly over her chest, emphasizing her shapely figure. She carried an insubstantial-looking parasol and a straw hat jauntily perched on her abundant hair, which she'd twisted into some manner of knot.

She came to a halt in front of him and looked up, her chin tilting in a challenging manner.

"Do you plan on ignoring my questions today, sir?"

John frowned. Questions? What question did she ask?

"And do you also plan to scowl at me?"

He bit back a smile at her tart tone. "Neither activity is part of my plans, Miss Page."

"Good."

He waited for more, but that appeared to be it.

It must be his turn to talk. "Shall we go?"

Once outside, she came to a sudden stop, her wide eyes fastened on the curricle.

John looked from her expression of stupefaction to his new equipage. "Do you like it?" he couldn't help asking.

She studied the carriage. After a moment or two, she said, "It was startling at first, but the longer I look, the more… striking it is." She glanced up at him and gave him a smile that he felt all the way to the soles of his boots. "I do like it. And it suits you." Her eyes seemed especially green today.

"How so?" John felt compelled to ask as he led her toward the curricle.

"You are not one of the common herd, are you, Mr. Fielding."

That sounded more like a statement than a question, so he didn't answer. Instead, he helped her onto the cushioned bench, which was narrow enough that her body pressed against his from knee to hip and again at the shoulders.

John hardened being in proximity with her soft, womanly flesh—not to mention her subtle, faintly floral scent. Such a response didn't surprise him. It did, however, cause him a good deal of physical discomfort.

He arranged himself as comfortably as possible, picked up the ribbons, and nodded at the groom to release their heads.

***

Thoughts of today had kept Cordelia awake most of the night. Even after she'd drifted into an uneasy slumber, she'd dreamed about the man beside her.

What could she have been thinking to accept his offer to ride in Hyde Park?

What had *he* been thinking to make it?

What would everyone who saw her think?

Cordelia was not a stickler, but her sister, the duchess, was.

And yet Ophelia was pressuring Charles to marry a merchant's daughter. Surely her sister would not be too displeased if she learned Cordelia was riding in the park with a merchant?

Well, Cordelia would find out soon enough. Even though the ride wouldn't take place during the fashionable hour, there would be plenty of people who would see them, and no doubt at least one would be eager to tell Ophelia.

While she didn't look forward to being scolded by her sister, she had to admit that today was the most exciting day she'd had in years. It was also one of the most perplexing.

Mr. Fielding's interest in her—if indeed he had any—was both unexpected and unusual. Just what were his intentions? Or did he even have intentions? In Cordelia's very limited experience, men didn't ask women to accompany them for rides in the park for no reason. Indeed, it usually was an early step in a courtship.

Could he be *courting* her?

The shocking thought made it difficult to breathe.

No—surely not!

Calm yourself, Cordelia. Don't think about tomorrow; think about the moment—about right now. Enjoy the opportunity to be without your charges for a few hours. And breathe. Breathe deeply.

Yes, she could do that.

She took a few deep breaths, until her heart had stopped fluttering, and then looked up at the huge enigma sitting beside her. "What are your horses called?"

He cut her a quick glance; his jet-black brows arched. "They have no names."

"Oh. You must have purchased them only recently."

"Yes, just this past week."

"So you are just getting to know them before you name them?"

The look he bent on her was one of disbelief.

"What? You do not think animals deserve names?"

His mouth twitched, but she could not tell from what emotion.

"Or are you too busy *laboring for your crust* to name them?" Cordelia did not know why she thought it wise to taunt such a man, but she couldn't seem to help herself.

The twitch became more pronounced—almost a smile—telling her he was actually enjoying her gentle teasing.

Emboldened, she went on, "Perhaps I might make a few suggestions?" She tapped her chin meditatively. "Hmm. How about Erebus and Eos?"

He eased back on the reins and slowed the glorious pair before turning to look at her, one eyebrow slightly raised.

Cordelia had begun to interpret his expressions. This one was the equivalent of a normal person saying, *I beg your pardon.*

"Greek deities of dawn and darkness," she explained. "Day and night."

"Ah."

"I can see you are not partial to those. Perhaps something more direct? Black and White?"

"My stable lad informed me the correct word is *Ivory.*"

Cordelia chuckled. "Yes, he is correct. I apologize for my inexactitude."

"How about Heaven and Hell?"

She gave an unladylike snort. "Perhaps Gabriel and Lucifer would be less shocking?"

"Don't you care for shocking things, Miss Page?"

Cordelia's face heated at the incendiary glance he cut her; she could formulate no clever response to such a question.

"Are you going to ignore my questions today, Miss Page?" he teased. "Are you going to *scowl* at me, Miss Page?"

Cordelia bit her lip, unwilling to show him how much she enjoyed his unexpected playful streak. "Why did you ask me to ride with you, Mr. Fielding?"

"Why did you accept?" he shot back.

"Don't you know it is rude to answer a question with a question?"

"Is it?" His face remained stern, but his dark eyes glinted with amusement.

"Very droll, Mr. Fielding."

"Are you happy minding your sister's children, Miss Page?"

Cordelia blinked at the sudden, far too personal, turn in the conversation.

Before she could object, he held up a staying hand. "Let me ask a different question. What will you do once you have married off your sister's children?"

"That is a personal question, Mr. Fielding."

"Yes, it is."

Nobody had ever asked her such a thing, although she'd thought about the subject plenty. None of her conclusions had afforded her much comfort.

Cordelia knew she didn't need to answer his question, but she wanted to. "I will return to my father's house, where I lived before my sister invited me to live with her."

"Do you look forward to returning to your father's house?"

She glanced up at him, but he was staring straight ahead, having navigated off the main path onto a more secluded one. Was he inquiring on this subject to any purpose, or was it merely idle curiosity?

She employed one of his tricks. "What of you, Mr. Fielding? I know nothing about you. Did you leave a family in Boston? Why are you in England? What are *your* plans?"

There, that should keep him quiet.

"I was born in St. Giles, not in Boston. I have no family—at least none who own me—I came to England in the employ of Mr. Stephen Worth, but I am now my own master. And my plans are not fixed. You never answered my question, Miss Page. Why did you agree to this ride today?"

How was a person to answer such a question? *Because I was bored? Because I find you intriguing? Because I've never met a more fascinating person in my entire life? Because talking to you makes my—*

"Was that question rude?" he asked.

"Yes." There, let him enjoy one of his monosyllabic answers for a change.

His laugh, like his voice, was deep and rumbling. But it had another quality: it was exclusive. Cordelia knew that John Fielding was not a man who took things lightly, yet she had made him laugh twice in the brief time they'd spent talking. Why did that make her so proud?

And why did she want to answer all his questions about her—no matter how inappropriate?

"I came for a ride because I wanted to," she said. "Why did you ask me?"

He looked down at her, unsmiling. "I asked you because I had to."

"You had to? I do not understand?"

He chewed at the inside of his mouth, and she could see he was displeased with the direction the conversation had taken. Well, he had started it. She folded her hands in her lap and waited.

He did not speak for several minutes but, oddly, it was not an uncomfortable silence. She could see he was considering her question when, too often, people simply spoke to have something to say. He was not such a man.

"I've thought of you often since the first time I saw you," he said.

Her chest tightened at his quiet declaration, and it felt as if her ribs were squeezing her heart. Cordelia ignored the uncomfortable sensation and asked, "You mean at Hookham's?"

"No, before then—the day I returned your niece's glove."

Cordelia's mouth opened, but she had no words. Why, they'd barely spoken at all, she'd scarcely—

And yet you, too, have often thought about that brief meeting, Cordelia.

That was true—she'd not been able to forget about him even when she'd had so very little to remember.

She swallowed again. "Oh," was all she could manage.

He stared at his massive hands, which were gloved in supple black leather today, and held the reins to his spirited horses with a masterful but gentle touch. He was a huge, powerful man, but he was no brute.

And he had been honest with her.

"I recall that day, too," she confessed. "Quite well," she felt compelled to add, earning a brief, disconcerted glance from his dark eyes.

For a moment, he looked as if he were about to say something more, but he shifted slightly and his gaze settled on the road ahead.

The atmosphere had become taut with all that was unspoken between them.

Rather than press him for a response—as a fearless, sophisticated woman might do—she behaved like a bloodless, polite lady and asked, "Have you visited many other parts of Britain?"

He paused so long that she thought he might not answer.

When he did, he sounded… subdued, perhaps even disappointed. "I spent time in Gloucestershire and Cornwall—both places where Mr. Worth keeps houses."

His answer eased the tension that had built between them, and for the rest of the ride they conversed about generalities. They were both halting, at first, but by the time Mr. Fielding guided his splendid pair up to the Audley Street house they were conversing with an ease she wouldn't have believed possible.

"Hold their heads," he told the groom when the servant would have helped Cordelia down from the carriage.

Instead, Mr. Fielding hopped down, came around to her side, took her by the waist, and gently set her on her feet. He didn't release her immediately and his hands were strangely hot, even though there were at least six layers of clothing between them. His jaw flexed, and he held her pinioned with his dark, heavy-lidded gaze.

There was no way Cordelia could have looked away, even if she'd wanted to.

"I want to ask you to ride with me again, but I don't know the proper procedure," he finally said.

Her heart leapt. "Just ask."

"Will you go for another drive with me?"

"Yes."

"Tomorrow?"

The question suggested a certain eagerness for her company—even if his tone and visage were expressionless.

Cordelia opened her mouth to accept, but then remembered. "Oh, I can't—I have to escort my nieces to Richmond."

He nodded; his gaze shuttered.

"But I'm at liberty the day after tomorrow." Only because she was staring did she catch the brief, unmistakable flash of pleasure that flickered across his normally unreadable face.

He walked her to the door, his hand covering hers, which rested on his sleeve, as if she were something unspeakably precious. "I shall come for you at the same time." And then he bowed and left before she could say a word.

But two days later, he was there again.

The afternoon progressed along the same lines. He was quiet—almost surly—but Cordelia could coax him out of his shell, until he was speaking if not expansively, at least willingly.

At the end of the ride, he asked her to accompany him again.

"When?" she asked.

"My days are unencumbered, so it is for you to decide," he said, his voice gruff, his scarred face stern. But the tension in his enormous body was that of a young boy—an eager boy—and it squeezed her heart so tightly that she ached for him.

"Tomorrow," she'd said, terrified by how badly she wanted to see him again. And again. Even when she wasn't with him, she thought of him. In fact, scarcely an hour passed when she didn't think of him.

Her nieces teased her about her *beau* and Charles looked pleased—like a cat who'd brought a mouse to their doorstep—at having introduced them.

Cordelia knew she needed to say *no* to his invitations—their rides were drawing attention, and not the right sort—and every day she swore she'd reject the next offer, and yet she could never make herself say the word.

So, here they were, again, on their sixth ride.

Cordelia had just asked him about Boston.

"It gets far colder than here—at least anywhere I've been in England or Scotland," he amended.

"What about the people?"

"What do you mean?"

Cordelia was pleased that he no longer ignored so many of her comments and questions. She flattered herself that he was more comfortable in her presence than he was with most people.

"What are they like?"

He shrugged, and she thought that would be all, but he said, "Society there is every bit as rigid as it is here—at least the rules seem to be, but the credentials needed for membership are far easier to acquire than they are here."

"You mean it only takes money?"

"To gain entrée, but a person must still work to maintain membership."

She chuckled. "By work, you mean a person must socialize and put themselves out."

He was in profile, but she could tell he was scowling. "Yes, that is exactly what I mean."

"And you lived there for five years?"

"Yes."

"Where did you live before?"

He turned to her slowly. They were riding down one of the side paths, which he seemed to favor, rather than getting caught up with the dawdling crowds.

She felt her face heat under the weight of his stare. He had the darkest eyes she'd ever seen. Even today, out in broad daylight, she couldn't tell the iris from the pupil.

"Mr. Fielding—you are doing that *thing* again."

The corner of his fascinating, scarred mouth twitched—an action she now knew was his equivalent of a smile.

"Where do you think I was before Boston?" he asked.

She blinked. "Goodness! How would I know?"

"You've not heard rumors?"

"No." Cordelia scowled at him. "I'm not in the habit of gossiping, if that is what you're asking."

He faced forward. "I was south of the equator."

It took her a moment to understand what he meant. She swallowed. "You were t-transported."

He nodded.

Dear God. Cordelia scrambled for something to say—but what *could* a person say? When she didn't answer, he turned to her again.

"What? Not so eager to chit-chat now? Fresh out of questions for me, are you?" he taunted.

"I have plenty of questions," she shot back, annoyed by his jaded, knowing smirk—as if he knew *exactly* how she'd react when she learned about his past. "How long were you there?"

"A lifetime." The muscles in his face pulled in strange directions, and she could see by the scars how carelessly the cuts had been stitched back together. "You want to know what I did to get transported, don't you?"

Why deny it? "Only if you wish to tell me."

That made him smile, the expression so cold she felt a chill even on a sunny day.

"Thieving. But that was only what they caught me doing. I did other things, too." He held her gaze with a brooding stare. "Worse things."

Worse things.

The words echoed in her mind as she struggled to digest their meaning.

Worse things like… murder?

She tried to shape the words, but she was simply too much of a coward to ask and too afraid of learning the truth.

Finally, when she remained quiet, he turned away, and they rode in silence, neither of them speaking until they reached Audley Street.

He helped her down, as usual, but did not linger after he walked her up to the door. Nor did he ask if she wanted to drive with him again.

Instead, he bowed and turned away, and Cordelia saw pride, defeat, and grim acceptance in his stiff posture and massive shoulders. He believed this would be the last time they met—that she would not want to see him again now that she knew the truth about his past.

Indeed, the duchess would be beyond livid if she ever learned that Cordelia had been riding in the park with a convicted thief. And worse.

He was halfway back to his carriage when Cordelia spun around and blurted, "I am free to go driving two days hence, Mr. Fielding."

Chapter 14

St. Giles
1802

John could hardly believe he'd escaped so easily. Well, at least he'd escaped the raucous, drunken celebration that had begun even before he'd won his fight.

Eddie had looked at him with actual liking as he'd come to him afterward to congratulate him. "You're a bloody force of nature, John Fielding." He'd smacked him on the shoulder. "Everything is on the 'ouse at Bella's."

But he'd not given John so much as a ha'penny as a reward for his lucrative win and obedient behavior.

That didn't matter.

What mattered was that he left quickly enough that John could shrug into his clothing and head directly to collect his earnings from Ronnie Hail, the lad who was to have placed his bet for him.

Hail owed him a favor because John had gone easy on the other man a year earlier when he'd collected an overdue debt without using his fists.

"I owe you," Ron had said. "I won't forget—you come to me when you need something. Anything."

Damn right he owed John. Jessup and Brown would have broken Hail's leg, at the very least.

Ron was to meet him close to where Ben would be hiding. That way, John could get the money, collect Ben, and then hop a stage for Bristol. There were closer places to catch a packet to Ireland, but John wanted to get away from London as fast as possible.

It was raining like a bugger by the time John finally got away from Marvin, so he waved for a hackney.

"I'll not take you all the way to Shay's," the driver warned when John told him where he wanted to go.

John wasn't surprised; the area was one of the worst in the city. "Fine, just take me as close as you can."

That turned out to be five streets away, so John was late—he'd told Ron to meet him at midnight and he could hear the distant cry of the Watch calling out one o'clock by the time he headed down the alley that led to the waterfront.

A solitary figure was pacing back and forth as John drew near. He squinted through the rain.

"Bloody hell," he muttered when he recognized the person. "Ben!" he called out, running faster. "What're you doin' out here? I told you to—"

John's head exploded with pain and white sparks of light and he staggered drunkenly when he tried to turn. "Wha—"

Hands closed around his upper arms and darkness fell.

John was drowning as he fought his way to consciousness, and for a moment he thought he was in the river.

But then he saw Jessup laughing and holding an empty bucket.

"John, John, John," a familiar, hated voice said as Eddie's equally hateful face hovered above him. "What a disappointment you are—trying to steal my property."

"I d-din't steal anythin'," he protested, the words badly slurred.

Eddie laughed. "You tried to steal young Ben—which I might have overlooked since he's as useless as tits on a bull—but then you tried to steal my best fightin' dog."

John stared blankly, the throbbing pain in his head making it impossible to think.

"*You*, John, *you*," Eddie said. "Now I'm gonna 'ave to punish you." He jerked his head toward where Ben stood, weeping loudly, flanked by Jessup and Brown.

"You told me you wouldn't 'urt 'im," John said.

Eddie's eyes widened with false innocence. "Oh, I ain't gonna touch 'im—neither are me lads." He turned and shouted at Ben, "You! Go jump in the river."

"But—but I can't swim!" Ben wailed.

The three men laughed.

"That's the point, you idiot," Eddie said. "Now, *go*."

Brown shoved Ben, and he stumbled.

"No." John stared in disbelief and struggled to get up. "No—you can't. He's just—"

Eddie put a heavy boot on John's chest and shoved him down. "You stay put."

"Don't, Ben," John shouted raggedly, his head exploding from the effort. "Run!"

Eddie kicked him hard, and it felt like something ruptured inside him.

"Run," John yelled again, but only a hoarse whisper came out.

Eddie leaned down and grabbed a fistful of John's hair, forcing him to watch where Ben stood on the edge of the pier, his body wracked with sobs.

"Don't steal from me, John," Eddie whispered, and then yelled, "Do it, *now!*"

Ben took a step back and disappeared.

"*Noooo!*"

Eddie stood and glared down at him. "Go back to the house, John. You've got a re-match in a month and I'll be keepin' you right under my eye from now on."

Eddie kicked him once more and then the three men strolled off, leaving him lying in the street like rubbish.

***

For two weeks John followed orders, trained with Marvin, beat money from debtors, and even caroused with whores when Eddie brought women from Bella's one night.

John's brief, and futile, period of resistance was over. He'd been a disobedient dog, but Eddie had brought him to heel.

Thirteen days after Eddie killed the last person who John cared for, he waited until the dead of night and then sneaked into Des's room.

Des hadn't fully recovered after his beating and his breathing was so loud that John could hear him even before he opened the door—which he'd oiled earlier that day—and slipped into Des's chambers.

As Eddie's brother, he was entitled to live in splendor—although he was a filthy pig who rarely bathed and never picked up after himself—and so Des was sleeping in a canopied bed that was fit for a king when John closed his hand round his spindly throat, choking off any sound before it could happen.

"'Ello, Des," he murmured against his ear, close enough that his lips brushed against his sour, unwashed skin. "Weren't expectin' me, were ye?"

Des tried to squirm, but John was easily twice his size.

"I've been dreamin' about this night for years, Des. Dreamin' about payin' you back for the misery you dealt. What I'm about to do ain't even close to payin' that debt. You should suffer like you made Lil do—like poor, scared Ben suffered and who knows how many others. But I'll have to be satisfied with just wringin' your neck like the dunghill cock you are."

Des's eyes were enormous in his misshapen head and tears slid down his battered cheeks.

His mouth shaped the words *please* and *mercy*.

Rather than make John feel pity for the other man, the tears and silent plea only enraged him more.

"Mercy?" he repeated softly. "How many times have you caused tears over the years, Des? And how much mercy did you show Lil, eh?"

The crack of bone on bone and a choked gurgle was Des' only answer.

John was surprised by how easy it was to take a man's life. Easy, but it hadn't made him happy like he'd thought it would all these years.

In fact, he felt dead inside as he climbed out Des's window, shimmied down the side of the building, and walked away from Eddie's house, leaving the last eight years of his life behind him.

It was as quiet as a tomb as he headed toward the better part of the city. He'd heard it called the Devil's Hour—that strange, hollow stretch of time between three and four in the morning—when ghosts were most likely to appear.

But John saw nobody—corporeal or spectral—as he made his way through the silent streets. His pockets were empty—Eddie had taken the money he'd laid on his last fight and broken poor Ron's arm in the process.

But that was fine—John wouldn't need money where he was going.

Chapter 15

London
1818

John sat in the corner of the Cock and Bull and nursed his third pint. It was long after midnight, but the Bull catered mainly to sailors, so it operated according to the tides rather than a clock.

The man John was here to meet, Jemmy Sharp, was not a sailor, but he made his money off their appetites, trading in whores and opium—a hunger that more than a few men had brought back from journeys to the Orient.

The Runner that John employed, a man named Riggs, had said that if anyone knew about Dolan, it would be Jemmy Sharp.

Riggs had told John about Sharp almost half a year ago, but the man was astonishingly elusive and it had taken John all these months to arrange a meeting.

"He's terrified of us for good reason," Riggs had said—*us* being Bow Street Runners, "so I can't be at the meeting with you or he'll scarper for sure."

Well, that was fine with John. He'd not wanted an audience, in any case.

John had shown up an hour early—wearing clothing as ragged as everyone else's, if considerably better smelling—just to make certain he wasn't stepping into a trap like the last time. Apparently Sharp didn't possess a watch because he was already an hour late.

John didn't mind drinking a few pints at the Bull, although he couldn't help wishing the pint glasses were a bit cleaner. He'd spent the bulk of his life in establishments far more unsavory and felt more comfortable at the Bull than he had at Worth's dinner table.

As he sipped his second pint and waited, he allowed his mind to wander toward more pleasant subjects—like Cordelia Page.

Tomorrow would be their first drive together since John had confessed the truth—well, part of the truth—about his past.

He'd expected her to run screaming into her house and slam the door in his face—not ask him for another drive. Not only because asking men to go on drives wasn't something proper ladies did, but also because he was a bloody convict! Didn't the woman have more sense? She should be furious at him for damaging her reputation.

She had likely realized exactly that the minute the door had shut behind her and John wasn't optimistic that she'd be waiting for him after she'd had some time to think—

A shadow passed over the table and John looked up to find a man wearing a green and red striped waistcoat, his thumbs hooked in the pockets of a lavender velvet frock coat.

He blinked at the blinding sight. "Er, you Jemmy Sharp?"

"Aye! Sharp in name and sharp in deed." Sharp's grin exposed three blackened teeth, and his smile never reached his eyes.

John turned to the serving wench who was sitting in the lap of a nearby patron. "Two pints."

She grudgingly disengaged herself from her companion, who—after one look at John—all but threw the woman toward the bar to fetch his beer.

John turned back to his guest, who'd watched the proceedings with open amusement.

"Speak."

"I don't fink so, guv. Show me the blunt first."

John sneered and leaned across the table. "The only thing I'll show you is the bottom of my bloody boot. Now, speak."

The other man shook with laughter and raised both hands, showing John his grimy palms. "Aye, aye, fair 'nuff, big lad." His beady eyes dropped to John's ungloved hands. "I've 'eard as 'ow yer right 'andy wiv yer fives." He grinned. "Or sixes in your case," he gave a hearty laugh at his own jest. "I can see wiv me own ogglers you've got a fierce pair o' raws." The scrawny thief leered at the serving wench as she slammed two pints onto the uneven table. "Fanks, luv."

John slid her some coins without taking his eyes from Sharp.

"Dolan," John reminded the man after the girl had gone.

Sharp quaffed fully half his pint in one gulp and wiped the thin foam from his smirking lips. "I ain't found 'im, but I know a bloke 'oo can tell ye more."

John sighed. Why was he not surprised? It was always this way—one more person between John and the elusive Dolan.

"Who is this man and why does he have information about Dolan?"

"Lamb."

"His surname is Lamb?"

"Nah, 'ee's from Wales." Sharp grinned and then swilled another third of a pint.

John got his meaning. Wales was known for its sheep. A lamb was a sheep. In the world of thieves, it all made perfect sense. "What is his *real* name?"

"Alan Moss and 'ee's a churchman."

Which did not mean that Mr. Moss was religious. A churchman was a man who removed recognizable symbols that might help to identify stolen property.

"Why would he know Dolan?"

"They polished the King's iron togevver."

Which meant they'd been in the same gaol. "When was this?"

Sharp shrugged. "You'd 'ave to ask Lamb."

John ground his teeth, but forced himself to say, "Where will I find him?"

"On the second floor of a crimping 'ouse, the one beside Dirty Mary's."

John knew of the whorehouse. Only a man who already had cock-rot would patronize such a place.

He took the small leather pouch from the inner pocket of his coat and tossed it onto the table. Sharp's hand shot out with a quickness that would have done a pugilist proud, and the money disappeared inside his stained lavender coat before John pushed back from the table.

Sharp picked up John's unfinished pint and raised it to his lips as John leaned over him, aware of what his bulk did to most men.

"If there is something nasty waiting for me at that crimping shop, I'll find you, *Jemmy*. And when I do, I'll squeeze your neck until your head pops. Do you understand?"

Sharp smiled, unperturbed by the threat of violence. "Aye, guv."

"Stay here for at least a half hour after I've gone." He didn't wait for an answer before striding out of the pub.

***

John was disappointed, but not truly surprised, when the building where Alan Moss was supposed to live was abandoned.

“'They all scarpered, guv—ain't nobody 'ome.”

The voice came from the narrow, gruesome smelling alley between the impressment house and Dirty Mary’s. John squinted into the darkness as a girl came out. She couldn’t have been over fifteen, but her eyes were old and hard.

“Crikey! Yer a big one.” She threw her non-existent hips from side to side as she walked toward him.

“When and where?” His sharp tone stopped her several feet away, which was still close enough for him to smell sweat and cheap scent.

She lifted her chin in a manner that would have done a duchess proud. “And why should oi tell *you* anyfink?”

John fished a coin from his pocket and held it up. Her eyes glinted in the dull red light from the lantern that hung over Dirty Mary’s door. It was a five-guinea piece. More than this girl—who was most likely diseased—would make laboring beneath a dozen men.

She laughed. “‘Ow do you loike that, lads? ‘Ee’s flush as a prince.”

John sighed as three rough-looking boys about her age emerged from the gloom behind her.

“Bloody ‘ell, Sary! ‘Ee’s the size o’ bleedin’ St. Paul’s,” one said, his high-pitched voice putting him younger than John would have guessed.

John took a few more coins from his pocket, one for each of his aggressors, and held out his palm. “Tell me what I want to know and you can have these. If you try to take them by force, I will leave you broken and bleeding and poor.” He hoped they'd take his offer because he did not wish to thrash a bunch of young, half-starved street urchins.

Four pairs of eyes burnt holes through his hand.

The biggest boy crossed his arms. “Tell ‘im.”

The girl cut him a dirty look that said she'd been hoping for violence. John didn’t blame her; she'd have good reason to hate men.

“Jemmy Sharp paid us to swaddle you. 'Ee said fists wouldn't do it—we'd need sticks." Her eyes swept over him. "For once 'ee didn't lie."

“Do you know a man called Lamb or Alan Moss?”

Her confusion looked authentic.

John wasn't surprised that Sharp had seen a way to make money and had lied to get it, but that didn't stop the leaden feeling of disappointment that settled in his gut at yet another dead end.

"Oi!" the girl shouted. "Give us the balsam."

John threw the coins, sending them sailing into the black alley behind them. The three boys wasted no time chasing the money.

"I know they won't share with you," John said, pulling a crown from his purse. "Here," he held out his hand. "Take it. I won't hurt you."

She scoffed, and he didn't blame her. Even though she was scared, she inched forward, glaring like a feral cat as she darted close enough to snatch the coin.

John watched her disappear into the alley like a rat into a crack, taking his latest hope of finding Dolan with her.

***

"I desire you, Miss Page," Mr. Fielding said the shocking words while looking Cordelia full in the face. And then, as if she might not understand what he meant, he said, "I want to bed you."

Cordelia was so startled that she would have toppled off the curricle seat if Mr. Fielding hadn't slid an arm around her waist and pulled her back.

"Careful," he growled.

Even after he released her, Cordelia felt the phantom imprint of his hand and arm on her body.

He was staring at her, as if waiting for a response.

Cordelia swallowed and then opened her mouth. And then closed it again.

"I'm sorry," he said stiffly. "That was inappropriate."

If Mr. Fielding's words hadn't knocked the air from Cordelia's lungs, she might have laughed. As it was, she struggled to keep down the hysterical bubble of mirth threatening to burst out.

Inappropriate? No. There needed to be a new word for what he'd just said.

Cordelia clung to the seat and stared straight ahead as the curricle jolted forward, frantically trying to regain her composure.

They'd been rolling slowly down the same path he always took and Cordelia had been talking—like she usually did—about life at Chelmsford Park, the duke's sudden illness last year, her father's house, and a half dozen other subjects, when he'd suddenly asked her if she enjoyed living with her sister's family.

His question had set her on edge for some reason—perhaps because she had not liked the answer she would have to give if she wanted to tell the truth: that she didn't like depending on her sister's good graces. And so—in a moment of annoyance—instead of answering *his* question, she had repeated the one that she'd asked him the first time he'd taken her for a drive. "Why do you ask me to drive with you, Mr. Fielding? What do you want from me?"

And, God save her, he'd answered her this time.

I desire you. I want to bed you.

The taboo words echoed in her head, disrupting her thoughts so profoundly she seemed to have lost her ability to speak.

He turned to her, his eyes as dark and intense as ever, his face a forbidding mask. "I've made a bloody hash of things." His eyes swept over her likely flaming face, leaving tingling awareness in their wake. "I will take you home now. And I will not call on you again." He turned his attention to the horses.

Cordelia forced herself to look beyond her distress to the man beside her and try to understand him. With his savagely handsome appearance and great wealth, he could have his pick of women. Why did such a man want her?

She had only been courted once in her life. The man in question, a local squire's son, had not been ardent in his pursuit and had lost interest in Cordelia and fallen in love with her best friend. That had been over a decade ago and she'd attracted no male interest—save for Charles's friend, the elderly Lord Deckleford, a man the same age as her father. And he'd not been especially ardent in his pursuit of her, either.

Certainly, he'd never looked at her with lust-darkened eyes as Mr. Fielding just had.

I desire you. I want to bed you.

Cordelia's head spun merely thinking the words, and she studied him from beneath lowered lashes.

The slashes at the corners of his mouth enhanced his appearance, lending him a harsh sort of beauty. Before the cuts, he would have been startlingly handsome, but now he was something else, something… more. Something mesmerizing.

Her gaze wandered over his glossy black queue and lingered on his massive shoulders as they flexed, effortlessly guiding the two frisky horses out of the park.

To put it bluntly, he was the most suffocatingly masculine man Cordelia had ever met.

I desire you. I want to bed you.

Her heart pounded hard and fast, sending flutters to her belly—and lower.

Nothing in all her years of mixing in society had prepared her for today.

Soon she would be back at her nephew's house and Mr. Fielding would help her down and then never return.

Say something.

But what? How could she respond to such an indelicate declaration? What was she supposed to respond? *Thank you, Mr. Fielding, how very kind you are. Oh, look—isn't that impatiens lovely? Have you ever seen such an attractive flower?"*

Who carried out a courtship using such shocking words? Who in the world—

A thought darted through Cordelia's head as fast and sharp as an arrow: What if he wasn't courting her? What if he'd just propositioned her?

Cordelia's jaw dropped.

Dear God! Had he just offered her a carte blanche?

I desire you. I want to bed you.

He's asking me to be his mistress, not his wife. She wanted to smack herself on the forehead. Of course, that is what he'd meant. How could she have been so stupid?

That made what he'd said beyond shocking; it made it… *offensive.*

Cordelia waited for anger to suffuse her.

But the feeling never came.

If what he'd said was so offensive, then why didn't she feel offended?

Why did she feel almost… excited?

***

Christ! What a disaster. But there wasn't a damned thing John could do to make it better.

You could offer to marry her. In fact, you should offer to marry her after making such a mull of things.

John almost laughed out loud. No doubt she'd be overjoyed to marry a convict—her sister, the *duchess*—would be thrilled to invite him into the family.

No, he'd destroyed what little they'd had with his outrageous proclamation and now any chance he'd had of being near her was finished. Which was just as well, because it couldn't have gone anywhere.

John was rarely astounded by his own behavior. In fact, he couldn't recall the last time he'd done something so impulsive and thoughtless. He was not an impulsive man, and he *never* blurted things out.

Except, it seemed that he did—at least when it came to Miss Cordelia Page.

They rode in silence, which suited John just fine. In fact, he thought he might never open his mouth ever again. Bloody small talk, indeed.

I want to bed you.

He ground his teeth so hard his jaw hurt. Yes, in the history of small talk, that had to be a monument. To be honest, he would have expected more of a reaction from her—slapping his face or at least screaming at him. But she'd just looked… thoughtful.

Stunned speechless, more likely.

Yes, that was probably true. But speechless was better than repulsed or insulted or frightened, wasn't it?

Stop. Dithering. He silently ordered himself.

John watched her from the corner of his eye; what the devil was she thinking about?

I doubt I want to know.

He sighed heavily. Why in the world had he said it? It was as if his mouth had been temporarily possessed by some other man—somebody like Worth, who frequently spouted whatever popped into his head.

John saw that her brother's house was just ahead and still he hadn't spoken, neither had she.

Perhaps that was because there was nothing else left to say.

Chapter 16

London
Coldbath Fields Prison
1802

"Thanks for saving me yet again."

John ignored the ginger-haired lad's gratitude.

They'd tossed the boy into the shed the day before and it had been like throwing bloody meat to sharks. John had watched the other lads torment him for a while, but had stopped the beating when it got out of hand. He didn't save the boy's hide because he was a good person; he did it because he despised the prick called Danno, the bully who ran things in the crowded shack, and had enjoyed giving him a bloody lip.

Of course, now he'd made an enemy of Danno, so he'd have to sleep with one eye open—not that he'd slept much before.

The redhead—Iain, he'd said his name was, inched closer and whispered, "They're coming for me tonight. You can go with me. My uncle will help you."

John's bitter laughter was loud in the little prison shed, drawing nervous looks from Danno's lads.

"What?" Iain asked, obviously stunned by his rude response to an offer of freedom.

He couldn't tell the boy that what had amused him was an offer to spring John from prison when he'd worked so very hard to put himself there.

No, he couldn't say that—nobody would ever believe him. Instead, he said, "The only place I'm goin' is Van Diemen's Land."

That's what the magistrate had told John after he'd broken into a toff's house in broad daylight, stuffed his pockets with valuables, and then taken a seat in the man's library, poured himself the best glass of brandy he'd ever tasted, and waited to be arrested.

Iain gasped. "You're being transported?"

"Aye, on the morrow, as *yer* luck would have it." He smirked. "I doubt you'd have lasted another day without me."

He could see by Iain's flushed cheeks he knew John was right; he wouldn't have lasted five minutes with Danno and his lads.

"Come with me tonight, John. We'll talk the guard into it by promising him more money from my uncle. Surely he won't care if two of us go if it means more coin in his pocket?"

"Tain't the guard puttin' me on the boat. My life ain't worth a bucket o' warm piss after gettin' on the bad side o' Fast Eddie. Leavin' this miserable shitehole of an island is the only chance I 'ave left."

"Fast Eddie?"

"Aye, Fast Eddie. He runs it all—from gin to whores, and he'd like me dead."

"Why does he hate you so much?"

"Never you mind. Just keep yer thoughts on getting' out." John turned away to show the discussion was over.

It was hard to imagine that Iain had never heard of Fast Eddie when he had loomed so large in John's life that he was willing to go half-way around the world to get away from him.

His plan, such as it was, wasn't much of a plan. But then what other choice did he have other than staying in Eddie's house and fighting until he was of no further use? He'd seen what Eddie did to cocks and dogs that had outlived their purpose.

As John had hoped, his quick confession to burglary had moved him speedily through the legal system. Thus far, none of the other criminals had seemed to recognize him. If things kept going his way, he'd be on a ship before Eddie realized where he'd gone.

"I'll never forget what you've done—how you helped me for no reason. Maybe someday I'll be able to repay the favor, John." Iain snorted at his ridiculous words. "Anyhow, I wish—well, I wish we'd had a chance to be friends. "

John turned to the talkative lad and met his gaze, surprised to see genuine gratitude in his eyes. He could have told Iain what happened to John's friends and that he should run as far and as fast away from John as he could to get, if he knew what was good for him.

Instead, he said nothing and turned away.

Chapter 17

London
1818

Charles, Cordelia, and her nieces had just sat down to dinner when a commotion broke out in the hall.

Charles gestured toward Tompkins, the young butler who'd replaced Sims after the duchess had pensioned him off. "P-Please see what that is about, T-Tompkins."

The door opened before Tompkins could reach it, and the duchess swept into the room.

"Mama!" Jane shouted, her fork clattering against her plate as she pushed out of her chair and prepared to launch herself at her parent.

Ophelia grimaced. "*Do* show a modicum of decorum, Jane."

Like a whipped puppy, Jane retreated to her chair. "Sorry, Mama," she mumbled.

Charles stood, his face an ashen gray. "Has something h-happened to—"

"Please inform Cook I shall dine with the family, Tompkins. And give us all a moment of privacy." Ophelia pulled off her gloves and handed them to a hovering footman. The door closed behind the servants and she lowered herself into the chair that Charles pulled out for her. "Be seated, Charles. I do not bear bad tidings." She glanced at Cordelia and her dark blonde eyebrows arched. "You look blooming, Sister."

Cordelia gaped at the unprecedented compliment. "Er, thank you, Ophelia," she murmured, but the duchess had already moved on to her eldest daughter.

"And so are you, my dear."

Melissa smiled, but her mother was not finished.

"I understand you have been frittering away your time and attention on the Earl of Madeley."

Melissa's mouth opened, and she shot Cordelia a heated glare, which the duchess intercepted.

"No, do not look daggers at your aunt, Melissa. She is not my informant on this subject, more's the pity." She gave Cordelia a look of disappointment. "No, I heard of your unfortunate partiality for Madeley from at least three separate sources."

There was a slight scratch on the door, and Tompkins stepped into the room.

"You may resume service, Tompkins," Charles said.

Conversation halted while the butler set a cover.

"That will be all for the moment, Tomkins," Charles said once the duchess's dining needs had been met. He waited until the door closed before turning back to his mother. "How is father?"

"His Grace's condition remains unchanged, but stable, which is why I thought I could safely visit for a few weeks." She glanced from her son to Cordelia. "No doubt my appearance has surprised you both. I made my decision so quickly I deemed it pointless to send word. My main purpose in coming is to help Jane prepare for her presentation." She turned to her youngest daughter. "I understand you visited Miss Priscilla Bowles last week. Did you enjoy yourself?"

Jane pulled a face. "She is very silly, but Mr. Bowles is building the most divine conservatory. It is only half-finished, but his architect said it will—"

"Am I to understand you spent your visit conversing with Mr. Bowles's laborers?" the duchess demanded; her gaze positively frosty.

"But architects are not laborers, Mama. They are—"

Ophelia raised a hand, and Jane shut her mouth with a snap. The duchess turned to Cordelia. "You accompanied her on this visit?"

Not only that, but Cordelia had arranged it, *and* she'd thrown the girls together at every opportunity, *and* she'd made sure that Charles was present as often as possible. But then her sister knew all that because she was the one who'd told Cordelia to do all of it.

Naturally, she didn't say that. Instead, she said, "Yes, Ophelia."

"You thought it wise to allow Jane to spend her time conversing with tradesmen?"

"Mr. Bowles was meeting with his architect when we arrived and he imposed on the man to conduct a tour for us. I did not feel it proper to contradict Mr. Bowles in his own home."

The duchess did not respond. Instead, her piercing gray eyes slid to her son.

Cordelia opened her mouth to say something that might divert her sister's ire from Charles, but Ophelia turned back to her before she could speak.

"I understand you have a beau, Cordelia."

Melissa snorted, which had the unfortunate result of attracting her mother's attention.

"That is a singularly unattractive sound, Melissa. If you cannot control such responses, then perhaps I should bring your old nurse out of retirement so that she could dine with you in the schoolroom."

Melissa's face flamed and Cordelia felt sorry for her. Her niece could be selfish and petulant, but she was only a girl and had no defenses against Ophelia, a woman who had snared a duke when she'd been two years younger than Melissa was now.

The duchess's gaze returned to Cordelia. "Well?"

"Beau is an exaggeration," she felt compelled to say. "I went for a drive in his carriage a few times."

"Do not be missish, Cordelia," Ophelia said as a butler and two footmen entered the room and laid out the duchess's meal. "Who is this paragon who has lured you into Hyde Park when so many other men have failed?"

Cordelia couldn't help noticing that her sister conveniently forgot the presence of servants when the subject was not one that touched her closely.

"He is a gentleman of my acquaintance," Charles said before Cordelia could answer. "I introduced him to my aunt. Mr. Fielding belongs to my philosophical cl-club." He gave Cordelia a sweet smile as he attempted to rescue her.

"Indeed?" the duchess said in a tone that made the hairs on the back of Cordelia's neck stand on end. "A gentleman? Now why did I think Fielding was a former employee of Stephen Worth, the American banker who was once a footman to Viscount Yarmouth and whose real name is Iain Vail?"

Charles goggled at his mother. Her nephew was no match for the duchess; it was like watching a puppy swat a paw at a cobra.

“He worked for Mr. Worth at one time, but no longer does. He is a wealthy man in his own right," Cordelia pointed out. Surely Ophelia could have no issue with a wealthy man—not when she was currently pressuring her son to chase after a merchant's daughter.

The duchess gave a bark of laughter. “He is indeed wealthy. I doubt he needs to work another day in his life after taking so much money from my husband in Worth’s colliery and canal scheme last spring. He certainly took enough to allow him to purchase Falkirk House for a song.”

Cordelia's jaw sagged. She'd known that financial exigency had forced the duke to sell Falkirk House, but she'd known nothing of Fielding’s involvement, or Stephen Worth’s.

"Mama," Charles said, his tone pained. "It was a business venture—Mr. Worth lost money just the same—"

His mother made a very un-duchess-like noise of disbelief. “Good Lord, Charles—can you really be that ignorant?”

Charles recoiled as if she'd slapped him.

Cordelia laid a hand on her sister's arm. "Ophelia—"

The duchess whipped around as quick as a viper. "It is just as well that I came to London! You two are no more fit than babes to manage matters.” She turned her sneer on her son. “Worth engineered that entire affair to destroy Yarmouth and his idiot son, not caring who else was ruined in the process.”

Cordelia raised her hand to her mouth to hide her shock; Charles looked like a marble statue.

The duchess let her son stew on the matter for a moment before heaving a long-suffering sigh. “I suppose I should not blame either of you as the subject was not noised about enough for it to have come to your ears. Worth has given compensation to *some* investors, but not—" Her mouth tightened and she looked from Cordelia to Charles. “That is neither here nor there. What I *cannot* understand is why any relative of mine would associate with men like Worth and Fielding to begin with.” The duchess's sky-blue eyes were as hard as glass. “Yes, I am glad I have returned. And just in time, it seems.”

***

John had briefly considered missing this week's philosophical meeting since it was to be held at Gaulton's house again.

Part of him wondered if Miss Page had told her nephew about his monstrous verbal blunder in the carriage a few days earlier.

Would Gaulton be waiting for John with pistols?

Would the door be barred to him?

As it happened, John encountered neither Gaulton nor a barred door.

But the butler seemed decidedly chilly when he greeted John in the foyer and then immediately—without divesting him of his hat or coat—led him to a smallish sitting room rather than the library.

John hesitated on the threshold of the room, which held only two occupants, neither of whom was a natural philosopher.

"You may go, Tompkins," the stranger said in a quiet but authoritative voice.

The butler bowed and left without a word.

"Come in, Mr. Fielding, we are expecting you. I am Ophelia Falkirk."

John was a yokel, but even he knew many peeresses used their husband's title as a surname. He inclined his head slightly and took the seat she indicated.

"No doubt you are wondering why you are here?"

John glanced at Miss Page, who met his eyes with a look he'd not seen before. Disappointment? Hurt? Betrayal?

He turned back to the duchess, not bothering to answer.

Annoyance spasmed across Ophelia Falkirk's face when he did not respond. "Very well, this conversation will proceed more smoothly with no contribution from you. I have informed both Gaulton and my sister of your role in our family's financial reversal last year. Why you and Mr. Worth have chosen to bedevil my unsuspecting relations further and make even bigger fools of them is beyond me. Given your past actions, I could easily ascribe the basest of motives to your current pursuit of my sister. As a Christian, however, I endeavor to rise above such thinking. Instead, I'll attribute your actions to a lack of sensibility and breeding." She paused after that salvo, as if giving him an opportunity to respond.

John almost applauded.

When he said nothing, her nostrils flared. "Because of her ignorance and lack of sophistication, my sister mistakenly accepted your offers to accompany her in public. That is at an end. Nor are you welcome as a visitor to this house." She stood, and then glanced down at Miss Page, who rose somewhat shakily, her face a sickly gray.

John hated the duchess at that moment. There was no reason to have Miss Page present for this conversation other than to humiliate her by rubbing her nose in her association with John.

He stood and inclined his head. "Ma'am, Miss Page."

The duchess glared at him, but her sister would not meet John's eyes.

Without another word, John turned on his heel and strode from the room.

***

Cordelia expected her banishment to the country daily.

To be honest, after the Fielding debacle, she welcomed dismissal. She wanted to get away from London—from the joy that had so briefly bloomed in her breast—and return to her parents' house where she could nurse wounds that were so painful; they felt almost physical.

It wasn't as if she'd really believed there could be anything lasting between her and Mr. Fielding, but it had felt so invigorating, so hopeful, to think that such a man wanted her.

While she'd never divulged her growing attachment to Fielding to Charles, she knew her nephew felt a similar sense of shock and betrayal.

Why hadn't he told her he lived in Falkirk House? What was his role in the investment scheme that had so shattered the duke's finances that he'd been forced to sell not only the family home, but one of Charles's properties, as well?

Cordelia despised herself for not asking those questions and more when Mr. Fielding had come to the house that last time. Instead, she had sat there like a silent lump, fear of her sister's displeasure keeping her mute.

She hated the way her sister treated her, but she loathed herself even more for tolerating such treatment. Why had she been so *spineless*? Why hadn't she demanded that—

"Cee?"

She looked up from her tambour to find Charles hovering in the doorway of the sitting room.

She gave him a welcoming smile. "Hello, Charles."

"May I d-disturb you?"

"Please do. I have not made a single stitch this half hour." She set her needlework aside.

He closed the door and came in, glancing at her current project—a handkerchief. "That is b-beautiful. Is it f-for Jane?"

She chuckled. "Who else would appreciate a tree?"

"I have m-missed going riding with you these past few m-mornings."

"So have I."

Neither of them said what they were thinking: that Ophelia had claimed the horse Cordelia usually rode and had dragged both Jane and Melissa along on their morning rides, forcing Charles to accompany them so they could project the image of a gracious family to the world outside.

"You were g-growing to c-care for him, weren't you, Cee?"

Cordelia's face heated, but she didn't bother with dissimulation. "It appears that I liked a man who did not exist. Or at least not the way we knew him."

"I liked him v-very much, too, although I scarcely knew him. There j-just seemed to be something about him…" He trailed off and shrugged. "He n-never lied to me, Cee. It is m-my f-f-fault for not inquiring into his background."

"A lie of omission, then."

"P-perhaps. Or perhaps we've m-misjudged his involvement in the canal scheme."

"That might be true, but what about Falkirk House? Why wouldn't he have said anything?"

Charles grimaced. "It seems odd that he wouldn't have m-mentioned purchasing our family's h-house, but then he's hardly b-been secretive about it; I discovered he lives there." He sighed. "The truth is that I didn't want to know who bought the house. It was too p-painful for me to lose the property and I avoided thinking about it. Like a c-coward."

Cordelia's brown furrowed. "Are you saying that you don't believe he and Worth are behind our financial difficulties?"

Charles shrugged. "I like to think of myself as a man of science, Cee, and I have no evidence for what Mama said. Rumors abound among the *ton*."

That was an understatement.

"I can't help th-thinking we might have done him a grave d-disservice by not g-giving him a chance to t-tell his side," Charles said.

Cordelia had thought the same thing half a hundred times. She could barely stand the shame that flooded her every time she recalled the way her sister had treated him—and the way Cordelia had sat there and allowed it to happen.

Still, her sister's suspicions were not entirely without basis.

"Do you think it is only a coincidence that he joined your club, Charles?"

"I have wondered that," he admitted. "But it was I who approached h-him that day in the c-coffee shop."

"What about the invitation to dinner at Worth's house—could he and Worth be up to something else?"

"I honestly don't see what, Cordelia. It was clear that I was there at Bowles's behest. The man has been about as subtle as m-mother when it comes to going after what he wants."

It all sounded plausible, but what did any of it matter? There was nothing they could do. Not after Ophelia had raked Mr. Fielding down like a servant—worse than a servant, really—and Cordelia had sat there like a chastened child and watched it all happen.

She was exhausted from lying awake and mulling over the matter.

There was no point. He was gone and was not coming back.

So Cordelia ruthlessly changed the subject. "How did you like Lady Courtland's ball, Charles?"

He looked relieved to drop the matter. "It was an unbearable squeeze, of course. The Season has started in earnest now, hasn't it? I will quit dragging my heels and p-put Mother and Bowles out of their m-misery and offer for Miss Bowles—soon," he added somewhat lamely.

"I don't wish to pry, but… is there someone else, Charles?"

"No, I am not in l-love with anyone else. I have no good reason *not* to marry Miss Bowles and a great many reasons why it would be an excellent match."

Cordelia wished she could comfort her nephew, but there was no avoiding harsh reality: the dukedom needed money, which meant that Charles would be forced to marry a woman he could not respect or love.

As for Cordelia and her confused feelings for Mr. Fielding? Well, that was all over. She had enjoyed a brief, tantalizing brush with somebody who might have been—

Cordelia stopped the foolish thought before it could bear fruit. She didn't know what might have been.

And now she never would.

Chapter 18

Somewhere in the Middle of the Atlantic Ocean
1803

John was grateful that he didn't suffer from sickness, but it was difficult to remain optimistic when at least half the men chained to him were violently ill day and night.

The ship he was on, the *Perseus*, would take seven months to get from Spithead to Río de Janeiro to Port Jackson. It was difficult to even comprehend that amount of time as he sat in the reeking, freezing, humid hold.

You did this to yourself, he reminded himself almost hourly on those first wretched days.

Yes, he had. And it had worked all too well to escape Eddie's wrath.

The first three weeks had passed in a blur of confusion, hunger, thirst, and intense discomfort. Somewhere during the fourth week, John had accepted that this was his life for the foreseeable future. Or, like the four men who'd already died from either sickness or neglect, this might be the *rest* of his life, full stop.

There were one-hundred and twenty-seven—one hundred and twenty-three, now—convicts on the *Perseus* and close to fifty crew who were there to *guard* the prisoners, but instead, ran the ship like their own private crime fiefdom.

In many ways, it was exactly the same as working for Fast Eddie.

John later learned that his journey on the *Perseus* was the only time that a ship employed private guards for convict transportation. All subsequent transports used soldiers to mind the prisoners. He wasn't convinced that soldiers would have been kinder or more humane, but they might not have been as easily and quickly corrupted as the private guards.

By the end of the first month, the crew had 'rewarded' the most obedient and strongest convicts by allowing them to work without pay. In other words, it was slave labor.

In John's opinion, that was far better than the alternative, which was spending the day locked in the hold, except for the half-hour when the crew would chase the prisoners around the deck with whips and cudgels to check for illness.

No, it was infinitely preferable to work like a drudge cleaning, repairing, and doing anything else the crew didn't want to do, which was almost everything except lazing about and drinking watered down rum.

And watching the men fight.

It was inevitable that his captors would learn of John's boxing experience.

He'd realized immediately that there was no point trying to keep his head down and hope that he attracted no attention; he was too bloody big to go unnoticed. The alternative to hiding was to assert his dominance—something John did by the end of his first week—and establish himself at the top of the pecking order in the hold.

But there was a whole other pecking order above deck.

The captain of the *Perseus* was a small, soft-looking man named Morris who rarely associated with the crew. What Morris did in his cabin all day was cause for endless speculation.

The captain left the management of the convicts—indeed, the running of almost everything except navigation matters—to a man named Barry Jackson.

John knew the moment he met Jackson that he was cut from the same cloth as Fast Eddie—they might have been brothers. Indeed, he was far more like Eddie than his own brother had been.

John came to Jackson's notice during his fifth week locked in the filthy hold—when he was almost to the point of regretting leaving Eddie's employ.

Two guards—one of them almost as big as John, but with a belly that said he'd not spent years training to fight—unchained him and frog-marched him up to a tiny room that was cluttered with charts, where Jackson sat sprawled in the only chair.

"You like the air up here?" he'd asked John, eyeing him from feet to head and lingering on his shoulders and chest.

That was easy to answer. "Aye."

"You ready to do what I say, when I say it, without askin' questions?"

John would have taken orders from Satan himself at that point. "Aye."

"You know Ned Bates?"

He nodded, already guessing where this was headed.

"Have it done by tomorrow and you can bunk and work with the lads the rest of the way."

By *bunk* he meant John could exchange one slightly less crowded room for another—but at least he'd not be chained hand and foot if he stayed with the crew—and by work, Jackson meant John would be their slave.

And by *have it done*, Jackson meant kill Bates.

The decision was easy. Not just because he would have done whatever Jackson wanted to get out of the hold, but also because John already despised Bates, who was a liar, a bully, and a rapist.

John didn't ask why Jackson wanted Bates dead; he didn't care. His soul—if he even had one—had been delivered to Old Nick the night he'd killed Des. What was one more murder?

When the guards returned him to the hold, they moved a skinny thief named Carter—the poor bastard Bates had been raping most nights—and chained John in his place.

Bates started babbling and whining almost before the hatch slammed shut.

"I've got money," Bates offered, pulling at the chains between himself and John, until he was practically sitting in the convict's lap on his other side.

John almost laughed; as if he gave a damn about money while he was locked in a tub in the middle of the ocean with homicidal guards in charge.

The next morning, when the guards opened the door to deliver the sour water and slop that counted as breakfast, they found Ned Bates cold and stiff and staring blindly.

After the guards took the body, Carter sidled up to John. "Here." He pressed a crust of moldy bread—his paltry share of the food—into John's fist. "Thank you."

John glanced down at the far smaller man—perhaps a decade older than his own sixteen or so years.

Carter was crying, but his eyes were fierce. "Thank you," he repeated.

***

It wasn't easy being a drudge on the *Perseus*, but it was far easier than living in the hold and surviving on scraps. And while John was always hungry and thirsty, as Jackson's prime boxer, he received more rations than any convict and even more than some of the crew.

All he had to do to earn his hammock and food over the coming months was fight whoever Jackson told him to fight, which usually meant he had to pound on men smaller than him; yet again, he was another man's dog.

As much as he hated being Jackson's dog, it was still better than being locked and chained in the hold.

Until the day that Jackson decided John should fight one of his own crew.

"The men need to be entertained—things have become… tense." Jackson paused, his eyes moving up and down John's body in an appraising way he was familiar with.

After over six months on board the *Perseus,* John's six-foot-five-inch body was nothing but bone, sinew, and gristle. At his last weighing in London, he'd been seventeen and a half stone. If he weighed even fourteen now, he'd be astonished.

Jackson's thin lips curved up into a snakelike smile. "You'll be fightin' Dixon next."

John had learned how to hide his reactions so well that he didn't give away what he was thinking by so much as the flicker of an eyelid. But inside his head, he imagined grabbing Jackson by his scrawny neck and ripping him limb from limb.

Facing Dixon—Jackson's second in command—in the ring was the last thing John needed. Dixon already hated him because he'd been Jackson's champion boxer before John came along. Not only that, but Dixon was popular with the rest of the crew—maybe even more popular than Jackson was.

John knew one thing for certain: if he fought Dixon, he'd need to lose the fight or he wouldn't make it off the ship alive.

He opened his mouth to point that out when Jackson said, "I want you to make it last a while before you take him out, John. I want you to bring him down a peg or two—he's been acting like he has ideas of his own," he muttered.

John wanted to howl in frustration. Jackson was using him as a tool to discipline Dixon—a whip to bring him back into line. Unfortunately, Dixon wouldn't see it that way; Dixon would take it as a personal attack from John.

Bloody hell. Barely one month left, and now it would be a long one.

***

Dixon was a big man, but he was soft and spent his days drinking and ordering other men around. By the third round, John was finding it harder and harder to keep Dixon upright, but Jackson refused to give the signal that would end the slaughter, so the fight dragged on two more rounds, until Jackson's men were grumbling and visibly upset to see one of their own endure such a severe beating from a convict.

When Jackson finally nodded, John sighed with relief and put Dixon down with an uppercut that knocked the big man onto his back.

"You'd better get below," Jackson muttered to John while the men clustered around their fallen comrade. Jackson hesitated and then added, "And you'd better sleep in the hold—at least for a few nights."

John hadn't hated anyone as badly as Jackson since Des. Thanks to Jackson, a hellish trip was now even worse, and he'd need to keep one eye open for the next three and a half weeks.

As it turned out, he only needed to wait three nights before Dixon came for him, along with three others.

It took those four and several more convicts—men who'd been unwillingly pressed into service—to hold John down while Dixon straddled his body, his razor flashing in the moonlight that filtered through the hatch.

"You're a serious lad, John—far too serious," Dixon said, his voice slurred with drink, the fumes that blasted from his mouth enough to turn John's stomach.

Dixon's cronies laughed and egged him on.

"You need to smile more, John," Dixon whispered. "From now on, you'll always smile."

In retrospect, the cuts probably wouldn't have been as bad—or at least not as jagged—if John hadn't struggled. But when the knife swooped down on his mouth, he fought harder than he'd ever fought in his life, his head exploding with pain when the blade ripped into his cheek. He'd experienced a lot of pain in his life, but nothing compared to that first slash of Dixon's knife.

Except the second slash, when Dixon's hand jerked and cut deeper, the blade nicking John's gums as it tore open his flesh.

"'Christ, ee's bleedin' like a stuck pig," someone said.

Laughter filled John's head, mingling with pain and the sound of somebody screaming.

"Shut 'im up before 'ee brings Jackson down 'ere," another voice growled.

More pain and brilliant white light.

And then darkness as black and thick as oil claimed him.

Chapter 19

London
1818

John's hands twitched as he stared at the Earl of Madeley, a man he would take great joy in thrashing.

Unfortunately, thrashing Madeley was not on the schedule for that evening because John was going to use the man to get what he wanted.

John had stalked his prey day after wretched day, finally bringing the earl to ground earlier that evening at another gambling hell, where Madeley had been losing badly. When John had suggested the earl be his guest tonight at Solange's, an exclusive gambling club and brothel, the young peer had latched onto the offer like a hungry infant on a nipple.

Without John to vouch for him, Madeley would never have been allowed into Solange's, not to mention given a seat at one of the tables. Hugo Buckingham, the man who ran the exclusive establishment, had no time for straw titles with no money to prop them up.

From the moment they'd arrived, John had plied Madeley with expensive spirits, signed for his debts, and now he was going to tighten the noose the rest of the way.

Madeley—too self-absorbed and drunk to notice the figurative rope closing around his neck—peered owlishly at John and said, "Explain it to me again, Fielding. Why isn't Bowles the one handling this?"

"As I explained earlier," John said with exaggerated patience, "I'm in the middle of a complex business negotiation with Bowles, but he's distracted by trying to marry off his daughter. I need him to focus on the business at hand, my lord, and you can help me do that—at significant benefit to yourself, I might add."

Madeley laughed. "You American chaps. Is business all you ever think of?"

John didn't tell him what he was thinking about just then.

Lord, but the man was thick! John was handing him a fortune on a platter, but he was too bloody stupid to realize it.

The earl poured himself another three fingers of expensive brandy and downed it in one gulp. If he drank like this every night, whoever he ended up marrying would be a young widow.

Madeley smacked his lips. "I've seen the girl—a thin, bran-faced chit—and danced with her a few times, too. Her chaperone is Keeting's widow—the woman fishes like a drink." He stopped and frowned, as if he knew he'd said something wrong, but couldn't quite discern *what.*

"Yes, that's the one," John said.

"But I thought Bowles had his sights set on Gaulton?" An ugly sneer twisted Madeley's handsome face. "Nothing but a duke for his precious daughter."

"He was interested in Gaulton," John admitted. "But then Bowles met the duchess."

Madeley hooted. "Ah, the lovely, grasping, starched-up Ophelia Page. The way she behaves, you'd think her family came with the Conqueror." He snorted. "Although she conquered old Falkirk quickly enough—for a while, at least. I'll wager she won't be casting herself onto the pyre when His Grace kicks off, will she?"

His words gave John pause. "What do you mean?"

Madeley leered and leaned closer, almost singeing off John's eyebrows with his fiery breath. "I mean, Falkirk has more bastards scattered across Britain than the Regent."

"That's hardly unusual," John said, although he had to admit he'd been surprised to learn that his father actually employed two of his bastards at Chelmsford—one as his steward and one as his huntsman—where the duchess would be forced to endure physical evidence of her husband's infidelity daily.

John dismissed the pointless thought and pulled Madeley's attention back to where he wanted it. "Bowles's talks with the duchess have hit a sticking point."

The earl snorted. "What? Bowles has decided that he doesn't fancy an avaricious harridan as an in-law?"

Bowles had put the matter far more succinctly. "The Duchess of Falkirk is a grasping virago," the iron merchant had complained to John and Worth when the three of them had met to discuss the new victualling warehouse Siddons Bank was financing. "She haggles like a moneylender, but with a more refined accent. She has bloody nerve demanding so much for her sprig, considering the duke is all but skint. Word of Falkirk's disastrous finances will be out soon enough," Bowles said with a grim smile. "And then the good duchess will be desperate to take what she can find. I've half a mind to wash my hands of her."

Although Bowles's threat had lacked conviction, John thought the man might be more amenable to a lesser title if it meant no longer having to contend with the duchess.

It had been Worth who'd planted the seed of an idea in John's head.

"Lord, but that man is title-mad," Worth said later, when it was just the two of them.

John had thought that was ironic coming from an erstwhile footman who'd schemed to marry an earl's widow.

"Hell, Bowles could have that idiot Madeley for a song, and he's not got half the debt Falkirk has. Of course, he's only an earl," Worth had conceded. "Still, I wouldn't be surprised if somebody came along and snapped up Priscilla Bowles while the duchess haggled. The girl is a sweet, biddable little thing; there will be plenty of men eager to take her off her father's hands."

John thought a lifetime spent with Bowles's insipid daughter sounded worse than transportation, but Worth's words *had* given him an idea. An idea that had led to this tiresome evening with Madeley.

"So," Madeley slurred, his empty glass clattering to the table. "Bowles will get a title for his daughter. I will get rescued from the river tick, the lucky Priscilla will get *me*, and—wait, what do you get, Fielding?"

I never have to see or speak to you *again.*

John repeated, for the fourth of fifth time, "Once Bowles is no longer distracted by the duchess, we can complete our business negotiations."

"Huh." The earl nodded, his eyelids heavy, as if he might fall asleep.

"Miss Bowles will be at Lady Moncrieff's ball tomorrow night," John said sharply enough to make the other man jolt and open his eyes.

"But I don't have an invitation for—"

John slid an expensive crested envelope across the table, along with a fat roll of banknotes.

Madeley's eyes opened wider. "Bloody hell! How much is—"

"A lot," John assured him. "Once I read about your betrothal in the newspaper, I'll give you the same, again."

Madeley swallowed and nodded, his gaze riveted to the money.

"But you won't get another penny unless you can get this done by the end of the week."

Madeley gasped. "The end of the week!"

"Do we have a deal?"

Madeley swallowed and nodded. "We have a deal."

John looked away from the drunken aristocrat and caught Hugo Buckingham's attention.

"My friend would like a room and a companion for the night," John said to the other man once he'd come to their table.

Madeley blinked blearily. "Wha—"

Buckingham gave John an amused look. "I'll see to it, Mr. Fielding. How about yourself? Mariel is free tonight."

John's cock didn't so much as twitch at the thought of the voluptuous whore he'd visited a time or two. "Not tonight." He didn't want just any woman—not even one whose mouth was like a velvet vise—he wanted Miss Page and only Miss Page.

"Shall I call a hackney for you?"

"No need." He wanted some fresh air and a long walk after his evening with Madeley.

Besides, he was in no hurry to get home. He doubted he would find sleep easily after what he'd set in motion tonight.

***

Cordelia could not recall hearing her sister raise her voice. Ever.

The duchess was standing in the middle of the Green Salon with the newspaper crumpled in her fist. "*How* did this happen?" she demanded of Charles for the third time since reading the betrothal announcement.

"I c-could not say, M-m-ama. You were there at the l-last meeting we had with B-Bowles. You know as m-much as I d-d-o."

Ophelia's jaw worked as if she were chewing rocks. Priscilla Bowles, the answer to the dukedom's financial woes, was betrothed to none other than the Earl of Madeley.

The duchess sank into an armchair, and the paper fluttered from her hand.

Cordelia caught Charles's eye and mouthed the words, *go away*.

Her nephew didn't need telling twice.

Once the door closed behind him, Cordelia went to sit beside her sister.

Ophelia glanced up at her, her gaze raw. "I do not know how we are to survive. Already the bills are oppressive. Some tradesmen have been so bold as to send dunning agents. First Falkirk House, and now we shall have to leave Chelmsford."

"*Leave*? Whatever do you mean, Ophelia?"

"I mean, lease it and retrench drastically. Chelmsford's rents simply are not enough to manage repairs on the laborers' cottages, the buildings, the farm, the—" Ophelia's voice broke and her shoulders shook, her sobbing almost noiseless.

Cordelia crooned softly and stroked her sister's back, at a loss for what to say. She'd always believed Ophelia to be implacable and unflappable. But she had her breaking point, just like anyone else.

"I am terrified I shall have to beg Papa to live with him. It would be so horribly *humiliating*." Ophelia cried even harder.

Cordelia gaped at her sister. "Mama and Papa love you and would do anything for you, but surely it has not come to that, my dear. As you said—"

"The girls *must* finish this Season, Cordelia! They *must* find husbands, as this will be their last chance to make decent matches. As for Charles?" She shrugged, her eyes flickering restlessly, as if there might be a solution in the surrounding room. "I have spent too much time on the Bowles chit, but there are others. There are—" she choked and squeezed her eyes shut, her body shaking.

Cordelia soothed her sister quietly while she wept.

Once the storm inside her had settled, Ophelia wiped the tears from her cheeks. "Lord, I must look a fright."

"No, you are one of those lucky women who looks lovely even when they weep."

Ophelia laughed, although it held no humor. "Yes, my looks. And see where they have landed me, Cordelia?" She snorted and said, so softly that Cordelia almost didn't hear, “After everything I did, it is all for naught.”

"What do you mean?"

Ophelia forced a smile and shook her head. “Oh, do not listen to me. I am half mad from worry. I make no sense." Her expression softened. "I know I have been dreadful to you, Cordelia, and to the children. I am terribly sorry, Cee.”

Cordelia smiled; her sister had not called her by her pet name for years. “We shall get through this, you'll see.”

Ophelia patted her hand, her blue eyes once again distant. “Yes, don't worry, my dear. Everything will be fine.”

Cordelia prayed her sister was right.

***

John was reading a report from his land steward in Massachusetts when there was a light scratch on the library door.

“Come,” he barked, not wanting to break his train of thought until he finished the paragraph. When he finished and glanced up, it was to find Sims standing in the doorway, looking as if he’d seen a ghost.

“Yes?”

“You have a visitor.”

John sighed; Worth. “I suppose you already told him I was here. You might as well show him in.” He turned back to his letter. He could ignore Worth as he finished it.

“It is not Mr. Worth, sir. It is the Duchess of Falkirk.”

That made him look up.

Well, well, well.

“Show her in.” John stared at the pile of paper on his desk without seeing it. This was it, then—his plan had worked, and far sooner than he'd hoped.

The door opened, and he stood. “Ma’am.”

John heard Sims’s shocked inhalation at his abrupt and disrespectful greeting. The duchess, however, gave him a regal smile.

“Mr. Fielding. How kind you are to see me. I trust I’m not interrupting anything?”

"Nothing I cannot put aside for a few moments." He gestured to the ragged brocade armchair. “Please, have a seat.”

Her lips tightened at his less than gracious welcome, but she came forward.

John raised his eyebrows at Sims, who was clearly expecting him to send for a tea tray or some such courtesy. "You may go, Sims."

The duchess gave him a steady look when he'd resumed his seat. "You are probably wondering why I am here."

It was not a question, so he didn't answer. Besides, he wasn't wondering at all: he knew she would come see him before she knew it herself.

"I am here to apologize."

John cocked an eyebrow.

Rather than look annoyed, she appeared almost amused by his taciturn response. "Even a duchess can make mistakes."

"And what mistake have you made, ma'am?" He wanted to hear her say it. He knew that was petty—especially since he had her over a barrel—but John did not like her. Not because of the way she spoke to him, but for how she treated her sister and for the three tatty-looking gowns Miss Page wore, while her nieces never wore the same clothing twice.

For the way she had forced Miss Page to sit silently while she'd upbraided her for allowing John to take her for drives.

For her willingness to sacrifice her son's happiness for money.

For many reasons.

And John knew with certainty that her belly roiled with hatred for him.

He could recognize her kind because he *was* her kind: a predator. If they had been alley cats, they would have been circling one another with twitching tails and arched backs, fangs and claws bared.

As it was, they circled each other with words as their weapons—at least she did; he didn't require any words.

Watching her grovel was fulfilling enough.

"I was hasty and unjust in my judgment of you, Mr. Fielding. It was brought home to me, rather strongly, that the ways of an American businessman are beyond the ken of a mere female."

John almost laughed at that. He didn't like the woman, but she was no *mere* anything.

"While I cannot feel you are a proper acquaintance for my son, or an acceptable suitor for my sister, it is not my place to ban you from their lives."

To John's credit, he kept a straight face.

Her eyes narrowed, as if she could read his expression if she looked hard enough.

John wished her luck with that endeavor; he'd had decades of practice concealing his emotions and the best of reasons to do so—to save his own hide. The duchess could stare at him until she was blue in the face; he would never allow her inside.

"So, that is why I came today; to extend an apology." She stopped, as if waiting for him to accept it—or offer one of his own.

She would wait a long time.

When he didn't speak, she stood, and so did he. "Thank you for your time, Mr. Fielding. I am most grateful." She inclined her head and turned without waiting for any response from John.

John did not like her, but he could respect her.

"Ma'am," he said.

She stopped and turned, the sinews in her slender neck as taut as piano strings.

"I would like to call on Miss Page."

An emotion flashed across her face far too quickly to identify—even if he had known her well enough to do so. But he suspected few could claim to know the duchess well, not even her husband. Perhaps *especially* not her husband.

"My sister is at home to visitors most afternoons." She turned on her heel and this time, he did not stop her.

He suspected today had been one of the bigger sacrifices the duchess had made in her life: that of her pride.

Cordelia Page would have to sacrifice far more. She wouldn't be able to get by offering mere words in exchange for John's money. Cordelia would need to give John her body and her future.

And like the cold, soulless villain that he was, John would not hesitate to take both.

Chapter 20

Van Diemen's Land
Hobart Town
1812

Thanks to Dixon and his mates, no beard could ever conceal the scar that bisected John's face, the same way no glove could ever hide his right hand.

John was and always would be, a freak.

Rather than diminish him, that knowledge fueled him like coals heaped on a roaring fire and he bunched his six-fingered hand into a fist and connected it with the other man's chin.

The resulting crack of bone and spray of blood fed his rage and nourished his hatred. It was a punch in the face of every person who'd played their part in sending him on his journey to the far side of Hell.

And it also earned him another handful of coins.

John watched with disinterest as his opponent went down with a dull thud. The crowd reacted with a primitive roar and John turned away and pushed through the maddened throng, ignoring congratulations and jeers alike.

Riddle, the man who managed John's fights, waited with all the rest of his ilk, men who sported cheap, too-colorful clothing and noses that had never been broken. Men who spoke in quick, sharp sentences as their watchful eyes darted ceaselessly and shrewdly around them.

Riddle grinned at John, the money he'd spent on his suit negated by the black gap in his front teeth. "Well done, lad," he yelled over the din, reaching up to clap John on the shoulder.

John shrugged away his hand and snatched his shirt off the wooden cart where he'd tossed it a short time earlier. He pulled the rough-spun garment over his head and turned back to Riddle as he tucked the tails into leather breeches, as battered and scarred as he was.

"I want my money."

"Aye, aye. Not so hasty, my boy. I've got yer pay. But I've got somethin' else, too. Something maybe worth even more."

John looked down a good eight inches into the other man's eyes. "My. Money."

Riddle nodded vigorously. "Aye, here 'tis." He placed a small pouch in John's bloody palm. John didn't need to count it. Riddle would be a fool to cheat him—a bleeding, bruised fool with broken bones.

He turned away.

"Wait, Fielding, don't you want to know who's looking for yer?"

What convict with even a teaspoon's worth of brain would want to know such a thing?

"He says he has information about yer da."

Riddle's words hit him like grappling hooks, sinking into his memory like it was flesh. John's feet became heavy, as if they still bore the manacles and heavy chains that had encircled his ankles all those years ago when he'd burned with fever and writhed in pain in the bowels of the *Perseus*.

After cutting his face, Dixon had put twice the number of shackles on him and the metal had chafed his legs until they'd bled. They'd left scars.

Always more scars.

John whipped around and demonstrated the skill that had earned him the nickname *Lighting John*. Riddle's neck felt like a dry corn stalk beneath his hand: delicate and breakable.

John squeezed. "Name."

The smaller man's Adam's apple fluttered against his fist like a tentative, anxious knocking against a door. John loosened his grip a little.

Riddle gasped and choked and then gasped again. "Worth, Stephen Worth. The banker from Siddons. The one who's come about the timber."

Riddle's high-pitched wheeze made John realize he'd squeezed the man tighter, this time in surprise. Stephen Worth was looking for John?

Riddle had to be lying.

He released the weasel-faced manager and turned away.

The crowd was already dissipating as he made his way back to Hobart Town. John smiled bitterly at the word town. Only a true savage would consider the pathetic collection of shacks a town; it was nothing but a prison that had spread beyond its walls, ensuring that those who'd already done their time were every bit as much captives as the inmates.

John had been laboring in a coal mine in Kingstown, boxing for one of the prison overseers when the man who operated Hobart Town first saw him. Shortly afterward, he'd been transported to the island.

That had been during the fourth year of his sentence.

The official who'd brought him to Hobart Town had died of a fever the year John's sentence was finished and he'd been living in a hovel ever since, too poor to purchase passage back home.

John had to use almost all the money he made from fighting just to feed and house himself.

He stopped at the house in question, having to yank hard on the warped wooden door before it gave way. The doorway was so narrow that John had to turn sideways to pass through it.

The house was a ramshackle structure that he shared with five other men, all *free* like John, but still slaving away at a variety of jobs because they couldn't afford to get off the island.

The short hallway was so dim that he didn't see the figure leaning against the door to his room until he was almost on top of the man.

"John Fielding?"

John eyed the big, well-dressed, ginger-haired stranger. "Aye, 'oo wants to know?" he asked, even though he already knew.

The American extended a hand, something convicts did not do. John stared at it until the other man dropped it back to his side.

"I'm Stephen Worth, with Siddons bank." After a long pause, he added, "Now."

John waited.

The other man smiled, amused, rather than annoyed, by John's silent belligerence. "I've heard a great deal about you, Mr. Fielding."

John raised one eyebrow.

"Oh, I already knew you were a good man to have beside you in a fight." He paused, and the smile dropped from his face. The look that replaced it chilled John's bones, a thing he wouldn't have believed possible anymore. Worth might be dressed like a gentleman, but he wasn't one.

John suspected that Stephen Worth was not a man to cross.

"You don't remember me, do you, John?"

Something about Worth's face teased at John's memory, but it was a wisp, a tendril of smoke and too tenuous to grasp. "No."

"You knew me by a different name back then—Iain Vail."

The memory was old—buried beneath a decade's worth of pain and violence and suffering—and it took him a minute to exhume it.

"Well, I'll be damned," he said, finally seeing a ghost of that scared boy in the grim man in front of him. John grinned—the expression so rare his face had almost forgotten how to make it.

Stephen Worth's eyes dropped to the savage scars on his cheeks, but his face remained unreadable.

John was impressed; it was an unusual man who could look him full in the face and show neither fear nor disgust.

"I've spent a great deal of time and money looking for you, Mr. Fielding."

"And all so's you can tell me about Lem Kennedy?" he mocked.

Worth—or Vail, or whatever the hell his name was—frowned. "Lem Kennedy?"

"Riddle said you knew me da."

"I know nothing about any Kennedy. But I *do* know about your father: the Duke of Falkirk."

John stared a moment and then burst out laughing.

When he could catch his breath, he said, "Ah, Mr. Worff—you've made me smile *and* laugh, today. Me, a duke's get?" He laughed again. "You need to stay outta the sun, guv."

"It's the truth—Falkirk is your father. I came across that interesting piece of information while I was looking into another matter. It is in your best interest to give me a few minutes of your time, Mr. Fielding. This is no trick—you can trust me."

Something about Worth's expression—could that be honesty he saw—made him hesitate before throwing the man out on his arse.

Not that John could remember what honesty looked like after nearly a decade spent in some of the worst hellholes, and with the most corrupt men, in the world.

Still, what else did he have to do today?

He sneered at Worth. "Trust? Well, that be as scarce as 'en's teef. But time? Well, you're in luck there, Mr. Worff. I 'ave all the time in the world."

John flung open the door to the dark, cramped hole he called home and waved the other man inside.

Chapter 21

London
1818

Cordelia was writing a letter to her youngest sister when the footman informed her that she had a visitor.

She glanced at his hand and saw it was empty. "No card, Marcus?"

The young man's mouth flattened into a disapproving scowl. "It's that Mr. Fielding, miss. Shall I tell him you're not at home?"

The room tilted and Cordelia clutched the edge of the desk, as if to steady herself. "Are you sure he's not here to call on Lord Gaulton?"

"Er, no, miss, he specifically said your name. And he also said, well..."

"Yes?" Cordelia urged.

"I beg your pardon, miss, but he said to fetch your bonnet, that he was here to take you for a drive."

"A drive?" she repeated faintly.

"Yes, miss." He scoffed. "In his… *curricle*."

Good Lord! What would Ophelia say when she heard about this?

Cordelia stared at the footman, who was still waiting for her response.

"Tell him… er, tell him I'm not at—"

You will regret it for the rest of your life if you don't see him.

It was amazing how much clarity the thought brought with it. It was past time Cordelia stood up for what she wanted. And, quite suddenly, she knew her own mind clearly. Today she had the opportunity to do what was right, and this time she would not be set to the side. If Ophelia did not like it; Cordelia would pack her bags and go home to Garry Court.

But she *would* talk to John Fielding herself before leaving.

Cordelia stood. "Tell him I shall be down directly, Marcus."

His jaw sagged, but he quickly recovered and bowed. "Yes, of course. Very good, Miss Page."

The second the door shut behind him, Cordelia leaned against the desk for support, her heart pounding so fiercely that she was dizzy.

"You need a hat and gloves," she murmured, the sound of her voice enough to push her toward the door, which opened before she could reach it.

The duchess stood in the doorway. "I see you have a caller, Cordelia."

Cordelia took a deep breath and squared her shoulders. "I did not know he would call Ophelia. But now that he is here, I will see him. I know you have made your position clear where he is concerned, but there are things I must—"

"I was hasty in my judgement of him, Cordelia."

Cordelia's eyes threatened to roll out of her head. Was that an *apology*?

Ophelia gave her an almost sheepish smile and took Cordelia's hand. "I'm sorry I hurt you. I went to Mr. Fielding yesterday and apologized for my behavior."

The Duchess of Falkirk had apologized to a mere cit?

Cordelia could not have been more surprised if Ophelia confessed that she'd gone out to the stables and shoveled manure.

"You—"

"After some thought, I realized I was hasty. Many other investors were hurt when the canal scheme collapsed. It was merely an unfortunate outcome of commerce. As for the house—well, he did not force us to sell it. We were seeking a buyer. Now," she said, suddenly brisk. "If you are to go with him, we must do something with that hair."

What in the world had happened to her sister?

"But—"

"Come with me, Cordelia. I've a new carriage gown and bonnet I was meaning to give you—it is a better color for you than for me. Nelson can have it hemmed up in a trice." She strode from the room, leaving Cordelia to stare after her.

It was as if some other entity had taken possession of the proud, haughty woman's body.

She was behaving for all the world as if she were sending Cordelia off with a beau—the same man she'd not even wanted in her house a mere two weeks ago.

What was she about?

Ophelia turned to her when she realized Cordelia wasn't right behind her. "Quickly, quickly, my dear. No dawdling. We've things to do."

Would wonders never cease?

***

Cordelia kept Mr. Fielding waiting for almost an hour, something she'd never done in her life.

"Pish-tush," Ophelia had when she'd pointed out how rude that was. "It is good for men to wait on us from time to time. It humbles them and makes them value us."

Cordelia wasn't sure that logic applied to Mr. Fielding.

And yet, when she went outside, expecting him to have left, there he stood, waiting patiently beside his magnificent, mismatched horses.

He looked rather magnificent himself in glossy Hessians, a coat that must have taken a league of black superfine, buff pantaloons that molded to muscular thighs that were bigger around than her waist, and a cravat that had been tied with care. He looked like a man who had set out to impress. Could this really be for her?

"I am sorry to have kept you waiting, Mr. Fielding." And she *was* sorry, and embarrassed, too.

His scarred face was as unreadable as ever. But his eyes? His eyes consumed her—that was the only word for it—from her blue, silk-lined bonnet to the slippers peeping from beneath the indigo carriage dress and matching pelisse.

"That is a new frock," he said.

His words left her speechless. He noticed her clothing?

They stared at each other for a long moment.

Another man would have told her how fetching she looked, how the color brought out the gold in her eyes and made her hair look like dark honey.

But Cordelia would take the look in Mr. John Fielding's dark eyes over a thousand words of flattery. Never in her life had a man gazed at her with such… desire.

He had a boy with him today, a lad of eleven or twelve, whose livery matched Mr. Fielding's equipage. It was tastefully designed: a black coat and breeches with shiny black boots and cream linen.

Although it was not done to comment on a servant, the boy was so obviously proud that he threatened to burst out of his clothing, so Cordelia smiled at him. "And who is this?"

Mr. Fielding glanced down a good two feet, as if he'd forgotten anyone else was there. It was his turn to look surprised, and his face, ruddy from spending time outside, darkened even more. "Oh, this is Barker."

The boy plucked off his hat and executed a deep bow. "At your service, Miss."

She cut Mr. Fielding a teasing look. "A tiger?"

Man and boy spoke at the same time.

"No!" he barked.

"Yes!" the boy said, grinning.

Cordelia had to bite her lip to keep from laughing.

Mr. Fielding heaved a sigh and then handed her into the carriage.

Soon she found herself pressed against his body, the sensation every bit as distracting as it had been the last time.

Barker released the horses' heads and sprinted to his perch on the back of the curricle.

Cordelia smothered a pang of disappointment. Whatever Mr. Fielding planned to say, it could hardly be personal if they had an audience of one hovering behind them.

***

John ground his teeth in frustrated silence as he tooled the carriage toward North Row. He'd been so addled that he'd given no thought to having Barker hanging over their heads. Saying what he had to say would be difficult enough without a servant earwigging.

He looked down at her, his breath catching in his throat when she turned her face toward him. John had once gone three days without water and his first glass had not been half as satisfying as his first glimpse of her after two wretched weeks without her.

She looked like a flower, the hat or bonnet or whatever the thing was called, was beyond fetching the way it framed her face.

When she raised her eyebrows at him, he realized she was waiting for him to speak.

Say something. Say anything!

Christ. She was turning him into a tongue-tied fool.

"Er, I thought we might leave the curricle and go for a walk," he blurted.

He'd thought no such thing, but with Barker listening to everything they said, it would be the only way he would have a word alone with her.

"That sounds lovely. I have had little chance to walk in the park of late." She paused, and he knew it was his turn to say something.

All he could manage was, "Oh?"

The corner of her mouth kicked up and John was sure she was going to tease him about being an uncivil lump, but she must have decided to have mercy on him, because she said, "Back home in the village we would see spring all around us and I would spend my time outside in weather far worse than what we have had lately. In that regard, I prefer village life. London makes us prisoners of our houses and,"—she paused and bit her lip—"I'm sorry."

"About what?" he asked, genuinely perplexed.

"I shouldn't have compared my minor inconveniences to a *prison.* Of course I don't know the first thing about prison. It was… insensitive of me." She faced forward, the sides of her headgear hiding her face.

John slowed the horses and guided them through the gates. The park was not busy at this time of day, which is why he'd chosen it, but the entrance still required his attention.

He took the first path that led off the main carriageway and then slowed the horses to a walk before turning toward her.

"Miss Page?" He waited until she turned to him before speaking. "You do not need to apologize to me—certainly not for something as minor as a mere figure of speech."

Her slender throat flexed as she swallowed, and then nodded.

God, how he wanted to grab her—hold her and comfort her. Take that haunted, anguished look from her eyes and replace it with pleasure and passion and physical satiation.

But John had sworn to himself that he would court her properly this time. No more brash, vulgar statements about how badly he wanted to fuck her—even if that was the truth—no touching her, even to comfort.

He would be a gentleman. Even if it killed him.

"There is no need to walk on eggshells with me, Miss Page. I am not ashamed of my past—nor does it offend me to mention it. I spent over a decade of my life in one prison or another, so I can hardly ignore that fact—or expect other people to do so."

In truth, his life with Eddie had been worse than his time on Van Diemen's Land in many ways. But she didn't need to know every gritty detail.

A loud gulping sound behind him caused him to glance over his shoulder. Barker's eyes and mouth were as round as wagon wheels.

John narrowed his eyes and the boy's mouth snapped shut.

He turned back to Miss Page to find her expression neither disgusted nor shocked at his admission but concerned—for *him*. Her capacity for compassion humbled him. She was too good for him—he knew that already—far too kind and decent.

But that wouldn't stop him from taking her for his own.

"There is a path ahead," he said. "I will stop and we can walk."

Barker leapt from his perch and ran to the horses' heads when he stopped the carriage.

John lifted her down and offered his arm. Within moments, they were alone on a pedestrian path.

She was tiny beside him, and her hand on his arm was light and insubstantial. When he looked down at her, all he saw was the top of her hat. He had a bewildering urge to pick her up, to hold her, to—

"Do you believe the Duke of Falkirk is your father, Mr. Fielding?" she asked, staring straight ahead.

John jolted slightly at the unexpected question and then allowed himself a grin, since she wasn't looking at him and wouldn't need to witness the horrifying sight.

"You might have done well in a boxing ring, Miss Page."

That got her attention, and she frowned up at him. "Whatever do you mean?"

"Only that you are not a woman to pull her punches," he explained.

Her already flushed cheeks darkened more. "I know it was an unpardonably rude question, but—"

"But you wish to know the truth."

She nodded.

"Is it so obvious that we are related?" John finally asked.

"You have something of the look of him—not to mention the odd coincidence of a six-fingered hand. Before his illness he was a tall, well-formed man, although not nearly so large as you—" She stopped and worried her lower lip, as if considering her next words.

John gave her the time she needed—he was in no hurry. Besides, he could watch her chew her plush lower lip all day long.

She sighed. "His Grace has not been circumspect in that regard."

John snorted at the polite euphemism. "You mean to say that I am not a rare specimen—that there are ducal bastards all over the country?"

She recoiled slightly at his crude language but nodded.

"Does the rest of your family know who I am?"

"I'm sure my sister has guessed, and I believe Charles suspects." She stopped in the middle of the path and looked up at him. "There are many things I can forget or forgive or which do not matter. But I dislike being kept in ignorance. Tell me, did you set out to hurt the duke because he is your father?"

"Yes."

She swallowed hard enough to make a gulping sound. "Did you—" she stopped, her eyes darting from place to place. "Did you have something to do with Madeley's betrothal to Miss Bowles?"

"Yes."

She squeezed her eyes shut and shook her head. "Why would you have done that? You had to have known that my sister and Mr. Bowles were encouraging a union between Miss Bowles and my nephew."

"I knew Gaulton did not want to marry Miss Bowles—that *you* did not want him to marry her. I also knew the girl did not care one way or another. Only your sister and Bowles wanted the marriage and Bowles had begun to question just how much he was willing to pay to get a duke for his daughter."

She kept her eyes closed. "But that is not all, is it?"

"No, it is not. I knew your sister would never let me near you if Gaulton married the girl. I also guessed that if your sister was willing to take the daughter of a merchant for a daughter-in-law that she could—with the right sort of pressure—be brought to accept a wealthy cit for a brother-in-law."

She opened her eyes and looked up at him, her expression raw and hurt. "I applaud your logic. My sister is indeed desperate and would accept you—if not joyfully, then certainly eagerly—as the family's savior. As for me? Well, I am a plain, poor spinster with nothing else to live for, so of course I would be grateful for your attention." Her usually warm eyes were cold and flat and the bitterness in her voice was like the lash of a whip.

John did not deny her words. They weren't entirely the truth, but they were close enough: he had manipulated and maneuvered her to get what he wanted, regardless of her feelings on the matter.

"It was not me you wanted—I was simply the unexpected byproduct of some Byzantine plot on your part. Any desperate woman would have—"

"No." John could not allow her to believe that.

When she wouldn't look at him, he took her chin and lifted her face until she was forced to meet his gaze. He wanted to lie—to say it was *only* her, but he owed her the truth. "It was both, Miss Page—both revenge *and* you." He looked from her eyes—which were unsmiling, for once—to her lips, which she'd chewed until they were red and puffy. "I want you, and only you. Badly. And no other woman would do."

Despite his better intentions, he bent his head and lowered his mouth to hers—slowly, to give her time to pull away.

But instead of rejecting him, her eyelids fluttered shut, and she sighed, her body swaying toward his.

Blood roared in his ears as he claimed her sweet, soft mouth, and every particle of his being throbbed with lust and the burning desire to possess and consume her—to keep her close and make her *his* and his alone.

But the innocent way her lips puckered and pressed against his brought John to his senses; she was a maiden and this could very well be her first kiss.

Leashing his desire was like trying to collar a rabid dog, and it took all the self-control he could summon to release her chin and step away when all he wanted to do was explore every inch of her.

John knew he should apologize. But he couldn't. It was the most chaste kiss he'd ever exchanged with a woman, and yet his body vibrated with need, his cock so bloody swollen and full it hurt.

Her eyelids fluttered open, and she gazed up at him, her lips still parted, her eyes soft.

John watched as she came back to herself and remembered who she'd been kissing and what he'd done.

Her warm hazel eyes hardened, and she gave a mirthless laugh. "Yet again you easily showed me what I wanted, didn't you, Mr. Fielding? Even my body doesn't belong to me and doesn't obey my will."

John did not deny it, nor did he regret it; it thrilled him how responsive she was to his touch even though she obviously disliked him.

"You are an evil genius of sorts, aren't you?" she asked, her tone marveling. "So cunning to have predicted our reactions to the letter. I have no choice but to marry you, do I?"

No, she really didn't, not being as kind and caring of her family as she was. John had gambled on the fact that she would do anything to save them, pay any price.

She gave him a tight, arctic smile. "You needn't ruin the knees of your fine pantaloons by making a formal proposal of marriage. We can agree—like businessmen do—that I will be your wife and you will save the people I love. Congratulations, you have bought your way into the Merrick family. You have also bought my body and all the rights of a husband. But know this, Mr. Fielding, you will *never* purchase my affection because it is not for sale."

The words would have hurt—would have been agonizing, in fact—if John had not lost the ability to feel such pain long, long ago.

But he knew *she* was feeling pain right now. And anger and betrayal and a sense of powerlessness—those emotions, at least, he could imagine and understand.

As for himself?

John felt no triumph, satisfaction, or relief. There was just… nothing.

He had won; he would decide their futures—the duchess, her son, her daughters, even the duke, although the old man did not know it, and probably never would.

He held them all in the palm of his hand, the way his father had once held John's mother and John, himself.

Yes, John had already devised a marriage contract that would leave him in charge of the people she loved, and he knew she would sign it.

Every move had been masterful and prescient. He had won.

So why didn't it feel that way?

Chapter 22

London
1818

To paraphrase Mr. Bowles, the duchess had haggled like a fishwife over the details of her sister's wedding contract, a protracted process that had left John feeling… soiled.

Her incessant demands had horrified his solicitors—two heartless bankers who worked for Worth and whom John had paid a great deal to protect and grow his fortune—who'd both pled with John to reconsider all that he'd agreed to give up to Miss Page's family.

But John didn't care about the money; he would have given everything he had to have Cordelia. Making more money was easy for him—Worth had taught him well—but finding another woman like Cordelia Page would be impossible.

John had hoped that he'd not have to see the duchess again after he'd given in to her demands, but she summoned him to Audley Street barely a week before the wedding.

"I will return to Chelmsford after your wedding."

Good. Bloody. Riddance.

Thankfully, the duchess had learned not to expect polite conversation from him—or any conversation at all, really.

"I do not know if Cordelia told you, but our younger sister—Miranda—will come to London for the ceremony."

Cordelia *hadn't* told him. But then she'd scarcely spoken to him, leaving everything to the duchess, who was more than willing to take charge. Of everything.

"Our parents are too old and fragile to make the journey," the duchess went on. "Miranda will remain in London to help with the girls, but she does not possess the requisite experience to shepherd them through a Season alone. I have asked Cordelia to remain in town and help her."

John crossed his arms, shifted uncomfortably in the tiny chair, and sighed—all of which should have told her what he didn't say: get to the bloody point.

"Where do you plan on living after you are married, Mr. Fielding?"

He was tempted to tell her it was none of her concern, but he knew she was Cordelia's only source of information on such subjects, so he said, "Wherever my wife wants." He experienced an odd tingle in his belly at the word *wife*. She would be his in a week. His. The thought made him harden.

John couldn't help being amused when he noticed his answer had momentarily robbed the duchess of speech. But not for long. "Oh. Well, perhaps my son's property in Shropshire—"

"No," he snapped. "That house will belong to Cordelia once we are wed, to do with as she wishes. But I will not live there." On that point, he was firm. "If she wants to live close to her nephew, then I will buy land and build her a new house."

John wasn't ashamed about driving the duke to the brink of financial ruin and likely causing his apoplexy, but he *did* feel a twinge of shame at stripping his half-brother of all his property.

While he hadn't given the Shropshire estate back to Charles, he'd done the closest thing by giving it to Cordelia. If she wanted her nephew to have it, then she could give it to him.

Charles Merrick was uniformly pleasant, friendly, and honest; he hadn't deserved what John had done to him. Astonishingly, the other man evidently bore John no ill will, whatsoever.

"C-Congratulations, sir! I am very g-glad things w-worked out between you and my aunt," he'd told John the night of their engagement dinner. "I am exceedingly f-fond of her and she deserves to be happy." His open, smiling expression had made John feel like a cad for all his scheming and plotting.

But although John regretted what he'd done to Charles Merrick, he did not regret trapping Cordelia Page into marriage. Nor did he feel any shame; he would do the same thing over again, and more, to have her. It was just Cordelia's poor luck that she was the first person he'd ever wanted.

Of course, he was sorry that she was angry at him—maybe even hated him—but he could not be sorry that he had secured her.

Secured her.

John snorted at the obnoxious words. He really was a ruthless bastard where she was concerned, but her effect on him was so powerful that he felt defenseless against her.

Although he'd touched many, many women over the years, he'd never been touched by one before. His need for her was frightening. For the first time that he could remember, he was reliant on another person, not just for his happiness, but for his peace of mind.

It was a humbling experience, and he didn't like it.

***

Cordelia allowed her eyes to linger on her wedding gown. The gown, like all her others, had once belonged to the duchess.

"I have only ever worn it once," the duchess said. "It is not the right color for me. I'm sure I don't know what I was thinking when I had it made."

Cordelia had briefly wished that her wedding gown, at least, would be something she got to choose, but she quashed such an ungrateful thought. After all, the money for the wedding was coming out of her sister's pocket.

Or that's what Cordelia had believed until the week before the wedding, when she'd learned the truth from her nephew.

She had gone to her sister's chambers to confront her. "I did not know Mr. Fielding was paying for this extravagant wedding, Ophelia."

"And whose fault is that?"

Cordelia's face had heated at her sister's sharp, but well-deserved, accusation. It was true that she'd avoided having anything to do with the financial aspects of her marriage, and Ophelia had every right to deride her over that.

Still…

"I do not think it proper to expect Mr. Fielding to pay for everything, Ophelia. That is Papa's province, *not* my betrothed's."

Ophelia scoffed. "Why should you complain when Mr. Fielding has not quibbled?"

"I don't want him to pay for this," she'd insisted.

Ophelia's pale cheeks had darkened at Cordelia's words. There had been several maids nearby, plying their needles to have Cordelia's re-made clothing ready by the wedding.

"Leave us," the duchess had ordered, and the maids had scuttled away like crabs fleeing the incoming tide. Ophelia had turned on her, eyes blazing. "You are behaving foolishly, Cordelia, and in front of my servants. Mr. Fielding wishes to bear the expense of this wedding. Papa has barely enough to keep body and soul together. Would you beggar him out of pride?"

"But it seems wrong, Ophelia. I am not even married and already taking his money?"

"Would you rather generate bills he could then pay *after* the ceremony?"

"I would rather not generate bills at all. We could have a small, simple—"

"You don't want to take his money. You are above such things, it would seem, and I—mercenary that I am—am not. Is that what you are saying?"

"No, I'm just—"

"You were too busy playing at being the sacrificial lamb to get involved, leaving me to appear acquisitive and grasping. So, here is my word on this matter: once you are married, you may manage him as you wish. Until that time, you have set *me* to dealing with him. I have done so, and this is the result. I will not have you changing everything and make me look the fool."

Her sister's words had been blunt, but they'd also held more than a grain of truth. Cordelia had been so angry at Mr. Fielding's manipulation that she *had* assumed the role of martyr.

Not only that, but she'd been even angrier at herself for wanting him so badly, no matter how badly he'd behaved. Part of her wondered what he would have needed to do to make her *not* want him—what other deviltry had he been planning before Ophelia exposed him, and would it matter to her? What in the world was wrong with her that she could want him so very, very badly even after discovering his true character?

The door opened and jerked her away from her self-loathing.

Her sister, Miranda, clapped her hands together. "Oh, Cee! You look lovely. That shade of rose is perfection on you and makes you glow. Just as a bride should."

Cordelia stood. "Thank you, Miranda." On impulse, she embraced her sister. "You look lovely, too, my dear."

"Oh, do be careful or you will crush your gown, Cee."

"I don't care." Her voice was muffled by Miranda's short, stylish curls.

“Poor Cee, you are shaking! You are having bridal jitters, aren’t you?” Miranda patted her shoulder. "Are you afraid of what will happen tonight?"

Cordelia pulled from Miranda's embrace and raised her cool hands to her hot cheeks. "Now you have made me blush."

"Did Ophelia tell you about—"

"Oh, yes, she told me," Cordelia interrupted hastily. She did *not* want to think about her sister's words on that subject, so it was just as well that the woman herself entered her chambers.

“You look lovely, Cordelia. That was indeed the perfect color for you.” Ophelia's cold, beautiful features softened slightly as they flickered over her.

“Cee has the jitters,” Miranda blurted.

Ophelia smiled wryly. “Well, if it is any consolation to you, so does your groom.”

“You have seen Mr. Fielding?” Cordelia asked, her voice strangely high and squeaky.

“He came in Mr. Worth’s barouche to collect Charles and the girls and take them to the church.”

Cordelia knew Stephen Worth was to be his groomsman. She had chosen Miranda as her maid of honor. Or, rather, Ophelia had done the choosing, pointing out, quite correctly, that she could not pick one girl without hurting the other. And Ophelia, with her husband in sickbed, was not an appropriate choice.

“Are you ready to go?” her older sister asked.

No! I'm scared—but excited and confused and—

Cordelia inhaled deeply, stilled her racing thoughts, and forced a smile onto her face. “Yes, I'm ready to get married.”

Chapter 23

London
1818

Cordelia paced her new bedchamber. It was the same suite of rooms that Ophelia had occupied when Falkirk house belonged to the family.

She was alone, having dismissed her new maid—a dour woman named Akers, whom Ophelia had insisted on hiring for her—an hour ago, not wishing to have an audience for her nervous fluttering.

The wedding breakfast had taken place at Audley Street, which meant it had been an intimate affair with only close friends and family—including the four guests Mr. Fielding had invited—the Worths, the retiring Duchess of Wake, and her gorgeous husband, the Earl of Trebolton.

Cordelia and Mr. Fielding had not returned to Falkirk House until late in the afternoon. She'd been dumbfounded to discover that the duke's ancient butler—Sims—was still in service.

Why was he still working at his age? Why hadn't Ophelia pensioned him off?

As much as she didn't want to admit it, it looked as if her sister had simply left him here—as if he were one of the tattered and worn pieces of furniture that filled the once-grand house.

There were other familiar servants, all misfits, who were too old or infirm to be employable elsewhere.

And there were some new misfits, too.

Like the huge footman, who was obviously a bit simple and yet he looked happy and seemed to do a more than adequate job.

Was it possible that Mr. Fielding—*John*—had hired him out of kindness? Or was it some housekeeping economy? And why—

The sound of a door opening behind her made Cordelia whirl around.

There was her husband, dominating the doorway like a second, far more imposing, door.

He was swathed from head-to-calves in a black brocade dressing gown. The robe bared what appeared to be acres of bronzed, muscular chest, making it obvious that he wore no nightshirt. He'd left his hair loose and the dark, glossy locks hung in thick waves to his shoulders.

He closed the door with a soft click and came toward her, a bottle and two glasses in his six-fingered hand.

Cordelia realized that her mouth had fallen open and closed it.

"Wine?" he asked.

She stared at the bottle and gleaming crystal, as mesmerized as a rabbit staring at a serpent.

Suddenly, her sister's words came back to her. "Sometimes it is best to have a glass of wine before he visits your chambers. If the man possesses any decency at all"—Ophelia had given her a skeptical look—"then it should take him only a few minutes to complete his business and bid you good night."

The duchess knew a great deal about getting with child and childbirth as she'd endured nine pregnancies, with only three children surviving to adulthood.

"Yes, I would like a glass of wine," she said in a breathy voice. Perhaps she might have several.

He made quick work of opening the bottle and pouring two glasses.

His black eyes glinted in the low light, and the corner of his mouth twitched as he lifted his glass. "To wedded bliss."

Cordelia's lips parted in surprise and his lips curved into a slight, teasing smile that charmed her.

He tapped his glass against hers, and she took a sip—a sizeable one.

She lowered her glass and then stared at it, unable to look at her new husband.

Her head throbbed, she'd begun to perspire, and she felt dizzy. Surely the wine wasn't affecting her so—

He took her glass from unresisting fingers and set it aside before stepping close enough that her nose was almost touching his naked chest.

Cordelia inhaled deeply before she could stop herself; he smelled *intoxicating.*

He slid a big finger beneath her chin and tilted her face, holding her lightly as his black eyes searched her face. She'd heard the phrase *watching like a hawk*, but now she knew what it truly meant.

"Do my scars disgust you? Would you rather I extinguish the candles?"

The question startled her. "Of course not."

His eyelids drooped, and he lowered his mouth over hers.

It was not like the gentle, brief kiss they'd shared in the park. No, this was a claiming: primal and raw and sensual. His tongue swept her lips, the tip penetrating in a way that made her gasp.

He made a low, rumbling sound, his huge hands angling her to allow him to probe her more deeply. The room seemed to rock and spin as he explored her with gentle, invading thrusts, tasting her lips, her tongue—even her teeth.

She clutched at his shoulders to keep from sliding into a puddle on the floor as he left a trail of kisses over her chin, cheeks, and down her throat. And then he opened his mouth wide over her neck and he *bit* her.

Cordelia shivered with pleasure and surprise; how could a bite feel so good?

"You are a maiden." It was not a question and his deep voice vibrated against the thin skin of her throat like distant thunder heralding a storm.

She swallowed convulsively at the shockingly personal question, which roused her from her daze, and gave a jerky nod.

"There is pain the first time but I will go slowly and be careful." He lightly stroked her jaw with the back of his six-fingered hand, a faint smile on his face. "I will make it good for you," he promised.

She nodded, and he lowered his hand and stepped away.

"I want to see your hair down."

***

John needed to slow down, but the smell and taste of her had driven him beyond reason within seconds.

He'd never wanted to bed a virgin, but the realization that he would the only man to penetrate, possess, and enjoy her body inflamed him. His cock, already hard, throbbed painfully at the heady thought.

It was *too* heady.

If he held her soft, shapely body against his, he would lose control and take her too quickly, too roughly.

This was a singular occasion, and he meant to savor it.

His gaze moved from her flushed cheeks and plump lips to her hair, which she'd braided into a heavy rope that hung over one slender shoulder.

"I want to see your hair down."

Her delicate nostrils quivered. "Don't you ever say please?"

"Rarely," he admitted, amused by her tart question.

"Perhaps you might do so when you speak to me."

His eyebrows rose, and he took a step toward her, aroused by the way her breathing quickened, her eyes widened, and her dark nipples tightened against the fine cotton of her gown.

He laid a hand on her supple waist and leaned in close. "Please take your hair down, Cordelia," he whispered into the fine hairs at her temple, smiling when she shuddered. It was the first time he'd said her name out loud, and he liked the sound and taste of it.

She made a soft gulping sound and took a small step away from him before she unwound the thick coil. It was not, as he'd believed, one braid, but three, twisted together, and the reddish-brown froth of curls fell to almost her hips when freed.

John reached out to run a hand through it, glad that he had six fingers to feel more of it. It was remarkably silky and thick.

"What is this color called?" he asked gruffly, lifting a loose curl to his face to inhale her scent.

"Er, I suppose it is closest to chestnut."

It wasn't like any chestnut he'd ever seen—either the nut or the horse—and it had vibrant yet subtle streaks of gold.

John wanted to see it against her naked skin.

The gown she wore was long-sleeved and high-necked, buttoned up to her chin and unlike any women's garment that he'd encountered. He was accustomed to either the cheap cotton shifts of women of his class or the easily accessible gowns of working girls. This was white and felt lighter than air, as if it had been spun from clouds.

And there were buttons—a horrific bloody number of them—and they were almost too small to see.

The fabric over her breast was rising and falling with small, rapid jerks and he glanced up at her.

"Are you frightened?"

"A little." Her eyes looked enormous and she appeared vulnerable with her hair down. She did not look like a competent, staid spinster aunt who spent her days watching over her nieces; she looked like a girl at her first bedding.

Her eyelids fluttered as he stroked his hand through her curls.

"Do you like that?" he asked.

She nodded.

He continued his gentle caressing, using both hands to soothe her, pleased when her breathing slowed and she inched closer to him until they were almost touching.

"Why do you keep it long?"

John blinked at her question and lowered his hands to her shoulders. "My hair?"

"Yes."

"Should I cut it?" he asked.

It was her turn to blink. "Would you cut it if I asked?"

"Yes." John could see that his answer startled her. "You have to look at me far more than I do," he pointed out. "So, if you do not care for it, I will cut it as short as you like." He'd never given his hair much thought, only allowing it to grow because he was too lazy to get it cut.

She smiled, looking more like old herself—well, what he thought of as her old self—the way she had looked before discovering that he was a manipulative, vengeful bastard.

"I like it the way it is. It is unusual, but it suits you."

Well, it wasn't much, but at least she liked one thing about him.

She cleared her throat. "I should like to say something now. Before we… well, you know."

John nodded, amused by her inability to say the word *fuck*. What did well-bred women even call fucking? Was there a polite word for it? He knew many *im*polite ways to describe it: pump, hump, rump, roger, strum, stuff, flog, jerk, do the goat's jig, and half-a-hundred other words and phrases.

He didn't use any of them. Instead, he said, "I know what you mean."

"I don't wish to be angry at you," she said. "I intend to be a good wife. In all ways." Her face flushed wildly, but she lifted her chin. "I would like to make you happy and be happy in return. I will set your house in order and make you comfortable. I know how to do things of that nature." She swallowed again, the little gulping sound she made oddly endearing. "But this?" She gestured to the bed. "This you must show me because I—"

"I will show you everything," he promised.

The pulse in her throat hammered twenty to the dozen.

"Shh," he murmured, stroking lightly over the delicate little drum, his huge, scarred finger obscene against the pale skin of her throat. "I want to see your body—all of you. That is one thing that will make me happy."

She made a soft trilling sound deep in her throat and turned an even darker shade of red.

"Please?" he added.

Her lips curled up slightly at that small courtesy, and she nodded.

John unfastened her gown, his gaze holding hers. He took his time—not because he wanted to, but because the buttons were so damned small—uncovering her with agonizing slowness, exposing first her rapidly rising and falling chest, then the soft upper swell of her breasts, and finally the thrusting, puckered tips.

John's mouth watered at the sight of her: she was fucking glorious.

His hand trembled as he brushed the sensitive underside of one breast and she sucked in a harsh gasp. He skimmed a thumb over a pebbled nipple and her eyes closed and her head tipped back. Her skin was like something between silk and velvet, but alive and warm. He nudged her gown off her shoulders, arms, and hips, until it slid into a soft, white drift around her feet.

She was the shape of an hourglass—a woman's body, not a girl's—her narrow waist flaring out to generous hips that begged to be grabbed. She opened her eyes and looked at him and then looked down, as if to confirm her suspicions that she was naked.

"Oh."

John slid his arms around her and lifted her sweet body, cradling her against his chest as he strode toward the bed.

***

Thus far, it was nothing like what Ophelia had told her.

First, the candles were blazing—it felt like hundreds, although she knew it wasn't more than five or six.

Second, he'd removed her gown, not merely lifted it to her hips beneath the cover of darkness.

And third, he was *looking* at her, his piercing eyes traveling over her body like feverish hands, touching her everywhere, leaving heated, tingling flesh in their wake.

But instead of feeling shy as she lay nude and exposed on the bed before him, Cordelia felt desirable and… aroused.

His hand went to the sash of his robe, and he paused. She looked from his waist to his eyes, which were as dark and unreadable as always.

Somehow, Cordelia knew that his hesitation was to give her a chance to look away.

"You won't ever have to see *it*," the duchess had assured her. "There will be an unpleasant pinch, but the entire process will be over and done before you know it. And, if you are fortunate, he will get you with child right away and you will not have to do *it* again for many months."

But Cordelia realized something amazing as she lay there before him: she *wanted* to see *it*—to see *him*.

She lowered her eyes, and he pulled on the tie and his robe opened and—

Oh, my goodness.

Her body's response to his was immediate and incendiary—every nerve burst into flame as heat and blood and desire pulsed through her veins, leaving her light-headed and breathless.

Cordelia had seen statues and paintings of nude men, but never an *aroused* nude man. While a statue was cold stone and a painting just pigment on canvas, he—John—was brilliant and coursing with life. Nothing she'd seen had prepared her for his sheer proportions and magnificence.

Muscles and sinews rippled like water beneath his skin, and everything about him was built on an enormous scale. His thighs were bigger around than her waist, his hips were powerfully muscled but compact and smooth. His tightly corded waist flared to a chest that was layered with chiseled slab upon slab of muscle, the skin that stretched over it satiny but marked here and there—like chips chiseled from marble, places where he had been hurt. To watch his body naked and in motion was to see the true artistry of God's design.

Her fingers itched to feel his skin, to touch the dark hair that grew between his small nipples and narrowed to a thin strip as it trailed down over the woven muscles of his stomach, only to become denser where it surrounded his phallus, which was thick and veined and ruddy and rose up proudly, curving against his taut belly.

Her mouth flooded with moisture as she looked from the thick length of him up to his face. His eyebrows arched and his expression was pensive, almost as if he were expecting her to faint or weep, or both.

Cordelia smiled—albeit tremulously—and he exhaled with obvious relief, the action causing the fascinating musculature of his torso to shift and flex.

"You should breathe," he murmured.

She gave a choked laugh and complied.

He shrugged off his robe and then lay down beside her, his weight depressing the mattress and tipping her toward him. His chest formed a wall that blocked out much of the light behind him. He smelled of soap and cologne and clean skin and she realized he had shaved again before coming to her.

He propped his head on his hand while his eyes roved her body, just as she had been studying his. What did he think of her? She was a woman well past her prime, a spinster whose bloom had faded long ago. Did he—

Cordelia hissed in a breath as he swirled his palm over one nipple, her body arching and thrusting her breast against him.

His nostrils flared as he caressed her, each languid pass throwing sparks out to the rest of her body. Her breasts tightened and became heavier and more sensitive until the feeling was close to pain.

Just when she thought she couldn't take another moment, his hypnotic stroking moved to her stomach. He massaged her abdomen in circles, pressing in some places, merely skimming others, working her body like an instrument, until she was all but purring under his touch—until she was so relaxed and loose-limbed that she scarcely noticed his palm rested over her mound.

"Spread your thighs for me, Cordelia."

As if she were in a trance, Cordelia opened herself, baring the most private part of her body to him without hesitation.

He made an appreciative noise and then parted her lower lips, hissing in a ragged breath. "You're so wet for me, sweetheart."

She shivered at his wicked praise, shamelessly spreading wider when he stroked her.

"Yes, that's right," he murmured, parting her swollen folds with his thick fingers and caressing from the sensitive nub of flesh to the entrance to her body, over and over and over again.

Cordelia whimpered, dug her heels into the bed, and pushed herself against his hand, chasing his tantalizing touch. Finally, maddened into forgetting herself—her pride—she clutched at his rock-hard biceps to yank his arm closer.

He chuckled softly and leaned forward to nuzzle her neck, his hot mouth moving to her earlobe. "Do you want more?" he asked.

Cordelia could only nod, her need too strong and distracting to form thoughts or words.

"Such a beautiful, responsive body," he praised. "I can't wait to be inside it." His words wrapped around her even as his fingers stroked and danced, pulling her nerves tighter and tighter until it was too much—until she *hurt* with sensation, until—

Cordelia cried out something incomprehensible as she exploded, her body convulsing and clenching as she gave herself up to mindless bliss. The sensation was both encompassing and far too fleeting and she was clinging to the diminishing waves of pleasure when she felt his knees between her thighs, nudging her legs even wider, spreading her like a butterfly.

Something thick and hard pressed against the entrance to her body and Cordelia's eyes flew open and met his, black and hot, inches from her face.

His jaw clenched, and it pulled his scars into a pale, jagged line that bisected his face

“I need to be inside you,” he rasped, his harsh, desperate voice sending an almost crippling wave of desire through her. "Are you ready to take me?"

She nodded without hesitation, her heart pounding with both excitement and fear as he breeched her body, biting her lip to hold back a whimper as his thick shaft penetrated her, his invasion slow but inexorable.

"It will be easier if you relax," he said in a strained voice.

She tried to do what he said, but he was so big—and the stretching so painful—that she felt like he was splitting her in two.

"John," she gasped.

His teeth bared in a feral snarl as he pushed deeper, not stopping until his hips rested against hers.

He groaned, and a shudder wracked his big body. "Christ! You are so fucking *tight*."

Cordelia gasped at his vulgar blaspheming, scandalized yet thrilled by the raw lust in his dark gaze—all for *her*.

"Try to relax," he said again, his arms shaking as he kept most of his weight off her.

She made a sound somewhere between a whimper and a laugh; relaxing was difficult to do when one was spread, skewered, and pinned like a butterfly to a board. But the pain eased and turned to an ache and then, finally, a not unpleasant fullness and her taut muscles softened.

He gave an indistinct murmur of approval when she became pliant beneath him. "Good—that's good." He shifted his hips slightly and then grimaced. "Maybe too good," he muttered, his eyelids flickered shut. "I just need a minute."

Cordelia wanted to tell him to take all the time he needed, that she was in no rush to speed this singular and quite fascinating experience.

She kept waiting and dreading the tearing pain that Ophelia had warned her about, but it had not happened yet. All she'd felt was a sharp stretch that had hurt like the dickens at first, but now felt lovely. The brief pain had been more than worth it to join with her husband—with John.

John was *inside* her.

Cordelia swallowed, both aroused and awed. For the first time since their ceremony that morning, she felt well and truly married.

His eyelid lifted a sliver. "Are you in pain?"

She smiled and shook her head.

He took his weight on one elbow and reached between their bodies.

Cordelia gasped when he stroked the source of her pleasure. She'd already discovered that his touch was far more skilled than hers and was mildly affronted that a man knew the secrets of her body better than she knew herself.

Her pique was short-lived, however, as he employed his entrancing skills to drive her toward her second climax in less than ten minutes.

"Yes," he growled as she bucked and ground against his hand. "Use me for your pleasure, Cordelia."

His erotic caresses intensified the sensual pressure building inside her until she felt as if she'd burst out of her own skin if he teased her even a second more.

"Please, John," she gasped. "Please—I need—"

His eyes burned into hers, and then he gave her what she'd begged for.

This time, when Cordelia came apart, John was inside her. The contractions that had obliterated her the first time were twice as powerful when shared. The waves of pleasure echoed as she lay stretched and full beneath him, suffused by a feeling of *rightness,* as if she'd been waiting all her life to discover this hidden part of herself.

She opened her eyes to find him looking down—his scarred face stern and beautiful.

"Good?" he asked.

She bit her lip and nodded, suddenly shy as she recalled her abandoned behavior.

He withdrew from her slowly, and then thrust again, deeply, driving her into the mattress and making her gasp.

"John!" She pressed her palms against his chest—as if she could possibly stop him if he didn't wish to stop.

But of course, he stopped immediately, his huge pupils flickering anxiously over her face. "Did I hurt you?"

He *was* hurting her—she'd never imagined this depth of penetration—but she could already feel her body adjusting and didn't want him to stop.

"I'm f-fine, now. It's… just—you startled me," she finished lamely.

He waited a moment before he moved again. This time, he worked her with shallow strokes, easing the pressure inside her.

Cordelia didn't realize that she'd tilted her body to take him deeper, to chase the sensation, until a pleased purring sound emanated from his chest.

"More?" he growled.

She nodded and his pumping became harder and deeper, the thrusts powerful and measured.

Cordelia sucked in a breath when he angled his body in such a way that he grazed her swollen bud. It struck her that he'd avoided the too-sensitive spot at first and somehow knew when his touch would give pleasure rather than discomfort.

Yet again, he knew her body better than she did.

The sensations gathered and built in her core; but this time, she was not alone on her journey. This time, John was with her.

He kept his weight suspended above her, his arms and shoulders bunching with effort as his hips drummed into her, his lips parted in a silent snarl, the cords in his neck strained to breaking.

His body was lightly sheened with sweat, the muscles beneath his skin rippling, enchanting her, making her brave enough to stroke a hand up his chest, her fingers sliding over slick, hot steel. He shuddered when she grazed his nipple, so she raised her other hand and swept her palms over him, as he had done to her, caressing the pebbled nubs.

"Yes," he hissed through clenched jaws, doubling his efforts, driving her up the bed, each thrust bringing her closer and closer to her own pleasure, until she cried out and arched against him, her body once again convulsing around his.

John hilted himself, his shaft spasming and thickening even more as he flooded her with heat deep inside her body.

The last thing she heard before drifting off to sleep was John whispering, "Cordelia," in a voice so low and gutted that she wasn't sure that she'd actually heard it.

Chapter 24

London
1818

John didn't fall asleep, even though he was spent—in every sense of the word.

Instead, he rolled to one side and flung his forearm over his eyes to block the light from the candles.

It would have been his preference to share a room with Cordelia, but he'd heard more than a few aristocratic men talk about their wives at the wretched club Worth had forced him to join. Those men had made it clear that proper ladies liked their privacy after engaging in intimacy.

So, he would get up and extinguish the candles and then go to the massive four-poster bed in his own room.

In a moment.

Right now, he'd just rest his eyes…

John woke with a start and glanced around, but it was dark and he could not see the clock. He was beneath blankets, so she must have covered him and extinguished the candles.

Her body was a warm strip along his left side, her breathing so soft he could not hear it.

John was a bit surprised how quickly—and deeply—he'd slept. He couldn't recall the last time he'd slept in a room with another person, but it was probably when he'd been a convict, which was also the last time he'd been forced to share his private space.

It had long been his habit not to sleep with lovers since that only led to conversations, something he strenuously avoided.

"John?"

He jolted at the sound of her voice, even though it was barely a whisper. "Yes?"

"I did not mean to wake you."

"I was awake."

"I would like to ask you something."

He blinked into the darkness as he gathered his wits. When she didn't ask her question, he realized she was waiting for him.

"Yes?" he prodded.

The bed moved as she turned to face him. "Will you tell me how you got those scars?"

It was the same question women always asked after sex, when they felt more comfortable with him; which was why he usually left before that could happen.

He'd never answered any of them honestly because his past was not a subject for idle pillow talk.

But this was different. This was his *wife* asking, and she deserved the truth, or at least a version of it. He would keep the more sordid details to himself because he adored her innocence, her goodness, and didn't want to ruin it.

"I angered some men on board the ship that took me south. To show their displeasure, they cut me."

"Angered… how?"

He considered her question for a moment. "Life on a convict ship was… complex." How could he make her understand that part of his life without disgusting or disturbing her? There probably was no good way to do both, so he erred on the side of caution.

"There was a hierarchy among the crew and I disturbed that."

"But—I don't understand. You were a c-convict,"—John smiled when she stumbled over the word—"how could what you did affect the crew?"

Oh, his innocent, sweet darling. John desperately wanted to catch her up in his arms and distract her from this ugly subject. But he suspected she would not appreciate such a protective gesture.

"The first mate used me to fight one of his men—for money."

She gasped. "They made prisoners fight sailors?"

He couldn't blame her for sounding skeptical. Most people—decent people—believed somebody law-abiding was in charge on those long, dangerous journeys to the southern colonies.

"Did—did you fight?" she asked when he didn't answer.

"Yes."

"And did they cut you because you lost?"

"No, they cut me because I won."

He could feel her shaking her head in the darkness.

John was not a praying man, but he prayed just then: *please God, make her stop asking questions about this before I'm forced to choose between ignoring her, lying to her, or telling her something that will change the way she looks at me.*

"How old were you?"

It wasn't exactly an answer to his prayer, but it was a less unpalatable question than many she could have asked.

"Fifteen, sixteen, maybe even seventeen—somewhere thereabouts."

"You don't know?"

"No." He hesitated, and then added, "My grandmother had problems remembering dates and told me conflicting years, so I'm not sure how old I am."

"How old were you when she died?"

Christ! It was like Pandora's Box—answer one question and two more popped out.

"Somewhere between seven and nine."

She did not speak for a long time. In fact, he thought she'd fallen asleep when he heard a muted sniffing noise.

"Cordelia?"

The unmistakable sound of a sob greeted his question.

"Are you weeping?" he asked stupidly.

"You were so very young to be sent half-way around the world in such harsh conditions."

John blinked into the darkness. Young? He'd never thought of it that way. By the time he stepped onto the *Perseus* he'd lied, stolen, fucked dozens of women, beaten dozens of men, and killed.

Had he ever felt young?

"You must have suffered t-terribly," she said, pushing her forehead against his shoulder, her cheek wet against his upper arm.

"Er, Cordelia—"

"Where did you go?"

"You mean which penal colony?"

"No, I mean, after your grandmother died?"

He grimaced, his brain scrambling for a convincing lie. He used to be quite good at lying, but he'd got out of practice, it seemed.

"John?"

"Er, I went to live with a neighbor." That wasn't entirely a lie.

"Thank God somebody took you in and showed you some kindness!"

John had to bite his tongue.

"May I—may I feel them?"

"Them?"

"Your scars?"

John had been asked that, plenty of times, too. His usual response was to get dressed and leave. But, again, this was his wife.

"Of course," he said.

Her touch, when it came, was as soft as a feather. She traced the scars with the tips of her fingers and choked on a sob. "It must have been agonizing."

"It no longer hurts," he assured her and then rolled his eyes at his stupid words.

To his relief, a watery chuckle interrupted her weeping.

But the slight bit of humor was distressingly brief.

"It must have hurt so much; did anyone help you?"

The agony of those feverish weeks of pain flickered through his mind. "Yes, there was a kind man on the ship." That much was true—Carter, who'd been grateful enough to John to risk angering Dixon and the rest of the crew—had stitched him up and given him enough food and water to keep him alive until they reached their destination. John had only a hazy recollection of a dull needle and the slight man sitting on top of him while other convicts held him down.

"A doctor?" she asked, her voice hopeful.

"Yes, a doctor," he said. Surely if there was a God, he would forgive such falsehoods?

"I can't even imagine the *pain*!" The last word was more of a sob.

"Don't cry. Please," he added hastily. But even courtesy did not stop her tears.

"Why are some people so *cruel*?"

John didn't tell her that in his experience, *most* people were careless, cruel, self-serving, or all three. Other than Lily, Worth, and Cordelia, he couldn't think of too many people who'd not wanted to use him for something. Well, he supposed Worth had used him, but not without giving something back.

Somehow, he doubted that observation would make her stop crying, so he lay there, helpless and frustrated, and let her weep, feeling as though somebody was scooping out his insides with a rusty spoon, scraping him clean, gutting him slowly with each shaking sob.

Finally, when he could take it no longer, he growled, slid his arms around her, and pulled her close. "Shhh, now, it was a long time ago," he murmured into her fragrant hair. "Don't waste your tears on what is past, sweetheart."

She snuggled closer and his cock—which had wilted like a coward when assaulted by her tears—twitched appreciatively as he held her voluptuous curves cradled in his arms.

Yes, he was an oafish lout. Here she was weeping—over him—and all he could think about was fucking her.

As much as John yearned to sheath himself in her delicious heat, he knew it wasn't done to mount one's brand-new wife as if she were a sporting wench—even if she wasn't sobbing all over one's shoulder.

John wasn't sure how long he should wait before he could have her again. He had only a limited experience with virgins: Cordelia and Lily.

Not that he'd been Lil's first, of course, but she'd sneaked away from the brothel after her first time and had come to John. She'd cried and cried that night—something he'd never seen the strong girl do before, not even when Des beat her—and all his twelve or thirteen-year-old self had been able to do was hold her for a while before she'd needed to go back to work and do it all over again.

Well, he hadn't been able to give Lily any time to heal and rest, but he could stay away from Cordelia.

Perhaps a week?

He grimaced. Maybe five days. He could last five days without her. It wouldn't be pleasant, but John didn't think this torrent of tears that was wracking her was just—or even mostly—for the boy he'd once been.

He strongly suspected that she was releasing pent up stress from the prior weeks. No doubt living with the duchess was trying.

Of course, living with John would probably be equally challenging. Not that he would try to crush her on purpose—no, he would do everything he could *not* to hurt her—but she was loving and gentle and he was… well, *him*.

Gradually, the wracking sobs became gentle weeping, which became sniffling, until she was finally breathing like a woman who'd cried herself to sleep.

John stared blindly at the ceiling, wide awake with a cock as hard as a bloody pikestaff.

Five days.

Chapter 25

London
1818

John was just finishing his meal when Cordelia entered the breakfast room.

She was wearing another new outfit, a shell-pink thing with a fiendishly low neckline that made him want to hurl his five-day vow out the window and bend her over the breakfast room table.

Not that wearing a sack wouldn't have generated those same impulses now that he knew what her body looked and felt like beneath her clothing.

She looked especially delectable in pink. The color was a different shade of pink from her wedding gown, but just as flattering.

Their wedding. Was that only yesterday?

John gritted his teeth. *Five more days.*

"Good morning, Mrs. Fielding," Fredrick said.

“Good morning, Fredrick. Could I have tea and toast, please?”

Fredrick’s cheeks tinted a bright pink at the fact that his mistress had recalled his name. "Right away, ma'am," he said, grinning ear-to-ear as he sped from the room like a comet.

John pulled out the chair across from him and then resumed his seat. She flushed as she thanked him, her mind no doubt on last night.

He'd stayed with her until she'd fallen into a deep sleep, and then he'd taken his erection back to his chambers and tossed one off. When even a second milking hadn't curbed his raging lust, he'd punished himself with a long, hard morning ride and then ordered a frigid bath after he'd returned home.

All that torture and here he was, hard again just from looking at her blushing face and the neckline of her dress.

Christ. Five days might kill him. He'd not been this rampant even when he'd been a lad. Of course, back then he'd never had to go five days without, either.

John forced his attention away from his cock and back to the beefsteak on his plate.

"I believe we are to have dinner with my sister tonight," she said a moment later.

There was news to kill his arousal. John nodded.

"You don't mind?"

"No," he lied, cutting another chunk of meat and lifting the fork to his mouth.

"The duchess wishes me to help with the girls, and there will also be a few functions I must attend." Her cheeks flushed for some reason.

John chewed his food, as well as the meaning hidden in her words, which wasn't hard to decipher: she meant invitations that would not include him.

She watched him with apprehension, her white, even teeth worrying her plush lower lip.

Her mouth was quite lovely, the upper lip slenderer than the lower one and—

"John?"

He pulled his gaze from her mouth. "Hmm?"

"I wish that I'd not made such commitments." She hesitated, as if waiting for him to tell her what to do.

John had no intention of starting down that road. What she did with her time was her own concern; the only place he had any interest in directing her was in the bedchamber. And then only until she discovered what she liked and directed *him*. Everything else in her life was up to her.

"Shall I tell Ophelia that I'm not available?"

John almost smiled. He would dearly enjoy watching his sweet, gentle wife defy her gorgon of a sister.

"You must do what you think is best." He could not tell if his answer pleased or disappointed her. But he meant what he said. He was her husband, not her master or gaoler. She would have to decide what activities pleased her.

She sighed but nodded. "I would like to speak to your cook and Sims. You do not have a housekeeper?"

"Not that I'm aware of."

She laughed, and he glanced up. Her smile was entrancing.

"What?" he asked.

"You were not jesting, were you? You really don't know who works for you?"

"No. Sims manages all that."

"I will manage *all that* from now on."

"As you wish," he said.

She shook her head, her kissable lips still curved in a wry smile.

Women; a mystery.

"You must hire whomever you deem necessary," he added, wanting her to know that he was not the sort of husband who held the purse strings tightly. "And the house no doubt needs"—he shrugged and waved his hand—"lots of things."

"It does feel a bit… bare."

He snorted. "Yes, a bit."

"I daresay my sister removed many family items when they sold it."

John thought she sounded defensive. Rather than be offended, he liked her loyalty to the duchess, even though the woman was a selfish, manipulative shrew who didn't deserve it.

He topped up his cup of coffee and added a heavy dollop of milk along with two heaping spoons of sugar.

Her eyebrows rose.

"I like sugar," he said.

Her expression was serious, but her eyes smiled. "So, I see."

***

Cordelia watched the door close behind her husband's broad, elegantly coated back and frowned. She had hoped that he might stay awhile so they could talk about… well, whatever married people talked about.

Perhaps they could have discussed the housekeeper he was not sure he did or did not have.

She chuckled again at his answer, but knew he was being honest. As a bachelor, he'd have been unaccustomed to a house this size and would have possessed no idea of how to go on. Her fingers twitched at the thought of setting the massive house to rights. It would be a challenge.

Perhaps she should have apologized to him about turning into a watering pot last night.

Cordelia cringed at the memory of her behavior. She hoped he did not think that was something she would make a habit of doing. She must have been very fatigued to lose control of herself in such a mortifying way.

The first part of the evening had been… well, eye-opening and quite delightful. Her face heated, even though she was alone.

The bedding had been nothing like her sister had forewarned, which made her wonder about Ophelia and the duke and what had made the other woman's experience so very grim and unpleasant.

Cordelia shied away from thinking too much about her sister's private life.

It was much more pleasurable to think about last night.

For all that her new husband was so quiet and reserved, he certainly seemed to know his way around the female body. He must have had many lovers to become so skilled.

Cordelia immediately wished she hadn't entertained that thought, which made her stomach churn with something that bore an unpleasant resemblance to jealousy.

Goodness! Had she ever been jealous before?

When Peter had married her friend Clara, rather than Cordelia, she'd felt sad, perhaps even rejected, but not jealous—certainly nothing like the sensation that had just rocked her.

Cordelia poured a little more tea and forced her mind away from the unsettling matter.

Instead, she pondered the day before her. She was her own mistress now and could do whatever she wished.

What *did* she wish?

She wanted to speak with Sims about the house, but she was simply too disquieted this morning to concentrate. Besides, she should give him some time to prepare for a meeting. She would tell him after breakfast that she would speak to him tomorrow.

Cordelia sighed. It was such a shame that her mother and father could not come to the wedding; yes, they were old, but she didn't agree with Ophelia that they were infirm. Her mother would have been a fount of information when it came to organizing Falkirk House, and her father would have delighted in an excuse to visit London booksellers.

It was too late to have them at her wedding, but perhaps she might bring a little London to her parents?

She smiled. Yes, that was what she would do. The last time she'd seen her mother, she'd noticed that she direly needed new gloves and her father always needed more books.

Cordelia's smile froze; she had almost no money. To own the truth, she rarely had any. Occasionally her sister would remember that there were incidentals, but, more often, it was Charles who gave her pin money, even though she hated to ask.

The door to the breakfast room opened a crack and Fredrick peeped inside.

"Ah, Fredrick. I was just about to ring for you."

A smile wreathed his face. "Yes, ma'am. How may I be of service?"

"Do you know if Mr. Fielding has left?"

"I do know," he said, sounding quite proud.

Cordelia chuckled. "And has he?"

"No, he hasn't. He is in the library, as is his way most mornings. Unless he does not get in until dawn, that is."

"He does not get in until dawn?" She wished she could take the words back as soon as they'd left her mouth. She should not be gossiping with servants, particularly not ones who were innocent and easily led into talking about their master's activities.

Cordelia burned to ask more, but stopped herself. If she wanted to know such things, she should be brave enough to ask her new husband.

***

John looked up at the light knock on the door. "Come in."

Cordelia stood in the doorway, hesitant.

John got to his feet. "Please come in."

"I hope I am not interrupting?"

"Of course not." He motioned her to the chairs in front of his desk. "Have a seat," he said, and then remember to add, "Please."

After she'd sat, he asked, "How may I help you?"

"I wish to purchase some gifts for my family."

What the devil was he supposed to say to that?

"Oh, good. That is, er, very kind of you," he finally managed.

"I—I have no money."

John felt like a fool. "Ah, I'm sorry." He took the ring of keys from his waistcoat pocket. "I should have given you more without making you ask for it."

"More?"

He glanced up while unlocking the desk. "Yes, more than the quarterly pin money I gave the duchess to give to you."

A crease formed between her eyebrows

"Your sister gave you no money?" he guessed, doing a poor job of masking his displeasure.

He watched as realization washed over her, and something else—probably embarrassment at her sister's clutch-fisted ways—and then looked away, uncomfortable with the pain his words had caused her.

Instead, he turned to the strongbox and removed a roll of notes. He was about to count out a sum—a habitual action—but then stood and gave her the entire amount.

Her jaw sagged as she took the fat roll.

"You have a private account at Siddons," he reminded her. "But you should have your clothing bills, house purchases, and other incidentals sent to me."

She stared at the money in her hands for a moment before looking at him, her eyes wide. "This looks to be a great deal."

He shrugged.

"It is too much. I only wished for a little." She peeled away notes.

"Cordelia." She jolted at the sound of her name. "Keep it."

She swallowed. "Thank you. I'm afraid I have behaved rather childishly by allowing Ophelia to manage my affairs before the wedding. I'm mortified that she would have, er…" she visibly struggled for words.

"Bilked both of us by keeping your pin money?" he suggested wryly. "Your sister is a worthy business adversary."

Humor mingled with mortification in her eyes. "Even so, I must apologize for leaving you to her machinations."

John looked down at his boot; the last thing he wanted from her was an apology. About anything.

"John?"

He looked up.

"Thank you for the money."

He squirmed under her open, honest gaze. "You wish to go shopping?" he asked, his voice harsher than he would have liked.

"Yes, just for a few things."

"I do not have a coachman." He pulled a face. "Or a coach, for that matter. I will place myself and my curricle at your service."

"Oh, you needn't do that. I'm sure you have a dozen—"

"I would like to," he said firmly. It was the truth. He'd watched her shop from afar for weeks; it would please him to chauffeur her about on her errands.

"Thank you."

"When do you wish to leave?"

"Would half an hour be too soon?"

He preceded her to the door and opened it. "In half-an-hour, then."

***

Barker was thrilled with the excursion, grinning big enough to split his face at the prospect of being seen on Bond Street.

"Barker," his wife said musingly, as John handed her into the carriage. "What is his Christian name?"

"I have no idea."

He walked around to his side of the curricle.

"You don't know his *name*?" she hissed.

"I'm sure Sims knows."

She continued to stare at him, scandalized. For a moment he thought she might pursue the issue, but she probably did not wish to do so where the boy could hear. And Barker made no bones about listening in on their conversation, as much as John had tried to break him of the habit.

"Where do you wish to go first?" John clucked his tongue and gave the horses their heads.

"I want to buy a pair of gloves for my mother. You could set me down somewhere on Bond Street. I'm sure you won't wish to waste your time in shops."

"I will accompany you. Barker can manage the carriage."

She cut him a look of disbelief. "But he is so sma—"

"I'm good wiv horses, ain't I, guv?" Barker piped up.

"Yes, you are. You are also good at engaging in conversations that aren't meant for your ears."

Barker's mouth snapped shut.

John gave his wife a pointed look and she let the matter drop, riding in silence on the short drive.

Bond Street swarmed with traffic of all sorts, even this early in the day, and he glanced at her feet. "Are your shoes comfortable for walking? Or should I stop outside the shop?"

"I would rather walk. Our coachman was always insistent on driving into the middle of the fray, as if we were too fragile to go such a distance on our feet. Then he would fuss and be agitated while he waited and I always felt rushed."

John pulled the curricle onto the very same side street he had favored for his spying expeditions. Barker hopped down, and he handed the lad the reins before lifting Cordelia down.

The day was going to be clear, which would bring the Bond Street Loungers out in force. Not that John worried about being shoved or crowded; that was one small benefit of his face: people gave him a wide berth.

"I should like to go to the Western Exchange first. There is a good glover there."

John led her in that direction and she gazed at shop windows while he gazed at her. He kept seeing her as she'd been last night, her hair wild, her eyes heavy with passion, her full breasts bouncing alluringly as he pounded into her—

"Oh, look." She stopped in front of a window containing a display of children's toys. "I had a doll very much like that one." She pointed to a vapid-looking porcelain baby with blue glass eyes and an improbably thick shock of blonde hair. "I gave it to Melissa when she was little. She loved the hair right off her head." She chuckled and looked up. "Did you have a favorite toy?"

He was about to say *no* when the image of a child's top flashed into his mind. A black and white painted spindle that had magically undulated when spun. John squinted, as if that would somehow make the memory clearer. Had that been his toy, or had he just seen it somewhere?

"I had a top," he said, when he realized he'd allowed the silence to drag on too long.

"Like that?" She pointed to a brightly colored thing the size of a melon.

"No, smaller and black and white."

"Charles had a black and white top when he was little. He was mad about it." She cut him a quick look. "May we go in? I believe that doll would be perfect for my friend Clare's youngest daughter."

The shop was all but empty, and they made their purchase without having to wait. John took the package, and they resumed walking, her hand tucked in the crook of his arm.

He felt foolishly proud—almost giddy—to be striding down the street with her. Part of him expected somebody—a constable, perhaps—to spring from the crowd and arrest him for impersonating an upstanding citizen.

John snorted softly. His obsession with his new wife had obviously softened his brain to the point where—

"You are from London, but you have no family here?" she asked, pulling him from his idiotic musing.

"No." The single word sounded too harsh, so he added, "My grandmother and mother came to the city after her husband died—she was from Dover and said she left no family behind." But Gran must have lied about her past because John had found no trace of her in Dover when he'd searched—and he'd spent a packet on trying to find any other relatives.

A pair of strolling dandies approached, ogling a passing female rather than looking where they were going. John scowled when they appeared disinclined to move out of the way, and the brightly dressed duo scuttled sideways when they met his glare.

"You said last night that friends took you in when your grandmother died. Are they still here in town?"

John was amused by her persistence in getting to know him, but he was also desperate to protect her innocence. In her world, the world of her quiet village and gracious duke's country home, people took care of children. They didn't sell them to workhouses or brothels. He hated to be the one to tell her how thousands and thousands of children lived in London, but at the same time, he did not want to build their future on lies.

"When I said that somebody took me in, what I meant is that I lived in a house with lots of other children." He gestured to a boy with a broom, waiting for a chance to sweep for a crossing pedestrian and earn a penny. "Like him, but without such an honest occupation."

"What do you mean?"

Here we go, he thought.

"When I was small enough, I was a cly faker."

"Cly faker?"

"A pickpocket."

"Oh."

"When I became too big to go unnoticed, I did other jobs, anything that required muscle." He carefully steered her around an oncoming matron with at least six poodles.

"What do you mean?" she asked, round-eyed.

"Oi fink you knows what oi mean, dontcher, luvvie?"

Her jaw dropped.

"That is what I sounded like; you married a common street urchin and thief." *And killer.*

She drifted beside him like a sleepwalker, and John felt more and more like a brute and a cad with every silent step.

"I apologize," he said, not that it would do any good. "Telling you all that was unnecessary."

She looked up at him with eyes that brimmed with pain and confusion rather than reproach. "But of course I should know about you! I'm woefully ignorant and have been sheltered all my life, but I want to know about you and your past. I am not too fragile to know the truth, John. Please don't mistake my compassion for weakness."

She was right; they were married, and she deserved to know the truth about him. If he'd been even halfway decent, he would have told her all the ugly details *before* trapping her into marriage.

John sighed. "I come from a part of London so dangerous and unpleasant that even Bow Street Runners have no desire to enter it. When I was fifteen, or thereabout, I ran afoul of an important man in that world and was sentenced to seven years' transportation. Like many others, I finished my sentence but could not afford a ticket back to England." He paused to toss a coin to a street sweeper. "Almost six years ago Stephen Worth came to Van Diemen's Land on business and took me back to Boston with him. For reasons of his own, it amused him to turn me into a gentleman." He snorted, "Well, to try. And when he came to England on bank business, he brought me with him." The tale was riddled with omissions, but it was enough—it would have to be. Many of the details he didn't tell her weren't his to share, but Worth's.

Her brow furrowed as she sifted through what he'd just dropped into her lap.

"You no longer do any work for Mr. Worth?"

"Not since last Fall."

"I am sorry if this is a foolish question, but what exactly is it you *do*?"

He barked a laugh. "Very little, actually. Most of my wealth works for itself, and don't ask me how investments operate. I leave the management to Worth and his army of bankers. I also own properties that earn rents. As for the things I *do* to earn an actual wage? I, er, oversee building projects."

She was right to look confused, because it was—if not an actual lie—then a blatant distortion of the truth.

"What does that mean?"

"I make sure that all facets of a large building project progress without interruption," that, at least, was not a lie.

"I never imagined such a job existed. And people pay for this?"

"Oh, yes, quite well, in fact." The least said about that, the better.

Thankfully, they approached the narrow, covered section commonly referred to as the Bond Street Bazaar and conversation became difficult.

John released her arm and followed close behind her, happily watching her progress through the multitudes of small shops. She was a thoughtful shopper, who clearly had an objective. She made her second purchase at a small bookseller's stall, where she found a fat tome on Roman history.

"For my father," she said, as the clerk wrapped her purchase. "He studies history."

John could only be glad his father-in-law lived in the country and that he'd be safe from having to discuss Roman history with the man. It had taken all his political skill—which, granted, wasn't much—to distance himself from Gaulton's tiresome philosophy club.

At the next shop, she was paying for the tan pair of gloves she'd picked for her mother when John added another pair. "I'll take these and pay for them both," he told the clerk.

His wife's eyes darted from the new gloves to him. "Those are the ones I tried on."

"I hope so." He pulled out his purse and handed the man enough to cover the purchase. "Wrap them separately, please."

"I don't need them," she whispered.

"Why did you try them on?"

"Because they are so pretty."

"Then you need them."

"But I have nothing to wear them with."

An image of her naked, on her hands and knees, wearing nothing *but* the gloves slammed into him with the force of a kick to the gut.

John kept that tantalizing thought to himself. Instead, he said, "Why not?"

"They are gloves for a ball gown."

"Don't you have a ball gown?"

"I do, of course, but these are too fine for it." She saw his frown and hastened to add, "I am *not* angling for a new gown."

"I didn't think you were."

"I don't even have a need for the ones I have," she added.

"Why is that?" he asked, taking both parcels from the clerk and leading her back to the promenade. "Because nobody will invite us to any balls?"

She cut him a quick look. "Do not think it is all your fault. I've never been important enough to garner invitations on my own merits and have only ever gone as a chaperone for the girls, so the gowns I own will do fine."

John tried to recall the dress shop that she'd frequented with her nieces. Surely it was around here somewhere?

"Now I have insulted you," she said when he didn't respond.

That made him smile.

"It is no reflection on you, John, I assure you. The circles my sister and her family socialize in are among the highest. I daresay even your friend Worth will not see invitations to many of those functions."

There it was—just ahead and across the street.

"Not that we shan't find our own circle, of course," she went on, her tone still appeasing, as if being ignored by the *ton* might hurt John's feelings. "But perhaps not this year as we are—" she broke off as he guided her across the street. "Where are we going?"

"You will see."

She remained quiet as he guided her toward the modiste shop.

"But why here?" She stopped in the middle of the pedestrian walk and he was forced to move her out of the way of two stout gentlemen engaged in a heated discussion and not minding where they were going.

"Because I want to go inside." John took her arm and guided her up the steps toward the shop of his nightmares. Shopping for *his* clothing was bad enough, and he girded his loins as he opened the door.

A woman haughtier than the Duchess of Falkirk examined them through a glass that magnified her eye. He'd seen toffs sporting such quizzing glasses and always wanted to ram them down their throats.

The haughty woman—no doubt Madame DuBois, the name stenciled in gold leaf on the shop window—motioned to an underling, who scurried like a mouse across the expanse of plush carpet.

"Good afternoon, sir," the mouse said, addressing his cravat. She turned to Cordelia and blinked. "Oh, Miss Page—but no, you recently married, didn't you?"

Cordelia smiled. "Yes, that is correct, Miss Pinker."

The woman, true to her name, blushed with pleasure at being remembered by a patron.

"You just missed the duchess and one of your nieces by half-an-hour—Her Grace commissioned several lovely gowns for her."

"My, they were up and about early." Cordelia glanced at John and he could almost hear what she was thinking: that her sister had wasted no time in spending John's money.

"This is my husband, Mr. Fielding."

"Please allow me to offer my sincerest congratulations, Mrs. Fielding." She turned back to John's neckcloth and congratulated it, as well.

He moved matters along. "My wife requires a new gown—something to go with these." He handed the clerk the opera gloves.

Cordelia made a distressed sound. "Oh, surely not—"

"She will need it by Friday—can that be done?" he asked the clerk, forcing her to look up. "I will compensate you for any extra labor." He glanced around and noticed there were gowns on display. "She will actually need several gowns. Perhaps some of those might suffice?"

"Of course, sir, of course." Miss Pinker led them to a room that must be used for private viewings. "If you will excuse me for a moment, I will have the gowns brought in here," she said, and then flitted away.

"John, I really don't need any new gowns."

"Duly noted," he said.

She gave a breathless laugh. "You really are a very stubborn man."

He didn't bother to dispute that.

Miss Pinker popped back into the room with the owner beside her.

Madame DuBois's expression was considerably warmer now that she knew John was wealthy enough to afford several dresses.

"It would be my pleasure to 'elp you today," the haughty woman condescended to say.

"My wife wishes Miss Pinker to assist her," John said.

The Frenchwoman's lips briefly parted in surprise, but she was a businesswoman before all else, and she forced a smile. "But of course."

Once that was settled, John picked up a copy of a sporting journal on the side table that was conveniently near a comfortable armchair.

"If you'll follow me, Mrs. Fielding, we can look through the readymade gowns to see if any suit you," Miss Pinker said.

When Cordelia hesitated, John said, "You will need something for the theater this Friday and I have it on excellent authority that we will be invited to at least two balls in the next few weeks." John saw no reason to mention that he'd not planned to accept either ball invitation until a few minutes ago.

She opened her mouth, but then closed it again and followed the clerk.

John smiled to himself as he flicked through the magazine, enjoying the rare feeling of getting the last word in.

Chapter 26

London
1818

Cordelia's new husband was mad. Utterly mad.

John had purchased half-a-dozen readymade gowns—insisting they be altered and ready in what must be a record amount of time for the shop—and another dozen were to be delivered over the next few weeks.

That had been several days ago and boxes had arrived every day, which had allowed her to wear a new gown each day that week.

The emerald-green silk dress that she was wearing tonight was one of the loveliest garments she'd ever possessed. The color made her hair look burnished, and the bodice was fashionably low and tight and pushed her breasts up in a way that made her blush whenever she glanced down at them.

"It's all the crack, ma'am, and, if you don't mind me sayin', you've a lovely figure for this style," Akers had assured her.

There was a knock on the door and Akers went to answer it while Cordelia pulled on the lovely opera gloves John had bought her.

Akers held out a black velvet case. "This just came for you."

"Thank you," Cordelia said faintly, taking the box with hands that shook slightly.

When she lifted the lid, she gasped at the parure—emeralds and diamonds set in gold.

"My goodness," Akers crooned. "Which pieces will you wear, ma'am?"

"It's just dining with family and then the theater. So perhaps only the necklace, ring, and earrings."

"Not the tiara?"

"You don't think it would be too much?"

"Not for the theater."

Cordelia smiled. "I suppose you are right. Very well, then I shall wear everything except the brooch."

Akers set about adorning her in jewels.

"This ring is especially lovely," Akers breathed as she reverently slid the monstrous square-cut emerald onto Cordelia's gloved finger.

She was not surprised that it fit perfectly. Her husband did not seem to be the type of man to miss details, although he did seem to have forgotten where her bedchamber was these last few nights.

Her face heated at the thought, even though Akers could not know what she was thinking.

Cordelia could not stop dwelling on the fact that it had been *five days*—tonight would mark the fifth—since John had come to her bed. Had she really been so awful? Or had her crying so revolted him that he was avoiding her?

Every day she swore she would ask him—although how one phrased such a thing, she didn't know—but every day was taken up with errands and functions for her nieces even though Ophelia, instead of leaving town as she'd said, had accompanied them on almost every outing, frustrating Cordelia no end. Why did her sister need *her* if she was staying in London?

At least tonight, for the first time, John would join the family when they went out, albeit just the theater and not a ball or party. Thus far, Ophelia had only invited him when it was just family for dinner. Cordelia was going to put her foot—

"Oh, emeralds do look lovely with your hair, ma'am. You look like a princess," Akers said, pulling Cordelia from her unhappy musing.

She laughed. "A rather *old* princess. " But her maid was right about emeralds suiting her coloring. Her only other jewels were the pearls her father had given her on her eighteenth birthday. This was… well, it was beyond anything she'd ever dreamed of wearing.

Cordelia knew she should be thrilled that he was lavishing her with jewels and gowns, but the one thing she wanted him to lavish her with—himself—he was steadfastly denying her.

I have become greedy and ungrateful, she chided herself as Akers settled her wrap around her shoulders and handed Cordelia her reticule.

Her husband was pacing back and forth across the vast entry hall when Cordelia descended the stairs.

He wore black pantaloons, a black coat, and an ivory waistcoat, the stark clothing a perfect foil for his dark hair. He did not register her arrival until she was almost on the bottom step. But when he did finally see her, he froze, his black gaze raking over her body in a manner that left her skin tingling.

As usual, he did not speak, but his poleaxed expression spoke volumes. His eyes lingered on her décolletage and she felt almost naked.

She laid a gloved hand on her necklace. "Thank you, John, these are quite ravishing."

He finally blinked. "Yes. Ravishing."

Somehow, Cordelia knew he did not mean the stones.

He held out his arm, and she laid her hand upon it. Outside, the curricle with its top raised waited for them.

He glanced down at her as he led her to the carriage. "The town carriage is taking longer than expected. I know taking a curricle to the theater is unconventional, but I thought you would prefer it to a hackney."

"The night is lovely; it will be nice not to be shut up inside a coach."

He handed her in and sprang the horses once Barker was on board.

Cordelia smiled as they sped along. This was their first evening out as a married couple. Perhaps later tonight he would come to her? If he didn't, she would gather her courage and seek him out herself.

***

Unlike the duchess and her family, who lingered in the theater to talk to a few acquaintances, John and Cordelia left as soon as the play was over.

The crowd was thickest just in front of the door and carriages lined both sides of the street, none of them his distinctive vehicle. Barker must have been kept out of the plum spots by older, wilier servants.

He turned to Cordelia. "I will take you back inside to wait while I go fetch the carriage."

"I wouldn't mind a bit of a walk. It was terribly stuffy and cramped in those seats."

Those were John's sentiments exactly. He didn't know why his sister-in-law had wanted to attend a play at the Colosseum Theater. The old playhouse was decrepit and his chair must have been a torture device that was no longer needed at The Tower.

Not only that, but the building was too close to the seamy side of the city for his comfort; he didn't like exposing Cordelia to such a rough neighborhood.

John suspected that his sister-in-law had chosen this venue—rather than the Royal or Drury—so she could keep him out of the public eye.

He glanced down at his wife's fragile looking slippers. "Are you sure you don't want to wait?"

"I'll be fine," she assured him. "Besides, we won't be going far."

"We'd better not," he muttered, tucking her arm in his and heading toward the street that bordered the south end of the theater. There'd been a line of carriages when they'd arrived, so possibly Barker had circled and stopped on that side. But when they reached the corner, there were only a half-dozen or so vehicles, and none was theirs.

This was ridiculous. He would take her back and try to catch—

A boy of about fifteen emerged from the alley they'd just passed and trotted toward them. "Oi! You Fielding?"

John drew Cordelia to his side, automatically angling his body to protect her.

Before he could answer, his distinctive curricle and pair came flying around the corner at the next intersecting street. Barker misjudged the turn and almost ran into a wooden cart that sold oranges and flowers.

"What in the name of—"

Movement out of the corner of John's eye set off warning bells—bells that should have gone off far sooner than they had.

John pushed Cordelia behind him. "Stay *right* behind me," he snarled, dropping into a crouch as two more men materialized beside the boy who'd tried to get his attention.

Unlike the lad, the men were brandishing knives.

The heaviest of the three lunged, sweeping his knife in a tight arc that would have caught John in the belly if he'd not leaned back. Before the man could bring the knife in another sweep, John kicked him in the knee, bringing down all his weight and breaking the man's leg with a sickening *crunch*.

His aggressor screamed, dropped his knife, and fell to the cobbles.

The other two men were staring at their fallen comrade in open-mouthed shock. The one with the knife quickly roused himself while the lad grabbed the prone man's hand and struggled to bring him to his feet.

John's new opponent dropped into a low crouch and brandished his knife.

"Keep behind me, Cordelia," John ordered in a low voice.

"Come on, ye big bastard," the other man snarled, lunging at him. But he was rattled and afraid and his movements were jerky and tight and easy to dodge.

Foolishly, he came within arm's distance and John delivered a cross body punch that hit the man right over his heart and almost knocked him onto his arse before he steadied himself.

"Guv!"

John didn't look away at the sound of Barker's voice and the distinctive clop-clop of hooves on cobbles—but his assailant did and that split second of inattention allowed John the time he needed to lift his foot high enough to deliver a kick to the groin that sent the other man right into the path of the approaching curricle.

Barker was on his feet as he drove, looking just like a miniature Roman charioteer, his small body straining to keep the horses from running full out.

John pivoted and grabbed Cordelia's arm, moving her gently, but quickly, out of the path of the approaching curricle.

Once they were no longer in danger of being trampled, John turned to her. "Are you hurt?"

"I am unharmed." Her voice was breathless, but steady.

He watched as the second assailant—who'd wisely rolled a few feet to the side to avoid the horses—struggled to his feet and shuffled back to the alley he'd emerged from, clutching his side.

"They're getting away, John!"

It would be easy enough to catch them—the badly injured man and lad were joined at the shoulders and doing an awkward three-legged hop—but he had no intention of leaving Cordelia alone even for a minute.

Barker managed to stop the carriage and John took Cordelia's hand. "Come," he said, surveying the street constantly as he led her toward safety.

"It was some sort of trap, was it not?" she asked, having to trot to keep up with him.

"It was. And I stepped right into it."

"But how could you have known?"

He didn't want to tell her he'd pulled similar shams himself countless times.

"I'm sorry, guv, but they *trapped* me." Baker's voice was high and shaky, and he sounded on the verge of tears.

"You did well, Barker. Hold their heads while I help Mrs. Fielding."

Within moments, they were rolling away from the theater and John turned to Cordelia, who correctly read the question in his eyes.

"I am unharmed," she assured him.

He nodded abruptly and turned his attention to the dark streets.

Fury bubbled inside him, strong enough to choke him; fury at himself.

First, for allowing her to walk with him when he should have known better.

And second, for being too bloody distracted to see a trap when it stared him right in the face.

He'd become lazy and careless, and tonight Cordelia had almost paid for his lack of vigilance.

***

Cordelia thought her heart might pound its way right out of her chest.

What an experience that had been!

Watching her husband single-handedly vanquish three men had been terrifying, exhilarating, and oddly stirring.

Was it wicked of her to find his intense physicality so… arousing?

Her face heated at the naughty thought and she was grateful for the near darkness as the carriage sped through the night.

Cordelia couldn't resist studying him from beneath lowered lashes.

His clothing wasn't mussed, he wasn't breathing hard, and he'd not even broken a sweat. In fact, other than a few strands of hair that had escaped his queue, there was no sign that he'd just severely damaged two knife-wielding men with only his body for a weapon.

He was magnificent—awe-inspiring—and more than a little intimidating.

And he was hers.

All night long she'd seen other women casting glances at him, their eyes drawn by his quiet confidence, his fierce good looks, and the aura of danger he exuded.

Her hand twitched to touch him—even just his sleeve—but she stopped herself, unsure that such an action would be welcome. His normally stern face was more remote than ever, and she sensed that anger simmered beneath his unflappable facade.

Cordelia wished with all her heart that he'd speak to her and take her into his confidence, but he didn't appear to need human interaction or conversation or friendship or *anything* that other people needed. At least not from her.

She knew that somebody wiser than her had once claimed that no man was an island, but John Fielding was about as close to an island as a person could get.

Chapter 27

London
1818

John sat in his chambers and drank. Alone.

He was drinking for a specific purpose: to get drunk. It was something he hadn't done for years. But tonight, he felt an almost crushing compulsion to feel numb, even if only for a short while.

Thus far, it wasn't working, even though he'd put away most of a bottle of claret.

Worth had given him a case of it as a wedding gift and would scream like a demented parrot if he ever found out how John was treating his gift.

John refilled his glass all the way to the brim.

Earlier tonight he had re-discovered an emotion that he'd not felt since he'd been a young boy: unadulterated, gut-churning terror.

When he'd realized that Cordelia might be hurt—or, God forbid, killed—if he couldn't stop the men who attacked them, the panic that had struck him had nearly paralyzed him into inaction.

Thanks to fear, he'd hesitated—only for a few seconds—before attacking, and that hesitation might have been crucial.

It had taken all his strength to behave normally on the endless drive home. Not until he reached the privacy of his chambers had, he allowed himself to react to what had happened.

For the first ten minutes he'd shaken so badly that his teeth had chattered, his hands trembling too much to even pour himself a drink.

That nothing *had* happened to her wasn't enough to make the fear go away. Because John had realized tonight that if he failed to protect her from those men's knives that she could very well *die* and abandon him to the solitary, pitiful life he'd been sleepwalking through before he met her.

John finally had something—some*one*—in his life worth keeping.

He shook his head in disbelief; how had this happened to him? Hadn't losing his Gran and Lily been enough to teach him a lesson? Hadn't he already learned how quickly a person could lose everything they held dear in the blink of an eye?

While he'd been scheming to ensnare her into marriage, Cordelia had—quite unwittingly—done him one better and stolen his heart.

John was in love with her—why lie to himself—and it bloody terrified him.

A light tap on his door made him jolt. When he turned, he saw his wife in the dressing room doorway. She was wearing either the same nightgown as their wedding night or one just like it.

He lurched to his feet.

When her eyes lowered, he looked down, too. He'd stripped off his coats, shirt, shoes, and stockings in a frenzy, scattering them about the room. Now he wore only his black pantaloons.

Shame flooded him as she looked at him—shame that she was forced to see him wallowing in fear and self-pity.

"Yes?" he growled, sounding just like a bear that had been disturbed in its cave. He cleared his throat and tried again. "Did you need something?"

She came forward, her gown floating around her like mist. He could see the outline of her body beneath the fine fabric, the curve of her breasts, the dark points at the tip of each, the shadowy triangle between her thighs.

Ferocious desire pulsed through him and heat pooled low in his belly; his prick hardened so fast that he actually felt dizzy.

"I know I should have waited until morning—you must be exhausted after tonight—but I didn't want to wait." She bent her head and sheets of chestnut-brown silk slid over her shoulders, hiding her face. "I could not go to sleep without thanking you."

John felt like he'd missed the first part of this conversation. "Thanking me for what?"

Her head whipped up. "For protecting me from those men."

He was often speechless by choice, but this time he was simply without words. What had she thought? That he would turn and run? Toss the men his money, her jewels, and beg for mercy?

"You were very brave."

He scoffed. "Brave?"

Her brow furrowed. "I don't understand you. Not at all. Do you not think that fighting off three men is incredibly valiant?"

"One of them was a boy and the other two knew nothing of fighting." He snorted and there was no amusement in the sound. "Your sister is twice as frightening as those three put together."

Her eyes and mouth became comically round—and then… she laughed. Not a delicate, lady-like titter, but a genuine belly laugh. She crossed her arms over her body—as if to hold her amusement close—unaware of how the action pressed the tissue-thin fabric against her breasts, her thighs, her sex.

She was far more intoxicating than the expensive liquor he'd been guzzling, far more potent.

John had promised himself that he'd leave her alone tonight because she needed to rest after being attacked by knife-wielding ruffians. But if he was to keep that promise, then she needed to leave *now*. Before he mounted her right there and fucked her into the carpet like the street cur he was.

He needed to ask her to leave.

John cleared his throat and opened his mouth.

"Well, you are to be commended then, aren't you?" she asked, wiping the corners of her eyes as her laughter ebbed.

"Commended? For what?" He'd forgotten what they'd been talking about.

"Because you took on both my *scary* sister and those men in one night and vanquished all of them." She stepped closer, her eyes darkening. "I have never seen a man fight before."

John scowled. "That was no fight, that was—"

"You moved so fast that I didn't even realize you'd struck the first man until he was writhing on the ground." Her eyes slid over his chest in a way that made his stomach clench and his jewels tighten.

She laid one small, slender hand over his heart and John stopped breathing.

"You were so fierce and graceful and strong." She swallowed, her hand trembling slightly. "You are the very definition of male beauty." Finally, she raised her eyes to his, and he shuddered at the heat and desire he saw.

John's control snapped, and he crushed her against him. "My God, Cordelia," he muttered, claiming her mouth roughly, like an uncouth beast.

She wrapped her arms around him and her mouth opened to his onslaught; he devoured her, thrusting deeply to claim, possess, and dominate.

A faint voice in his head suggested a little finesse would not be amiss—this was only her second coupling, after all—but John shoved the cautionary voice aside and slid his hands beneath her bottom, lifting her off her feet. He spread her thighs with his body and pushed her nightgown up until her hot, wet sex ground against the sensitive skin of his naked belly.

Her legs tightened around his waist and she made a soft moaning sound as she clumsily returned his kisses, her tongue tangling with his, stroking into him with increasingly bold thrusts, her hands sliding up his shoulders to his neck and then fisting into his hair, pulling painfully tight.

Her passion thrilled and astonished him in equal measures and he opened wider as she explored the exquisitely sensitive roof of his mouth, the inside of his lips, even his teeth, as if she couldn't get close enough and wanted to be inside his skin. It was a desire he knew all too well.

John walked her to his bed, loath to let her out of his arms but desperate to taste her. He gently pulled away and set her on the high, soft mattress. She looked bloody delicious, her lips slick and swollen from her erotic assault, her pupils huge and devouring.

Gone was the spinster aunt, the chaperone to nieces, and rescuer of persecuted old dogs.

Raw, sensual hunger defined her now. And it was all for him—*only* him.

"Take off your gown," he ordered, busying himself with his pantaloons. But even six fingers could not unfasten his buttons fast enough and he cursed his clumsy, drink-addled hands, pulling and tearing and sending at least one button flying before he could shove the skin-tight garment to the floor.

Cordelia had become tangled in her nightgown, one elbow cocked at a strange angle as she struggled to get free. She abruptly stopped squirming when her eyes landed on his cock. Like a child who'd just spotted a new toy, she appeared to forget what she was doing and just stared.

John unfastened the remaining buttons of her gown and slid his hands beneath the fine cotton, straightening her bent arm before lifting the garment over her head. Only to find it was now caught around her hair.

They both laughed, the sounds breathless and desperate.

John gave her a gentle push, and she flopped back on the bed, the action causing her magnificent breasts to shake enticingly.

He captured an already peaked nipple in his mouth, suckling and nipping until she thrust her fingers into his hair and held him close. He smiled against the breast he was sucking and slid a hand between their bodies, quickly finding what he sought between her thighs, which were spread and pinned by the weight of his torso.

She moaned and pulled his hair hard enough to make his eyes water when he caressed her sweet little nub.

John worked his way from her nipples to the sensitive undersides of her breasts, inexorably moving downward. He hovered over her navel, his tongue probing and swirling until she laughed and squirmed, her hands settling on his jaws to stay his teasing. He knew the instant she realized she was touching his scars because her body went rigid and she snatched her hands away.

John looked up and caught her wrists, finely boned and fragile in his grasp, and set her hands back on his face. "Touch me, Cordelia—anywhere you wish." He lowered his mouth to the gentle swell below her navel and sucked the thin skin of her belly into his mouth.

She hissed and arched against him, her nimble, curious fingers tracing his scars, his jaw, his nose, his eyebrows.

John sucked hard and then released his mouthful and briefly admired the mark he'd left before turning to his ultimate destination.

He parted her lips with his thumbs, exposing her swollen petals to his greedy gaze.

She gave a soft, guttural cry and her hands froze on his head as he circled her exposed bud with the tip of his tongue, flicking and teasing.

Her thighs spread wider, and she lifted her hips to grind herself against him.

He smirked against her sensitive flesh and then sucked her engorged bud into his mouth.

"John!"

He worked her until she was writhing and whimpering and muttering incoherent pleas, orders, and prayers, not stopping until she came apart beneath his lips.

She was still cresting on a wave of pleasure when he positioned himself at her tight opening and entered her with a long, slick thrust, holding himself deep inside her to share the echoes of her climax, until she sighed and became boneless beneath him.

John anchored himself firmly between her thighs and pumped his hips, invading her deeply with each pounding thrust and exerting enough friction against her sensitive bud to work both their bodies toward the same destination.

***

Cordelia had not believed the night could get any more exciting, and she had been wrong. The wicked thing that he'd done to her with his mouth was… delicious.

"Yes," he murmured beside her, his voice raspy. "You are."

Cordelia squeezed her eyes shut, mortified. "I did not mean to say that out loud."

"Why not?"

She laughed. And then realized his question had been serious. "That was not what my sister told me to expect in the marriage bed."

His chest rumbled with laughter. "I daresay it wasn't."

She turned to face him, mesmerized by the way his dark eyes glowed with amusement. "But she has had nine children. *Nine.* Surely she must know what she is talking about?"

"You think bed sport and getting with child are the same thing?"

"Well… yes. I mean, is there some other way?"

His mouth twitched. By now Cordelia could recognize his smile, even though he always tried to suppress it or hide it from her. She suspected he did that because it twisted his face and made him look like he was snarling.

"A man can pump a woman full of seed in several ways." He reached out and took her naked breast in his right hand, the gesture all the more shocking for how casual it was, how possessive, as if he had every right to touch any part of her body that he pleased.

He did. Under the law, she belonged to him as surely as this house or his unmatched pair of horses.

The thought should have terrified her; she barely knew this man. But, for some reason, she was certain that he would never hurt her—at least not intentionally.

Cordelia shivered under the warmth of his huge hand, subtly arching her back like a cat that wanted more petting.

He thumbed her nipple, and her body responded with a hungry ache that frightened her. He could arouse her so easily, so quickly, and she knew *nothing* about how to arouse or pleasure him. What if he became bored with her? What if—

"If I were a gentleman," he said, interrupting her rapidly spiraling thoughts. "I would come to you under cover of darkness, lift your shift to your waist, penetrate your body, and spill inside you after a few hard thrusts." His voice was low and harsh as he uttered the crass words. "That is the way a proper gentleman would fuck you."

There was that thrilling, shocking word again.

Cordelia knew she must be a deviant because her breasts and sex seemed to come alive at his earthy language.

"It would be quick and joyless for you, but I would still enjoy the pleasure of an orgasm."

Orgasm. An exotic word for an exotic experience. Every nerve in her body tingled at his blunt speaking.

He pushed to his knees and nudged her thighs apart, looming over her as he pinched her nipple with one hand and slid the fingers of his other hand through the private curls between her legs.

Cordelia spread her thighs in eager anticipation of his intoxicating touch, her face unbearably hot at her wanton begging.

He leaned lower, his expression stern and hungry as he stroked a thick finger through her wet, swollen folds.

Oh my, oh my, oh my…

"There are men—and women, too—who believe that a woman cannot and should not experience sexual pleasure." His thumb circled her sensitive nub while another finger gently probed the entrance to her body. "But the truth is that women's bodies were made to enjoy orgasms—you can have five or six in the time a man can only have one."

Cordelia wouldn't have known what he meant only a week ago, but she knew his words were true. She had climaxed—*orgasmed*—again and again and again.

He grinned down at her, as if she'd spoken her thoughts out loud. The feral expression was there and gone in the blink of an eye. "I don't just wish to empty my seed inside you and breed you, Cordelia—I wish to *own* you."

She gulped. "O-Own? You already do."

He gave her an inquisitive look.

"Under the law, a husband—"

He scowled dismissively. "Know this, Cordelia—the law may say that you belong to me, but you are not chattel in *my* eyes. You belong to yourself."

Cordelia appreciated what he was saying, but, as a woman, she knew all too well that she was still at the utter and complete mercy of her husband no matter what he promised her.

"That is not the owning I am talking about," he said in a gruff voice.

"What kind of owning do you mean?"

He chuckled; the sound so low she felt it rather than heard it. "I mean that your body will be so attuned to mine that you will become wet and eager after only a glance from me or a touch from my hand." John swooped down and claimed her mouth while he pushed a finger inside her.

Cordelia cried out at the unexpected pleasure, and he captured her cry in his mouth before pulling away.

He watched her through hungry eyes. "Well, Cordelia?" he asked, his breathing ragged as he worked her with deep, measured strokes and scattered what remained of her wits. "Should I blow out the candles, creep beneath the covers, and use you for my pleasure like a gentleman would? Or should we see how many times I can make you orgasm in one night?" A second finger joined the first, stretching and filling her.

She blinked as her pleasure-fogged brain struggled to comprehend him. Was his question some sort of trick?

"Hmm?"

"Your way," she blurted without hesitation. "I want you to own m—" Cordelia moaned and bit her lower lip as he pinched and teased a nipple with his free hand.

His dark eyes glittered, and his smile was tight and fierce. "That is just as well, since you already *own* me… Wife."

Cordelia could only stare, stunned by his words. Was he telling the truth? Could a woman like her possibly have ensnared a man like him?

"It is true," he said, making her wonder if she'd spoken out loud again. He paused his delicious fondling and distracting thrusting. "I am yours to command," he said, lazily flicking her bud with his thumb. "What do you need—my hand, my mouth, or my cock?" He looked down and Cordelia followed his gaze to said *cock*, which was once again thick, hard, and long.

She swallowed. "I thought you said you could only d-do it once?"

"You inspire me."

Her eyes narrowed at the humor in his voice. “I can see you find my ignorance humorous.”

John shook his head slowly from side to side, his expression serious as he reached out and ran a finger over her lower lip. “I find you desirable and beddable, and I want to wreck you with pleasure.”

Her mouth dropped open at his erotic declaration and he continued to stroke her lip, exerting a little more pressure with each pass. Cordelia touched the tip of her tongue against his finger, eliciting a low, hungry growl.

His nostrils flared as he pushed his finger deeper and then withdrew, stroking into her mouth the same way he'd just penetrated another part of her body. Cordelia's eyes threatened to roll out of her head as she took his meaning.

She glanced at that most fascinating and male part of him. Did he want…?

He smiled faintly and removed his finger with obvious reluctance. “I will teach you that later," he said, reading her mind so easily it was unnerving. "Right now, you must tell me how you want me.”

Her gaze dropped to his *membrum virile*, although she could not bring herself to say the shocking word *cock*.

"Excellent choice." He rolled onto his back. “I want you to ride me."

"R-Ride you?"

"Yes. Climb on top and straddle me. Place your hips over mine.”

She could see what he wanted and hesitated.

"It is your choice, Cordelia. I will not make you to do anything you do not wish to do."

She gazed at the length of his body spread out before her, a buffet for her senses. If she sat atop him, she could look at all of him and even touch him more easily.

Cordelia clambered to her knees; only after she'd already lifted one leg to straddle him did she realize how exposed that left her.

The corners of his mouth twitched, and he openly stared at her sex.

"It is ungentlemanly of you to look," she chided, her entire body on fire with embarrassment as she quickly lowered herself onto his breeding organ, which was hard and impossibly hot.

"Yes," he agreed, unabashed, as he lifted his hips—and her—off the bed, the action pressing his shaft between her sensitive folds.

Cordelia's eyelids fluttered; the friction was exquisite, and she had to bite her lip to keep from moaning.

"You like that," he said, doing it over and over, until her she vibrated with need.

"Lean forward and take hold of my arms," he ordered gruffly.

She did so, resting her hands on biceps that were like hot, smooth stone.

He rolled his hips, and she whimpered, digging her fingers into his muscles as he rocked beneath her, the sound of their labored breathing filling the room.

Cordelia was on the cusp of giving in to her body's demands when she remembered his words.

I want you to ride me.

She gritted her teeth against the pleasure threatening to crest inside her and then walked her hands across his hot, hard body until she was again up high on her knees. He watched her through slitted eyes, his lips parted, and his breathing labored.

Cordelia looked down to where he jutted out from her private curls, as if he were part of her body. She laughed. "Why, it looks like it belongs to me."

"It does belong to you." He slid a hand between them and gripped his shaft. "Rise up higher and mount me."

Oh, the things he said to her!

Cordelia's body was shaky with desire as she obeyed. Once he was positioned at her entrance, she bit her lip and then sat down hard, taking every inch of him fast and deep.

"My God!" His hips jerked up violently enough to raise them both off the bed again. "I think you are trying to kill me," he murmured. "Please continue."

His playful words surprised a laugh out of her.

He smiled and lifted his arms. "Use me for balance, if you like."

Cordelia used his hands to steady herself as she lifted off him and then lowered again, just as hard as the first time.

John gasped, every muscle in his chest, arms, and abdomen taut and defined, like steel beneath silk. His body was the most sensual thing she had ever seen, and she loved the sound of his gasps and moans.

She wanted to force even more noises from him.

She wanted to make him whimper, beg, and squirm, just as she had done.

In short—and to use his words—she wanted to *wreck him with pleasure*.

It did not take great experience or intelligence to know that right now would be an excellent time to do all that to him.

He watched her intently, his lips curved in a slight, sensual smile that made her inner muscles tighten.

Again, he gasped. "Yessss." The word was a long, sibilant hiss.

Cordelia concentrated and squeezed the same muscles again as she rose up on her knees.

He groaned. "Ride me hard, Cordelia. Please…"

His feverish begging severed the last of her reservations and Cordelia posted him in earnest, clenching and releasing and taking him deep inside her with each stroke.

He shuddered beneath her, his strong hips rocking to meet her on each downstroke, his eyes closed and his expression one she'd never seen on his face before: pure bliss.

It was a look more valuable than gold or jewels; a look she would do anything to see again and again.

***

John was back in the room—Lily's room—and her eyes were staring sightlessly, her body splayed, Des Houlihan crouching over her.

John was frozen with terror. He couldn't move; he'd never be able to get to her in time because he couldn't move so much as a muscle!

Lily! The word tore out of his throat as he strained toward her.

"*John!*"

John's eyes flew open, and he looked around unseeingly. A hand landed on his shoulder and he grabbed it, crushing it in an iron grip. "No!" he snarled. "No, you can't—"

"*John.* It is only a dream. You must release my arm. You are hurting me."

He whipped around and saw her—Cordelia—her eyes glinting in the glow thrown by the fire. He instantly released her, his heart pounding as if he'd been running.

John gulped mouthfuls of air, squeezing his eyes shut. *Christ! It was a dream. Just a dream.*

A small, cool hand stroked his hair off his forehead. "You were having a nightmare."

He lay motionless, reveling in the soothing, sweet sensation of her touch.

Her other hand came up, and she cradled his face, tilting it up toward her. "Are you all right, John?"

He opened his eyes. "Did I hurt you?" he asked, his voice raspy.

"No, you did not squeeze hard enough to hurt." She tucked a strand of hair behind his ear, the gesture so tender it gutted him. "Come, lie down beside me." Cordelia stretched out on her side, smiled, and patted the bed. "Please."

He hesitated a moment and then lowered himself beside her.

"Do you remember the dream?"

"No," he lied. It was better to lie—better for her. She had cried like a babe at the story of his maiming. If he told her about Lily, she would probably weep for a month. He didn't want to make her cry. He wanted to make her sigh, beg for more, scream out her passion, laugh, scold—anything but cry.

"Who is Lily?"

John sighed. When was the last time he'd heard that name spoken out loud? "She was somebody who died a long time ago."

"Somebody dear to you?" She hesitated for a long moment, her body becoming tighter. "A lover?"

"No, not a lover. She was a friend—more like a sister."

"Ah."

John felt the tension drain from her. His own body, however, remained taut and wary as he wondered—and dreaded—what she would ask next.

"I hardly ever dream," she said. "Do you dream often?"

"No."

She chuckled. "Have you always talked this much?" she teased.

"Tell me about your parents, your village, your friends."

"You're only asking me about them so *you* don't have to talk."

That was true.

"Very well," she said after a moment. "I will allow you to divert me—*this* time."

And so she told him of her happy childhood, her loving parents, and her friends, who were all still alive and thriving.

John also discovered what happened to the old dog that she'd rescued—not that she knew he'd seen her that day.

"He lives in the country now, on one of my father's tenant farms. There are five boys in the family and they adore him. They named him William, after the Conqueror." She giggled, the sound girlish. "With his ragged ear and snaggleteeth, you could hardly find a less prepossessing conqueror, although he is very valiant and protective of his people."

Her words came slower and slower, until they finally stopped entirely and her breathing became regular as she drifted into a deep, hopefully dreamless, sleep.

John kissed the top of her head and pulled her tighter until they were as close as two spoons in a drawer.

He stared into the gloom and waited for dawn, unwilling to close his eyes and risk returning to his nightmares.

Chapter 28

London
1818

John had barely left his wife's bed when he wanted to be back in it. Every day he swore he'd exercise some restraint and let Cordelia sleep—rest and recover—but every night he went to her.

And every night she welcomed him with open, eager arms.

Although he took her several times a night, he was clinging to a shred of self-control and had managed—thus far—not to slake his lust on her in the morning, too.

John slipped soundlessly through the door that connected their chambers and swiftly dressed for riding.

Sims came to the foyer as John passed through. "This was waiting for you this morning, sir."

John took the envelope, which was unmarked. "You didn't see who delivered it?"

"I'm afraid not, sir."

John broke the cheap wafer that sealed it and unfolded the thin parchment.

"Come to Fat Bailey's place near the wharf at midnight if you want to know more about what happened outside the theater. Come alone and bring fifty pounds."

The handwriting was that of an educated person. As far as traps went, this one was clumsy and obvious. John had no intention of going to the river with bulging pockets at midnight—at least not without gathering some information beforehand.

Instead of going for a ride in the park, John hailed a hackney.

The wharf looked even more desperate in the cold light of day and most of the buildings that lined the streets were so decrepit they looked in danger of collapsing at any moment.

Fat Bailey's, which was a gaming hell-slash-brothel, wasn't the worst looking building on the street, but it was close.

John pounded on the flimsy door and glanced around as he waited. There wasn't a person in sight and only the birds were active this early and with this particular tide.

"Open up!" he shouted, and then pounded some more.

He was just about to kick the door down when it opened a crack and a querulous voice demanded, "Who's making all that racket?" A watery blue eye met his, widened, and the door began to close.

John rammed his shoulder against the splintery wood hard enough that it probably knocked whoever was behind it off their feet.

Squawking and scuffling emanated from the dim interior as he shoved his way into the building, which smelled so strongly of onions, unwashed bodies, and stale beer that John's eyes ran as if he were weeping.

He reached down and grabbed the scrawny arm of an ancient man and hauled him to his feet.

His captive glared up at him and gingerly touched his bleeding nose. “Oi fink it’s *broken*.”

“I can make sure it is, if you like.”

"No—no, don't 'it me, please!" The man tried to back away, but John didn't loosen his grip. "I din't do nuffinck."

“Why were you trying to close the door in my face?”

“Cor Mister! 'Ave you *seen* your face?”

John laughed. “Well, you’ve got a point there, old man. Where is Bailey?”

“Ee's sleepin', ain't 'ee? Just loike any normal bloke at this hour.” His glower told John he did not fit into that category.

“Go wake him up," John ordered. He dropped his skinny arm, snatched the candle from the sconce, and—not bothering to see if the old man had obeyed—ventured deeper into the building. He followed the stench of sour beer, which led him to a small, gloomy tap room.

John grabbed one of the ragged drapes and yanked it off the rod, hoping to shed some light into the room.

Dirty brown light leaked through the window, which had been boarded up in several places, and illuminated the grimy pump room. John dribbled some wax on a nearby table and secured the candle in it.

He paced the room restlessly while he waited for Bailey, struggling with the fury that had been building inside him since receiving the note.

So, somebody had planned that attack last night? An attack that might have left Cordelia hurt—or worse. John could only assume this was backlash for prying into Dolan, which meant he must be getting closer to the man.

Whoever had orchestrated that attack had made a critical mistake if they'd thought it would dissuade him, because John was more committed to finding the elusive criminal than he'd ever been.

His body spun around before his brain had even registered a sound.

A man as thin as a fence post, wrapped in a tattered and stained dressing gown, shuffled out of the gloom. He squinted at the shards of bright light coming through the boarded window and winced, his gaze sliding to the torn drape on the floor.

"Was ripping that down really necessary?" he asked, shading his eyes and turning toward the small sideboard laden with smudged bottles and decanters. His hand shook badly as he filled a glass.

John was momentarily surprised by the man's cultured accent. But his fury shoved the other emotion aside.

"Fat Bailey?"

The man gave a weak chuckle. "As you see. And you must be the infamous John Fielding."

Bailey lifted the glass to his mouth and John darted toward him and slapped it out of his hand, sending it crashing into the wall.

Bailey stared in open-mouthed shock as golden liquid dripped down the faded, filthy wall-hangings. "Bloody hell, you're fast! The sobriquet Lightening John is well deserved, I see."

A fraction of a second later, Bailey found himself looking at John down the length of his outstretched arm, his own hands scrabbling frantically at the six-fingered hand around his throat.

"Who?" John demanded, not bothering to explain what he meant.

Not so much as a peep or gasp issued from the other man's mouth, and John realized he might be holding him too tightly.

He relaxed his grip and tried again. "Who?"

"F-f-fassshhht Eddie. Arggh!"

John startled at the named. “Fast Eddie died years ago.” That was one of the first things John had checked into upon returning to Britain.

“Drink,” Baily gasped.

The other man's skin had turned an alarming shade of red and he looked like he might lose consciousness, so John abruptly released him.

Bailey slid to the floor, his hands around his throat, as if that might protect him from further attack.

"You'd better talk or I'll squeeze you harder next time," John threatened, ungently nudging Bailey's narrow arse with his boot. "Get up," he ordered, and then poured another glass of something that looked like claret but smelled like vinegar.

Bailey pushed himself up with a pitiful groan, and John handed him the glass.

He took it with badly shaking hands and slurped half the glass before sighing and slumping against the wall.

“Now, who was it, really?”

“It was Fast Eddie Houlihan—” He cringed away when John reached for him. “*I swear*!" he insisted in a shrill, terrified voice that was more than a little convincing. "I *saw* him. He was here, in my pub. I overheard him talking about you with some woman. She was paying him to grab you and he wanted more money—he said you were too bloody dangerous." Bailey snorted, sizing up John's body with a wide-eyed look. "Now I understand what he meant. Anyhow, they haggled over the price, but I never heard what they agreed on."

John was momentarily nonplussed. "A woman wanted him to take *me*?" he repeated with disbelief.

"Yes—she wanted you. I'm telling the truth."

"What woman?”

“I don’t know."

John lunged toward him, and Bailey shrieked. "I don't *know*! She was covered head to foot in black and had a heavy black veil over her face. All I can tell you about her is that she wasn’t dressed like anyone from around here.”

John's head spun; none of this made any sense. "Fast Eddie died, and I heard that from a Runner."

"Yes, well, Eddie went to a lot of effort to make people believe that."

"He used to be the king around these parts—why would he pretend to be dead?"

Bailey stood straighter, suddenly angry. "And I used to be the Right Honorable Thomas Bailey and look at me now. Oh, how the mighty have fallen." He reached for the bottle to pour himself another glass and John let him.

"What happened?"

"I got caught accepting a bribe."

John scowled. "I don't give a damn about what happened to *you*. I meant Eddie."

"Oh." Bailey frowned, obviously offended.

John didn't care. "If you don't start talking, I'm going to—"

Bailey held up his hands in a defensive gesture and his words tumbled out in a rush. "Eddie got hit by a night soil carter, of all things, about ten years back."

John snorted.

"It sounds amusing, but it was serious. It broke both his legs and did something to his chest and jaw. He was laid up for months; by the time he could move and talk, his territory had been carved up like a beefsteak, with Charlie Clifton taking the lion's share."

John knew about Clifton, so that much was true.

"Eddie owed a lot of money to a lot of people—none of which he could pay. He thought it was safest for his health to stick to the shadows. You know how it is—Clifton wouldn't want Eddie around his turf, no matter that his fangs had been pulled."

It was bloody difficult for John to imagine Eddie without *fangs*. But he knew what the other man meant—it was just smart business practice to eliminate your enemies when you had the opportunity.

Bailey had filled the glass to the rim and had to bend low to take a drink without spilling. When he straightened up, he glared at John, no longer afraid now that he'd imbibed some liquid courage.

"You sent me the message to meet you at midnight—why couldn't you meet me right now to tell me this? At a decent hour?"

Bailey snorted. "Because I couldn't deliver Eddie to you in broad daylight, could I? It was hard enough to lure him here at night," he muttered under his breath.

"Why would he come back here?"

"Because I told him I would tell *you* that he was behind the ambush if he didn't show up with money."

John laughed. "And you want to charge me as well?"

Bailey eyed him sullenly. "Go ahead, laugh all you want. I do what I have to do to get by."

"You expect me to trust you after hearing this?"

Bailey shrugged. "Take the deal or leave it. But if you decide to take it—it will cost you seventy-five quid."

"It was only fifty this morning."

"That was this morning. Besides, I know how wealthy you are—that money means nothing to you."

"You won't get so much as a penny until I have Eddie where I want him." John's hand shot out and closed around Bailey's neck and he squeezed, shutting off the lies. "Have him here tonight as promised, you skinny turd, or the next time I visit, it will be just for *you*."

He released Bailey and turned away without waiting for an answer, his head spinning so wildly that he could barely see: Fast Eddie was alive and he was looking for John. It seemed the old crime lord wanted retribution for killing Des all those years ago.

Apparently, John's past sins weren't in the past, after all.

Chapter 29

London
1818

The evening had been interminable.

Cordelia had decided—as she stood and exchanged idle chatter with the same women she had always conversed with—that these evenings had *always* felt interminable.

But never had she chafed so badly at the boredom.

She'd hoped to see John before she left for the tedious dinner and ball, but Sims had informed her that John would not be home for dinner.

Cordelia knew she should be happy for him and pleased that he wasn't dining alone. Hopefully, he'd gone out to his club with Stephen Worth. Or perhaps he was dining at Worth's house with their other friends.

But instead of being happy, she'd been angry—not at him, but at herself for being so spineless and allowing Ophelia to monopolize her time. She was a newlywed and should be spending this time with her husband, not attending functions from which he had been specifically excluded.

Tomorrow, she would tell Ophelia that she could not help her with the girls.

Cordelia was tired of superficial Season functions and she was tired of London; she dearly missed their parents and wanted to go see them.

She was eager to introduce them to her new husband; they were gentle, kind people who would look past John's intimidating façade and appreciate the loyal, wonderful man beyond the brusque manner.

With that thought to bolster her, she had faced the wretched dinner party, which had finally ended around midnight.

Unfortunately, she returned to Falkirk House—excited to see her husband—only to learn that John was not at home.

That had been hours ago, and she couldn't sleep. Instead, she was pretending to read and waiting for him.

Cordelia yawned and looked at the clock; it was two-thirty, three minutes after the last time she'd looked. She yawned again and rubbed her eyes, which felt heavy-lidded and gritty. Perhaps she might just rest her eyes for a few moments…

Cordelia jolted, awakened from a deep slumber by a loud thud.

She squinted at the clock; it was just after five. She'd not had a quick nap; she'd slept for hours.

There were more sounds beyond the connecting door. Was John only coming home now? What would a man do until this time of the morning?

Poor, naïve Cordelia—what do you think *men do when they stay out until morning?*

Her brother-in-law—the Duke of Falkirk—flashed through her mind. Right behind the duke were images of the dozen or more baseborn children he'd fathered over the years.

Cordelia swallowed several times to rid her throat of the lump that had formed. Is that what she had to look forward to? Illegitimate children and mistresses and—

She seized control of her rapidly spiraling thoughts; she was behaving like a hysterical wife, which she very much hoped she was not.

But she *was* a curious wife, so she slipped on her robe and passed through her dressing room, listening at the connection door. When she heard nothing, she opened the door and tiptoed inside, not wishing to wake him if he'd gone to sleep.

His bed was empty. Cordelia frowned; then what in the world had she heard?

She stared at the empty bed for a long moment, as if she might find answers there, and then shook her head and turned.

Her hand was on the doorknob when a soft grunt come from the direction of the fireplace.

She whirled around and squinted toward the sitting area. "John?"

***

John had hoped to enter his house unnoticed.

He should have known better.

Fredrick was asleep in a too-small chair he'd dragged into the foyer. His eyes had blinked blearily as John entered.

"Mr. Field—"

"Go get some sleep, Fredrick," he said, not ungently. "I'm fine."

The big lad nodded and tried to unwedge himself from the chair. "Yes, sir. Goodnight."

John grunted and trudged toward his chambers.

Rather than go to the dressing room to disrobe—he didn't want to risk waking Cordelia—he stripped to his breeches in front of the fire in the small sitting area.

He tossed his coats and shirt onto the floor—they were fit for the rubbish bin—and lifted his left arm, turning to the side to examine himself in the big mirror over the fireplace. The cut was longer than he'd thought, but only part of it had been deep enough to require stitching.

John was a lucky fool. And an arrogant one for going to the meeting alone. It hadn't been Bailey who'd set a trap for him. No, Bailey's pub had been locked up and dark and silent.

When nobody had come to the door John had finished the job he'd begun that morning and kicked it down. Inside, he'd seen signs of a hasty departure.

He'd been fuming—not paying attention, *yet again*—and had been jumped from behind several streets away from the waterfront.

He grunted with disgust at his stupidity and gingerly lowered himself into an armchair. Truly, he was no longer fit for the streets.

He should stay home from now on. Sims could tie a bib around his neck and feed him gruel like the infant he'd become. What would—

"John?"

John gave a startled yelp and twisted in the chair, hissing when the motion tugged on the wound.

"I'm sorry. I didn't mean to startle you. I—I heard a noise and came to look." Her eyes were enormous in her pale face, and her normally smiling lips were turned down at the corners. "You are home," she said, her words oddly wooden.

"Yes," he agreed, unsure of what she wanted. "I am home."

She nodded and turned to go.

John raised his eyebrows; what had that been about? He shrugged off the thought and lifted one boot, needing to bite his lip to keep from whimpering like a babe.

"I just want to ask you one thing."

Again, he jolted, but at least this time, he didn't make any embarrassing noises.

She wanted to *talk*? Now?

Christ, he could barely lift his foot without sniveling. "Could we talk later, Cordelia? Now isn't really—"

"Were you with your m-mistress tonight?" She blurted the words out so fast they all slammed together, and it took him a moment to untangle them.

Mistress?

He blinked, stupidly wondering if he had accidentally tucked away a mistress somewhere without realizing it.

"Please don't ignore me," she said, mistaking his confused silence for something else entirely.

She'd crossed her arms, an action which pressed the fabric of her nightgown—a lacy thing he had not seen before and approved of very much—against her body.

"Won't you answer me?" she asked as he swallowed the copious moisture that was flooding his mouth.

"Er, I don't have a mistress." He turned to the boot he still held and tugged and then winced.

"You don't?"

"No." He tugged again, harder, and the boot came off. His forehead was cold and clammy from the effort. John placed the boot on the floor with exaggerated care, husbanding what remained of his strength for the next one.

Or perhaps he would just go to bed with one boot on? Who was there to stop him?

"I suppose you were in some brothel."

He turned to stare at her. "Why on earth would you suppose that?"

"My sister told me to expect that. She said all married men have their—their—" She flung up her hands as she searched for the word she wanted.

"Whores?" John suggested

She flinched. “I was going to say *distraction*, but your word is probably more accurate.”

“No, I don't go to whores.” He paused for a second, and then added for good measure, "and I have no intention of acquiring any such *distractions* in the future."

"Really?" The single word pulsed with emotion—disbelief, gratitude, and amazement among the ones he could identify.

"Yes, really."

"Oh. Well. Good, then."

He turned back to his boot, gritting his teeth.

“What is wrong with you?”

"Nothing," he grated.

"No, you're wincing—and grimacing." She was suddenly beside him, and when she saw the plaster on his side, she gasped. “Why—you are *hurt*!"

John didn't have enough strength left to explain that it was minor.

"What happened?"

He didn't have the strength to describe *that*, either.

He was already too ashamed of his idiocy to share it with another person. The fewer people who knew about tonight, the better.

She dropped to her haunches. “Who *did* this to you? Did you care for the wound yourself? Are you sure you cleaned it properly? I will ring for some clean cloths and hot water and—”

John caught her wrist and stopped her when she stood to go. “Stay, Cordelia.”

“But—”

“Please.”

She pressed her full lips together and nodded, obviously reluctant.

And then her gaze moved to his boot. “At least let me help you.”

She did not wait for him to answer, but took his boot heel and then straddled his leg.

“I used to help Papa remove his boots after he would go out on one of his tramps.” She grasped his boot heel in one hand and toe in the other and tugged, bending over more as she did so. The sight of her shapely bottom against her night gown caused blood to roar in his ears.

"There, see how quick and easy that was?" She released his leg and turned to place his boot beside the other. When she would have moved away, he caught her hand again, and this time he pulled her down onto his right thigh.

"Oh!" she said, her spine ramrod straight, her cheeks rosy, and her eyes straight ahead.

"Why are you awake so early?" he asked.

"No particular reason."

She was a terrible liar.

John eased her gown up, using only one hand, the other arm still wrapped around her.

She stared at his hand with a rapt look on her face, as though she'd never seen it before.

"Lift the hem up, Cordelia," he said, once he'd bunched it up to her knees.

She obeyed him with a noisy gulp, her breathing quickening.

"Higher," he said when she stopped just shy of her mound.

She lifted her gown higher, squirming as she exposed her brown curls to his gaze, her knees pressed together, her feet ankle-to-ankle.

He tapped her thigh. "Open for me."

Her body jolted at the quiet command, but she spread her legs a miniscule amount.

John grinned. "Wider—yes, that's good. But maybe even a bit more."

When she'd opened herself enough that he could reach her, he traced the seam of her sex up and down a few times.

She shuddered.

"Shh, I won't hurt you," he promised as he pushed a finger between her pouty lips.

It was his turn to shudder when he discovered wet, swollen heat waiting for him. He rested his forehead on her arm and closed his eyes as he probed her. Good God. She was so ready for him.

She whimpered and spread her thighs wider as he stroked her slit from her entrance to the tight bundle of nerves above it.

John could feel the tension in her muscles as she fought a losing battle, struggling to maintain control of her body against the tide of pleasure that was cresting inside her.

He nudged her arm aside and kissed her through the lacy fabric of her nightgown, sucking and nuzzling the side of her breast, nibbling the sensitive skin above her ribs.

"Relax and let go, love," he murmured, shifting her torso enough that he could take her erect nipple in his mouth and suckle her while still strumming her with his slick finger.

Not until her body went soft and pliant did John breech her. They both groaned with pleasure at the penetration.

"Such a sweet little cunt," he whispered, smirking against the damp fabric plastered to her nipple when she startled and squirmed at the filthy word.

John knew he was a bad, sinful man to corrupt her, but he couldn't make himself behave. He loved the little sounds she made and the bright colors she flushed whenever he said something crudely sexual.

He pumped her tight channel gently, until she began rocking her hips and grinding her pussy against his hand, her body begging for more, harder, deeper.

For several bliss-filled minutes, the only noises in the room were her harsh breathing and the wet sucking sound of his stroking. All too quickly, she shuddered and clenched around him.

"That's right," he urged. "Come for me, Cordelia."

"John!" she cried out against his shoulder, and then bit him, as if to stifle the sounds of her passion, her hips bucking as she rode out her pleasure.

John wrapped his arms around her and held her tightly as she came back to herself, back to awareness.

He could sense the exact moment she remembered where she was and what she'd been doing because her body stiffened and her eyes lifted to his with painful slowness. Even in the low lighting, he could see her flush.

"You must think me wanton."

A smile that could not be stopped stretched his mouth. "Yes. Thank God."

She bit her lower lip, but it could not stop her answering smile. "That is wicked of you, Mr. Fielding."

"I know, Mrs. Fielding."

She gurgled at that. "You should—oh!" She raised her hand to her mouth. "*Look* what I did to your poor shoulder."

It was his turn to chuckle.

"This is no laughing matter—don't you see what I did?" She stroked the bite mark with gentle fingers. "It is… savage."

John glanced at the mute evidence of her passion on his shoulder and his prick—still hard and aching—thrust against his placket.

Cordelia looked down at his eager cock and touched it with the same lightness she'd touched his shoulder.

He wasn't quick enough to stifle the groan that burst out of him and she looked at him with wide, startled eyes. "I'm sorry. I just wanted to…"

She trailed off and John waited, burning to know what she wanted.

"Is it possible to, well, to give you pleasure with my hand? As you have done to me?"

Lust thundered through his body and his shaft throbbed painfully at her innocent yet erotic words.

It was a bloody challenge not to just bend her over the back of the chair and plow into her with all the finesse of a bull in rut, but the last thing he wanted to do was frighten her with the urgency of his need.

Slowly, John. Go very slowly.

"Unbutton me," he said in a voice hoarse with suppressed desire.

Her hands went to his fall and unfastened buttons and catches with nimble efficiency. He lifted his hips off the chair and she stood just long enough to pull down his pantaloons and drawers.

His prick, hard and leaking like a spigot, sprang free, and she made one of those soft noises in her throat that strained his self-control.

John had never been with a woman who didn't know what to do. How should he—

She reached out a finger and touched the bead of moisture.

John bit his tongue hard enough to taste metal, and his entire body tightened.

Cordelia was too intent on exploring him to notice his body's reaction and the next few moments were some of the most ecstatically agonizing of his life. She touched and poked and prodded while he almost chewed off his own tongue.

Finally, when he feared he might go mad, she looked up.

"It is almost like it has a mind of its own."

His head dropped against the back of the chair, and John laughed.

***

It was fascinating—far more interesting than her own private parts. But it also seemed vulnerable. Would not one accidentally knock it about—on the edges of tables or the doors of carriages or other such objects?

It seemed so fragile and was the smoothest, softest skin she had ever felt, even softer than a baby.

The way it was rearing up right now she could see all of it, even where it joined his body, which was almost as interesting as the fat crown on top and the slit, which was weeping. And it jumped when she touched it in certain places. Really, it was quite riveting.

When he'd stopped laughing at her silly comment, she said, "Show me what to do, John."

He took her hand and placed it on the shaft, wrapping his own massive fist around hers and moving their joined fists downward. The thin skin that encased him slid with their stroke, fully exposing the red, bulbous tip.

"I am most sensitive here." He gestured to the area right below the mushroom head and then moved their fists up and the protective skin slid up to his crown.

His grip was almost painfully tight and his eyes locked with hers as he pumped his powerful hips while simultaneously stroking. Looking into his dark, smoky gaze made her woozy, and her breasts and womb felt fuller and ached.

Cordelia now recognized the signs of her own arousal and was astounded by how eager and relentless her body was in its quest for pleasure—and how arousing it was to give *him* pleasure.

His eyes closed, and he released her hand, but the measured thrusting of his hips continued—harder now and faster.

Cordelia worked him just as he'd demonstrated, becoming more confident and defter with each stroke, until he began to buck wildly, his hips driving them both from the chair, until, quite suddenly, he froze, a guttural sound coming from deep in his chest.

She stared down in amazement as jet after jet of pearly liquid covered her fist, his shaft swelling with each spasm, until his hand came up to still hers.

"Too sensitive," he murmured, and then let his head fall against the chair back.

His muscular body went limp beneath her and his breathing fell into a regular, deep rhythm.

Cordelia smiled in amazement; he'd fallen asleep.

***

John must have been exhausted, because he didn't so much as twitch when she left his lap.

After washing her hands in the cold basin of water, she wet a cloth and warmed it in front of the fire before wiping away the evidence of his passion, fearful that her ministrations would wake him.

But he slept on, giving her an unprecedented opportunity to study his naked body.

His breeding organ slumbered along with him, heavy and sated on his muscular thigh. The light from the fire washed him in its glow, making his skin look reddish-gold. He was so *big*. His fingers were easily twice as thick as hers.

The muscles of his shoulders and biceps bulged even when he was at rest, and she lightly traced the blue vein that pulsed beneath the thin skin of his upper arm.

His forearms were heavily roped with muscle, his golden skin littered with old scars and the nail on one finger missing entirely.

Cordelia stroked a cruel-looking wound that was dangerously close to his heart, horrified by the conflict, pain, and suffering he'd endured. His past was so harsh and yet he was so gentle and kind—not just to Cordelia, but to poor simple Fredrick and fragile, ancient Sims, both of whom loved their work and would have been devastated to be discarded.

Her gaze dropped to his six-fingered hand and her mind tried to skitter away from what that meant. But the truth—that John was the baseborn half-brother of Charles, Melissa, and Jane—was undeniable.

Although she didn't know the Duke of Falkirk well—she doubted anyone could truly know such a proud and reserved man—she'd seen several of the children he'd fathered out of wedlock. Although not all of them resembled the duke as much as John did, every single one of them had the distinctive right hand.

Ophelia had never mentioned her husband's many infidelities—she was even prouder than her husband—but his behavior must have enraged her over the years.

Cordelia swallowed as she looked at her husband's distinctive hand. John was probably a constant affront to Ophelia, although he was old enough that he might have been born during the duke's prior marriage. Or perhaps not—since he did not know his age, it was difficult to say.

Still, she would need to keep all that in mind when she became angry at Ophelia's hostility toward him—even though he'd most certainly saved the dukedom.

Cordelia pushed away the unhappy thoughts and stood, covering his big body with his robe. She considered allowing him to sleep, but a bath would be good for his aching body and he could crawl into bed afterward.

Once she returned to her chambers, she rang for a bath to be brought up to his room.

While she waited, she searched for an herbal salve an old woman who lived on the Chelmsford estate had once given her. Mrs. Twicket—or Twickey, as everyone called her—was ancient and had long ago been the nurse to the first duchess, but had lived in her little cottage for as long as Cordelia could recall. The old Welsh woman made many herbal remedies, and this balm was good for fending off infection.

Rather than summon her maid, Cordelia plaited her hair before slipping into one of her older morning dresses, wishing to be comfortable rather than fashionable.

By the time she'd finished dressing, she heard activity next door and knew the servants were setting up the bath. She waited until the murmur of voices ceased and then knocked on the dressing room door.

"Come in."

John was already in the tub, which was in front of the fireplace. The cut on his side was high enough that the water did not disturb the dressing. She could see now, in better light, that whoever had bound the wound knew what they were doing.

"I brought you this." Cordelia stayed near the door, not wishing to intrude.

He fixed her with his dark, almost brooding, gaze. "Come closer."

Cordelia smiled."I believe you need a larger bathtub."

His knees were bent almost to his chest, and water sloshed over the sides even though at least half of his body was not covered.

"This was the biggest of the three."

"It's not big enough. You look like a big frog in a small puddle." She couldn't help laughing.

His eyes narrowed as he stared up at her. "What do you have in your hand?"

"It is an herbal remedy for your cut."

He held out his palm.

When she handed it to him, he grabbed her wrist, his hand moving like a blur and sending the tin clattering across the floor.

Cordelia gasped.

"There is just enough room left in the tub for you," he said.

She shrieked. "No, please! I've just dressed, I'll get wet."

"Perhaps I won't pull you in if you apologize for laughing at me." He gave a suggestive tug when she hesitated.

"I'm sorry! I'm so sorry for laughing at you."

"And?" He pulled her a little closer.

"And *what*?"

"What are you going to do to make it up to me?"

"Wh-what would you like me to do?"

His eyelids lowered into sensual slits, reminding her of what she'd done for him only an hour earlier.

He smirked faintly. "Not that—at least not just yet."

Her body clenched at his suggestive look, and a wave of heat rolled through her. "You are wicked," she murmured.

"I am," he agreed. "You could wash my hair. It is uncomfortable to raise my arms."

Cordelia didn't know if she was relieved or disappointed that he wanted something so… mundane. "Of course."

She unbuttoned the six buttons on each of her sleeves and pulled them up to her elbows. There were two pitchers of water beside the tub, and she knelt and poured a little over his head.

"Too cold or hot?"

"It's good."

Soon she had his hair lathered, marveling at how thick the strands were when compared to her own. She scrubbed the nape of his neck where the hair grew to a point, massaging the taut cords beneath his satiny skin.

"Mmm." His muscles flexed and rippled beneath her fingers.

Cordelia inhaled deeply at the sensual sound, her heart pounding as she allowed her fingers to become bolder and knead his massive shoulders, concentrating on those areas where he made approving noises.

By the time she picked up the second pitcher of water to rinse him, her hands were shaking and her skin was damp and prickly. Who could have guessed that washing somebody's hair could be so very, very *arousing?*

Cordelia was lowering her shirt sleeves when he looked up at her, his gaze hooded "Thank you, Cordelia."

Her breath caught at the unguarded—almost shy—expression on his face and she froze like a stunned hare.

But he wasn't finished shocking her, yet. "If I ring for breakfast in my study, will you join me?"

And that was the moment Cordelia realized that she'd done something that was both frightening and foolish: she had fallen in love with her husband.

Chapter 30

London
1818

A few mornings after the debacle at Fat Bailey's pub, John was reading his paper and putting away vast quantities of food while Cordelia ate her usual breakfast of tea and toast.

She'd been unusually quiet since the night of his injury—well, since the morning after, to be precise.

They'd eaten in his room and she'd asked again about the cut on his side, seeming to accept his explanation that he'd been assaulted by footpads on his way back from a new building he'd been supervising.

"You seem to attract such trouble," she'd mused.

But, after begging him to promise that he would not walk alone after dark, she had left the matter alone. He had not seen her the next two evenings as she'd had functions to attend, but he'd gone to her chambers both nights and she had welcomed him, seemingly as insatiable as he was.

But even as thick and insensitive as John was, he thought she seemed subdued.

"Is aught amiss?" he asked, watching her shred a piece of toast rather than eat it.

"No, it is nothing. I was just thinking of tonight."

He waited.

"We are to dine again at my sister's. Again."

He knew of their plans and waited to see if she had anything else to add. When she did not speak, he turned back to his food.

"I can see I will need to become accustomed to long silences and unreadable looks."

He glanced up to find her smiling, to soften her words.

"I didn't realize there was a question," he said. "As far as I am concerned, our social schedule is a matter for you to decide. You needn't ask my permission before making plans for us. Just give me some notice."

Her eyebrows shot up and her smile grew larger.

Good. He had pleased her. He lifted his loaded fork to his mouth, and they ate in silence for perhaps five minutes.

"Ophelia told me you agreed I should stay in London to help chaperone Melissa and Jane. That is not true, is it?"

John chewed and swallowed before answering. "No."

"Why would she have told me that?"

Because she's a manipulative, controlling harpy.

John doubted she would enjoy hearing that.

"Probably she took my lack of comment as assent." He considered putting the last piece of meat in his mouth, but decided it was too large to do so politely, so he cut it in half.

"Ah, you see the danger in that sort of laconic behavior?" she teased.

John grunted, making her laugh with even more *laconic* behavior, which had been his intention.

"So, you have no preference for what we do?" she asked.

He'd prefer to avoid the duchess's company entirely, but once again, he kept that uncivil response to himself. Instead, he said, "No."

The door opened, and Fredrick entered with another pot of coffee for John.

"May I get you more tea, Mrs. Fielding?"

She smiled up at the footman. "Thank you, but I require nothing else."

Fredrick bowed and left them to their meal.

"He is very gentle and eager to please," she observed once he'd gone.

That was the type of befuddling comment people were forever making in John's presence. What the devil was he supposed to say? *Yes, he is?*

He looked up from his plate to find her staring at him.

"Yes, he is."

Her face relaxed, and she plucked up a piece of toast from the rack and took a bite, rather than tearing it to bits.

Huh. So that was all it took? Three words? Even John could muster three words for most occasions.

She nibbled her toast while he finished the last few pages of the paper.

"I don't want to stay in London," she said a few moments later.

He looked up.

She wasn't looking at him, but at her toast, her expression mulish, as if it had somehow offended her.

He opened his mouth.

"I'm tired of the Season," she added, even more forcefully. "I should like to visit my parents."

This was unexpected news—and very welcome.

And also a splendid opportunity to try out his new Rule of Three. "Today or tomorrow?" he asked.

She gave a startled laugh. "Can we just leave whenever we want?"

"Why not?" He had no pressing business. As for his other activities—his pursuit of Dolan and Fast Eddie—well, he could use a break from all that. Besides, he had two Runners searching for Eddie. He didn't need to stay here to supervise them.

Indeed, it would be safer for Cordelia out of the city—safer for John, too, if he was going to keep behaving like a muttonhead and let himself get attacked every other day. He had a wife to take care of, now, and needed to stay alive to do his job. If the knife from the other night had gone deeper, he would be dead. Of course, that would make Cordelia a wealthy woman who could marry the man of her choosing.

John smirked. While he wanted to make her happy, he didn't want to make her quite *that* happy.

"Don't you wish to know why I have changed my mind?" she asked.

He was about to say *no,* but thought better of it. "Only if you wish to tell me."

"I've wanted to tell Ophelia for days that I don't wish to stay in London, but I've been too much of a coward to face her."

John couldn't fault her for that; he'd go leagues out of his way to avoid having to speak to the woman.

"I have decided to gird my loins and tell her today."

He did not envy her that conversation. The duchess was unused to being thwarted, especially, he guessed, by a younger sister she viewed as a servant-slave.

"You wish to leave tomorrow?" he asked.

She looked up and gave him a vague smile, no doubt thinking about the afternoon ahead of her. “Saturday will be soon enough. That way, we don't have to miss Lady Trentham’s ball.”

John bit back a grimace. He'd been hoping she’d forgotten about the blasted ball.

“Do you like dancing?” she asked, changing subject with lightning speed, as women liked to do.

Did he? Worth had rammed lessons down his throat and John had attended some entertainments back home—when Worth had forced him to—but nothing in England. He'd found it to be a waste of time.

Again, he decided the truth was not the best option. “I've not done it often enough to form an opinion," he lied.

As he'd feared, even that simple statement piqued her interest. “Did you go to many assemblies in America?” She frowned, the action causing a charming crease to form between her eyebrows. “Do they call them that there?”

"I went to functions where people danced, but I don't know what they were called. Worth made me go when I worked for him," he added.

“In Boston?”

“And in New York.”

“New York! That sounds so romantic.”

Romantic would not be the word he would use for the huge, violent, filthy city. Before she could think up any other unanswerable questions, he tossed back the last of his coffee, wiped his mouth with his napkin, and stood.

She glanced up. “Are you sure you do not mind?”

“Mind what?” he repeated blankly. "Dancing?"

She smiled. “No, leaving London so soon. I know you have a business here.”

“Nothing that cannot wait.”

After all, most of his business had been waiting for over twenty years already.

***

Somehow, or other, John found himself engaged to dance every single set at the Countess of Trentham's ball that Saturday night.

He could conceive of no way to get out of it other than sprint from the ballroom and leave his wife behind.

He was positive that Worth was behind it. The man hated to see anyone else relaxing and enjoying themselves if he had to work, and Lady Trentham had made sure that her husband would not run low of partners tonight.

But at least John was finally dancing with Cordelia, now and it was a waltz, a dance he didn't usually like as he felt guilty about putting his scarred face so close to strange women—especially young, easily frightened, ones.

However, he was enjoying this dance a great deal. Far too much, in fact, and his cock was half-hard, a condition that was difficult to hide in pantaloons.

“I have danced every set, John.” Cordelia's cheeks were flushed with pleasure. “I think the same is true for you, is it not?”

"Unfortunately."

She laughed.

"I'm not jesting," he insisted. "Worth is determined to torment me.”

“Are you suffering right now?” Her eyes looked especially green and twinkled with mischief.

He drew her fractionally closer, his hand dropping slightly, until his smallest finger rested in the cleft of her buttocks. “In a completely different way.”

Her eyes grew comically large. “John! Was that a… compliment?”

He cocked an eyebrow at her.

“It was!”

He tried to keep from smiling, but couldn't.

“And a smile to go with it. Stop, or you shall spoil me beyond mending.”

“Are you saying I do not compliment you? Or smile at you?”

She appeared to think his question over. “You compliment me with your eyes—sometimes you smile with them, too.”

“Is it possible for eyes to smile?” he teased, looking down into hers, which seemed to smile all the time.

“Oh yes, I believe it is possible for eyes to communicate all types of things.”

John’s body heated at what he saw in the velvety blackness of her swollen pupils and it was all he could do not to scoop her up and spirit her out to their carriage.

Instead, he calmed himself and whirled her around the dance floor.

"Tomorrow will be an early day," she said.

He looked up from her cleavage, which he had been unapologetically admiring. Was she saying what he hoped she was saying? This was her special night—her first ball where she didn't have to mind two girls—and he couldn't bring himself to suggest leaving early. But if *she* did—

"Would you be terribly disappointed if we left a little early tonight?" she asked.

John gave her the second smile of the evening. "I'll send for the carriage as soon as this dance ends."

***

Cordelia was shameless. Utterly wanton. And rude.

It was unspeakably uncivilized to leave a ball so early, but she had known, when she was waltzing with John, that she had not wished to spend even another minute with any man but him.

Besides, he'd looked positively miserable as he'd stood up with one giggling chit after another.

And so she'd taken pity on him and pleased herself at the same time.

John worked miracles to get their carriage brought around quickly and was handing her into it less than half-an-hour later.

He closed the door, took her by her waist, and swung her into his lap.

Before Cordelia could so much as squeak, his mouth lowered over hers with a hunger that robbed her of all thought. Cordelia eagerly, if clumsily, matched him stroke for stroke, their tongues engaging in an intricate dance.

"Mmmm." One big hand slid up her leg, lingering where her stockings gave way to the skin of her thighs. "Are these the ones with the flowers?" he murmured against her throat.

She laughed at the unexpected question. "Yes, roses."

"You will leave these on later, so I can see them when I spread your beautiful legs and take you," he whispered, quickly finding her opening with a blunt finger and plunging deep inside her.

Cordelia bit her lower lip to keep from crying out.

"You're so beautiful, Cordelia. I couldn't take my eyes off you tonight," he said, working his magic on her body with both his adoring words and clever hands.

Cordelia reveled in his fervent tone, marveling that this was really *her* who was driving this glorious, passionate man mad with desire.

Although he'd never said the words, had she ever felt so loved, so cherished?

If she had, she could not recall it.

***

John wanted to mount her in the carriage, but they were only a few moments from home and he did not want to rush once he was inside her delicious body.

And so, once the final shudders of her climax faded, he reluctantly removed his hand from her silken heat, smiling at the small sound of reproach she made.

"Soon," he promised, kissing her one last time before lowering her onto the seat beside him, where she quickly went about setting her mussed clothing to rights.

The carriage rolled past a streetlamp and he saw her cheeks were red, either from his night beard or from passion or both. He rubbed his jaw; yes, it was scratchy even though he had shaved again before dinner, but then that was over six hours ago. He would shave again before—

The carriage shuddered to a halt and John blinked; they were home already?

Thank God!

John didn't wait for the footman before hopping out and turning to lift her down.

"Drat! I dropped my glove."

John bent to fetch it just as the crack of a pistol filled the air, instantly followed by breaking glass and Cordelia's scream.

He grabbed her hand and yanked her down to the cobble before throwing his body on top of hers.

"Are you shot? Cordelia?" His ears rang from the gunshot, his eyes flickering over the darkened streets, searching frantically for the shooter. "Cordelia," he repeated when she didn't answer. "Are you hurt?"

"John… can't breathe."

He rolled to the side, his gaze moving over her body, looking for blood, before darting back to the seemingly empty street.

"Mr. Fielding?" his coachman called out, the sound of boots hitting the cobbles.

Something flickered across the street—near a large rubbish bin—and John squinted.

"My God, sir! I'm sorry, there was a man layin' in the street, but when I stopped, he—"

"Follow the shooter!" John yelled, pointing. "He ran down that alley—do *not* try to stop him, just see where he goes and report to me. *Run,* dammit!"

The coachman bolted toward the alley, boots clattering as he rapidly disappeared from view.

John turned to look at his wife and cursed; there was blood smeared across her pale skin.

"Fuck!" he hissed, frantically checking her head for wounds, and using all the tenderness of a vegetable shopper inspecting a cabbage.

"I'm fine. I'm *fine*," she assured him. "It was just glass that hit me, not a bullet."

He saw the wounds, then, five or six cuts along one jaw. They were bleeding, but none were deep.

John crushed her to his chest and muttered, "Thank God."

"If you hadn't bent to pick up my glove you—you would be—" she broke off and sobbed, burrowing into him.

If he hadn't bent, he'd be dead.

She pulled away to look at him, her face wet with tears. "It was you they were trying to shoot—wasn't it?"

John didn't answer.

Instead, he helped her to her feet, inspected the seat for glass, and then tucked her into the carriage. "I'll drive us home," he said, not waiting for an answer before closing the door.

Rage bubbled up in his belly like acid as he strode to the front of the carriage.

Yes, they'd shot at him, but they'd hurt Cordelia.

John wouldn't stop until he found whoever had done this.

And when he found them, he was going to kill them.

Slowly.

Chapter 31

London
1818

Please, John, I'm well enough to leave today—I *want* to leave. Everything is packed and ready. I want to go."

Cordelia *needed* to go. Suddenly, she missed her parents desperately, more than she'd done since she'd been a small child.

John stared, his expression brooding and the scars on his face strangely livid, as if the color had drained from the rest of him.

He'd come to her room only briefly last night to ask after her health. Once she'd assured him she was fine—that the cuts were minimal—he'd taken his leave.

Cordelia had waited and waited for him to return. Hours later, when she'd gathered the nerve to knock on the connecting door, she'd discovered he was gone, his bed still made.

She'd barely slept last night, tossing and turning and twisting in the sheets until she'd finally heard movement in his room just after dawn.

And now it was after ten o'clock and she was dressed for traveling and ready to leave. "Please," she said.

"We'll be getting a late start so we shan't get far," he warned.

"That is fine. I just want to go."

John gave a sharp nod and stood. "I'll go speak to the coachman."

Barely an hour later, they were on the road out of London, their departure delayed slightly by a tearful Barker.

"But, guv, I *need* to go."

"You need to do as you're told," John had snapped, for once losing his temper with the stubborn boy.

Barker had looked stricken at drawing his hero's ire.

John's stern face had softened. "We'll only be gone a few weeks, lad, and it will be a holiday for you. You can lie about the house and do nothing but stuff yourself with Cook's cakes and biscuits."

Unconvinced, Baker had sobbed once and then fled to the mews

Cordelia knew John feared for the boy and didn't think it was safe for him to ride on any of his carriages. The only reason Barker hadn't been on his perch the night before was because he'd had a sniffle and Cordelia had insisted that he go back to bed.

She shuddered to think about what might have happened to the boy if he'd been with them.

It was soon clear that Barker was not the only one that John was worried about.

Cordelia and Akers rode in the coach while her husband rode alongside on a massive dun-colored beast that Cordelia had never seen before. The animal was exceptionally ugly, not to mention bad-tempered, if the way it had kicked and lunged at the groom was anything to go by. But she couldn't help noticing that the horse behaved the moment John took his reins.

Their escort included two mounted grooms, another servant beside the coachman, and two on the back box, for *six* male servants, all of them armed.

While John had said nothing to Cordelia, it was obvious that something was afoot—something connected to the attack last night.

To be honest, she didn't want to know what was going on. If that made her a coward, so be it. She could live with that. Perhaps later, once she'd put some distance between herself and the terrifying episode—and London—she might ask him the meaning behind it all.

Cordelia held her book in her lap, unread, and stared out the window to where John rode, his expression as grim as a hangman's. His buckskins were a burnt umber, his coats and boots black. As huge as he was, the dark clothing only served to make him look bigger and more formidable; he was monolithic astride his steed, the only horse she'd ever seen that looked like it was scowling.

What would her parents make of him? Her gentle, bookish father and her sweet, gentle mother?

Ophelia clearly thought him a barbarian—although she'd taken his money readily enough—and Miranda had been too terrified to even look at him. Melissa hadn't seemed to notice him, too absorbed in her own affairs. The only members of her family who'd exhibited any interest in him were Charles and Jane.

And the duke—John's father—what would he think of his son? Not that it was likely he'd emerge from his comatose state to see John, or even know of his existence. But perhaps he already knew about him? After all, he'd created John; what did he make of his son, the ex-convict turned wealthy businessman?

Cordelia sighed. To be honest, she often wasn't sure what to make of her husband herself. Most of the time, he was as easy to see through as a block of stone; his gaze so guarded it reminded her of a window that had been bricked shut.

And yet when they were in bed together…

Cordelia's face burned at the images that flickered through her mind. When they were alone and tangled in each other's arms, he became somebody else—somebody passionate, playful, and hypnotically erotic.

The things he did and said were gloriously shocking.

John glanced at the carriage window just then, as if he sensed her wicked thoughts. Their eyes locked and her heart lurched into a gallop. Cordelia's response to his coal-black gaze was instant and visceral; she squeezed her thighs together to stop the throbbing in her sex, but that only intensified the sensation and made her want him more.

Still expressionless, he turned to face the road.

Cordelia slumped bonelessly against the plush velvet seat, her body hot, sweaty, and wrung out from merely a look.

***

John stopped for the night far earlier than he would have done had he been traveling alone. But, for all her protests, there were dark smudges beneath Cordelia's normally vivid hazel eyes, and she looked exhausted.

He'd cursed himself more than once for giving in to her pleading to travel, but then he hadn't felt good about remaining in London, either.

"Is the room not to your liking, sir?"

John looked down at the sound of the timid voice. Ah, yes, the innkeeper. He'd forgotten all about the man.

"This will serve," he said, not bothering to glance at the tiny room.

"And where should I put your lady wife's maid? Er, normally she would have this room," he pointed out, as if John didn't realize that he'd taken the servant's room—so that he could be closer to Cordelia.

"Put her in the room two doors down, the one you offered me."

"Of course, sir."

"Have a bath brought up for my wife immediately," he ordered. "I'll have mine after she finishes. Have a servant fetch me from the taproom when it is drawn."

"Very good, sir." The innkeeper scuttled away, visibly eager to put some distance between them.

John couldn't blame the man; he'd been in a foul mood since some bastard had almost killed his wife.

He descended the stairs and made his way to the small taproom that was off the dining room. Rather than sit at the bar, John took a corner table that faced the door—a habit of longstanding.

The inn was small but meticulously clean and John had stayed in it several times, as it was conveniently on the way to one of Worth's houses.

"Well, look who has decided to show his face again."

He looked up and blinked at the serving wench, struggling to place her.

She propped her fists on her generous hips and gave him an exasperated look that was only partly feigned. "You don't even remember me, do you, Mr. John Fielding?"

He didn't.

However—judging by the proprietary way her eyes roamed over his body and the fact that she was just the sort of tall, well-padded woman that he normally fancied—John assumed he'd bedded her in the past.

"It's Maggie," she said with a saucy smirk. "I can see that I must've made quite an impression."

What did a man say to *that*? He'd fucked more women than he could count—he suspected Maggie was his match in that way—but he'd never bothered to remember any of them.

She gave an earthy chuckle. "Cat got your tongue?"

"Ale."

Her eyes widened slightly at his terse response, but she laughed again. "Aye, just as talkative as you always were. You want a meal?"

"Just the ale."

She snorted and came close enough to grind her pelvis against his upper arm. "You want dessert later tonight? I can bring it up to yer room after eleven."

John could just imagine Cordelia's reaction to *that.*

"Just the ale."

She sneered, tossed her head, and flounced back to the bar, her lush bottom swinging from side to side.

He found it interesting that his cock didn't so much as twitch as he watched her go. He'd felt the heat of her pussy when she'd rubbed against him and her backside was a thing of beauty, and yet he'd felt nothing, while just thinking about Cordelia's smiling eyes could make him as hard as a poker.

That's because you're a fool.

Yes, he most certainly was. And a careless one, at that; his carelessness had almost gotten the one person in the world he cared about killed.

John clenched his jaws, terror at what might have so easily happened last night curdling his guts.

After taking Cordelia home, he'd returned to Fat Bailey's, not allowing the door—which somebody had hastily repaired after his last visit—to impede him. He'd torn the building to pieces, searching for any information that might help him find the disgraced judge so he could beat some truth out of him.

But there'd been a shocking lack of anything personal. All he'd found were a few pages of newspaper beneath a stained mattress, stories about Bailey's fall from grace a decade earlier. It was true that he'd once been a well-respected judge until his connections with the criminal underworld had landed him in one of the jails where he'd sent so many others.

After sacking Bailey's home and business and finding nothing, he'd returned to the pub where he'd talked to Jemmy Sharp. But no amount of money or threats had convinced the bartender to share any information about Sharp *or* Bailey.

It was as if somebody had shone a light on the nastiest, darkest places in the city and all the roaches had run for cover.

Before leaving town, John had hired two more Runners—for a total of four—arranging for Riggs and another man to trail behind the carriage at a discreet distance, just on the off chance that somebody followed them from London.

Meanwhile, the two Runners who remained in London searching for Bailey or Eddie would send any new information to John via messenger.

It might take a while, but he would bloody well get to the bottom of this mess.

The bartender, rather than the serving wench, approached his table with his pint.

Good. The last thing he wanted was more taunting and pouting from Maggie.

John drank off half the pint in two gulps, sighing with contentment when he lowered the glass. It had been a tension-filled afternoon; all day long he'd expected attackers to leap out of the trees or emerge from ditches.

Nothing like that happened, of course, especially not with seven armed men surrounding the carriage. Still, the anxiety had taken its toll.

He'd clearly disturbed something nasty and dangerous by poking around and looking for Dolan. John knew he should cease all his snooping—for Cordelia's sake—but something told him that his unknown assailant would keep coming for him even if he stopped searching.

Maybe that was just something he told himself to justify what he wanted to do.

He turned the pint around and around on the table, leaving rings of condensation.

It was a battered old table, but somebody had expended effort and beeswax to give it a pleasing veneer. Not unlike John, with his expensive clothing to cover his battered, scarred body—not that any amount of polish or money would ever disguise the fact that he was from the gutter. Sometimes he wondered why he even bothered. At first, he'd looked after his appearance because he worked for Worth, and Worth insisted on certain niceties.

Now he kept up appearances, so he didn't shame his wife. He couldn't do anything about the scars or the unseemly bulk of his body, but at least he could dress himself decently.

His wife.

The words alone were enough to get him hard.

John had wanted her desperately last night, as if sheathing himself in her warm, welcoming body was the only way to convince himself that she was safe.

It had almost torn him in half to leave her unmolested in her bed.

But he ached for her and wasn't sure he could deny himself the comfort of her body two nights running, no matter how much she might need her privacy and rest.

"You're a selfish idiot," he muttered beneath his breath. The woman had just been shot at and terrified to within an inch of her life. Because of him. She deserved some time to heal without John humping on her leg like a frenzied cur.

He scowled and squeezed his cock hard enough through his buckskins to subdue it.

And then he shoved all thoughts of his wife, her body, and his needs into a room in his head and slammed the door.

Somehow, John suspected it wouldn't be so easy to *keep* the door shut.

***

John held back from all the embracing and kissing and chirping going on between Cordelia and her diminutive parents, momentarily reminded of the little people in *Gulliver's Travels.*

For some reason, he'd not expected them to be quite so old, even though he knew the duchess was a good fifteen years older than Cordelia.

Although John saw no resemblance between the slight, snowy-haired Pages and their own children, Mr. Page and his granddaughter, Jane were remarkably similar. Or perhaps that was more the spectacles they both wore and their identical expressions of studious intelligence and forbearance, which said they were only tolerating socializing until they could get back to their books.

All too soon, the fragile-looking pair turned to John.

To say there was fear in their faces as they stared up at him would be too strong, but it was clear they were apprehensive of the scarred giant in their midst.

But then, who wasn't?

"I'm sorry, Mr. Fielding," Mr. Page said, stepping forward. "It was rude of us to ignore you, but it has been some time since we've seen our daughter. Please call me Adam, and this is my wife, Christine."

John knew that smiling wasn't a good idea, so he merely bowed and fell back on his trustworthy *Rule of Three*. "Call me John," he said, wishing that he didn't sound so very *harsh*.

"You must call me Mother Page," Mrs. Page piped up, her eyes bright and brave as she peered up at him, like a tiny finch facing down a huge black raven.

John glanced at Cordelia to see if her mother was serious.

When she gave an imperceptible nod, he turned back to the older woman. "Er, it would be an honor, Mother Page."

He imagined Stephen Worth howling with laughter at this exchange.

Adam looked at John's army of servants and his eyes widened, as if he'd only now noticed them. "I'm not sure we'll have room—"

"The servants—except for Akers—will take the carriage and horses to stay at the inn. Only John's mount will stay here."

Adam nodded to an ancient male servant. "Richard can take your horse to our stables and see to him, John."

John could just imagine how that would go over. His savage horse bit and kicked every single person who came near him. Well, not John, but that was only after they'd reached an accommodation.

"One of my grooms will see to him before they go," John said quickly.

Wilson, his head groom, took the stallion's bridle and deftly pulled back when the beast lunged and snapped at him.

Mrs. Page and Cordelia gasped, and Mr. Page chuckled. "Spirited, is he?"

A quarter of an hour later, they were settled in their room—as in singular.

Apparently, they were to share a chamber, something that both surprised and pleased him.

As Cordelia and her maid disappeared into the dressing room, John looked out the window, his attention not so much on the scenery as the number of places where assailants could hide.

The two Runners would keep an around-the-clock watch on Garry Court. He'd specifically sought out men who'd been raised in the country, aware that lurking successfully in the city and doing so in the country required different skills.

Even if the men knew country ways, they'd inevitably be noticed as strangers. But then so would anyone his adversary was likely to hire and send after him.

"Thank you, Akers, that will be all until later."

John turned from the window at the sound of his wife's voice. Cordelia wore one of the new gowns he'd selected at the modiste's—a greenish blue silk that suited her to perfection. It was probably too fancy for country dining, but it was the plainest of the new dresses.

"That looks well on you," he said, wanting to strip it off her.

Her cheeks flushed. "Thank you. I'm sorry about the room—if you wish to have one of your own, I can—"

"I don't want to put your parents out."

She nodded, her expression still tense, and he knew she wanted something more.

"I hope my restlessness will not keep you from your sleep," he said.

"No, I am usually a sound sleeper," she said.

"But you have not been sleeping well since the attack," he guessed.

"I haven't."

Guilt and anger—neither far from the surface these days—roiled in his belly.

"I sleep better when you are in my bed," she blurted.

John's head whipped up and his mouth opened, but no sound emerged.

She dropped her gaze, her cheeks so dark she looked to have been burnt by the sun. "I'm sorry, I didn't mean to—"

"So do I—sleep better with you, that is."

She blinked. "You do?"

John nodded, ignoring the part of his mind that was telling him he sounded like a fool and a weakling to admit such a thing.

Well, so what if he sounded like an idiot? He was one.

He hesitated, and then decided: *why the hell not?* and added, "I've only stayed away from you the last few nights because I thought I might disturb your rest."

"But I like it when you disturb my rest—" She bit her lower lip and rolled her eyes. "I mean—"

"I know what you mean." John felt a rare smile pulling at his mouth. "So, this is where you grew up."

She nodded, visibly relieved at the change of subject. "Yes, and this was actually *my* room when I lived here."

The room was a soothing blend of greens and blues and he should have guessed she had a hand in decorating it.

She came to stand beside him at the window. "You cannot see it from here, of course, but Chelmsford Park is on the other side of those trees—almost five miles from here."

"How did your sister meet the duke?"

"It is quite a romantic tale," she said, smiling. "She'd been riding and her horse pulled up lame. The duke found her and brought her back to Garry Court on his horse."

"She was riding on his land?"

"He owns almost all the land in these parts, so he allows the local populace to use some of it. And of course, the hunt trails are on his property."

"Does your sister hunt?"

"She has always been hunting mad, and Papa kept a horse for her. He couldn't afford the hunters she keeps now, of course." Cordelia bit her lip, and he could almost hear what she was thinking—that the duke couldn't afford those hunters, either.

But John could.

"She rode with the Chelmsford pack even back then," Cordelia went on. "When His Grace noticed her skill, he allowed her to ride his own hunters because he said he hated to see such a skilled rider without a worthy mount."

Not to mention the fact that Ophelia Page must have been a ravishing young woman—something his father was known to collect the way other men collected paintings or livestock.

"The duke was most eager for Ophelia to continue hunting after they married since his first wife had not enjoyed the sport, a fact which apparently displeased His Grace greatly."

"You knew his first wife?"

"I vaguely remember seeing her only once, not long before she had her baby."

"The one who died in some sort of drowning accident?"

"Yes. It was a terrible, both the nanny and baby died in London."

John had read all there was to read about it—not much—in his exhaustive search of the duke's past.

"Ophelia was devastated."

John frowned. "What do you mean?"

"She was the one who brought the baby to London because she doted on him so and didn't wish to leave him behind. She was pregnant, herself, at the time."

John knew the duke's first wife had died not long after giving birth to their only child but he'd not realized the two marriages were so close in time.

He turned to look out the window. "How long after the duchess's death did he remarry?"

"It was less than a year, if that is what you are asking," she said rather tartly. "But he needed a mother for his child." She paused and then added, "There was nothing going on between them before they married, John."

He turned to her. "I never implied there was."

"I'm sorry, of course you didn't. It's just that there were ugly rumors at the time—I remember hearing them, although I didn't understand what they meant until later. The duke allowed several people to exercise his hunters, but you know how people can be—they only noticed one of those people: the pretty young woman." She sighed, a fond smile on her face. "Ophelia at seventeen was—well, she was surpassingly lovely."

John believed it; the duchess, at almost fifty, was dazzling. Not that her beauty would ever be enough for him to overlook the fact that she was a grasping, cold-hearted bitch.

"Ophelia was so ill with grief over the baby's death that we were all concerned she might not carry to term. As things turned out, she had a stillbirth, and it took several more tries before she delivered Charles. We didn't think he would live, either; he was such a tiny, sickly baby. Only Jane was robust, but Ophelia almost died during the delivery and the doctor counseled against more children. Nine times she was brought to bed," Cordelia said, more to herself than to him. "It took its toll."

John understood what she was trying to say to him: that those tragedies—combined with a husband who was incapable of being faithful—were part of why the duchess was so cold and hard.

A faint bell sounded somewhere.

"Ah, it is time for dinner," Cordelia said, grinning up at him. "My mother had to institute the use of a bell because my father always missed mealtimes. Are you ready to go down?"

"Of course," he said, inwardly gritting his teeth at the thought of making empty civil conversation with strangers.

It would be a long, long two weeks.

Chapter 32

Garry Court
1818

Before his marriage, John's early morning rides had been the high point of his day.

Now, however, he found it increasingly difficult to pry himself out of his wife's bed and leave the warmth of her body behind.

A few mornings after they'd arrived, John was creeping from their room when Cordelia's voice stopped him.

"Are you going riding?" she asked, yawning as she pushed up onto one arm, her other clutching the bedding over her bare chest.

"I am."

"I would like to go with you sometime."

"You ride?" He felt like an idiot. Of course, she rode; women of her class were practically raised in the saddle.

She nodded, her hair a chestnut tangle around her face, her eyes still heavy with sleep.

Christ, but she was stunning!

Although he'd made love to her each night, he'd done so quietly and quickly—extremely aware that they were in her father's house—rather than in his usual fashion, which involved making her cry out as loudly, and as often, as possible.

"What sort of rider are you?" he asked.

The way the color flared in her cheeks told him exactly what memory his question evoked.

He couldn't resist teasing her. "Do you prefer a vigorous ride—until your mount is lathered and winded? Or are you more interested in something slow and relaxing?"

Her jaw dropped, but—just when he thought she would duck beneath the covers—she surprised him. "I prefer to ride hard and break a sweat." Her smile grew. "And I like a big, powerful hack beneath me."

John groaned and gripped his cock, which filled so quickly at her words that it left him lightheaded. "That was very naughty, Cordelia."

She grinned, clearly pleased with what she'd done to him.

He hesitated for only a second before going to the bedroom door and locking it.

"John?" Her voice—higher than usual—vibrated with interest and excitement. "What are you doing?"

He shoveled in more coal, poked the embers until heat rippled the air and then adjusted the big wing chair across from the fireplace, glancing a few times at the big mirror over the mantle as he did so.

"Why are you moving furniture, John?"

He ignored her question, not stopping what he was doing until he'd positioned everything the way he wanted it.

When he was done, he turned to his wife, who'd pushed up higher to watch.

"Come here."

He turned, not bothering to see if she obeyed, and lowered himself into the chair.

The rustling behind him told him she'd paused to don her robe.

Good. He'd enjoy making her take it off.

John closed his eyes and relaxed his body, savoring the ache in his balls, the throbbing in his shaft, imagining what he was going to do to her. Imagining her reaction.

He felt the air shift around him and opened his eyes to find her standing in front of him, staring down at his groin.

His dressing gown had slipped open, baring him from stem to stern. His cock, already hard, throbbed under her curious gaze.

John spread his thighs, the motion pulling the robe open wider, the cool satin sash slithering over his prick and balls, the touch light and tantalizing.

"Take off your dressing gown."

She startled at his abrupt command but tugged clumsily at one of the slim ties—there were five in all—that closed the garment, not lifting her gaze from his groin.

He smoothed a hand over his chest, pinched one of his nipples hard and hissed in a breath.

Her lips parted and her breathing sped up as he stroked down the hard ridges of his belly, grunting when he brushed the leaking head of his cock.

"John," she said, the word breathy and choked.

He wrapped a fist around his aching shaft, groaning as he slowly pumped himself, enjoying the way her hands shook and fumbled with the last of the ties.

She shrugged the robe off her shoulders, and it slid to the floor.

"Christ, you're gorgeous," he muttered, releasing his cock. "Come sit on my lap."

Her already flushed cheeks darkened, but she quickly obeyed, turning to the side, as if to balance her lush bum on one thigh.

"No—straddle me. Put both your legs over mine and face away, your back to my front." John brought his knees together before gesturing for her to do as he bade.

Her brow furrowed adorably. "This is most… unusual," she said, her gaze darting from his face to his lap a few times.

John smirked as he thought about just how unusual it was about to get.

She lowered herself gingerly, sitting just the way he'd wanted, her shoulders tense, spine rigid. He snaked an arm around her soft belly and pulled her back until his shaft was sandwiched between his abdomen and her lower back.

Her body jerked a time or two, but finally her muscles relaxed.

John spread his thighs, spreading hers in the process.

"Oh, my goodness!" She scrambled to pull her legs together, but he slid his palms around her lush thighs to keep her from closing them, easily holding her immobile as he spread her wider and wider.

"But, er, John, this is—" she gasped, no doubt looking down and getting one hell of an erotic picture.

"Lean back against me, Cordelia."

She gulped and stiffly obeyed.

John slid down lower in the chair until he could see their reflection in the mirror over the mantle.

He gave a low, animal grunt at the sight. Great. Bloody. Hell.

Cordelia's head was still bent, her gaze obviously riveted to her spread sex.

When she tried to cover herself, John swiftly caught her hands and pinned them easily between his palms and her thighs.

She twisted to look at him.

"No, sweetheart, don't look at me. Look straight ahead—at the mirror."

Her head whipped around and her eyes bulged when she met his in the glass, her cheeks a fiery red.

John chuckled and prepared to shock her even more. He released her hands just long enough to lift her and notch his cock between the spread lips of her sex, groaning when he pulled her back down, the feel of her hot, wet flesh on the thin skin of his shaft heavenly.

"There, that's better."

She stared, entranced, at where his big ruddy shaft nestled between the delicate petals of her sex.

"Just like a flower," John murmured, pumping his hips slowly and stroking his length between her slick, swollen lips. He nudged her tight little bud with his crown, the sensual friction making her gasp and shiver.

"Take me in your hand, Cordelia."

Again, she met his gaze, her eyes round with wonder.

He nodded, as if she'd spoken. "Do what I say."

Her fingers trembled, as light as a feather on his shaft.

John grunted and thrust, chasing her touch. "Grip me harder, love, squeeze me."

Her fist clenched—probably from shock—causing moisture to bead at his slit.

"Ah, yessss." He bucked his hips, pumping his sensitive crown into the tight tunnel of her fist while his shaft rubbed against her sex.

"See how lovely you are," he murmured, his hands free to caress her magnificent breasts now that he didn't need to keep her pinned and open. Indeed, she had spread her thighs wider so that she could watch what she did to them.

"Do you like watching, Cordelia?"

She swallowed noisily, her expression hungry and her eyes dark with desire. "I do," she admitted in a gruff voice, and then bit her lip and dropped her gaze, suddenly shy.

John smiled, slid an arm around her waist and lifted her until his slick crown rested against her tight opening. "Hold me steady, darling. I want to be inside you."

Her hand stilled, and John lowered her with torturous slowness.

"Good lord," he groaned, as his thick shaft disappeared into her body. "I've never seen anything so beautiful in my entire life."

Cordelia cut him a quick, startled look before dropping her gaze back to where they were joined, clearly as mesmerized as he was.

Once he was buried to the root, he gave them both a moment to adjust to the exquisite pleasure.

"Use your hand to feel where we are joined," he urged, when she couldn't seem to look away.

She gave him such a scandalized glance he chuckled. "Touch both of us," he said. "I want to watch."

And, by God, she did exactly that, her slim fingers shaking and tentative at first, but her touch quickly growing more confident when she realized how much pleasure it yielded.

Her stroking moved from her body to his and John thought his head would explode when she caressed his tight sac, cutting him another startled look, this one accompanied by a shy smile. "You feel like a furry animal here."

He barked a laugh and then almost shot out of the chair when her hand slipped to the sensitive spot behind his balls.

She jerked her hand back. "Did I hurt you?"

"No—no, not at all." He cleared his throat and confessed, "I'm perhaps, er, a little too excited." That was an understatement; he was dangerously close to embarrassing himself.

Her smile grew into a grin. "John Fielding! Are you blushing?"

"Of course not," he said, shamelessly distracting her with a sharp thrust of his hips.

She gasped.

"Did you like that?" he asked.

She nodded and watched him with heavy-lidded eyes.

So, John did it again, and again, lifting her a little as he withdrew and then bringing her down to meet each upstroke, mesmerized by the sight of his prick moving in and out of her body.

It didn't take long before his thrusting became less controlled, and he knew he'd not last much longer.

"Yes, John," she whispered, her inner muscles fluttering.

Only at the last moment did John recall where he was. Instead of shouting out his pleasure as he sheathed himself to the hilt, he bit his tongue, his body jerking soundlessly as his cock swelled and flexed inside her, filling her with his seed.

Cordelia shuddered and shook as she gave in to her climax, her inner muscles squeezing his pulsing shaft and milking him dry.

John's heavy eyelids threatened to close, but he forced them open and slid his arms around her body and held her close, trailing grateful, heated kisses down the tender knobs of her spine.

For one endless, charged moment, their eyes met in the mirror and John swore that her piercing gaze cut straight to his soul.

He lowered his forehead to her back and squeezed his eyes shut, but still a hint of moisture leaked from the corners.

What the hell was wrong with him? Why did he feel as if his chest was too small to hold his heart?

***

Three mornings later, John woke Cordelia up at dawn.

That, in and of itself, was not an unusual occurrence, but what happened after they'd enjoyed each other's bodies was.

"Get up and get dressed to ride—a horse," he added with a smirk. "Meet me down in the stables in thirty minutes." And then he'd rolled out of bed and disappeared into the dressing room.

Cordelia had sputtered at his domineering order, but—curiosity eating at her—she'd scrambled to obey.

John's dun stallion was already saddled when she reached the small stable, and she paused in front of the ill-tempered beast.

"Hello," she murmured.

The stallion—she hadn't heard his name—put both his ears back, whickered softly, and stamped one huge hoof.

She held out her hand, flat and palm up. "You're as grouchy as your master, aren't you?"

The horse tossed its head, but didn't lunge or bare its teeth, so she gently stroked his velvety nose with her palm.

The stallion froze and so did she, both of them as still as statues. She'd not yet put on her gloves, and his whiskers tickled her skin.

After a long moment, he nickered and gently lipped her.

"There, that's nicer, isn't it?" She rubbed his nose and then slid her hand beneath his jaw. "I don't think there is anything quite as lovely as a horse's nose," she confided, stepping closer to use her second hand to scruff him between his ears when he lowered his head. "Except maybe a horse's chin. People will tell you that dog noses are better, but I disagree."

He gave a sharp toss of his head—as if to scoff at the notion—and Cordelia laughed.

***

John froze at the sight that met his eyes: his wife had not one hand, but two, on the Hell Beast's head—dangerously near his mouth.

Cordelia looked up and saw him, smilingly unaware of the pain and possible mutilation that awaited her only inches away.

"He's delightful, John. What is his name?"

"Cordelia, step back—slowly," he added softly when she looked worried.

Once she'd walked far enough away that the stallion couldn't reach her if he lunged, John sagged with relief.

"What is wrong?" she asked when he slid an arm around her and moved her even farther from the horse's teeth.

"He's not friendly."

"That's not true, he was very—"

The Hell Beast saw Wilson approaching with Cordelia's little gelding and lashed out. It was only because Wilson was accustomed to the stallion's ways that he could avoid a nasty bite.

"Oh, goodness," Cordelia murmured, looking concerned. "Why, he was so sweet a moment ago."

He had been—John had witnessed it. Perhaps the beast was coming up with a new strategy.

"What is his name?"

John could hardly tell her he called him Hell Beast, so he shrugged. "He doesn't have one."

"Did you just get him?"

He sighed, already knowing where this was going. "I've had him since coming to Britain."

"That's terrible! No wonder he is so hostile and angry. Every creature deserves a name." The look she was giving him was the look most people reserved for murderers and rapists.

"Fine. Name him." He gestured the gray. "You can name this one, too—because he's yours."

Cordelia suddenly noticed the horse Wilson was holding. "Why, he's a *darling*. Did you get him for me, John? Where did he come from?"

John answered her last question. "I sent word to the Duchess of Wake and told her what I was looking for. She operates a stud operation and is a fine judge of horseflesh so she had one of her grooms bring him here for you."

"She is so kind—and so are you. Thank you, he's lovely."

The next few minutes were taken up with cooing and petting, and John took the opportunity to lead the Hell Beast a few feet away and have a little chat. "You bite her, kick at her, or even look sideways at her and I'll have your balls, my lad—understand?"

The Hell Beast gave him a dismissive sneer and pawed the ground, a reaction that told John he'd have to watch the temperamental stallion closely.

Ten minutes later—after his wife had thanked him profusely, embarrassing John and amusing Wilson no end—they were on their way.

"You'll have to lead because I don't know the area well," he said.

"The path I'll take us on will lead us through the prettiest part of the duke's property."

John just grunted, even though his scalp tingled at the thought of going so near his father.

"You'll be able to get a glimpse of Chelmsford Park this way."

He didn't tell her he'd already seen the house once—both the outside *and* inside—not long after he'd returned to England, he'd made a pilgrimage to see the home of the man who'd thrown him away like rubbish.

Back then, the duke had still been healthy and fit and living in London with his wife and children, and a pretty little auburn-haired opera dancer conveniently tucked away.

While the duke and his family were absent from their country estate, John had employed his rusty housebreaking skills. The opulence of the ducal residence was breathtaking. Even Worth's magnificent homes couldn't compare when it came to ancient grandeur.

The duke possessed all that—and more besides—and yet John had grown up in squalor and his mother had died in poverty, his grandmother murdered by a thief for her scissors.

"—if you don't, John."

He turned at the sound of his name. "I'm sorry?"

"I was just saying that I'll understand if you don't want to see Chelmsford."

"Why is that? Do you think it will be painful to see the place where my father lives?"

She recoiled slightly at his tone.

This was the first time the subject had come up since she'd mentioned it that day in Hyde Park. What was there for either of them to say on the subject?

And yet, when she remained silent, John felt compelled to speak. "I came here once before."

"When?"

"After I first returned; I wanted to see where he lived."

"Oh. We might have met, then."

"No, the family was in London."

"Ah, this was before he took ill."

"Yes."

"Did you—is it true—" she stopped, sighed, and shook her head.

"Did I purposely lure the duke to invest his money in a scheme that was set up to fail?"

She nodded.

"Yes."

They had to ride single file for a few moments and John stared at her stiff shoulders, wondering if he'd just doomed himself in her eyes.

He told himself that he didn't care if he had.

But that was a lie. Somewhere along the line, he'd come to care more about Cordelia's opinion than his own hunger for revenge.

Oh, how Worth would laugh and laugh, if he knew.

"I understand," she said a few moments after they were back on the wider trail.

"You understand what?"

"Your desire for revenge."

"You do?"

"Do you think I am without envy, jealousy, or baser emotions, John?"

"I've not seen any sign of them in you."

She laughed.

"What?" he asked.

"I was so envious of my sister for years that I could scarcely bear to visit her even though she lived a scant five miles from me."

"You were envious of *the duchess*?"

"You sound so surprised."

"I am."

"Why? She is beautiful, accomplished, well-respected, and she is a duchess."

He shrugged.

"Oh no, you don't get to escape that easily. I want your words, not shrugs."

"I'm not sure you want to hear my words about your sister."

"I know she is arrogant and can appear cold—"

"She *is* cold," John cut in. "I've seen the way she looks at Charles—as if he were a chess piece that she is willing to sacrifice. I saved him from Miss Bowles, but his mother will find another—just as unsuitable—heiress for him to marry."

"She *can* be cold, but she loves her children and only wants—"

"That is not my idea of love," he retorted, annoyed by the raw emotion he heard in his own voice. Christ! He sounded like a fatuous fool.

They rode in silence for a while, and when Cordelia finally spoke, it was to talk about benign subjects like local flora and fauna.

When they approached a low bridge stretched over a pretty stream, John's horse strained at the bridle. "Is that what you want?" he asked the horse, speaking out loud without thinking.

Cordelia looked over at him and raised her eyebrows.

John's face heated at getting caught talking to his horse and he hastened to explain. "He likes water, so we'll meet you on the other side."

With very little encouragement, the Hell Beast bolted down the bank and frolicked in the stream like a foal, kicking and jumping and sending water diamonds flying.

He could hear Cordelia's laughter as he allowed the stallion to gambol a moment longer before saying firmly, "That's enough—we can come back later and I'll let you act like a fool when nobody is watching."

Cordelia was grinning when they climbed the shallow bank. "Did he get you wet?"

"Only a little."

"I think I have a name for him."

"Oh?"

"Morvac'h."

He squinted. "Say again?"

"Morvac'h, it's Breton for *sea horse*. There is an ancient tale—my father told us the story when Miranda and I were little—but I can't remember much other than the horse's name. I'm sure he'd recite the poem for you if you like."

John imagined being forced to endure hours of poetry and ignored that last comment.

Instead, he tried out the name, "Morvac'h."

He was amused when the Hell Beast's ears flickered. "You like that, do you?"

The horse whickered, and both Cordelia and John laughed.

"There is your answer," she said.

"All right, then—Morvac'h, it is."

"There is a meadow just ahead, if you and your sea horse wish for a gallop?"

"I could do with a bit of a run," he admitted.

He was more interested in watching Cordelia than racing her, impressed by her elegance and ease in the saddle. The little gelding was perfect for her—a bit more spirited than she was probably used to, but they could grow together.

While John had always enjoyed his solo morning rides, he suspected—as he watched Cordelia fly across the meadow—that he'd enjoy them even more from now on.

***

Two mornings later, Cordelia woke before John and barely made it to the basin on her dressing table before voiding her stomach.

"Cordelia?"

She looked up from the basin to find John crouched beside her, his body naked and warm in the cool morning air, his pitch-black eyes creased with worry. "You are ill. I'll go fetch a doctor—"

Cordelia set a hand on his chest and shook her head.

And then promptly threw up again.

John slid his arms beneath her and picked her up, the basin still clutched to her chest.

Once he'd deposited her on the bed, he left and then quickly returned with a damp cloth.

"Thank you," she muttered, using it to wipe her mouth before setting the basin aside.

"No, I should keep it near," she said when he would have taken it away.

"What is wrong? Is it something you ate? Perhaps the oysters—"

She couldn't help laughing.

He looked so affronted by her amusement that it only made her laugh harder.

"Cordelia? Are you—is there—"

"I'm with child, John."

His jaw dropped, and his expression of astonishment was so adorable it set her off again.

"Are you quite sure? Shouldn't it take longer?"

"What? You don't believe you've been doing a thorough job?"

He goggled, his sun-darkened cheeks turning brick red. "Are you *sure*?" he asked again. "We've not even been married a month."

"I'm sure."

She had finished her courses a little less than a week before their wedding night. A midwife had once told Ophelia that was the most fertile time of a woman's cycle. It appeared that was correct.

She smoothed a hand over her roiling belly.

"How is it that you know?" he asked in a strangely hushed voice. "Is it—can you already feel it, er, her or him?"

The foolish question sent her into the whoops and he looked so perplexed and wounded that she just laughed harder.

He shot to his feet. "I'll fetch your maid," he said over his shoulder as he hurried from the room.

Cordelia hugged herself, so filled with joy she thought she might explode. She was pregnant with John's baby—could her life get any better?

***

John rode Morvac'h until they were both sweaty and winded, and still his thoughts whirled chaotically.

Cordelia was pregnant; John would be a father.

Why was he so surprised by that information? She was right—they *had* made love a remarkable number of times in the past weeks.

But it still felt like it had happened quickly; after all, they'd only been married twenty-seven days.

John's ignorance of the process—which had obviously amused Cordelia to no end—had shocked him. But then there was no reason for him to know about such things, was there? He'd never been around a pregnant woman before—well, other than Lily, and he'd never seen her naked, so he did not know how she'd looked. Not that Cordelia looked any different; her belly was still soft and gently swelled. How did women know these things?

Cordelia is pregnant.

The words rang out in his head and he realized he was grinning.

"I'm an idiot."

Morvac'h snorted, as if in agreement.

He desperately wanted to share his news with somebody. But who? There was Worth, of course; the man already thought he was responsible for John's marriage since he'd seated them together at his dinner party. No doubt he'd like to claim credit for his child, too.

John laughed at the thought.

Suddenly, he wished like hell that Worth was there, riding beside him. He'd never had a damn thing to say to the man in the past, but now—

The *bang* and searing pain in his scalp were almost simultaneous.

John's body knew what to do before his brain had categorized the sound as a gunshot and he leaned low over his horse while calculating the damage he'd suffered to his head—it felt like a graze—and urging the stallion into a gallop, which wasn't hard since the horse was already terrified.

Morvac'h's enormous body jolted when the second shot rang out. This bullet took John in the shoulder, embedding itself in the meat.

Why couldn't it have taken my left side?

He laughed like a maniac at the pointless thought and flexed his arm; it hurt like hell and was bleeding like a bastard, but he could still use it.

The next shot missed him entirely, striking the trees beside the path, sending leaves and splintered wood flying and giving Morvac'h—who was already running flat out—a burst of speed.

John reached for the small pistol he kept tucked at his lower back.

"Dammit," he muttered when the gun snagged on the strap that held it. He tugged hard enough to tear the leather and the damned pistol slipped from hand, which had become slippery with blood from the shoulder wound.

John cursed and ducked beneath a low-lying branch just in time to avoid being brained.

How many damned shooters were there? One man with several guns? Several men? One man who could load a pistol with inhuman speed?

What the hell did it matter?

Morvac'h had to slow to take a corner and two more shots zinged, one stinging his side in what felt like another flesh wound.

John's shoulder throbbed as the bullet wound made itself known. He needed to get off the damn path before he ran into a tree. His best bet was to head for the main road.

Thank God the Runners were watching Garry Court, day and night; Cordelia would be safe.

The rush of relief that hit him at that thought was so strong he almost let go of Morvac'h's reins. Only the horse's wild, angry neighing shook him from the strange daze that seemed to be descending on him.

"Good boy," he muttered drunkenly.

Why was he so groggy? He shouldn't be losing that much blood.

And why did his throat hurt?

He reached up to feel the source of the pain and hissed. When his hand came away it was bloody.

Christ, he'd taken another hit without realizing it.

Morvac'h jerked abruptly, lunged off the path, and he felt the horse's massive muscles bunching.

He's going to jump! John's brain screamed right before he was flying, the feeling of weightlessness magical.

The landing, however, felt like a bomb exploding in his head, blinding him with white spangles of light followed by bone-deep pain.

He heard himself cry out and slid to one side.

"Can't fall," he mumbled, burying his fingers in the stallion's mane.

Morvac'h's body bunched, and he jumped again.

This time, everything went dark when he landed.

Chapter 33

Garry Court
1818

Cordelia did not truly become worried until dinner.

John was a lot of things—surly, uncommunicative, and reserved—but he was never purposely discourteous.

"He would not miss dinner," she told her father, after she'd learned from Wilson that John hadn't returned from his morning ride.

Her father's pale cheeks darkened. "I'm sorry, Cordelia. I should have noticed he wasn't here. But you know how I get… "

Yes, she knew how he was when he got caught up in a book.

"I will send Richard to the inn, unless—"

"Wilson has gone and will organize a search if John is not in the village."

He chewed his lip, a gesture she'd inherited from him. "Do you think he might have gone somewhere? Perhaps to visit a friend?"

"He doesn't know anyone around here—" she broke off and frowned; surely John wouldn't have gone to Chelmsford to see the duke? The doctor and nurses her sister had engaged didn't even allow his children in for an unsupervised visit. Certainly, they'd never admit a stranger to see their patient. Would they?

"Cordelia? Would he visit friends?" he asked again.

She couldn't tell him about the duke—it wasn't her story to tell. "No, I don't think he has friends in the area."

Her father gave her a sharp look.

"What is it Father?"

"His hand and that jaw say he has Merrick blood in him, my dear."

Cordelia was struck by the astute observation.

Her father chuckled wryly. "Just because my head is often stuck in a book does not mean I can't see what is right in front of me."

"No, of course not. I'm sorry."

There was a light knock on the door, which spared her from having to say anything more on the subject.

Richard, her father's servant, stood in the open doorway. "Mr. Fielding's men are here, Miss Cordelia." He opened the door wider and five men trooped into the study.

"Beggin' your pardon for disturbing you, sir," Wilson murmured to Cordelia's father before turning to her. "Mr. Fielding hasn't been in town today, ma'am. He left a little later this morning, around nine."

Cordelia knew that because her morning sickness was the reason that he'd gone late.

"He usually comes back around ten," Wilson continued, "so if he started two hours later, he should have been back no later than noon. That's an extra six hours that he's been away."

Cordelia felt as though he were looking at her accusingly for not noticing earlier and felt compelled to explain herself.

"I left before noon and returned home at four—after paying calls with my mother—so that's why I didn't know he hadn't returned. Did he mention going anywhere today?"

The groom shook his head. "No, but his mount isn't back, which tells me he hasn't been injured badly or unhorsed. Unless—" He stopped and dropped his gaze to the hat he was twisting in his hands.

Cordelia knew what he'd been about to say: that it was possible both John *and* his horse had been too badly injured to return.

"We don't know anything yet," her father soothed. He looked at the men. "You will start searching tonight, I hope?"

Wilson nodded. "Aye, but none of us know the area, so I've asked at the inn and have five locals to partner with us. We'll go out looking, ma'am, and we won't stop 'till we find him."

Cordelia shivered at the implication that John would need to be found.

***

"Look at you, so big now," a low, sing-songy voice crooned in John's ear.

Small, icy hands stroked his fevered brow and John pushed his burning head against them, wanting more.

"No, no, no—don't thrash. You'll pull out all my careful work." High-pitched cackling jarred his aching head. "Drink a bit more of this, Master Dommie. It'll set you up all right and tight."

I'm not Dommie, he wanted to say, but no words came out.

"Drink up, now."

John struggled weakly against the sickly-sweet liquid, but his body was heavy, too heavy...

"Sleep, Dommie."

Dommie. Why did that sound so familiar?

Once again, blackness claimed him.

The next time John woke up, he could open his eyes a crack, enough to see daylight blazing through a small, lace-covered window.

But when he opened his mouth to speak, all that came out was a moan.

A wizened face appeared above him and he jolted.

"Shhh, now. Don't be frightened."

The voice was so… *familiar.*

He squinted up at her, his eyes watering and his head *raging.*

"Who—who are you?"

"Don't you recognize me?" Her wrinkled mouth puckered, like a child who'd suffered a disappointment. "I'm Nanny Twicket," she said, peering at him, looking for signs of recognition. "Remember? You called me Twickey."

John blinked. "Twickey?"

"Aye, that's what all my children called me, Twickey. Why, I don't even remember my real name." She gave another vaguely witchy cackle. "I've been Twickey for most of my life." Her face screwed into a fierce scowl. "Until *she* took you away, Dommie."

"John. My name's John," he rasped, wincing as he pushed himself up.

"Of course you are," she soothed, a child-sized hand patting his shoulder. "No—you can't be getting up. You'll pull out the stitches."

"Stitches?"

She nodded vigorously, fluffy wisps of hair the color of fresh snow flopping on her brow. Although her hand on his shoulder was firm, her eyes were frosted as white as her hair.

"Do you want some water?"

He didn't, but the way she was staring was making him feel… nervy, even though he suspected she couldn't see much.

"Yes, please."

"So polite." Her lips curled into a gentle smile, and she patted his shoulder again before turning away. She touched the various pieces of furniture on her way to the tiny kitchen. She might not be completely blind, but she was probably close to it.

Lord. Had *she* been the one to stitch him?

When he glanced down, he saw that he was naked, the only thing covering him a sheet.

Although the air in the cottage was cool, his skin was clammy and hot. He hurt in at least four places: his hip, shoulder, neck, and head.

A quick look at his hip showed a wound covered with a poultice. He felt the same thing on his shoulder and pressed lightly—which was still hard enough to make his eyes water—but could feel no bullet beneath the dressing.

The wound on his neck hurt like the devil, even though he knew it was only a scratch because otherwise, he'd be dead.

"Don't be touching those, now," she said, making him realize she could see well enough to notice movement.

She shuffled slowly toward him; a glass of water clasped in both hands.

"Who stitched me?" he asked, taking the glass from her.

"I did."

"But—"

"Oh, I can see well enough—I have the magic eye." She pointed to the small table beside the bed, where a fancy magnifying glass sat. John looked around him as he drank. The little house seemed to be composed of just the one big room and perhaps a lumber room off the back. The bed he was sleeping in was the only one, which meant that he'd ousted her.

She pointed to an armchair in front of the fire. "I'm more comfortable in the chair," she said, reading his mind with an ease that unnerved him. "Besides, I don't hardly sleep anymore." She absently smoothed a hand through his hair, the gesture rhythmic and soothing, the way you'd stroke a child.

"Such nice hair," she purred. "That's how young men wore their hair when I was a merch."

John frowned at the word. "Is that… Welsh?" he asked, not sure how he knew that.

She looked pleased. "You remember!"

He almost asked, *remember what*? But then he decided he didn't want to know. "How'd I get here?" he asked instead.

"I brought you here." She beamed down at him proudly.

"How—" he stopped; what did it matter how she'd brought him inside? More important was *where* and *when.*

"I found you yesterday afternoon." She chuckled. "Well, it would be more accurate to say that *you* found *me.* Or at least your horse did."

"Where is he?"

"Don't worry about your horse. I took him to the Schuyler cottage—they kept horses and there was a stall for him. It's musty, but he likes it well enough."

The thought of this *tiny* woman leading his vicious horse made his temples pound.

"The hay is no good," she went on, oblivious to the violence to life and limb she'd somehow avoided. "I let him out to eat by the stream and he doesn't run away." She gave a burble of laughter. "He wanted to follow me home—I think he misses you." She pulled a face. "Your saddle is a fright—covered in blood and—"

"Where am I?" he asked rudely.

She cocked her head, the gesture birdlike. "You're on the duke's land—that's where you are. This is Rook's Roost and I've lived here ever since I quit working for His Grace." Her mouth turned down at the corners at that disclosure, and he thought she was done.

But then she added, "I don't go out much these days, but I know I've never seen you about." She reached out and touched his face before he realized what she was doing. He was so startled that he simply sat there, unmoving, as she stroked the scars. "These must have hurt."

Before he could answer, her hand dropped to his shoulder and then slid down to his wrist. "Six fingers," she said in a confiding tone, as if he might not have noticed. "You are one of his, aren't you?" Her eyes narrowed, and she suddenly looked almost evil, like a witch from a fairytale. "He's always had his women." Her eyes glinted maliciously. "But he's not had any of late, has he? Now he's like a fly caught in a web. And *she* watches over him like a big fat spider hovering over a fly."

John squinted, trying to make sense of what she said, but his mind was suddenly stuffed with cotton wool.

He cleared his throat several times and twitched his hand out from under her cold little claw. When he ran his tongue over his teeth, he felt a sickly-sweet film.

Fear penetrated the thick haze that was descending over him, and he struggled to shove himself up again. "Did you—"

"I only gave you enough to settle you—just like I did yesterday when you woke as I hauled you inside. You're quite large, so it took more than I'd expected."

Laudanum.

John gritted his teeth; he *hated* laudanum. No wonder he was having such wild thoughts. But if she'd given it to him yesterday, then—

"And I put a little in the water you just drank because I could see you were getting agitated."

He glared at her. "How much?" he snarled and then blinked as his vision darkened around the edges.

"Enough." She hummed softly beneath her breath and the tune was haunting. "You need to sleep."

"I need to get back and warn…" John lost track of what he was saying.

"Hmm, what's that, Dommie?"

"Not Dommie," he slurred. "Why're you calling me that?" he sounded petulant, unlike himself.

"Oh? Did I?" She chuckled, and the sound vibrated the air strangely.

John gagged on the sudden dampness that flooded his chest, his lungs struggling to pull in enough air. "Can't—can't—"

"Shhh, now." She patted him, and the bed rocked wildly from side to side. John fisted the mattress with both hands to hang on as the room spun.

"Sleep, Dommie."

This time, the darkness came for him with claws and fangs to drag him under.

***

Cordelia could not sleep, even though she knew it was foolish; her exhaustion didn't help John, and it was bad for their child. But every time she'd drifted off to sleep last night, she'd found herself in the middle of the same dream.

They were back in London, in the carriage on the same dark street. Bullets were hitting the carriage but this time they hadn't missed John. This time—

She'd woken in a cold sweat three times before she'd given up and stared into the darkness.

At first light, she'd sought Richard—who'd gone out to help the searchers—but she'd known by his weary, shaken look that there was nothing to report.

How could John just disappear? And here of all places! This was where she'd grown up. It was safe here and nothing bad ever happened.

Until yesterday.

The door to the sitting room opened, and her head jerked up. It was her father. "There are two Runners here, my dear." He cleared his throat. "Er, they say your husband hired them to watch the house. Our house. Shall I talk to them for you?" The deep crease between his large, sensitive eyes told her how distressed he was by all this. Guests didn't just *disappear*—at least not from Garry Court.

"No, father. I'd rather talk to them. Er, alone."

"I will bring them to you," he said, not arguing with her decision.

Cordelia didn't know what she'd expected—she'd never seen a Bow Street Runner before—but the men who entered the room a few moments later were both slightly built and neatly dressed, looking more like bankers than men who chased dangerous criminals.

Before they could speak, she blurted, "My father says that my husband hired you to watch our house?"

"Yes, ma'am. My name is Donald Riggs, and my associate is Horace Stamp." They both bowed. "Mr. Fielding believed there might be some sort of attack given the three that happened in London—"

"*Three?*"

"Er, yes, ma'am."

Anger, fear, and helplessness swelled in her chest. "What is going on? Has somebody followed him here from London? Is that what happened?"

The men looked at each other before the leader, Mr. Riggs, spoke. "It looks like somebody shot at him while he was riding yesterday morning. We found some blood on—"

Cordelia gasped and covered her mouth. "Oh God. Is he—"

"It wasn't a lot of blood, ma'am, and what we can see of the tracks shows he escaped his pursuers—two, perhaps even three, horses were after him." The man scowled slightly. "If we'd gotten there before half the village traipsed all over, we might have been able to gather more information. As it was, we brought in a local hunter and even he couldn't tell where your husband's horse went, although they followed the other horse's tracks back to the main road. His big dun stallion has a distinctive tread, and we found some tracks that might be his beside the stream that—"

"Mr. Fielding's horse likes water—loves it, actually."

"That's what his groom said." He cut her a cautious look. "We know there are abandoned mines all over the countryside, so we're checking as many as we can in the area, just in case—"

"Yes, I understand," she said, not wanting to hear him say the words. "If you know about the mines, then the men who attacked him might look there, too."

"We've got three dozen men, many with dogs—"

Raised voices came from outside the study right before the door flew open and the duchess strode into the room, garbed in a magnificent royal blue travelling costume that made her look like a peacock with two peahens—her mother and father—both hovering anxiously beside her.

"My God, Cordelia, I just arrived at Chelmsford and heard what happened; I came right over."

"Ophelia… I, er, thought you were staying in London?"

"His Grace has taken a bad turn." She turned to the Runners and said sharply, "Who are these gentlemen?"

"I told you she had company," their father said, casting an apologetic look at Cordelia.

"Come inside, Papa, Mama. You should know about this, too—" A wave of nausea washed over her and she lurched to her feet and staggered to her father's desk. Beside it was a small rubbish bin; Cordelia dropped to her knees and emptied the contents of her stomach.

Pandemonium erupted as everyone started talking at once.

Cordelia raised a hand when she was sure she'd finished and the room went silent as she drew her handkerchief from the sleeve of her morning gown and wiped her mouth.

Her father helped her to her feet.

"I will send for Doctor Arnold immediately," her mother said, scurrying for the door.

"There is nothing he can do for me, Mama."

Her parents looked confused, her sister suspicious, and the two Runners looked as if they'd rather be someplace else.

Cordelia smiled apologetically. "Thank you, gentlemen. Please report back regularly, even if you have no news."

The men bowed and hurried from the room.

Cordelia turned to her wide-eyed family.

"I am with child."

"Oh, darling!" Her mother's face flushed with joy.

"Congratulations, my dear!" her father said, patting her shoulder gently, as if she might break.

Ophelia's face was a pale mask of civility, and Cordelia knew that she'd embarrassed her proper sister by blurting out such a private matter.

"Congratulations, Cordelia," she murmured. "But as to your husband's disappearance—"

Cordelia flushed at the imputation that she was celebrating while her husband was missing.

She quickly told her parents and sister the little she'd learned from the Runners.

"Bow Street Runners," her mother echoed in shock. "But—why do people want to hurt Mr. Fielding?"

Three sets of eyes settled on her questioningly.

"I don't know."

"You know nothing about these attacks?" her sister repeated.

Cordelia recoiled at her abrupt tone and disbelieving look. "Yes, that is correct," she retorted. "I know nothing."

Ophelia's skeptical expression melted away, replaced by one of concern. "I'm sorry, my dear, that was ill done of me. It's just that I was hoping there might be something we could *do* if we knew more. But as things stand, I shall, of course, lend all the male servants to the search effort."

"Thank you, Ophelia."

Her sister nodded and stood, suddenly brisk. "I must go," she said, pulling on her gloves.

"Are the children with you?" Cordelia asked.

"No—I didn't wish to alarm them. His Grace has suffered similar episodes in the past and it always comes to nothing."

Their parents looked distressed by her callous answer.

Ophelia glanced at them both and frowned. "You may think me cold and uncaring, but the strain on the children has been terrible."

"But he is their father, my dear," their mother pointed out timidly, gazing up apprehensively at this magnificent daughter she'd somehow brought from her body.

Cordelia was briefly reminded of David facing Goliath.

Her sister fixed her mother with a look of weary cynicism. "A fact of which I'm more than well aware, Mama." She turned to Cordelia. "You must stay at the house, of course. It will make more sense to conduct the search from there." When Cordelia hesitated, her sister's gaze flickered to their parents.

Cordelia knew what that look meant: this ordeal would wear on her aged mother and father.

"She must stay here," her father said while her mother nodded her agreement.

"I think Ophelia is correct," Cordelia said gently. How many times in her life had she been forced to utter those same words? "It will make more sense to stay with her—where we can coordinate the search more easily."

Her father sighed. "If you wish, my dear."

"Good, then that is settled," Ophelia said. "I will send the carriage for you later this afternoon."

"No need," she had the pleasure of saying. "John's carriage is at the inn, along with the servants."

Ophelia hesitated, and then nodded. "Of course. Come tonight and bring his servants with you—there is ample room for them." She brushed kisses on her parents' cheeks and bustled from the room.

Once she was gone, her father turned to her. "You may stay if you wish; we do not want you to leave."

Cordelia embraced them both, torn. "I will go," she said, hiding her reluctance.

Something inside her railed against returning to her sister's house. Not just because of the subordinate position that she would naturally assume, but because the house had been in a state of near mourning for almost a year. One entire wing was sealed off against everyone except the duke, his doctor, and several nurses who served him around the clock and never mixed with the rest of the household. It created an unpleasant tension.

But it would be far easier on her parents if she stayed at Chelmsford and conducted the search from there.

God, where was he?

The thought drove all her concerns about moving to her sister's house from her mind.

He'd been missing for over a day and not even his horse had returned.

Cordelia did not know if that was a good sign, or a terrible one.

Chapter 34

Garry Court
1818

It was dark, the next time John woke and his mouth was so dry it felt like he'd been eating dust.

His head felt like a boulder, his stomach pitched, and he would have murdered for even a teaspoon of water, but his wounds, he had to admit, had settled into an ache rather than a sharp pain. The only light in the cottage was the glow from the fire, which illuminated his surroundings just enough to show the glass on his nightstand. Not that he had any intention of drinking from it.

The last thing he wanted was more laudanum.

How long had he been there? How had his horse gone unnoticed at an abandoned stable? Where was this woman's cottage? Did nobody visit her? How did she get her food?

John grimaced; none of that was his concern. He needed to haul his arse out of bed and go find Cordelia.

He had no idea how long it took to stand, locate his clothing and boots—all cleaned and pressed and shined—and get dressed, but he was bloody exhausted by the time he'd finished.

He dropped on the bed, sleep clawing at him.

"Dommie?" A pair of eyes glittered in the near darkness.

"I need to leave." His voice was even rougher than usual. "How do I get back to the road from here?"

She hesitated long enough that he thought she might argue. Instead, she pushed up from her chair. "If you fetch some water from the pump, I'll make tea."

John snorted, and she gave him a cheeky smile. "Don't worry, I won't put anything in it you don't want."

He sighed. "Where's the pump?"

It was cool and clear outside, with only a few clouds skittering over the half moon.

The fresh air was good for him, as was moving about, and he felt almost human when he returned to the house carrying a bucket.

She'd lighted a lantern and set her small table with plates, cups, and a platter of biscuits. Good God! How could she bake if she couldn't see?

"I don't make them," she said, once again guessing his thoughts. "Everything comes to me from the village." She scowled. "His Grace pays for it all," she added, as if he'd asked. "Thinks I'm too batty to use the stove for anything other than heating water."

John thought that might be a fair guess, given how often she'd called him by some other man's name.

"How far is my horse?"

"Ten minutes—have your tea, first, then you can go."

He hesitated, glanced at his watch—it was not quite two o'clock in the morning—and then sat, the chair squeaking ominously beneath his weight. "Nobody came looking for me?"

"Nobody comes to this part of the woods if they can help it." She looked up from the tea she was preparing and waggled her eyebrows. "I am a witch, you know."

John's face heated, and he hoped it was dark enough to hide his reaction. Now that he wasn't higher than a kite on laudanum, he felt guilty for thinking such thoughts about her. She didn't look like a witch; she looked like an old woman with a tenuous grip on reality.

And she sounded lonely.

"Who is Dommie?" he asked, although he could guess.

She took a while to answer. "Dominic Streeter Andrew Merrick, the Duke of Falkirk's son and heir. Sugar? Milk?"

"Three and yes."

She chuckled. "Such a sweet tooth you have."

John took the teacup and saucer from her shaky hand. "So, you were nurse to the first Duchess of Falkirk's son?"

"Yes, and I was *her* nurse, too. I came with Miss Martha from Cardiff when she married His Grace. She insisted on it. *I'll only want you to look after all my babies, Twickey*, Miss Martha said to me." She smiled fondly. "She was so excited to marry him—so *honored*, even though he was as cold and proud as a king on his throne. It should have been *he* who was honored." She clucked her tongue and sipped her black tea.

"Miss Martha's father would have let her marry anyone—he worshipped her—but she had her heart set on a peer. And if I told her once, I told her—"

She prattled on and John drank his tea, eating several biscuits to settle his stomach.

By the time he'd drained his cup, he still felt queasy and weak and should probably wait until morning to leave, but he needed to get back to Garry Court. He knew the Runners were watching over Cordelia, but he couldn't rid himself of the sick feeling that something bad was about to happen to her.

"—and I know what she told His Grace." Twickey's heated words broke into his thoughts. "But he didn't care. She could do whatever she wanted, just so long as she didn't interfere in *his* business."

John squinted at her. "What did you just say? Who told His Grace—" He winced as the room tilted slightly. "Bloody hell!" he snapped when his head stopped spinning. "Did you put more laudanum in this tea?"

"No, Dommie—I swear—"

"John! My name is John."

She nodded, clutching her cup in a way that made him realize he was shouting.

"Who told His Grace what?" he repeated more calmly.

It took her a moment to recollect what she'd been saying. The moment she did, an ugly sneer settled on her face. "The duchess—the *new* duchess—disliked me right from the start. She said I wasn't a proper nurse, and she made me leave." Tears slid down her papery cheeks. "He listened to her, even though I promised Miss Martha on her deathbed that I would care for you and—"

"I'm not *him*. I'm John Fielding."

Her hazy eyes were suddenly as piercing as a falcon's. "You wait." She got up and shuffled slowly to the door he thought led to a lumber room. When she opened the door, he saw the small room was piled high with furniture and crates.

She rooted around inside for a moment and then began tugging on something that was obviously heavy.

John rushed to help her as she dragged out a portrait—heavy gold frame and all—that was taller than she was.

"What are—"

She yanked the painting around until it faced him. "Look!"

The woman in the portrait wasn't pretty—her features were too strong for that—but she was handsome in a dignified way. She was also tall and sturdily built, her features firm rather than fine.

Her hands were normal, of course—the six fingers came from the duke's side of the family—but her hair and eyes were the color of coal.

"Where did you get this?" he asked, unable to look away from it. There were rips and gashes in the canvas which somebody had tried to repair.

"*Herself* had it thrown out with all Miss Martha's other things"—she flung a hand toward the lumber room—"she told her servants to get rid of everything. *Everything*, even her clothes." She was crying again, but tears of rage this time. "This is your Mam, Dommie, can't you see that?"

He inhaled deeply and held it a moment before shaking his head. "I'll admit there is a resemblance, but—"

"You are the *spitting image* of her," she hissed.

John heaved an exasperated sigh. "That boy *died* years ago. I'm a bastard—one of many. You said yourself the duke spread his seed far and wide"—he held out his arms—"so behold yet another ducal by-blow."

"No. You're Martha's boy, as sure as day turns to night."

John turned away, disgusted with himself for arguing with her. She was a lonely old woman who'd been driven mad by losing the ones she loved.

"They never brought back his body," she said.

John swung around. "How old was the boy? Not even two? If he and the nurse fell into the Thames—a place where entire boats get lost in the sludge—they're lucky they found the woman or they might never have known what happened."

"It wouldn't have happened if *I'd* been with him!" she raged, her voice choked with sobs.

John scowled and snatched up his coat. As he slipped it on, he glanced at the pile of his possessions that Twickey must have taken from his various pockets. "Where's my gun?"

"There wasn't one."

John had vague memories of yanking at the pistol and tearing his leathers.

He picked up his watch, silver tinderbox, and the stubby pencil he always carried with him—the little leather-bound notebook was nowhere in sight—and slid them into his coat pocket.

He opened the small purse and emptied the thick wad of paper money and few coins onto the table. "Take this for your efforts. I'll bring—"

"You've a birthmark—right in the middle of your back, between your shoulders—and it looks like a splash of hot tallow, a pale brown color that is unusual. You had it when you were born."

"I didn't even know I *had* a birthmark in the middle of my back—it's not a place I often look."

"Go see the duke if you don't believe me. He will remember it."

John snorted, not bothering to hide his disbelief that a man like the duke would even step foot into a nursery. "Why in the world would he know about—or remember—a birthmark on an infant?"

"The doctors told him about it when you were born."

"That wasn't *me*," he growled. "My mother was a whore who spread her legs for money and I'm the result of a quick fuck and a few spurts of spunk."

She didn't blink at his vulgar words. "He will know you as his own."

John sneered. "He doesn't know anything anymore—does he? He's no better than a bloody vegetable, from what I've heard."

"*She* keeps him there—locked away—and doesn't even allow the doctor he's known all his life to look at him. Why does she keep him hidden like a dirty secret under lock and key? You could go see him—you could—"

"I'm leaving," he said firmly. "But I'll come back. I'll bring my wife to meet you." Cordelia would find the strange old woman interesting.

She grabbed his arm as he turned to go, her fingers like the hooks of a grapnel. "When you go see him—"

"I'm *not* going to see him."

"Just be careful, Dommie. She's dangerous."

"She? You mean the duchess?" he couldn't keep the amazement from his tone.

The old woman nodded. "She gets what she wants; she always has."

"Which way to my horse?"

"Follow the path west and you will come to the abandoned cottage. Then you must go to Chelmsford Park and talk to him."

John turned away, and this time, he kept going.

***

"Drink this, Cordelia. You need to sleep. When did you last rest?" Ophelia asked when Cordelia didn't immediately reach for the sleeping draught.

"I want to be awake in case—"

"Somebody will wake you. You have my word." Ophelia set the glass on the nightstand. "It is only a bit of laudanum in some warm milk and won't harm your baby, if that is worrying you. I know a great deal about being with child. You must listen to me."

Cordelia smiled up at her. "I will just finish reading this chapter and then take the draught."

"Good. You will know the minute I get any news."

"Thank you, Ophelia—for everything."

"Sleep well, my dear."

Cordelia put down the book once the door closed behind her sister. She'd lied about reading another chapter—she'd not read even a word over the last two hours.

Instead, she'd stared at the wall and waited for news, the minutes crawling past like hours.

The search had moved off the duke's estate and was now concentrated in the shallow hillsides that were riddled with old mines. Many of them collapsed.

Cordelia chewed her lip and glanced at the milk. She should drink it and sleep—even a few hours of oblivion would be welcome after almost two days of constant worry. Worry not only for John but also for her child after the uncomfortable conversation she'd had with the two Runners.

"We can't protect you if you stay with the Duchess of Falkirk, Mrs. Fielding; there are only two of us and Chelmsford Park is just too large. I would respectfully ask that you stay at Garry Court," Mr. Riggs had said when she'd told him she was moving to stay with her sister.

"I don't need any protection—it's clear they are after my husband. You should be looking for him, not watching after me."

"That's not what he paid us to do, ma'am." He'd spoken with the wholly masculine assurance that he knew what was best for her.

"Well, *I* am in charge in my husband's absence and I'm sure he would want you to take orders from me. Or are you saying he'd want you to disobey me?"

Riggs hadn't been saying any such thing, and Cordelia had known it. But she wanted the two Runners on John's trail, not wasting their time watching her.

Riggs had merely stared at her, his gaze both respectful and stubborn.

"I order you to join the search for my husband and stay away from the duke's house—it would only cause me embarrassment to have my sister know you were lurking about. It would suggest that I didn't think I was safe with my own family. Are we understood, Mr. Riggs?"

"I understand you, Mrs. Fielding."

Cordelia wasn't stupid. She'd known that his simple statement and cool look had meant that he'd do just as he pleased.

As angry as she'd been that he'd refused to obey her, she couldn't help being relieved that the Runners were out there, watching over the house. If there was even a sliver of a chance that the men who'd attacked John might come after her, then it was wiser to err on the side of caution.

Cordelia eyed the glass her sister had set on the table.

It wasn't that she hadn't slept at all—she'd catnapped this afternoon and once before dinner—it was just that she couldn't seem to sleep at night.

In truth, she wasn't all that tired and the last thing she wanted was a laudanum-induced sleep, complete with strange dreams.

She picked up the glass and took it to the big sash window she'd opened to enjoy the fresh air. After emptying the contents, she replaced the empty glass on her nightstand.

Tomorrow she'd thank Ophelia for her kindness and her sister would never know that she'd not taken the draught.

Cordelia shoved the comfortable wing chair closer to the window, which overlooked the long curving driveway; if anyone returned with news of John, they'd come from that direction.

After she snuffed out the candles and wrapped her fleecy shawl around her, she curled up in the big chair and tucked her legs beneath her, making herself comfortable for the long, sleepless night ahead.

Tonight, she would keep vigil for her husband.

Chapter 35

Chelmsford Park
1818

The big stallion nickered when John entered the small stable, almost as if he were happy to see him; although, more likely, he was just bored after being locked up all day.

"You're a mess, lad," John muttered as he briefly examined the dun's coat by the light of a makeshift torch and then led him outside, where he snuffed out the burning twigs.

Fortunately, there was enough moonlight that he could see well enough to pluck out the worst of the briars and twigs.

His arm hurt was hurting like a bastard by the time he lifted the saddle and he worried that he'd torn the stitches. Once he was mounted, he carefully felt the wound; it hurt, but it hadn't started bleeding again, so the stitches must have held.

Even with the halfmoon there were plenty of shadows on the narrow path that led to the road, so he moved slowly, even though he was burning to get back to Cordelia. As soft-hearted as she was, she was probably miserable with worry.

Having somebody to worry about him was a new and not entirely unpleasant phenomenon, and it made him want to get home to her as quickly as possible.

And yet when John finally arrived at the road that would either take him back to Garry Court, or on to the duke's house, he hesitated.

John had never been a ditherer. Life simply hadn't offered him enough time to dither at the critical junctures. A man or woman who lived the way he had—by his wits—often had only seconds to decide.

But he was dithering now.

He sighed heavily and turned left, heading toward the very man he'd put in a sickbed.

John had never wanted to kill the duke; that would have been far too quick. He'd wanted to toy with him until the restless feeling that constantly lived inside him went away.

Putting the Duke of Falkirk into a near-death state so quickly had denied John the full flavor of his revenge and robbed him of the opportunity to meet or talk to the man. To confront him.

Indeed, he'd only caught two glimpses of the duke, once, very briefly, when he'd strode from his club to his coach, and again when he'd come out of his mistress's pied-à-terre early one morning, when he'd paused to pull on his gloves.

He'd had a good look at him that time and had been close enough to his tall, elegant person to see how sleek and well-maintained he looked.

John had desperately searched for any resemblance to the duke—other than their distinctive right hands—but had come away with nothing.

If not for the proof that Worth had found—John's christening record in the parish registry where his Gran had gone to church—he might have believed their relationship was a product of his imagination.

Although his father's name had been listed—Alastair Robert Merrick—he knew the Duke of Falkirk would never have attended the christening of a whore's brat. In fact, he doubted either of his parents had attended. It would have been his Gran who'd ensured the safety of his immortal soul by getting him blessed.

John felt Morvac'h tense beneath him and saw his ears twitch.

"What is it, lad?" he whispered, just as he heard voices.

He quickly guided Morvac'h into the trees. Anyone out at this time of night wouldn't be up to any good—and John was in no shape to fight—so it was wiser to hide.

"—urprised Ballard said we were to hang back and not go look with the others."

John heard the voice before he saw the men—two of them, riding fine-looking horses.

"I'll just bet he did—the toad eater. You know Her Grace would be thrilled if he was never found," the second man said, giving an ugly laugh. "Then she could have all his money without the bother of having *him*."

"Shhh. You know the others could be around—what if somebody heard you?"

"Just relax, Gerry. We're the only two on this section of the road." He snorted. "Besides, you think any of them would say anything different? And it's the truth, ain't it? It must be eatin' her up to know she was saved by a convict."

"I never heard what he did to get transported?"

"What does it matter? He came back rich. Miss Cordelia was lucky to get him, if you ask me."

"She's always been kind to me."

"Aye, unlike her sister."

"I wonder why Miss Cordy is back at Chelmsford?"

"Her Grace would have made her come—you know how she likes to be in charge of everything. It's like me sister, and how—"

"I never thought Miss Cordy would marry," his friend interrupted, clearly uninterested in hearing family stories. "Especially not to somebody like *him*. Have you seen him?"

"Aye, he came into the King's Arms when I was in there—could barely fit through the door. He's a right scary looking—"

The voice faded away as the men disappeared over the slight rise John had just come down.

So, those were his dear sister-in-law's servants, who'd been told to hang back in the search for him.

To be honest, he was impressed there *was* a search. But that would be Cordelia's doing—or maybe the two Runners. And it sounded as if Cordelia was at Chelmsford. Why the devil would she go there?

John grimaced; he didn't like that at all. Hopefully Riggs was somewhere about to keep an eye on her.

He waited another few minutes before getting back on the road. If what the man had said—that most of the male servants were out wandering around—then breaking into the duke's house might be even easier than he'd hoped.

Twickey said the duke was in the east wing along with a live-in doctor and some nurses. She'd made it sound as if the duchess were isolating her husband, but why would she do such a thing?

John cursed himself for believing anything the old woman said. After all, if she was to be believed, then John was Falkirk's real heir.

The dark, looming monstrosity that rose up before him shoved all his thoughts aside and John paused a moment to take in the sight. Chelmsford was *huge*, easily the size of one of the enormous government buildings John had seen in London. It astounded him that he was connected to such history and grandeur—even if the connection was on the wrong side of the blanket.

"Let's go," he muttered, urging Morvac'h onward. John wasn't interested in sneaking. If he were discovered, what would his sister-in-law do? Have him arrested? Shoot him? What a scandal *that* would cause.

John snorted and cut across a lawn that was as lush as velvet, heading for the east wing, where only three windows were illuminated, all of them close together on the top floor. Something told him that was where he'd find his father.

When he reached the corner of the building, he dismounted and turned Morvac'h loose to graze on the thick grass. He wouldn't wander far with such forage beneath his hooves.

John found a narrow, unadorned door just a few steps below ground level. He surmised it was a servant entrance that would likely lead to a servant corridor or stairwell. The lock on the door was ludicrously simple to pick—probably easier than carrying around the heavy key that fit the ancient lock.

It was darker than a coal pit inside, but he felt around on the wall beside the door and quickly located a sconce with a candle stub. He fumbled with his flint for a moment before he could light the candle, and then he closed the door and raised the light. As he'd thought, it was a servant stairwell, plain and functional.

When he reached the top floor, he paused on the landing and listened at the door for a long moment before opening it a crack.

The corridor beyond had tall windows along one side and they allowed in moonlight that illuminated the opposite wall, which bore several doors that were spaced in such a way to indicate they led to suites of rooms.

The light he'd seen from outside was the glow from two wall sconces, one on either side of the third door down the corridor.

John strode down the plush carpet runner that ran the length of the hallway, stopping in front of the third door. Once again, he laid his ear against it and heard nothing. The doorknob turned without resistance; he took a breath and pushed it open.

John didn't know what he was expecting—armed men? The duchess sitting beside the bed, holding her husband's hand? Nurses and a doctor bustling?

What he encountered was none of those things.

The room was like any of the bedchambers at Falkirk House in London, except the appointments were far, far grander. Against the far wall was a massive four-poster bed with a stick-thin figure lying almost exactly in the center.

His chest was moving up and down so slowly that for a moment, John thought he was dead. He'd expected to feel something when he looked upon his father, but he'd not expected the emotion that filled him: pity. The man in the bed was skeletal and pale, a shadow of his former self, and it looked as though the right half of the duke's face had slid.

John had seen that look before. An apoplexy it was called, when a person lost use of their body, sometimes all, sometimes part.

He pulled his gaze away from his father and did a quick investigation of the two adjacent rooms, more than a little surprised to find both were unoccupied. Where were the duke's doctor and nurses?

A table had been moved beside the bed and it was cluttered with bottles and jars, a mortar and pestle, and a lancet and bleeding cup, among other doctoring paraphernalia. Somebody had placed a chair beside the bed, raising it up on slabs of wood so it would be on the same level as the bed's occupant.

There were no slippers beneath the bed, no robe draped over the foot and a quick glance into the dressing room showed it held only a few garments, telling him that the duke had come to this bed and never left it.

John turned back to the bed and started when he saw that one of the duke's eyes was wide open, the other closed. His mouth had opened, too, and drool ran from the corner that was distorted. But the working half of his mouth was struggling to speak.

He gestured to John with his hand—his six-fingered hand. "Zhom… zhom—" His uncooperative tongue choked off whatever he was trying to say and a look of impotent rage flickered across half his face, leaving no trace on the other half.

He lifted his six-fingered hand and shook it at John.

"This?" John raised his own deformed hand.

The duke's eyes fell shut, and he sagged against the pillows piled behind him, his nod almost imperceptible.

John approached the bed, anger now warring with pity. "Yes, you're my father."

The eye opened, its crystalline blue blazing up at him.

"Zhom—"

"John Fielding."

The duke made a guttural, exasperated noise and made a writing motion with his functioning hand.

John glanced around the room, looking for a writing desk. There wasn't one, but there was a piece of parchment beneath one of the bottles on the table. It looked like it had directions for dosage on one side, but the back was empty of writing.

On the nightstand was a Bible.

He took the paper and book and set it on the bed before pulling the pencil stub from his pocket and placing it in the older man's hand, which was cold, boney, and pale, making John's fingers seemed mockingly tan and healthy by comparison.

The duke breathed like a man hauling a boulder rather than pushing a slight piece of wood and graphite. The first word was messy, but short and easy to read: son.

John nodded. "Yes, I'm your son. My mother was Mary Fielding. She—"

The duke made an agitated gurgling sound and tried to write something else, but the pencil shot from his fingers.

John replaced it and his father tried again, but his hand shook so badly it was almost impossible to decipher.

He squinted. "Is that a 'd'?"

"It is," a voice behind him said.

John spun around, his hand automatically reaching for the nearest weapon, which was the lancet on the table.

"You won't need that," the duchess said.

Two people stood in the doorway and John recognized both.

Eddie grinned and raised his hand, which looked almost as fragile as the duke's, with one critical difference: it held a pistol.

"It's been a long time, John."

"Not long enough," he shot back.

Eddie chuckled hoarsely, his laughter turning into a moist-sounding cough.

John looked from the duchess to Eddie, his brain scrambling to put together the pieces.

"Put down the lancet," the duchess repeated.

"Why should I? Old Eddie looks a bit shaky; I could get to you before he could shoot me anywhere lethal."

The duchess cut Eddie a look of contempt. "That is probably true." She lifted her hand from her skirts. "But my aim is *quite* true."

John replaced the lancet on the table.

"Put both your hands where I can see them and step away from His Grace." She gestured with the pistol. "All the way back against the mantle."

When John complied, she went to the bed, glanced down, and gave a bitter bark of laughter before snatching up the piece of paper.

"Really, Alastair?" She cut her husband a hate-filled look.

The duke glared up at her with eyes that blazed with fury and no small amount of fear.

The duchess crumpled the piece of paper and turned to John.

"You look like your mother." Her mouth curled into an unpleasant smile. "Although her large, bovine features are slightly more attractive on a man than a woman."

"Why?" John asked.

"Why what?"

"Why *all* of this?"

"Oh, you poor, stupid man—you've not figured this out yet, have you?"

John squinted at her in disbelief. "Are you saying—"

"Yes, for God's sake, you're that cow's son."

He could only stare.

"Alastair saw you with Worth, saw the hand, saw the resemblance, and asked a few questions about you. Which is when he learned *you* had been asking about *him*. He came to me and accused me of—oh, the things he said and threatened me with. It's simply too upsetting to repeat them. He was so angry—so worked into a lather—that suddenly he froze and stopped speaking and collapsed, just like a defective automaton." She gave a derisive laugh and cut a dismissive look at her husband.

The duke had closed his eye, but his clenched jaw told John he was still conscious.

John jerked his chin at Eddie. "What's he doing here?"

She turned to Eddie, who was leaning against the door, his face gray and tight with pain. "You should thank Mr. Houlihan—he's the reason you're still alive."

The old gangster grinned, showing a scant handful of teeth. "It's true. I didn't want to kill you—you made me too damned much money." He shook his head. "If I'd known what you were goin' to do to poor Des," he clucked his tongue. "Well, I would 'ave done you myself. That was clever of you to get yourself shipped south."

"Yes, brilliant," the duchess said, her eyes burning with loathing as she looked from Eddie to John. "I feel like I've been trying to kill you for half my life," she gave a disbelieving laugh. "Over and over and over again, and each time—" she shook herself. "But that doesn't matter. Tonight is going to be the last time."

"Let me guess," John said. "Somebody—one of the duke's gaolers, oh, I mean caretakers—shot me by accident, believing I was a burglar breaking into His Grace's chambers? Or will you have Eddie take me off someplace private and dispose of me less… messily?"

"'Oh, goodness, no." The duchess chuckled bitterly. "I trust *him* even less than I trust you. You'll die right here in this room—where I can make sure you're actually dead."

Suddenly, Cordelia's head popped up behind the duchess and Eddie; she was in the room they'd just emerged from.

John caught the squawk of surprise that tore out of his mouth and tried to mask it with a cough. He cleared his throat loudly and shuffled his feet, making as much noise as possible to keep his armed adversaries from noticing there was a woman only five feet behind them.

Christ! What the hell was she doing there?

The duchess narrowed her eyes at him. "Why, I believe you are frightened—I can see it on your face.

She was right about that; it was all he could do to keep from screaming hysterically at his wife to get the hell out.

The duchess laughed. "You're nothing but a big coward! You look on the verge of fainting."

He bloody well was—his heart was beating faster than a hummingbird's—and he was looking anywhere but at Cordelia, who was pantomiming something behind her sister's back.

Finally—after an excruciating eternity—his wife disappeared from view.

John's legs went watery with relief and he had to lean against the mantlepiece to keep from sliding to the floor like a butchered cow.

The duchess turned to Eddie, quickly losing interest in such an unmanly coward. "Put him where you want him before you shoot him; I don't want to be dragging him about before servants come running."

"A condemned man's last request?" John said before Eddie could speak.

The duchess hesitated, but then smiled at her husband, the expression even colder and crueler than the look she'd given John.

"What do you think, Alastair? Should I give your son one last request before I kill him? Again."

The duke was watching the proceedings with an eye that threatened to roll out of his head, his breath wheezing in and out like a punctured bellows.

She chuckled and turned to John. "Let me guess. You want to know what happened?"

He nodded.

"I paid two fools—Kennedy and Bower—to get rid of you and the nurse." Her mouth tightened, the expression making her look ugly. "The idiots took care of the girl but gave you to some gutter hag—an old woman whose daughter had just died in childbed."

Hatred flared in John's belly at the word *hag* and he had to force himself to be calm as he asked, "How did you find out I was alive?"

"I didn't know for several years, not until Mr. Dolan paid me a visit at Falkirk House. You see, he'd stolen the old woman's things when she died. There was the baby's clothing—loving stitched by the old duchess's Welsh nurse and complete with his name on the garment—along with a little notebook."

John recalled the notebook. He had always wondered why his Gran had it as she couldn't read. As for the baby clothing, that must have been what was inside the leather pouch in Gran's bag, the one she'd always told him she'd give him when he was older.

"What was in the notebook?" he asked.

"Ah yes, the notebook." She sighed. "Kennedy told me that he'd written about what they'd done to you and the nurse in great detail, including who'd paid them. He said if I decided to pay somebody to kill him and Bower—which I'll admit was my plan—then his written confession would go to the duke." Her lips twisted unpleasantly. "I kept expecting that he'd blackmail me himself at some point, but both he and Bower seemed to have disappeared into thin air. In any case, after six years had passed, I'd begun to think it was all behind me."

"But then Dolan came to you with the garments and notebook," John said.

"Yes. He also told me something else."

"He told you I was still alive," John guessed.

"He offered to keep all my secrets, for a price."

"He blackmailed you."

"Indeed, he did," she said, her eyes glinting with malice. "For several years I fed his greed, until it became apparent that I'd have to do something about him or end up a pauper. So, I went over his head."

He turned to Eddie, who grinned at him. "And that is where Eddie came in," John said.

The duchess nodded. "Mr. Houlihan had his own price to get rid of Dolan, but at least he agreed to get rid of you, too—unlike Dolan, who'd wanted to keep you around as… insurance."

She turned toward Eddie and must have given him quite a vicious look because the old criminal paled.

He wouldn't be surprised if the servants arrived to find *two* dead men in the room, rather than just John.

The duchess turned back to John. "Imagine my surprise and displeasure when *you* showed up alive and well last year after Mr. Houlihan had assured me that he'd *taken care* of you years ago."

"So, you were behind the attacks in London and the one here," John said.

"Yes. I paid Mr. Houlihan to organize those debacles." She shifted the heavy pistol from one hand to the other, flexing her fingers and shaking out her hand before dropping it to the mattress and twisting her torso toward Eddie, making John glad that Cordelia wasn't peeking from the other room just then. "The fool couldn't even get that right," she said, her voice dripping with loathing.

Eddie recoiled from her gaze.

The duchess snorted. "I'm sure you can—" she shrieked and stumbled back from the bed just as a gun went off.

John's body acted on instinct and he dived for the settee, the only cover between him and his two gun-toting captors. He'd scarcely hit the floor when two more bangs went off.

He frowned; *two* more? How had—

"John!"

The familiar voice startled him into jerking his head up. He'd forgotten about the settee above him and whacked his head—right on the plaster-covered wound.

"Dammit!" he muttered.

"Oh, John!" Small hands grabbed his shoulders and Cordelia dropped to her knees beside him. "Did you get shot?"

John shifted onto his damaged hip, winced, and then met his wife's anxious gaze. "Not today, darling."

"I thought you were gone." She flung her arms around him and sobbed.

"There, there," John murmured, glancing over her shoulder to where the two Runners stood.

Riggs was holding the duchess while the other man bent over something, Eddie, he guessed.

John gently put Cordelia at arm's length. "Did you bring them here, love?"

She nodded, her chin trembling. "I thought you'd died. I thought you'd fallen into a mine shaft, I thought—"

John kissed her—thoroughly, only coming up for air when her body stopped shaking.

"Shhh, love," he murmured. "Everything will be fine."

She shoved her face into the side of his neck, her slender arms tight around him. "I love you so much, John and I was so afraid. I didn't want to raise our baby alone. I—"

"Mr. Fielding?"

John looked up to see Riggs standing on the other side of the settee, grinning down at him. "Glad you're alive, sir."

"And I'm glad to see you, Mr. Riggs. I'll admit I was hoping at least one of you would be around when I learned Mrs. Fielding was here."

"How'd you find out, sir?" He nudged back his hat and scratched his head. "And where were you, if you don't mind me asking?"

"I don't mind at all," John said, pushing to his feet and helping Cordelia to hers. "But perhaps we might find a more comfortable place to have this discussion."

"Zhom!"

The muffled yell came from the direction of the bed, where the duke was lying on his side, his limbs sprawled across the bed.

John hurried across the room and climbed onto the bed so he could lift his father up and then lay him on his back.

"Good God!" His father's fingers were curled around the stubby pencil and covered in blood.

"He stabbed her in the hand," Riggs said beside him. "It's quite a nasty wound for a pencil."

Not to mention the man wielding it was severely crippled.

Tears ran down the duke's face—from both eyes—and his unparalyzed side was twitching.

"Zhom."

That's when John realized that the word the duke had been trying to say, repeatedly, was Dominic—John's name. His real name.

He locked eyes with his father.

A father who was gazing up at John as if he was overjoyed to see him.

A father who had never abandoned John or his mother.

John swallowed and ignored the prickling behind his eyes, setting a hand on the duke's fragile shoulder. "Everything will be fine now… Father."

The duke flailed out a bloody hand for him and John caught it, clasping it tightly while the older man sobbed out his grief.

Somebody took his other hand, and he turned to find Cordelia beside him, crying just as hard as the duke, hope shining in her eyes.

Yes, it's possible that John might have shed a tear or two, himself.

Chapter 36

Chelmsford Park
1818

Nobody slept that night, except the duke, who remained awake only long enough to make his intentions toward his wife clear.

"No jail," he wrote on the parchment that now lay on the bed so that he could easily use it.

John understood that his father's words didn't mean that he didn't value John—or the woman Ophelia had killed—but that only more pain would come of making the matter public at this point.

"We will keep her in this wing since it is already isolated," John told Riggs. "At least until His Grace decides what he wants done with her."

The Runner—who was well-versed in the ways of justice for aristocrats and how it differed from that for the masses—nodded.

"You and Stamp should go take care of Fast Eddie. Tell the constable he was caught breaking into the duke's room." It was better to stay as close to the truth as possible.

"Yes, sir."

John turned to Cordelia. "Which of the servants is most likely to keep his or her mouth shut?"

"Jameson is the butler. I believe he can be trusted to be discreet, although I don't know him well." Cordelia cast an unhappy glance at her sister, who'd sat motionless and speechless in a chair in front of the window ever since the Runner had tied her hands behind her back and put her there. "Ophelia replaced most of the upper servants over the past year."

And now they all knew why: so, she'd face little curiosity or resistance about the duke and just what was going on in these rooms.

Which reminded John, "Where *are* the nurses and the doctor who were supposed to be with the duke?"

"I saw them leaving the house around ten o'clock and thought it seemed odd," Cordelia said. "I couldn't sleep, so I watched and waited for news of you. That's how I saw *you* when you rode Morvac'h across the lawn, as bold as you please."

"And then you barged into a room where two people were waving around guns," he added dryly.

"I never imagined they'd have guns," she protested. "I'd just sneaked in to listen."

"Hmm. We'll talk about that sort of reckless behavior later. But for now, will you go fetch the butler?"

She nodded, hesitated, and then kissed him on the cheek before scurrying from the room.

John's face heated at the sweet sign of affection. Thankfully, the two Runners were busy with Eddie and didn't see him blushing like a lad of fifteen.

Only the duchess watched him, her gaze hostile. "You have everything now—the title, Chelmsford, and a child on the way. You'll throw them out, won't you?"

"If you mean my half-siblings, the answer is *no*; I won't punish them for your sins."

She gave a bitter, unamused laugh. "You did everything you could to destroy us from the minute you stepped foot back in England. Why change now?"

John couldn't argue with that. "I did," he agreed. "But I've lost my hunger for revenge."

"Why should I believe you?"

"Why would I lie to make you feel better?"

She snorted. "I suppose that is true enough."

Although the woman didn't deserve any comfort, John couldn't bring himself to continue the cycle of hate and violence. "They are my brother and sisters—my family—and you stole them all from me. I'm hardly in the mood to throw them away again."

She merely glared.

John shook his head. "Why did you do it? You were a country girl who'd done the impossible and landed a duke. You are a duchess—why risk all that?"

"A *duchess*." Her eyes burned as they darted from John to the man sleeping on the bed. "Being his duchess is nothing but humiliation and embarrassment. Do you know how often I had to watch him acknowledge his by-blows—or the whores who gave them to him? One of them even lived in the servant quarters when I moved in." Her eyes narrowed with spite. "I soon got rid of *her* and her strapping young offspring. But there were always more, more, more. Even last year before he became ill, he had a mistress in London. At his age!"

John knew all that; he'd been startled by the number of bastards the man had. But what had startled him more was how he'd taken care of them—at least financially—along with their mothers, something that had made his apparent neglect of John all the more painful.

"Why did you keep him alive if you hate him so much? You must have known what would happen if he ever got well enough to leave this bed."

"I did it because I *enjoyed* watching him suffer," she hissed. "Trust me; I would have made sure that he never left this room alive."

He could only marvel that this woman was related to Cordelia and her gentle parents.

"You'll tell them, won't you—Charles, Melissa, and Jane?"

"The duke will decide what to tell his children."

If it were up to John, he'd let them live in ignorance of their mother's sins. None of them deserved the burden of such knowledge.

Cordelia entered the room with a sleepy looking, hastily dressed servant in tow.

"Will you come and tell the servant what you wish done, Lord Gaulton?" Riggs asked.

John was about to turn and look for Charles when he realized the Runner was talking to him.

Bloody hell! He was a peer.

He couldn't help smiling a little; just wait until Worth heard about *that*.

***

Cordelia waited until the four men were busy with the dead man before approaching her sister.

Ophelia's shoulders tensed, but she continued to stare out the window.

"What was in the glass you gave me tonight, Ophelia?"

"You didn't drink it, I take it?"

"No—but I almost did."

A bitter smile curved her sister's lips. "Don't worry, it wouldn't have been enough to kill you. Just make you ill."

Cordelia raised a hand to her mouth to smother a gasp. "I cannot believe you would do such a thing!"

Ophelia whipped around, her eyes sparking with anger. "You would have been fine—so don't look at me that way."

"My b-baby?"

Ophelia's haughty, dismissive look said everything her mouth did not.

Cordelia stared in horror and disgust at the creature her sister had become. Or had she been this way all along? Certainly, she'd been warped for decades to have murdered a woman and tried to kill a helpless infant.

And she was a monster to keep her husband locked up like a prisoner and deprive him of access to his children.

Ophelia suddenly lurched toward her. "Please, you can help me get out of here—we're *sisters.*"

Cordelia stepped back. "You just confessed to attempting to murder my child, and I heard what you said earlier—you've tried to kill John multiple times. And you want me to release you on the world?" She shook her head, nauseated. "You will be more fortunate than you deserve and the duke will put you in a comfortable house somewhere. What you truly deserve is what you visited upon my husband—to be cast into the world alone and powerless." She turned away, too sickened to even look at her.

When she saw John was watching her with concern in his dark gaze, she stumbled toward him and he caught her up in a protective embrace, holding her tightly.

"I can't believe my sister tried to kill our baby," she sobbed.

***

"Shh, sweetheart. You're safe now and so is our child." John caught her up in his arms and carried her to the settee, where he laid her down, away from the duchess's cruelly mocking gaze.

He dropped to his haunches and took both her hands while she wept.

"I heard everything she said, John. I wanted to go to you directly, but Riggs made me wait—he wanted Ophelia to incriminate herself. I was so *scared* for you."

The Runner had been wise; a confession was powerful evidence, which they might have needed if the duke didn't recover enough to give his version of events.

"I'm so ashamed, John. All your problems—every single bad thing that happened to you is my sister's fault. If not for her, you would—"

"Hush, darling. Even if your sister was the worst thing that ever happened to me, I still have one reason to be grateful to her: she brought *you* to me."

She goggled.

John couldn't help laughing.

"I can't believe it."

"Hmm?" he asked, covering her hands and wrists with kisses.

"You just laughed."

"Did I? Impossible!"

"And I think you just made a joke, didn't you?"

He smiled against her soft skin. "It's been known to happen."

She gave a watery gurgle, and pulled her hands away, but only to bury them in his hair and yank him close for a kiss.

"Mmm," he groaned against her. "You are distracting me, when I need to—"

Shattering glass and shouts cut off the rest of what he was about to say, and John leapt to his feet.

"Good God," he hissed.

The duchess must have thrown herself at the window; she was slumped partway out, a huge shard of glass projecting from the side of her neck.

John turned to grab Cordelia and stop her from looking, but she was already up and running toward her.

She dropped to her knees beside the duchess. "She needs a doctor!" Her hands fluttered around her sister's neck, uncertain of where and how to stop the flood of blood pumping from the shuddering body.

John knew without a doubt that her sister would be dead before anyone could step out the door to call for a doctor.

There was a flicker of movement from the bed and John locked eyes with the duke, who must have been awakened by the commotion.

His father looked from the body of his wife to John.

There was no anger or sadness in the other man's eyes. Only relief.

Epilogue

Chelmsford Park
Nine Months and a Little Bit later…

Enough for today, Father?" John asked, replacing the chess pieces on their squares.

The duke nodded, the motion stiff, but far smoother than it had been even a month ago.

"Again tomorrow," he said, a slight slur marring his speech. "Maybe I'll beat you then."

John chuckled. "You can try."

The duke's valet—who'd happily returned to his employer after the duchess had forced his retirement—pushed his wheeled chair alongside John.

"You and Cordelia will bring my grandson to see me later?" his father asked, the sentence becoming more garbled by the end.

"Of course, Father."

As he often did, the duke caught John's hand and squeezed it, his gaze sweeping over him with a look of pride and love that he never would have believed such a proud man could feel toward a son—even one who wasn't a scarred, convicted criminal.

The journey from his father's chambers to the ones he shared with Cordelia was only the distance of a hallway. Indeed, all the family now shared the same wing of the house.

John peeked inside Cordelia's chambers but saw only her maid.

Akers smiled warmly at him. "She's not here."

"In the nursery?"

"Where else?"

John chuckled and closed the door, heading to the suite of guest rooms they'd converted into a nursery.

"I won't have my baby all the way in the old schoolroom," Cordelia had insisted.

"Our baby," he'd reminded her. "And I won't, either."

And so they had their baby just a few steps down the corridor.

John found Cordelia sitting in the big rocking chair he'd discovered tucked away in the massive attics, which were among his favorite parts of the house to explore.

"It was yer Mam's chair," Twickey had told John when she'd seen it. "She'd sit in it and rock for hours when she was pregnant with you."

Cordelia raised a finger to her lips and pointed to their sleeping child, his dark head resting quietly—for a change—on her shoulder.

"*May I?*" he mouthed, gesturing from himself to the baby.

She nodded and John carefully picked up Broderick Alastair Adam Davies Merrick, the Earl of Pensford.

John grunted softly—only partly in jest—when he lifted his heavy son. "Have you been feeding him bricks?" he whispered, laying the remarkably dense, hot little body on his chest and carefully cradling his dark, fuzzy head.

"He needs to be big to carry all those names," she whispered right back. "I'm going to tell Twickey we're putting him down for his nap."

He nodded, stroking Broderick's back in the circular motion he'd discovered the baby liked.

"You'll be big enough for all those names, won't you, lad?" he murmured against his child's fragrant temple, sneaking a kiss or two while he bobbed up and down like a pigeon, the motion yet another thing his son liked.

It was true that he had a great many names: Broderick was his maternal grandfather's name, Alastair the duke's name, Adam Cordelia's father, and Davies was John's mother's surname.

Cordelia had accused him of using up all the names on the first child.

"I hope to have at least a half-dozen-more," she'd told him a shockingly short time after Broderick's birth, an event which had driven John almost out of his mind with worry.

"It was painful," she'd admitted when he asked. "But I forgot about most of it the moment I saw him."

John would have to take her word for that because he'd not be forgetting his wife's screams any time soon. Nor would the doctor who attended the birth and had discovered himself several feet off the ground for one long, tension-filled moment.

Cordelia had made John promise never to do that again. "One doesn't lift people by the throat when one is angry, my dear. Especially not when one is the heir to a dukedom."

"Well, this heir does, doesn't he, little man?" John asked his son, who rudely ignored his father's question.

Cordelia's arm slid around him and he turned to find Twickey already waiting, hands extended.

He carefully set the child in her arms and watched as she navigated the short distance to the crib.

"I've never dropped or hurt a child in my life," she'd retorted when he'd asked if she was sure she could care for a baby. "You'll need to engage some younger lasses to help, but I can carry a baby ten feet to a crib or rock one in a chair."

And so that's what she did—loved their child—while sharing a lifetime of knowledge with the two young nursemaids they'd hired.

Cordelia looped her arm through John's and steered him purposely toward the door.

Once they were outside, she chuckled. "You'd live in there, if you could, wouldn't you?"

"Said Pot to Kettle."

She grinned up at him. "I'm so excited to see Charles and the girls—it seems like forever since Christmas. Do you think they had a good time?"

John snorted. "Why would three young people, on the loose with minimal oversight, and with virtually unlimited funds, have a good time in Paris, my dear?"

Cordelia laughed. "Well, when you put it *that* way."

John had been concerned how the loss of the title would affect his sweet younger brother, but he should have known better than to worry.

"I'm so relieved I could weep," Charles had said upon learning he was no longer the heir apparent. "Not only has an unwanted weight been lifted from my shoulders, but I have the brother I always wanted."

"Do you realize you said all that without stammering once?" John had pointed out.

Charles had laughed. "You see—already I am better for getting out from under all that responsibility. Ungrateful dog that I am, I feel no guilt about dumping it all on *your* broad shoulders. Please never think I resent you, brother; you rescued me. You rescued all of us."

Really, the man was so good and gentle and kind that John wondered how they could possibly be blood relatives.

"I can't believe they are coming back from Paris a whole month early," Cordelia said.

"Charles's letter said they would have stayed longer if Melissa hadn't fallen for that Frenchman."

"*John.*" She squeezed his arm

"Hmm?" he asked, opening the door to her chambers, which Akers had prudently vacated.

"Can we agree not to call our new relative *That Frenchman* while he is here?"

John grunted. "I can't believe Melissa married That Frenchman."

Cordelia smacked his shoulder. "What a stodgy, insular Englishman you are for a man who has been all over the world."

"Never to France," he pointed out, unbuttoning the large buttons on her gown. It was made to be convenient for nursing infants. John had to admit he personally found the design extremely convenient.

"What time is it?" she asked, squirming to see the clock.

"We've plenty of time to get ready before they arrive."

"The last time you said that we arrived in the sitting room a quarter of an hour after our guests got there!"

"Worth didn't care about that; it just gave him more time to snoop around in our things. And it also spared us having to listen to more of his bragging about that son of his."

"Said *Pot,*" she teased as she held up her arms and he pulled the gown over her head, tossing it aside in a cavalier way he knew would make her laugh—it did—and then turning her to unlace her stays.

"How was His Grace today?"

"He almost won."

"I can't believe he's not beaten you even once."

"Neither can he."

Cordelia laughed.

John knew she didn't believe it, but he'd probably spent a tenth of his life playing chess. Almost every convict knew the game and made their own playing pieces from rocks, chunks of wood, or whatever was at hand. Although his father had never asked how he'd gotten so good, he thought the older man had guessed.

Thus far, the duke had asked only a few tentative questions about John's past. But John's candid answers had distressed him too much, and he'd soon stopped, too upset about all those lost years. Not to mention the guilt he felt that he'd brought a woman into their lives who'd tried to kill John—more than once.

When John had told him, the only time they'd spoken about it, that he wouldn't change a thing in his life, the older man had looked stunned.

But if there was one thing John had learned over the years, it was that good endings often came out of bad beginnings.

Like the first time he ever saw Cordelia, for example. He'd been bent on revenge and up to no good, and then he saw her and—

"John?"

He realized he'd removed her chemise and was staring at it.

She gave him a quizzical smile. "You looked so far away; what were you thinking?"

John considered giving her some glib, Rule of Three response—he still didn't feel comfortable talking about his thoughts and feelings—but he loved her and wanted to do better when it came to sharing himself with her.

"I was thinking about the first time I saw you."

A smile spread slowly across her face, and she slid her arms around his waist.

Lord! What was it about the juxtaposition of her nakedness and his being fully clothed that made him so hard, so fast?

"I remember," she said. "I was at Hookham's and you fetched a book from the top shelf for me."

He shook his head.

A crease formed between her glorious hazel eyes. "Do you mean the time you returned Jane's glove?"

"No, I saw you before then."

"But—where?"

"Open my fall and take me out."

"Mmm." She didn't hesitate to reach between their bodies. "Where, John?" Her eyes were dark and intense.

"It wasn't far from that dressmaker's shop—" He groaned as her small, warm hand wrapped around his shaft, giving him a few skilled pumps.

John cupped her bare bottom and lifted her high while Cordelia wiggled her hips slightly, until he was positioned at her opening, and then she sank down slowly, taking every inch.

"Cordelia," he whispered, his eyes fluttering closed.

"Tell me where you saw me," his little tyrant ordered, flexing her inner muscles.

John moaned. "Do we have to finish this conversation right *now?*"

The wicked jade laughed at him. "I'm not moving until you tell me."

"Some boys were tormenting a dog, and you rushed in and saved it—risking your neck." The words came out in a rush.

"You were *there?*"

He nodded, tilting his pelvis to penetrate her more deeply while trying to pull her down onto him.

But she was like a monkey stuck to a tree, immoveable.

"Were you *spying* on me?"

"Yes, I was. Now can't we—"

"I can't believe you didn't tell me this already."

At that moment, John couldn't believe he'd ever mentioned it.

She raised one eyebrow as she stared down at him.

"Cordelia, *please.*"

"I love it when you beg. It reminds me that I *own* you."

He'd created a monster.

She grinned, and then ever so slowly, sank down on him again.

John shuddered as he buried himself in her tight heat. "Thank God."

"We're not done with this conversation, John."

"Mm-hmm," he dug his fingers into her arse and thrust.

"We'll talk more later," she added in a breathy voice. "The only reason I'm not—*ah*! pursuing this matter right now is that we've got company com—*oh John*!"

Every night—several times—he demonstrated how much he loved her with his body.

But for once, John used his words. "I fell in love with you the day you risked your life for an old dog in an alley. You were fierce and beautiful and bold; how could I possibly have resisted you?"

His gorgeous normally articulate wife stared up at him with wide eyes, her lips parted in wonder as she uttered a soft, indistinct sound and melted into his arms.

John smiled, pleased to finally have the last word.

Dear Reader:

I hope you enjoyed John and Cordelia's story! This book has been a long time in the making and they are one of my favorite couples. I especially love John and it is always a challenge to find the right partner when you have such a strong character.

It was fun to write a hero who just refuses to talk! Luckily his inner life is rich and active and that is how I finally got to "know" him as I wrote the book.

Like all of my books, this one started out a LOT longer. I think my initial manuscript was about 115,000 words. The final book clocked in at a svelte 103, 000!

People ask me if it is painful to cut so much out. Well, yes and no.

I wish I could include all the extra stories and background information that I have to cut simply because it's TOO much.

At the same time, I feel like I am "finding" the story, so sometimes I need to shave a bit more off (think sculptor) to get to the true book.

A lot of the "naughty" words and slang that I used in this book (and all my books) I found using *Green's Dictionary of Slang* and the *Grose's 1811 Dictionary of the Vulgar tongue.* The second source is pretty interesting since it was printed at the time, and Green's will give you a good idea when the word or phrase first came into use.

THE BASTARD was the last book I had planned for this series, but I might one day add a story about Geoffrey from book 2, THE POSTILION, since he seems to have enchanted a lot of readers with his bad-boy behavior.

I love hearing from readers, so please don't hold back.

Is there a character you'd like to know more about?

Questions about this story?

Upcoming stories?

Stories you think *need* to be written?

If so, you can drop me an email at: minervaspencerauthor@gmail.com or leave a comment or visit my website: www.minervaspencer.com.

As always, I humbly ask that you take a moment to write a quick review—even just a few words—if you liked my work.

I don't pay for reviews, so I rely on my lovely readers to share their genuine opinions and help others decide to give them a try. It doesn't have to be long, just a few words will do and will make book vendors happy.

Until my next book, I wish you all the best and lots of great reading!

Minerva Spencer & S.M. LaViolette

Who are Minerva Spencer & S.M. LaViolette?

Minerva is S.M.'s pen name (that's short for Shantal Marie) S.M. has been a criminal prosecutor, college history teacher, B&B operator, dock worker, ice cream manufacturer, reader for the blind, motel maid, and bounty hunter. Okay, so the part about being a bounty hunter is a lie. S.M. does, however, know how to hypnotize a Dungeness crab, sew her own Regency Era clothing, knit a frog hat, juggle, rebuild a 1959

American Rambler, and gain control of Asia (and hold on to it) in the game of RISK.

Read more about S.M. at: www.MinervaSpencer.com

OUTCASTS SERIES

DANGEROUS

BARBAROUS

SCANDALOUS

THE REBELS OF THE *TON*:

NOTORIOUS

OUTRAGEOUS

INFAMOUS

THE SEDUCERS:

MELISSA AND THE VICAR

JOSS AND THE COUNTESS

HUGO AND THE MAIDEN

VICTORIAN DECADENCE: (HISTORICAL EROTIC ROMANCE—SUPER STEAMY!)

HIS HARLOT

HIS VALET

HIS COUNTESS

HER BEAST

THEIR MASTER

THE ACADEMY OF LOVE:

THE MUSIC OF LOVE

A FIGURE OF LOVE

A PORTRAIT OF LOVE

THE LANGUAGE OF LOVE

DANCING WITH LOVE

THE MASQUERADERS:

THE FOOTMAN

THE POSTILION

THE BASTARD

THE BACHELORS OF BOND STREET:
A SECOND CHANCE FOR LOVE (A NOVELLA)
THE ARRANGEMENT (A NOVELLA)

Keep an eye out for two BRAND NEW series coming in 2022:

THE BELLAMY SISTERS
PHOEBE
HYACINTH

THE WILD WOMEN OF WHITECHAPEL
THE BOXING BARONESS
THE DUELING DUCHESS

Made in United States
North Haven, CT
26 May 2023